RED MOUNTAIN

A NOVEL

BOO WALKER

ALSO BY BOO WALKER

Red Mountain Rising

A Marriage Well Done

Red Mountain Burning

An Unfinished Story

The Singing Trees

A Spanish Sunrise

Writing as Benjamin Blackmore:

Lowcountry Punch

Once a Soldier

Off You Go: A Mystery Novella

This is a work of fiction. Names, characters, organizations, places, events, and incidents are either products of the author's imagination or are used fictitiously. Any resemblance to actual persons, living or read, or actual events is purely coincidental.

For Red Mountain, a place that found me when I needed finding.

1

A COYOTE WITHOUT A PACK

Late September, Washington State

Under the light of a wide-eyed moon, Otis Pennington Till strolled into his syrah vineyard, puffing on an unlit briarwood pipe. At sixty-four, and despite a lower back still tender from lifting a wine barrel earlier in the year, he moved with a fair amount of grace.

Not too far away, the coyotes called up into the moonlit big sky night, their howls and yelps disturbing the calm of Red Mountain. He could hear the uneasy *baas* of his flock of Southdown sheep stirring in the pasture below, and he knew his huge Great Pyrenees, Jonathan, was on high alert.

"*Baa* back to you, friends!" he shouted with a British accent, the leftovers of his London childhood.

Kicking aside a tumbleweed with his work boot, Otis plucked a few grapes from one of the ten-year-old syrah vines and put them in his mouth. He closed his eyes, and as the skins burst between his teeth, the juice coated his tongue. He hoped to be overwhelmed by the complexity of the fruit, the mouth-watering acidity, the velvety tannins, the elegance. But the nuances he'd grown used to tasting in ripening Red Mountain grapes didn't treat him tonight.

For a couple of weeks now, Otis had been struggling with his sense of smell and taste. When he first noticed the symptoms, he chalked it up to a cold or a hiccup of growing old; perhaps a result of too many hours spent with his tobacco pipe as of late. But his condition was getting so bad that he might be incapable of making wine this year.

Otis spat the seeds to the ground like he was spitting in his opponent's face. He cast his pipe into the dust, cursing.

Trying to wrangle his anger, he filled his lungs with the cool, clean air and gazed at the harvest moon, the bright orange eye of the night. "Please don't take my wine away from me," he begged. "It's all I have. You might as well kill me now."

Otis tossed his tweed cap to the ground. He removed his cardigan and plaid button-down shirt, his boots and trousers and the rest. Naked, he stood tall and proud. Chill bumps rose on his arms. He lifted his hands in the air, as if ready to catch a star. He drew his right hand to his face, kissed his palm, and blew that kiss up towards the heavens, up towards the rest of his family—his sons and wife. "I could be joining you sooner than later, my loves."

Lowering to his hands and knees, he looked back to the moon and howled. Without a trace of self-consciousness, like a child, he howled. As loud as his body would let him, he imitated the wild dogs out there, pacing in the darkness, calling out, singing their songs.

Ahhhhhh-ooooooooooo! Ahhhhhh-ooooooooooo!

Stopping to catch his breath, Otis noticed the coyotes had raised the volume of their own song, perhaps welcoming him. He could hear the higher pitch of the young ones and the deeper haunting sound of the eldest, and Otis howled even louder and with more heart.

Ahhhhhh-ooooooooooo! Ahhhhhh-ooooooooooo!

Feeling better, Otis dressed and made way back toward the house at the western end of his forty acres. He took pride in the fact that every square foot of his property was tidy. Despite the occasional strong winds that often brought trash from the road, not even a bottle cap could be found on his land. Every hose was coiled to Army standards. Weeds were virtually non-existent. You could have slept in the sheep corral or dined in the chicken coop. All his energy, all the usual precision of a Virgo that was normally channeled toward the loving and caring of other humans, Otis redirected toward his animals, his property, and his wine.

He entered the stone home he and his wife had built and made way to the study. Most evenings, when he felt too lethargic to tackle anything constructive, he found at least a modicum of solace in gazing at the wall-to-wall shelves lined with his collection of books, all well-read, thoroughly enjoyed, and dog-eared, especially those written by English authors, like Shakespeare, George Orwell, D.H. Lawrence, Graham Greene, and Churchill. He felt a kinship with them, even though he'd been an American citizen since his early teens.

At the touch of a button, Art Tatum crooned from the CD player. Otis poured himself a peaty twelve-year-old scotch from a crystal decanter and carried the glass over to his recliner. Since his wife had died five years before, he hadn't slept in their bed. He couldn't even bring himself to lie down in it. He couldn't bear to revisit their intimate moments there—their naked bodies wrapped around one another, Rebecca stroking his hair and murmuring in her soft morning voice that he missed so dearly, their silly pillow fights and their once-a-month lazy Saturday mornings when they wouldn't get out of bed until noon. Since she passed, he had slept on the couch or in this recliner, a beast of a chair he'd worn in so well that the outline of his body was visible in the cracked, worn leather.

Using a letter opener that had belonged to his father, a journalist who wrote for the *London Telegraph* and the *Bozeman Daily Chronicle*, Otis rifled through the stack of mail. Eventually he drew out a letter addressed in large, flowery handwriting. He recognized it as being from his maternal aunt, Morgan. She didn't believe in computers, she loved to brag, so her correspondence was by virtue of the United States Postal Service.

Just seeing her name on the return address made Otis moan. Morgan was the Queen Bee of Montana—the belle of the ball, but Otis could handle her only in small doses. Her personality matched her handwriting—too big and forceful for her petite body. She'd outlive him by thirty years; he was sure of it.

As always, the letter began innocuously. But Otis was wise enough to expect a surprise. He found it, and the words made him jump to refill his glass. He could hear her high-pitched voice as he re-read the end:

I'm coming to see you, sweetie pie. What's it been? Five years? Since the funerals? Not acceptable. Seems like you and I are the only two of our blood who are managing to survive this sometimes awful world. We should share secrets. I'll be there on Monday. According to the lovely lady at the post office, you should get this letter on Saturday. I didn't want to give you the time to stop me. Make sure you pick up some Folgers and half and half. You know I can't stand that Seattle single-origin crap.

See you very soon,
Morgan

OTIS REACHED for a half-eaten bag of pork rinds and worked his way through them while pondering her intentions. He raised his eyes to the urn that held the last of his wife's earthly remains, the turquoise vessel a gift from a potter friend in Sonoma.

"You wouldn't believe who's coming to town, Bec," he said, setting down his snack. "Aunt Morgan. She's still trying to pair me up with some other girl." He shook his head. "Morgan loved you so much. I don't know why she'd ever want me to replace you."

No one knew Otis had kept his wife's ashes. He'd told her brother and her best friend that he had spread her remains in their vineyard on Red Mountain, as she'd wished. But he liked having her in their home, and he wasn't ready to say goodbye. He stared at the urn for a while, revisiting old memories—trying to focus on the happier ones. Then he bid his dead wife goodnight and returned to thoughts of his impending visitor.

Aunt Morgan. Coming to Red Mountain. What a disaster. She'd been hinting at this trip for months now. She'd decided he was lonely and sad, and it was time he started dating again. She made him feel like he was fifteen with her overprotective smothering. And now she was coming to town.

Involuntarily, Otis's imagination played a series of disastrous scenarios resulting from her visit; all of them centered on his being embarrassed in front of his friends and fellow Red Mountain inhabitants. Otis knew his reputation on the mountain. He was a respected leader, a pioneer, the wisdom bearer, the godfather, the man the young winemakers and grape growers came to see. How easily Morgan could burst this persona, leaving him vulnerable and exposed, to be picked apart and laughed at by the vultures of youth. His thoughts finally faded to black.

He woke in the chair hours later. The window faced the top of Red Mountain, which was about 1,400 feet at its highest point. The sun hadn't quite peaked over the mountain but had brightened the night to a tarnished silver, illuminating the silhouettes of the vines running along the hills. Twenty yards out, a lone coyote—his spirit animal—stood there looking at him, white-gold eyes glowing in the early morning light. They'd met a few weeks before, in the same place.

The two stared at each other for a long time before Otis tipped his tweed cap and closed his eyes again.

2

THE LOST ART OF CHASING DREAMS

Rory was standing in their Vermont kitchen, wearing one of his cheesy pinstriped suits. A red tie was pulled away from his neck, his typical after work appearance. With his politician's smile—the one Margot had grown to hate more than anything in the world—he asked, "What's for dinner?"

Margot raised her eyes at him from the cutting board, where a Santoku knife waited next to a pile of chopped garden carrots. "Hi, Sugar. So glad you're home." And with that, she took the knife by the blade and threw it at him with the expertise of a ninja. The blade embedded in his throat. She laughed, a sinister, devilish cackle, as he fell to his knees and bled to death on the kitchen floor, the last gurgles of his life a symphony of joy to her ears.

Margot Pierce reached for the glass of merlot she'd poured, sighing as she sank into the bubbles and savored the last moments of her daydream. Taking a bath in the early afternoon had become a ritual. So had imagining how she'd kill her ex-husband.

He had been the mayor of Burlington, Vermont, the father of her only son, the man who tracked her down after seeing her in *Crazy for You* on Broadway in New York, put a ring on her finger, and dragged her back to Vermont. The man she'd left her promising career behind for: Rory Simpson. Just his name disgusted her now.

How unlucky she was to have been Margot Simpson, even temporarily. The name had invited an exhausting amount of teasing in comparison to the matriarch of *The Simpsons.* She'd changed her name back before he'd even signed the divorce papers. The bastard. The man whose affair was exposed by a journalist who managed to capture images of Rory's cock in his secretary's mouth—a slutty little whore named Nadine—a news story that made its rounds internationally and made Margot the most pitied woman in America.

These kinds of daydreams—admittedly disturbing as they were—had kept her from going insane since she'd left him. She attempted to keep each fantasized murder civil by only using objects found in the kitchen. It was the one rule to her cathartic game. One day, she'd have to quit killing him and move on to something else. It couldn't be healthy. Maybe she needed to see a therapist, but she didn't have time right now. She had a business to get off the ground, and things weren't off to the best start.

In a way, she had to appreciate his infidelity. Her half of their money had allowed her to move to Washington to realize her greatest dream: opening an inn and farm sanctuary. The inn was already being built, but the associated hemorrhaging of cash was starting to threaten the possibility of the farm sanctuary, a place where abused and neglected farm animals could live out their lives.

Since childhood, she'd been a protector of all living things, not even letting her friends squash a bug in her presence. Philippe, her rescued three-year-old terrier mutt, was curled up on the cool tile floor against the wall. His wiry gray hair and royal gait made Margot think he belonged at the feet of Queen Guinevere while she held court. Margot spoiled him accordingly.

She'd bought her home and the land for the inn before she'd moved out to Red Mountain, but she couldn't yet purchase the adjoining ten acres for the sanctuary. At this rate, someone else might swoop in and buy the property out from under her. Every time she drove by, she wanted to grab the "For Sale" sign and put it in her trunk.

The inn was supposed to be open by now, but delays in construction had held up the project. Her contractor, a man she was learning to distrust, had assured her he'd be finished by September 1. Now, she'd be lucky to open the doors by June. And she'd be even luckier if she wasn't painfully over budget. *That's what I get for trusting someone, especially a man*, she thought. If her contractor wasn't careful, she'd be daydreaming about him in the bathtub too. She had no shortage of kitchen weapons in her arsenal.

She dressed and went downstairs, Philippe following closely behind. Her home stood on the lower part of Red Mountain, below Col Solare, a winery owned by St. Michelle and the Antinori family. She'd bought the house from a Microsoft couple who'd built it only five years earlier. She never knew why they left, but the house was everything she ever wanted. It wasn't very big, but she didn't need much space for herself and her son. The white stucco and red roof, that Santa Barbara kind of look, fit so perfectly with the desert climate and the vines that ran in rows as far as you could see in every direction.

The Microsoft couple had done an exceptional job inside too, sparing no expense on fixtures, appliances, and the little details. Due to the escalating nature of real estate on Red Mountain and the seller's market they were in, Margot paid top dollar, but she believed in her purchase. Red Mountain was only beginning to show its potential. One day, people would compare the area to Yountville or Calistoga.

She heard a car door shut and walked out the front door. Her seventeen-year-old son, Jasper, was getting a backpack out of his car. The sight of him brought her so much joy. Though Jasper hated her to say it, he was the most adorable boy, or man, she'd ever seen. He was barely 5'8", weighed maybe 150 pounds, and had this baby face that made her want to gobble him up. He'd attempted to hide his youth by growing a beard, but the effort was so patchy that it somehow only enhanced the cute factor. He had exceptional taste in clothes and took great pride in his dress.

Today, he was wearing a pair of red John Fluevog brogue shoes with dark jeans and an ironed white button-down shirt. And he'd been the one to iron it! His brown hair was shaggy and he wore glasses with thick rims. She'd offered him LASIK but he had no interest. He liked looking sophisticated. His beat-up wool fedora rarely left his head. The whole look especially worked when he got on the bench behind the piano, which is where he had spent the majority of his life. He had this kind of budding-jazz-star look, "the mad scientist on the ivories," as one of the college recruiters trying to poach him had said.

Margot was learning more and more that the only person she could really trust in this world was Jasper. Somehow, despite all the crap she and her husband had put their son through—the media bullshit, the agonizing divorce, her own mental breakdown—her son was still solid as a rock. As long as he was in her life, everything was going to be all right.

He reached down and greeted Philippe.

"How was school, sweetheart?"

"Not bad. I'm figuring it out. By graduation, I'll be running the show." Jasper was generally very quiet, a great listener, but he was rarely short of words with her, even if sometimes sarcastic. He had put all the anger he felt toward his father into taking care of her. *What an amazing man,* Margot thought. That's right: man. He was a man now. Jasper was an old soul, always acting twice his age. Alas, because of this maturity, he had a hard time making friends, finding little in common with kids his age.

He approached her, put his hand on her shoulder, and gave her a peck on the cheek. "What's going on with you?"

"About to make *culurgiones*, your favorite."

"Can I help?"

"Don't you have homework?"

"Yeah, but it can wait."

"Wait a minute. So you want to help your boring old mom make dinner tonight? How did I get so lucky?"

"I enjoy making dinner with you. Especially Sardinian. I could use some comfort food."

"Why don't you take an hour and play the piano? I know you're dying to." Jasper had proved to be an exceptional classical and jazz pianist, and staff from Julliard, the Berklee College of Music, and the New England Conservatory, among others, had been bugging them for years. Half of their decision to come to Red Mountain was for Jasper; one of the top piano teachers in the country lived close by in Richland.

As Jasper started inside, Margot noticed someone had stuck a piece of paper to his back that read *I love boys*. She caught up to him and ripped it off. He didn't notice and kept moving. Did he really like his new school? Without his father as mayor, she was worried people would treat his strange side with a bit more teasing. She didn't want to baby him, though. He could take care of himself. At least, she'd keep telling herself that.

Before following him back inside, Margot took a minute to look at the inn, or what was to be her inn. Her contractor was on vacation, and he'd failed to line up work while he was gone, so the site on the other side of her property was a ghost town. Actually, the only signs of life were her five hens pecking and scratching diligently at a patch of dirt near the yet-to-be-working fountain in the front. The actual exterior of the inn, built of concrete block, was up, but they hadn't even started stuccoing yet. The only landscaping they'd done was the line of young black locust trees along the driveway and parking area.

She named the inn Épiphanie, homage to her mother's side of the family, who came from Carcassonne in the southwest of France, no doubt the roots of Margot's deep love for cooking and European cuisine. Épiphanie stood two stories high, with eight rooms upstairs for guests, each with a private balcony. The architecture matched the Spanish style of her home. Downstairs, there was a giant dining room, a commercial kitchen, a wine cellar, two bathrooms, and a large entryway that would feature a grand piano for Jasper to dazzle guests with when they entered. On a clear day, from any chair on the back patio, you could see the snowy top of Mount Adams off to the west.

Margot went in to finish dinner. Jasper was on the Steinway in the living room warming up. She'd always enjoyed his playing, even when he was stabbing out "Heart and Soul" when he was five. Now *and* then, she could listen to him for hours.

Today, he was teasing Debussy. She pulled out the piece of paper she'd ripped off his back and looked at it again. Her blood boiled. Youth could be so damn cruel.

3

FROM THE WOMB TO THE GRAVE

Looking back, Emilia Forester could have so easily said no. She'd wish for many years that she had. It wasn't fair that even as a young seventeen-year-old, the choices you make can affect your life so drastically. There was no room for mistakes. The human condition is relentless, from the womb to the grave.

And it all started with a question: If you could change anything about yourself, what would it be? Answering that question was her assignment, handed down by Joe Massey, her Twelfth-Grade Creative Writing teacher at Belmont High School in Richland, Washington. He'd encouraged them to write from the heart, to search deep, to write with passion and honesty. She'd done just that, answering the question with ease because she'd always known the answer, turning in a paper a week later that peeled back all her layers. Finally, someone else knew the truth about Emilia Forester, and she found comfort in sharing the burden.

Mr. Massey had earned her trust, though. She wasn't offering up her soul for free. Ever since she'd started there in August, leaving her privileged kids' private school in Seattle for a taste of the real world in an eastern Washington public school, he'd been there for her, encouraging her to work harder, to tap into her true potential. In fact, she suspected that he had already come to know the truth through her writing. Mr. Massey might be the only person on earth that knew the real Emilia, the one she worked so hard to hide.

Today, Mr. Massey was walking up and down the rows of his classroom returning the papers, folded in half to hide the grades. Murmurs of excitement, relief, and disappointment teased the air as each student saw their grade. When Mr. Massey reached Emilia, he raised one corner of his mouth and set her work in front her.

She met his eyes through his wire-rimmed glasses and returned a slight smile of her own. Mr. Massey wasn't that much older than the rest of the class—Emilia guessed twenty-six—but his confidence and poise in the classroom earned him respect among his students. She and her friend, Sadie, had innocently flirted with him since school began in August, and they'd gotten to know him fairly well.

He was good-looking in a professorial kind of way. He had sharp cheekbones, inviting brown eyes, a pronounced Adam's apple, and an orderly divide in his hair reinforced with a touch of gel. He dressed the part of the professor, never scared to walk into class with a bow tie or khaki pants hemmed way too high. Somehow, he could pull off the look with style. He was as tall as the basketball players in the class, and he had an obsession with bicycling, which kept him in great shape and full of energy. Emilia saw him most mornings pedaling along George Washington Way with his messenger bag slung over his shoulder.

Mr. Massey continued down the row as Emilia unfolded her paper. She found the *A* written in red ink in the right corner. Below it, he'd written: *Come see me after class.*

As the other students filed out, Emilia flattened out her sundress and poked her head into his office. "Mr. Massey?"

"Come in," he said from behind his desk.

His office was small, tidy, and sparse. A Trek road bike leaned against the left wall and window, pressing against the closed plastic blinds. A red helmet hung from the handlebars.

Emilia guided the door closed and sat in one of two chairs opposite him. She always chose the left chair for some reason. She'd fallen in love with writing in the past couple of months, all thanks to him, and was no stranger to his office. A picture of his wife in a gold leaf frame leaned on top of a collection of literary magazines on his desk. Emilia had never spoken to his wife, but she occasionally came to have lunch with him at one of the picnic tables on the front lawn.

Holding her books on her lap, Emilia said, "You wanted to talk to me?"

He smiled without showing his teeth. After considering his words for a moment, he said, "You wrote a great paper."

"Thank you."

"You wrote like you were breaking out of chains."

She nodded.

"Have you ever talked to anyone about this stuff? About your parents?"

She shook her head, beginning to regret having poured her heart out.

"You know, most people wrote about how they didn't like their name or something about their body or some tiny quirk. You told me something very private. You certainly earned your *A*." He scratched his head.

"But it's not the writing I want to talk about. You're a great writer, and I love how you're not afraid to take chances, to push the rules. And you definitely dug deep. But the subject matter alarms me some. What can I do to help?"

"I don't think there's anything anyone can do. Unless you can go back in time and take the guitar out of my dad's lap. And take the beauty from my mom's face."

"Why do you feel like you have to be tied to all that? Like you have to achieve their same status? Yes, they're famous. And I can only imagine what it's like growing up in that kind of environment, people looking at you, taking pictures of you. I bet it can be horrible. Everyone expects the world from you."

"They say I won the genetic lottery."

"Who is 'they'?"

"Everybody. Look at my life. My dad is Jake Forester. Even if you're not into music, you know that name. And of course my mom has to be a supermodel." She laughed, knowing how absurd she must sound, complaining about what every other girl in the world would kill for. Not Emilia.

Though she'd gotten it all, Emilia didn't want her mom's wavy and thick cinnamon hair or her long legs or her slender body. She didn't care about her own olive complexion or her big brown eyes or her long eyelashes. In fact, she hated how boys and even older men stared at her. It's not like she dressed to invite all these looks, the double takes, the whispering and whistles. Most of the year, all she wore was sundresses. She didn't even wear makeup.

She'd done nothing to earn these features, so therefore she didn't deserve them, and she couldn't ever be proud of them or find confidence in them.

"I was born with the ultimate silver spoon in my mouth. There's no worse curse. I'm supposed to look like my mom, sing like my dad. Get perfect grades. Never get down or depressed. And then go on to save the world. My life is one big failed attempt to reach the bar my parents set."

"Oh, come on, Emilia. You're awesome in your own right."

"How do you know?"

"Because I've been reading your writing for two months. I know how your head works. You're brilliant. Deep down, you're a good person. A kind person."

"I'm a fake. I'm like the president's daughter growing up in the White House. I'm not allowed to make mistakes. I'm not allowed to be a kid. I can't even be human. Everyone expects me to act like the perfect adult."

He nodded. "I get it. It's a heavy cross to bear. But you don't have to be that person. You don't have to be trapped by your parents. Fame isn't the benchmark of a person's worth in life. Neither is money or medals or awards. You don't have to grow up to be like your parents. All you have to do is realize your own potential. That might be by becoming a mom. Or a TV reporter. Or a nurse. Or a writer. Or the most noble of trades, you could become a teacher."

She allowed herself to smile and he said, "The most important thing you have to find is happiness. Be who you're supposed to be."

"You don't understand. I don't know who I really am. Nothing is my own. Nothing I've done is my own. Nothing I am is my own." She gripped the books on her lap tighter. "The way I look: that's my mom. My singing and guitar playing: that's my dad. All the cool experiences, all the travel, the restaurants, the people I've met: that's my parents. What am I? A lost trust fund kid. People like me end up on TV shows about what went wrong." She felt tears coming and brought a hand to her face. "Who am I?"

Mr. Massey stood from his chair and came around to her side of the desk. "Hey, hey," he said, putting his hand on her shoulder.

"Who am I?" She burst into a staccato cry, covering up her face with her hands. He put his arms around her, whispering comforting words, saying everything was going to be all right.

He knelt in front of her and pulled her hands away from her face. He said, "It's okay to cry. It's okay to be confused." She met his eyes for a moment and then looked away. He touched her chin and lifted up her face, bringing her eyes back to his. "Everything I like about you...it has nothing to do with your parents."

Those words meant so much to her, and she could tell he really meant them. He did understand her. He'd read her deepest thoughts. He knew that she was broken inside, that she'd created this alter ego, this White House kid thing, this persona that didn't even exist. She wasn't always happy; in fact she was often lost in the darkness. Her parents weren't perfect. At times, far from it. Though she did a great job of hiding it, there was an insecure and scared little girl who was creating noise in her head, fueling the fire of her self-doubt. In a way, this alter ego had been the only way for her to survive all the scrutiny of growing up as Emilia Forester.

Mr. Massey was now the only one on earth who knew what was going on inside. And he was okay with it. He did indeed understand her. That's why, when he moved toward her, guiding her lips to his, she let it happen.

The kiss sent shivers through her body, and as her books slid to the floor, she felt something sexual stirring inside of her that she'd never experienced before. For a long time, she had worried that she'd never know these feelings, the ones Abby, her mom's assistant, talked about.

A craving came over her, and she had an urge to rip her teacher's clothes off. She was ready to give him her virginity right then and there. He touched her stomach and glided a hand up to her breasts, and she felt it in between her legs, an orgasmic earthquake. The sensations were too overwhelming, though, and she pushed him away. She didn't like the feeling of losing control.

She licked her lips and kissed him again, telling him without words that she wanted more but that she couldn't. "I've got to go," she said. She had to get away and try to make some sense of it all.

"I like you," he said.

She nodded.

"Maybe we could see each other."

"I think so."

"Could I have your number?"

She scribbled her cell number on a piece of paper, collected her books from the floor, and rushed out of his office.

4

THE WOMAN WITH SECRETS

Brooks Baker stood from his desk and walked to the massive window overlooking the world-class cellar down below, a view currently filled with workers sampling barrels and tanks, moving wine, cleaning—the business of harvest at a winery. Amidst the action, he saw her.

Abby Sinclaire.

She was a mirage in his mind, this woman of such epic beauty and greatness that his imagination had lifted her up into the clouds and made her nearly untouchable. Getting intelligent words out and sounding witty in her heavenly presence was like prying screws loose from fresh wood with the claw of a hammer. What a shame he didn't have a chance. Sure, Brooks had a high-profile job as the head winemaker for Jake Forester's winery, Lacoda, and people considered Brooks good-looking in a "bad boy" kind of way, but he didn't have the guts to try taking their relationship from professional to romantic.

How could he possibly muster the courage to ask out Abby Sinclaire? Yes, they were both in their mid-thirties. No, she had never been married and she didn't have children. What if she was as lonely as he was? Or—a big fat *OR*—what if she wasn't? Was being Carmen Forester's assistant all she was looking for on this mountain?

His resistance to asking her out came down to one fear: what if she said no? Brooks worried that rejection would rub all his old wounds raw and expose who he used to be.

Abby must have felt his prying eyes and looked up at the window. She wore a gray trucker hat with the Lacoda logo, her brown hair poking out the back in a ponytail. She offered a little smile and a quick wave. He waved back, trying hard to hold her gaze. Those warm wet-sand eyes tore into him, intimidating him with her confidence, boiling up his nervous energy, exposing his imperfections. *Don't let her see how I really feel right now*, he told himself. *Don't let her see the butterflies in my stomach, the extra kick in my heart, the wanting in my eyes, the way she makes me feel. Don't let her see how badly I need her.*

His eye flapped an unintentional wink. Brooks turned in shame and hurried back to his desk, hoping she didn't notice his capability of creating awkwardness. Why this insecurity? He wasn't like this with anyone else. Only her. *Oh, Abby Sinclaire, what you do to me. What you do to me, woman!*

His past fed this insecurity. While others were working hard in high school to get into a nice college and then working hard in college to land a nice job, Brooks was busting out of foster homes, breaking laws, thumbing rides, and jumping trains. Other than this absurd self-doubt and the fear of somehow waking up back in that awful past life, the tattoos covering his arms and the stacks of dental bills from earlier neglect were the only real reminders.

He pushed these unhealthy thoughts away and went back to looking over his work orders, making sure he had taken care of each vessel of wine. Some tanks needed punch downs, which meant the grape skins needed to be punched back down into the juice to ensure the proper extraction of color and flavor. Some tanks needed a change of temperature. Thankfully, all the wines he'd tasted so far were showing great promise.

A knock on the door and she was standing there.

"Hey, Abby," he mumbled through the marbles in his mouth. "It's good to see you."

She strolled into his office—though to Brooks, her entrance was more goddess-like, more like an angel floating in on a magic carpet. She couldn't hide how attractive she was if she spent all day every day trying. Brooks had gotten to know her through long lunches and dinners at the winery and at their bosses' home right down the road. She was one of those women who never exploited her beauty.

Abby never attempted to outdo or compete with Carmen Forester, her ex-supermodel employer, who now was close to fifty but still dressed in Isabel Marant and Marni and Proenza Schouler, designer names Brooks had gotten used to hearing. In fact, Carmen had an entire room with three walk-in closets to house her wardrobe. Not that Carmen dressed too young for her age—she didn't at all—but she dressed with great care, and her love for clothes was perpetually evident.

Though Abby had inherited tons of Carmen's clothing, she tended to wear the less flashy items: jeans and t-shirts, long dresses and sweaters, more conservative skirts and blouses, almost like she didn't want people looking at her that way, the way Brooks saw her. Brooks thought Abby's shyness might be one of the many reasons Carmen had hired her to be her personal assistant. Carmen probably liked the fact that Abby was beautiful but didn't feel a need to compete with Carmen, outdress or outdo her. On the other hand, Brooks had this feeling that Abby was hiding a wild side that no one on Red Mountain had yet seen.

In Brooks's eyes, Abby was much more attractive. Where Carmen's face was sharp and almost pretentious, Abby had a face of warmth, innocent of hidden agendas, and a sexy and confident smile that came out often. Where Carmen's body was extremely slender and tall and nearly daunting, Abby was more average height with more curve. Abby's brown hair had light streaks in it, and Brooks thought that her highlights were the only thing she did to enhance her image. That's what he liked about her. She wasn't trying, she just *was*.

Her tortoiseshell glasses were further proof that she made a conscious effort not to use her looks to get by in life. Maybe she was slightly insecure and went out of her way to hide her beauty, and that was okay by Brooks. If that idea were true, he would love that. He loved the way her mind worked too. In every conversation they'd had, he found himself caught somewhere between working hard not to seem infatuated and trying desperately to keep up.

She was a great conversationalist, something Brooks was working on improving in himself. Her mastery of the art of conversation is what had really excited him. Sure, her looks had stopped him cold and always did when she floated into the room, but it was that mind of hers that kept making him want to share the same space with her again. When they started talking, they'd have to be interrupted to stop.

Brooks was worried, though, that she might be that way with everyone. She might be one of those kinds of women who make everyone she speaks with feel like she's interested in them.

Along with her warmth and innocence, there was something "bad girl" about Abby that appealed to the motorcycle guy in Brooks. At parties, she was the one to instigate the first—and sometimes second round—of Jose Cuervo shots, and she was often the last one standing when the lights went out. She laughed the loudest—no, she roared—at poop and fart jokes and usually had a few crude jokes of her own to tell. Morning, noon, or night, she welcomed a good argument, especially one involving church or state; and she'd bury you if you insulted women. At times, not often, but at the most opportune time in a back and forth, she would drop the *F* word and she would use it with such confidence and calculated timing that it worked to great effect. Brooks wanted to get to know her, to learn about her past, about her skeletons in the closet.

Brooks asked, "How's your day going?"

"Easing along." She gestured to his chair behind the desk. "Please sit down." He sat and she continued. "Thought I'd stop by to say hello. Looks like everyone's busy."

"Yeah, that time of year," he said, nodding.

She smiled. A few seconds of awkwardness filled the space between them. Brooks was reminded that she was much easier to talk to after a glass of wine.

"Carmen sent me up to grab a few bottles for the dinner tonight. Got any ideas?"

"Are they having company?"

"Having a few friends in from Seattle. Didn't Jake invite you?"

"First I've heard of it."

"Why don't you come? I think we're shooting for seven. I'm smoking salmon."

"You're smoking salmon?"

"Why not?"

"I know you're a great cook, but wow."

"Oh, is smoking fish supposed to be a man's job? The whole 'a woman belongs in the kitchen' thing. 'A man should handle the grill.'"

"That's not what I meant."

She smiled. "I'm kidding. Seriously, why don't you come?"

"I'm sure Jake will ask me if he wants me there."

"I want you there. I mean...I could use someone to talk to. You know how long these dinners can be."

Brooks lifted his eyebrows. "Yes, I do."

"Hey, did I catch you winking at me a minute ago?"

Caught off guard, Brooks sat up in his chair and put his hand to his face, covering his eyes. "I was hoping you didn't see that."

"Oh, I saw it."

"I didn't mean to. Really, I didn't mean anything by it. It's an involuntary thing that happens sometimes."

"Brooks," she said.

"Seriously, don't read into it."

"Brooks," she said again.

He stopped his retreat and looked at her.

"I'm picking on you."

He took a deep breath and a few moments went by. She smiled and he couldn't help but smile too. "I'm feeling slightly defensive today, obviously."

"Ripe for the picking, that's for sure. Now lighten up and tell me you'll come down to dinner. If I keep waiting for you to ask me out, we're not going to get anywhere." She tilted her head down and stared at him.

He met her gaze, speechless. They both broke into a laugh.

"Is it that obvious?" Brooks asked.

"Is what obvious?"

"You know."

"Tell me," she said. "I want to hear the words come out of your mouth."

He surrendered with slumped shoulders. "Is it obvious that I'd like to ask you out?"

She pinched her fingers together. "Just a little."

"Well, it's true. I have wanted to ask you out for a while."

"Why haven't you?"

"What can I say?" He put up his hands.

"I know what it is. You're scared of rejection."

Brooks's eyes widened. What was it with this woman?

"All men are. Don't worry. I won't reject you. Maybe I will for a second date but I'll at least give you a chance. Don't mess it up, though. I'm selective."

"I bet you are." Brooks started to feel more comfortable and a surfable wave of confidence rolled in. "If I ask you out, my dear, you'll want a second date."

"Oh, there's the Brooks I know."

He beamed. "Now, you better get out of here before I change my mind."

"Ha. Touché. I'll see you at six. You can help me cook."

"I'll be there at 6:15 just so you know I'm not wrapped around your finger. And I'll bring some bottles down."

She kissed the air. "Bye for now."

Brooks didn't say another word. He didn't want to mess up the rhythm. He waved and smiled and watched her leave his office. Once she was gone, he raised a fist in the air in triumph. He finally had his chance.

5

THE SURVIVORS

Otis was blowing off his driveway when Aunt Morgan pulled in. His brood of hens was dust-bathing in the sun near the woodpile, enjoying the glorious weather. Jonathan, his 120-pound Great Pyrenees guard dog—the Great White Beast, Otis often called him—lay on his back on the front porch with his paws in the air. When Morgan's SUV came bumping along the gravel drive, the dog flipped up and ran toward the intruder, his ferocious bark startling the chickens. It was seventy-six degrees outside, a few patches of white in the sky, and it would drop down to the high forties tonight. The Weather Channel promised two more weeks of the same, satisfying news for Red Mountain inhabitants.

"Lord," Otis said, crossing himself, watching her park next to his truck. "You have to be playing tricks on me. I say this with all the love in the world: please get her out of here quickly."

Morgan stepped out of her SUV dressed to the nines, with jewelry everywhere. Her white hair had thinned quite a bit since he'd seen her last, but her face still evoked youth with her big bright blue eyes and "satisfied with life" smile, and he knew before she spoke a word that she was still as sharp as ever. Morgan had made the eight-hour drive in closer to seven, all by herself. Who else could do that at her age? Otis thought she actually might have found the Fountain of Youth somewhere outside of Bozeman. She really didn't look much older than Otis, maybe the opposite. In fact, he had more wrinkles than she did. And she was definitely not a proponent of Botox or plastic surgery or even heavy makeup. She was simply bent on staying young.

"My precious Otis. It's so good to see you, darling." They embraced. She was several inches shorter and quite petite, and he swallowed her with his large arms.

"Morgan, so great you came."

"I had a feeling you needed a visitor. Now get my things and show me to my room. I'm sure you've primped for me. I have my little bag in the front and two in the back. Grab my paints and brushes too. And the easel."

Otis popped open the back and saw two huge bags bursting at the seams next to her painting arsenal. He wondered how she had even gotten the bags zipped. "Wow, looks like you're traveling for a while. Where else are you headed?"

"I'll go back after this. Johnny is watching my cats, and I can't trust him for too long. I told him two or three weeks, tops."

Otis nearly collapsed. "Two weeks." He swallowed his despair. "That's wonderful."

"Aunt Morgan knows when one of her own blood needs some love," she said. "I'll never forget your family moving back from London to help while Jim was sick. Now it's my turn to take care of you."

While she spoke of life back on the farm in Bozeman, Otis showed her around and led her to her room. She visited every couple of years, so it wasn't her first time seeing the home. He left her to get cleaned up and went into the kitchen to start dinner. A skirt steak was marinating in herbs and wild garlic on the counter. He'd selected one of his early vintages of chenin blanc to start the evening. He popped the cork and took a sip. It tasted just as dull as every wine he tasted lately, but he tried not to let it get him down.

Morgan joined him a little while later. Otis was pouring heavy cream into a pot of mashed potatoes. "Looks wonderful," she said. "Oh, how I've always loved your cooking."

"Do you like skirt steak?"

"I gave you your first bite of skirt steak, sonny. You're talking to one of the original Montana cattle girls. Where's my glass?"

He was already on his way to the fridge. "Hold your horses." He filled a glass and handed it to her. He'd forgotten how much he enjoyed her feisty nature.

"Now," she started, smacking her lips together. "I have to tell you something that might come as a surprise. In fact, you might be upset with me, but I don't care. At my age, I can do however I please."

He dropped a huge knob of butter into the potatoes. "I can't wait for this one." Anything was possible with this woman.

"I've invited someone for dinner."

"That's okay, I guess. I didn't realize you knew anyone here." Truthfully, Otis didn't like this news one bit, but he knew he'd have to be flexible if he was going to survive her residency.

"She's a woman I met at the grocery store in West Richland on my way here. I stopped to get a few necessities, and we started talking. She doesn't live too far away, and I thought it would be nice to offer her dinner. She's a lovely woman."

"Morgan."

"What?"

"I know you're joking."

"Do I look like a joker? Her name is Joan. I've forgotten her last name. She really is a doll. And stunning too."

"Morgan, you've been here less than an hour, and you're already stirring up trouble. I'm not going to let you set me up with every woman you run into while you're here."

"Oh, I wouldn't do that. Only the ones I see fit to date my nephew." Otis started to open his mouth, but she jumped ahead of him. "Otis Pennington Till, you will entertain my new friend tonight and that's the end of it. I'm an old lady with very little time left, and this is my wish. You wouldn't dare take that from me. You don't have to date this woman, but you do have to spend the evening with her."

She raised the pitch of her voice. "You never know, it could work out. She's single."

"Morgan, I am perfectly happy by myself. I don't need—"

"Oh, nonsense. You're alone. Every line on your face shows your desperation for love. You haven't gotten laid since the Ice Ages. Now if you want me to stay for the rest of the year, I can do that, but I'll tell you right now. I'm not leaving until we find you a new girl."

"A girl? I'm sixty-four. I'm past dating age."

"Oh, nonsense. I went on a date two days ago. He was twenty years younger than I am. We made love three times in the evening and once the next morning! Don't tell me you're too old. Now, quit your moaning and accept the fact that we have a guest for dinner tonight. Raise your glass and let's drink to our reunion."

Otis paused long enough to let some anger go. Long enough to calm the inner dragon that wanted so desperately to come out breathing flames. If this was how she was going to spend her two weeks with him, he might not survive. The audacity of this woman! She stared at him as he let his emotions settle. Otis knew fighting her would only make things worse.

He chose his words carefully. "It's fine. But I would really appreciate it if you don't pull this again while you're here. At least not without asking me. I know that you want me to remarry, but I'm not interested. It's not that I can't let go of Rebecca. It's that I'm old and busy, and I don't think about love any more. I have my animals. My vines. I have my wine. I already have too much going on."

"You have your animals?" she asked. "You're not poking the sheep, are you?"

"Don't be absurd."

She put a hand on his arm. "I promise, no more surprises. You'll have fun tonight. I know how to pick them."

"Is she twenty years younger?"

"She's just your age."

∼

THE DINNER GUEST arrived at seven. Otis and Morgan sat in chairs in the back yard watching the sunset over his cabernet sauvignon vineyard. They were discussing the struggles of getting old—bad knees, bad hips, bad doctors, more medicine, upcoming surgery—when Jonathan barked. Otis walked to the driveway, ready to apologize for his crazy aunt.

Joan stepped out of an electric car and nearly knocked Otis over with her beauty. She had short silver hair, light brown eyebrows, olive green eyes, and rounded cheeks from an apparent lifetime of smiling. Small diamonds shimmered on her ears. She had very proper posture and a great figure, but there was something deeper about her that was even more striking. Otis felt very comforted by her presence. Before even exchanging a word, he felt like she was an old friend. When they looked at each other, he almost said, "I know you," even though they'd never met.

"You must be Otis." Her voice was warm like Mozart, warm like an Irish coffee.

"I am." He approached and shook her hand. She had a gentle touch and an even more gentle gaze, and they looked at each other for a long while.

"I'm Joan Tobey. Before we say another word, can I please apologize? I can only imagine how shocked you were that your aunt invited someone to dinner. Let's be honest. Trying to set us up."

Otis felt his face reddening.

"She took my shopping cart hostage and wouldn't let me go without agreeing."

"I'm the one who should apologize. Morgan is a wonderful woman, but she loves to pry."

"She's adorable. I hope this is okay."

"It's more than okay. I'm happy you're here. Please come in."

Inside, Morgan greeted Joan, and the women jumped into a conversation about how beautiful Otis's home and property were. Of course it needed a woman's touch, but they could help with that. Otis brought Joan a glass of wine and noticed Morgan beaming with joy as he invited them to sit in the chairs facing outside to the west, where the sun was an hour away from disappearing beyond the horizon.

"I'm so glad you came," Morgan said to her. "And you look radiant."

"Thank you, Morgan. It was very nice of you to force me to come. I'm much less nervous now than I was a few moments ago."

"You have nothing to be nervous about," Morgan said. "We like company. What is life, after all, without human connection?"

"So true."

Otis decided to skip past all this banter that could lead into some very dangerous territory. "So Joan...who are you? Where do you come from? If we let Morgan steer the conversation, you and I will be embarrassed to no end."

"Nonsense," Morgan said.

Joan set her glass on the small table next to her and sat back, resting her hands on her lap. "I suppose the American answer to who I am would lie in what I do for a living. I'm a life coach of sorts. A gardener. A yoga teacher sometimes. Retired other times."

Otis admired the proper manner in which Joan carried herself. She had a way about her, a quiet confidence blended with humility, a poise that was nearly irresistible, a magnetism that made you want to sit closer to her. "What exactly does a life coach do?" Otis asked, noticing Morgan and her devious smile, his aunt relishing Otis's interest in Joan.

"I have clients around the state. Sometimes they come to me. Sometimes I go to them. I help with their problems. I help them repaint their reality, if you will. It's a long and involved topic, but I guess the short of it is that I help people realize their potential. Teach them how to love again. Teach them how to love themselves. How to take care of themselves; how to eat; how to take care of their bodies; how to break free." She spoke as much with her olive eyes as with her mouth. "I teach them about the present moment."

"Well, you've met your greatest challenge," Morgan said, pointing dramatically at Otis, waving her finger up and down, up and down. "If you're for it."

"Oh, come on," Otis said to Morgan, blushing. "I hardly lay on the couch and suck my thumb." He shook his head and looked at Joan. "She has this uncanny ability to make a sixty-four-year-old feel like he's ten again."

"What a wonderful ability," Joan said, smiling and winking at Morgan.

Morgan smiled too. "See, you little squirt? I know what I'm talking about."

He threw his hand in the air. "Oh, forget it."

Joan said, "You two are so cute."

"She drives me to drink."

"Everything drives you to drink," Morgan said.

Otis crossed his arms. "Back to Joan. She makes for much more interesting conversation."

"Agreed," Morgan said. "When can we get Otis into your yoga class? I'd love to see that."

"You'd be surprised how flexible I am," Otis said.

Morgan belted out a laugh. "I bet you couldn't touch your toes if your arms were a foot longer."

Otis shook his head, realizing that the more he fed her fire, the taller the flames. At least Joan looked to be enjoying herself. He was keeping an eye on her glass. She wasn't drinking quickly, which made him slow down himself. "So Joan..."

"Yes?"

"Ask her if she's married," Morgan interrupted.

"Oh, my god," Otis said to Morgan. "Can you please behave for five minutes?"

Morgan snickered and finally nodded.

"I was married once," Joan began. "A long time ago. I grew up in Seattle, went to U-Dub, where we met. We were married right after college and he took a job at PNNL, you know, Pacific Northwest National Laboratory. He was a scientist." Otis knew what they called "The Lab," well. PNNL's campus was only about twenty minutes from Red Mountain. Among many epic accomplishments, PNNL had pioneered compact disc technology in the 1960s.

Joan said, "He worked right up until he died ten years ago. We were married thirty-four years. I live by the river in Richland and have a wonderful life. That's me. How about you two?" Joan bounced her eyes from Morgan to Otis.

"Oh, I'm just an old retired Montana cowlady," Morgan said. "I grew up on our ranch and spent most of my time raising a son and daughter with my husband. I've outlived them all. Now I spend most of my time managing our land."

Joan shook her head. "I can't wait to hear more about your ranch." She turned her eyes to Otis. "And how about you?"

"I'm a winegrower."

"This is yours?" Joan asked, raising her glass. "It's really gorgeous wine. What a talent."

They dined and moved through wine like old friends, and as Otis said goodbye to Joan later in the evening, he asked if he could see her again. He could hardly believe the words as they exited his mouth. She wrote down her number, and he pecked her on the cheek. Something stirred deep within his heart, a feeling he hadn't known since he'd met Rebecca so many years ago.

As Joan drove away, Morgan said to Otis, "I told you I can pick them."

"I won't deny that," Otis said, feeling sudden pains of guilt in his stomach, wondering if he'd betrayed Rebecca.

"Sonny boy, some things are meant to be."

Otis crossed his arms and put his head down. "If only all beginnings didn't come with endings."

Morgan touched his arm. "You can't think that way."

"It's all I've ever known. My life is one big black cat crossing in front of me."

6

THE UNIQUE BOY

Emilia drove home after school with the buzz of life charging through her. Finally, someone understood her. She wanted so badly to be with Mr. Massey right then, to share with him, to confide in him, to dump all her secrets and for once, enjoy being exposed. But he was probably back home with his gorgeous wife, kissing her and touching her just like he'd done to Emilia hours before.

She turned onto the main thoroughfare of Red Mountain, Sunset Road. The waning sun sprayed golden hues of light onto the patchwork quilt of harvest colors, each vineyard block its own shade of greens, oranges, purples and yellows. Moving to Red Mountain was the ultimate culture shock, but today—especially today, Joe Massey acting like a defibrillator shocking her heart back to life—Red Mountain was one of the most beautiful places on earth.

She sped up and passed a John Deere tractor putting along. She and the driver waved and smiled at each other; she wondered if he could see how good she felt. Farther up the road, horses were pulling a wagon of happy tourists with glasses raised, as if they were toasting to Emilia's new lover.

She turned left onto the dusty road that led to her home and her family's winery, Lacoda. The winery was a quarter mile down the road and buried deep into the earth. The desert-colored stone made the winery nearly camouflaged. During the building process, her father was all about the idea of the-less-footprint-the-better. "I don't want anyone to know we're here," he'd said. *Nice try, Dad. Not on this planet.*

Her dad had spent two years scrutinizing architectural drawings and material decisions before giving the green light. He'd decided to take advantage of the cool temperature of the earth and built a state-of-the-art underground gravity-flow building. As Emilia had heard a million times, a gravity-flow winery allowed the production team to de-stem and crush the fruit on the ground level, drop the juice through hoses into the floor for fermentation on the next level, and through hoses again into aging vessels on the next level. Gravity led the way, no pumps necessary.

Another half-mile past the winery, she reached her home, designed by the same architect and built at the same time as Lacoda. A mammoth stone wall surrounded their home, a necessary evil of celebrity life.

In 2004, a man who was now in prison had broken into their home in Seattle and attacked her mom. Luckily, her dad had been there and was able to subdue the intruder, breaking his arm and nose in the process, which only proved to further ignite record sales. They'd employed a bodyguard for several years after the attack, but as the band members aged, they'd lost some of their spotlight on the world stage, and her parents had decided things had become much safer.

Emilia pressed the button on the gate-opener, and the metal doors swung out. Her mother hurried to her car, clearly troubled. Though Emilia loved her mom, she couldn't help feeling scorn for the woman. Carmen Forester had made her name and her living off her cover girl looks, and her exterior defined her. It drove Emilia crazy. Even in her fifties, the woman was severely concerned about her appearance: her wrinkles, her sags, her makeup, her clothes, blah

blah blah, as if age was consuming her identity one gray hair at a time.

"We can't find your brother," Carmen said, wiping tears from her eyes. Her makeup, which Emilia thought she often overdid, was melting on her face.

"How long's he been gone?"

Carmen sighed. "We thought he was upstairs in his room. Maybe an hour, I guess."

"Where's Dad?"

"Out on the ATV."

"Where's Abby?" referring to the woman who spent much of her time helping with her brother, Luca. Scratch that; Abby had pretty much raised Luca. She's also the one who'd taught Emilia about men and sex. Emilia so wished she could tell Abby about Joe Massey; that dirty secret would blow her mind.

"Abby's on her way home now."

"Did you call the police?"

"Not yet. I'm getting all the vineyard workers involved."

Emilia knew why they hadn't called the cops yet. The media vultures loved to find something to put out there on the Foresters, and her parents did everything they could to keep their kids out of the press. "We'll find him, Mom. It's okay. I'm going to run upstairs and search his room. It could have to do with one of his latest projects."

Carmen nodded. "Okay, I'm going to get in the car and drive down Sunset again."

"Take mine." Emilia got out, leaving her car running. She hugged her mother and said, "We'll find him. Don't worry."

"I told Jake to keep an eye on him. Your dad gets so involved in his damn music sometimes. The whole world could explode, and he'd be the last one to know it."

"Mom, this is nobody's fault. We'll find him."

Luca was eight and too young to be out on his own, but he was often hard to manage. Her brother was different. In many ways, he acted and thought like an adult, an odd characteristic in an eight-year-old. He would sit at the dinner table and listen to grownups talk for an hour or two, only chiming in when he saw fit. He understood concepts far beyond the average eight-year-old's ability and very rarely acted up—intentionally, at least.

He had an imagination so vivid at times that he often lost grasp of reality. Emilia understood and loved that about him, and most of the time, so did her parents, but every once in a while his imagination would lead him into trouble. Most likely, Luca had wandered off, chasing one of his imaginary friends; he had seven of them.

Emilia ran up to his room. There were glow-in-the-dark stars stuck to the ceiling. Twin beds with airplanes on the blue comforters. A trunk spilling out with toys. More toys on the floor waiting to trip whoever came rushing in. She navigated her way to his desk and took a stack of drawings that he'd been protective of last time she'd entered his room.

She sat down on the floor and rifled through. Most of the illustrations were of machines and robots, good efforts for a little guy. She came across one drawing that caught her attention, a chain-link fence surrounding a series of radio towers. Much like the towers on the top of Red Mountain. Without hesitation, she ran back downstairs, trying fruitlessly to reach her dad by cell.

She ran into the garage, pushed the button opening the sliding door, and climbed onto one of the other ATVs, something she'd spent plenty of hours on in the past. She revved up the motor and sped out onto the driveway and turned into their vineyards. Going over thirty miles an hour, bouncing up and down, she roared past Lacoda.

She slowed as she started the steeper part of the climb to the top of Red Mountain, which wasn't the tallest mountain in the world, but certainly a daunting piece of geography for an eight-year-old. She saw him, two miles from the house, hiking up the last of the slope with a walking stick and a backpack.

"Luca!" she screamed. She sped up and soon caught up with him. He made no effort to run. That was the way with him. He wasn't trying to disobey or cause problems. He was just being an adventurous boy. She stopped and turned off the ATV. "What are you doing?"

"Hi, Sis," he said, not a care in the world. Luca looked more like his father than his mother, the big head, the dark hair, the intense eyes. "I've devised a new way to contact the Moon People," he said, "but I thought it would be best if I were closer to the antennas. They'll help with the transfer rate."

"That sounds brilliant, Luca, but you know we've been looking for you. You've worried Mom and Dad to death. Do you remember you're not supposed to go too far from the house?"

"Yeah, but this mission is vital to the future of mankind. I was coming right back."

As the immediacy of the situation subsided, Emilia's thoughts drifted back to Mr. Massey's office, back to their kiss. She'd never known a kiss like that, a feeling like that. She got the shivers simply thinking about his tender touch, his handsome face, his kind words.

She eventually said, "Well, I think we'll have to postpone your journey today and go back home. Mom and Dad will need to see you."

"But, Sis, we don't have much time left. The Moon People will be leaving our solar system and traveling to Enceladus soon. They need my help."

"I see." Emilia decided to humor him. "Where is Enceladus?"

"Oh, come on, Sis. It's one of Saturn's moons. Another alien race lives there. The Moon People know them pretty well."

"You are so bright, little brother." Emilia thought for a moment. She, like her parents, did not discourage this incredible imagination. "Let me call Dad."

Their dad came riding up the mountain in his ATV. To everyone else, Jake Forester was some sort of god. Jake fronted a band called Folkwhore that came up during the Seattle grunge era with the likes of Pearl Jam, The Smashing Pumpkins, Nirvana, and Soundgarden. Platinum and gold records decorated the walls of his studio.

But to her, and to Luca, he was just Dad. Sure, he looked more like a musician than most dads, with his tattoos and leather bracelets and younger clothes, but still, he was Dad. He pulled up beside them and hopped off the ATV. Today he had short hair and a five o'clock shadow. Some days it was a beard or mustache or long hair. Emilia was used to it changing. He lifted Luca up in the air and embraced him, talking into his neck. "Luca, you scared me. Haven't I asked you to take me along on your adventures? Red Mountain can be a dangerous place, and it's much better to travel with a sidekick like me." He set Luca down.

"I'm sorry, Dad. It's the Moon People. They wanted me to come alone. They're trying to get to Enceladus for the Space Conference. All the alien races are worried about Earth, the way we're destroying our planet. I'm kind of the ambassador, since the U.S. President is such a bonehead."

Jake and Emilia laughed.

"You say that all the time, Dad. Reception in my room wasn't strong enough. I think their radios are running out of batteries. So I thought I'd get a better signal near the other antennas above." He pointed.

At the top of Red Mountain, a tall chain-link fence protected a series of Wi-Fi, radio, and cell antennas climbing a hundred feet into the sky. They'd walked by them many times when they hiked the trails as a family.

"I see," Jake said. "I need you to talk to me, though, whenever you leave the house. Unless you are playing in the yard. If you leave our property, we need to know where you are. Your mother was terrified. Remember the coyotes I've told you about?"

"Oh, the coyotes are not a problem." He pulled his Star Wars backpack off and reached inside, pulling out some wheat crackers. "I brought these to feed them. They'll be happy."

"Luca," his dad continued, "coyotes aren't like Pepper or Wilson. They aren't normal dogs. They are dangerous and will hurt you."

"I don't think so, Dad. I've seen them before. They're very nice."

"Sometimes you have to trust me, son. I will let you finish your mission, but you have to make a deal with me. You will never go far from the house again without bringing your mom or me or your sister along. When you're older, you will understand."

Jake took Luca, and the three of them rode to the trail on the top of the Mountain. There were no trees, only sagebrush and large boulders of granite. Almost moonlike. The wind blew hard, as it usually did at the top. Emilia twisted her head, taking in the view for many miles in each direction. The farmland, the Columbia and Yakima Rivers, the Horse Heaven Hills, the plume of smoke rising from the Hanford site, the cherry and apple orchards on the northern and eastern slopes, the multi-colored vineyards of Red Mountain, the roof of their house.

They rode the trail to the towers and dismounted. The gate leading inside the fenced-in area was locked, and a sign warned off trespassers.

The three of them approached the fence. "You can't get inside," Jake told Luca.

"Oh, I don't need to. Just watch, Dad."

He set his backpack down and emptied it onto the ground. There was masking tape, coat hangers he'd unraveled, batteries, and two paper cups.

"What do you have there, Luca?" Emilia asked, holding back her wind-blown hair, still revisiting her kiss with Joe Massey.

"Remember when Dad showed us how to talk to each other with two cups and a string? I didn't have string long enough to reach the moon, so I had to devise a stronger method. Just watch, okay? I can't teach you in the middle of the mission."

He taped several straightened coat hangers to the two cups and taped the two double AA batteries to the side of the wire. He shook it in the air, apparently ensuring its stability, and said, "I'm ready." He reached back into his backpack and pulled out a long rubber glove from the cleaning closet and a pair of ski goggles. He put the over-sized glove on his hand. "With this kind of power, you have to wear a glove. Otherwise you get burned. Now stand back, please. My invention is in the early stages, and I'm not sure exactly what to expect."

Luca put on the goggles, got on his knees, and held one cup to the fence. He spoke into the other. "Moon People, this is Luca Forester. I'm checking in from Red Mountain. Are you out there?"

He moved the cup to his ear and back. "Coming in loud and clear. Are there any other things you need me to do? It could be light years before we connect again. Will there be anything to add to my list of missions?"

Emilia looked at her father who was smiling.

"I will reach out to the U.S. President soon. I don't speak Russian or Chinese yet, but I will find a translator. For now, I will make sure people are recycling here on Red Mountain. Yes, and the nuclear site here is only a clean-up now. No more plutonium. I read about it all the time. As far as the pollution in the river, I'll talk to the mayor. I think my Dad knows him." Luca shook the cup. "You're breaking up. We must terminate the call before they track me." He listened intently.

"Ten-four," Luca replied. "Roger," he said a moment later. After two minutes of listening, Luca said, "Tell your leader that I would like to come visit him one day. I'm only eight now, but maybe when I'm eleven. I'll be taller and stronger. And my Dad will probably let me go for a day or two." He listened and then, "Yes, that's fine. I will complete the missions. Over and out."

~

WHILE CARMEN and Jake gently scolded their son, Emilia followed her mom's assistant, Abby, over to her place to help unload groceries. Abby lived in a tiny villa the Foresters had built for her down the hill from their own home. She lived for free as part of her compensation. Her place was more a bungalow than anything else. A bedroom and bathroom upstairs with a balcony, then an adorable living room, kitchen, and half bath downstairs. Abby had made the place even cuter with her own abstract paintings from artists in Bainbridge, Whidbey, and the San Juans. Abby loved color and her place was a rainbow.

Emilia often hung out there, learning more from Abby than she ever would from school. Abby could talk politics for days, and she was a big proponent of women's rights. And she was so unique and refreshing. As Emilia lifted her last bag onto the counter, Abby said, "That was scary, wasn't it? I feel like we need to put an ankle monitor on him."

"He'd probably figure a way out of it."

"Hey," Abby said, "wanna hear a good joke?"

"Of course." Emilia loved her jokes; the more off-color, the better.

"There was this woman named Mary from Benton City. She went to Seattle for the first time and when she got back, all her friends wanted to know what it was like. She said, 'there are men who kiss other men.' 'What!' one of her friends screamed. 'What are they called?' Mary said, 'They call them homosexuals. And there are women who kiss other women.' 'You're kidding me!' her friends said. 'What are they called?' Mary said, 'They call them lesbians. And there are men who kiss women in their private parts.' 'Shut your mouth,' one of her friends said. 'What do you call them?' 'I don't know, but when he was done with me, I called him Precious.'"

Emilia burst into laughter. "Where do you get these things?"

"Dark alleys," Abby said, sitting down on a stool in the kitchen. "Anyway, how's life? You look like you're on top of the world. All bubbly. Like you've fallen in love. Are you and Tex getting serious?" Emilia had been dating the star football player since the first week of school.

Emilia shook her head. "Definitely not. Life's really good right now, but Tex has nothing to do with it. I'm trying to figure out what I ever saw in him."

"I know what you saw in him. He's a southern hunk."

"He is a hunk. But he's...he's just that. A hunk. I don't remember ever having a thought-provoking conversation with him."

"I know that type. Look at me, Em. I'm thirty-six and never married. There aren't a lot of perfect guys out there. Most men are just blocks of muscle running around bumping into things and groping for your goodies."

"He's the only guy who has asked me out in a long time. I felt like

I was obligated to say yes. Then it snowballed into something. It was never going to last." The truth was that it was that fake side of her, this identity she'd created for protection, that had said yes. The real Emilia had never been into him.

They moved to the couch. "Welcome to every relationship of my life. Guess what, Emilia? The reason no one asks you out is because you're intimidating. Look at you. You're the full package. No one feels worthy."

"My parents are intimidating. I'm not."

"Who cares about your parents?"

"Everybody I know."

"Oh, come on. Yes, you're going to have to be extra careful the rest of your life dating. I'm sure any guy would want to say they're dating Jake and Carmen Forester's daughter. But Em, you're going to have to shake them off. Really. Get over it. Nobody is going to feel bad for you. You're a catch, regardless of your parents. So Tex is history, huh? Then who is the new guy?"

Emilia jerked her head up.

"Do you think you can hide things from me? I've known you since you were a little girl. And I'm a woman. Nobody bubbles like you unless they're falling in love."

Emilia smiled, desperately wanting to tell Abby. She so badly wanted Joe Massey to touch her again. "There might be someone else."

"Who?"

"I'm not ready to divulge that information." Oh, God, she wanted to. She wanted to tell Abby that for the first time in her life, she felt something for someone.

"It must be someone you shouldn't be seeing."

Emilia let a smile out. "I can't tell you."

"You naughty girl."

And Emilia thought: *It's so fun being the naughty girl for once.*

7

A RED MOUNTAIN DINNER PARTY

A t Lacoda, Brooks Baker slipped on his work gloves and rubber boots and climbed through the door of a fermentation tank with a shovel. They'd drained the free run juice of some east block syrah. Now the bottom of the tank was filled with pomace, the remaining skins and seeds from fermentation that needed to be pressed. He didn't have to get in and do the dirty work, but he liked being a role model. Shoveling tanks was good, hard work.

After twenty minutes of shoveling, he hopped out to let the cellar rats wash the tank. He needed to be at the Foresters' place soon and still had to grab some wine and change. He made small talk in broken Spanish with his guys while taking off his boots. He took the elevator down to the bottom level, where the finished wine aged and remained until shipping. Following the light of wall sconces, he hung a left and walked down one of the arched walkways. The temperature hovered just under sixty degrees at all times, and it very much felt like walking through caves.

Brooks reached the Foresters' personal cellar. He pressed his thumb to the reader and the giant wooden door opened, revealing what a wine geek would consider a dream collection of over three thousand bottles from around the world, dating back to the late 1800s. Ahh, the benefits of stardom. Brooks had the honor of being the only non-family member other than Abby who was granted access.

He made his way to the white Burgundy section and chose two bottles of 1973 Comtes Lafon from Meursault. One is never enough, he reasoned. He put them in a wine bag and went toward the Red Mountain section, selecting a couple of bottles of Hedges Family Estate and Kiona from the late nineties. It was going to be a good night.

Back on the ground level, he washed off in the sink. He couldn't get the purple off his hands, though; the mark of a winemaker. He'd been working ten-hour days since harvest began and the purple just kept coming. When he closed his eyes at night, he saw purple.

Shortly after six, he climbed onto his Triumph Scrambler motorcycle and rode down to the Foresters', wine bag in hand. He pulled inside the open gate, went around to the front door, and rang the bell. The family's two Weimaraners barked inside.

Abby opened the door wearing an apron, and Pepper and Wilson burst out, greeting him. "Hey, boys." He let them smell his hand and he patted them on their heads.

"Hi there, handsome," she said.

He kissed her on the cheek and followed her in. The house was immaculately clean, thanks to their housekeeper. The ceilings were ultra-tall, and the modern interior focused on oranges, blues, and golds, the walls a mixture of brick and exotic wallpapers. The art was more Matisse than Monet; the furniture was wavy and abstract like the art and covered in extravagant and colorful pillows.

"Everyone's out back," Abby said, leading him through the house. "Want to help me finish things up in the kitchen?"

"Yeah, sure. Take me to your microwave."

"You know, Brooks, you're going to have to learn how to cook eventually. You can't be in the wine business and not know your way around the kitchen."

"Everyone on this mountain is a chef. Someone has to focus on the eating. I am a master of sticking a fork in my mouth. What did you make?" he asked, as they entered the kitchen. It was the kind of culinary dream you design in your head for years, featuring an Italian six-burner stove, three ovens, an oak island covered with fruit and vegetables. There were plastic-wrapped plates of food on the white quartz counter, ready to go.

"Nothing too fancy," she said. "A kale and Brussels sprouts salad, Caprese with the last of our garden's tomatoes, my smoked Copper River salmon. Cheese, cornichons, olives, my pickled asparagus. Oh, and I've got some baguettes in the oven. Do you mind grabbing them?" She tossed him a hot mitt.

He removed the mouthwatering crusty bread. "By the way, you look beautiful tonight."

"In my apron? I'm a mess."

"Definitely in your apron. Just the way you are."

With the wine bag slung on his shoulder, Brooks picked up two plates and headed out the back door. The pool was lit up, and a Balinese statue of Devi spat water from the middle. Hearing laughter, he walked to the upper deck, which was as high as the gate and offered a gorgeous view west. Everyone turned to greet him.

He shook hands with Jake and Carmen Forester, and they introduced him to the others. One of the men was a writer from *Rolling Stone*; Brooks had an interview with him in the morning. One of the women was an old friend of Carmen's whom Brooks had met before. He kissed Emilia on the cheek and shook her boyfriend's hand.

Tex Gentry was the captain of the football team, a great receiver, a muscular and handsome blond—and to Brooks, a real douchebag. Brooks thought Emilia could do better. She was out of his league. Tex didn't have the depth that she had, or the character. Brooks felt like Emilia's older brother, and he hoped for and expected more from her.

He went back inside to help Abby and then joined the rest at the long rectangular table, Brooks taking the far end from Jake. Behind Jake, the sun was setting. The western sky was lit up in wild streaks of color, and the desert and the rolling treeless hills glowed in lilac and purple. You could just as easily be in Spain or Italy. Red Mountain had a distinct European feel. Mount Adams, the second highest mountain in Washington, stood proudly on the horizon, and the circling clouds glowed like a stack of halos, perhaps angels looking out over the land.

That night and every night, the characters of Red Mountain and their conversations were even more colorful than the big sky sunsets, never allowing a dull moment to last too long, often crossing lines that shocked those newest to this spot on the globe.

Carmen was usually one of the first to cross those lines, and this evening was no different. Halfway through the meal, someone got on the topic of how desperately Red Mountain needed accommodations, and Margot Pierce's name came up. A Vermont transplant was building a place not too far away on the mountain called Épiphanie, a small inn and restaurant. She'd brought spicy ginger cookies to the winery earlier in the year when she'd first moved to Red Mountain, and she and Brooks had shared a glass of wine and swapped stories. Anyone who brings cookies was okay in his book.

Carmen jumped into the conversation; she'd obviously been drinking all day. "I hear Margot is vegetarian. Is that all she's going to cook? We finally get a restaurant, and all she's going to serve is peas and spinach and tofu. What a waste!"

"Come on, Carmen," Jake said. "That's not very kind. I'm sure the food is going to be delicious."

"Well, I don't see how she's a vegetarian. She's completely over-weight. I bet she sneaks hot dogs when no one is looking. Everybody moves out West and has to turn vegan. It's just such a cliché."

The table went quiet, something Brooks had gotten used to. If you couldn't handle uncomfortable silences on Red Mountain, it would be a hard place to live. He glanced over at Jake and could see his disgust. Carmen hadn't always been this way. She'd become so jaded and angry over the past year. Brooks wasn't sure why, but he wondered how long Jake could take it.

Their son, Luca, appeared and crept up to the table in his paja-mas, a video camera in his hand, the red light blinking. He ran to his dad as everyone said hello. Abby stood to take him back upstairs, but

Brooks jumped in. "I'll get him. Luca and I have some catching up to do." He'd grown very close to Luca too. Without a family of his own, the Foresters and his mentor, Otis Till, were all he really had.

Brooks snatched the video camera and lifted Luca into the air. Luca giggled loudly. "Aren't you supposed to be sleeping, you booger?" Brooks slung him onto his shoulders.

"No. It's not even nine o'clock yet."

"Nine o'clock? What eight-year-old goes to bed at nine o'clock?" Brooks asked with the whole table listening.

"I have straight A's in school. I can do whatever I want."

"I can't argue with that. But how about you show me what you've been working on? I heard about your newest project."

"Well, it's top secret."

"Then let's go upstairs and you can debrief me. You know I have top secret clearance, right?"

"Who gave you top secret clearance?"

"If I told you, I'd have to tickle you."

"You're full of crapola."

Carmen jumped in. "Watch your mouth, Luca Forester."

A round of laughter circled the table.

Brooks carried Luca up the stairs and sat on the rug with him, amongst a circle of wooden chairs usually occupied by Luca's imaginary friends. Brooks had met them many times. "Let me see if I can remember everyones' names," he said.

"Okay, go for it."

"Daga, Gobles, Stanbar, Chandemier, Seuvy Doo, Dillo, and...Mido."

"Yep! That's pretty good."

"So I heard you scared your parents today?"

"Yeah, I was on a secret mission. I'm helping the Moon People."

"Is that what the video camera is for?" Brooks asked.

"How did you know?"

"I know things."

"Oh. Yeah, they've asked me to make a movie of life on Red Mountain, so they can understand humans better. My sis is a really good editor and is going to help me. She did a movie for school last year."

"How long will the project take?"

"Probably another month or so. Depends on how good my footage is."

"Will I be able to see it?"

"I'll have to ask the Moon People. Since my dad's famous, he could probably get it into a few select theaters for a release if I want to. Maybe I'll take you to the premier. Abby can be your date."

Brooks was floored. "How do you know about me and Abby?"

"I know things."

"You are one smart kid. You know that?" Brooks put his hand on Luca's head. "Can you keep Abby and me a secret?"

Luca nodded.

"It's really good talking to you. I've got to get back to the table."

"Are you going to kiss her?"

"I hope so." Brooks said goodbye and walked back downstairs, touched by the boy's greatness.

8

CRAVING LOVE

Margot Pierce didn't want to get out of bed. It was one of those mornings. She was still in her nightgown. There was a box of tissues spilling out next to her. Philippe was on the end of the bed chewing on her back-up tampon. Her favorite movie of all time, *Under the Tuscan Sun,* played on the screen. She'd been texting with her best friend who lived in Vermont and thumbing through trashy magazines while binging on leftover pasta and pistachio gelato. She hated her ex-husband even more than usual; could barely wait until the afternoon to get in the tub and play out a new fantasy—perhaps this time with the garbage disposal. She was completely fed up with her contractor and couldn't believe yet another day was passing without workers on site.

Seeing the empty bowls of gluttony next to the clock reading 10:04 a.m. completely disgusted her, and she paused the movie long enough to hide the evidence and climbed right back into the covers to finish the movie.

Margot had seen *Under the Tuscan Sun* so many times that she could quote every line. She loved Frances, the woman Diane Lane played in the movie. They had so much in common: their vile exes, their love of good food, their desire for romance. The movie had inspired Margot to follow her dreams and start Épiphanie. *Under the Tuscan Sun*, on a very admittedly unhealthy level, was her guiding light, a fact she hadn't told a soul and would take to her grave.

Her favorite part came on. Frances has met Marcello, her Italian dream man, in Tuscany. After an unexpected twenty-four hours of blissful passion, she starts jumping on the bed, dancing and singing ecstatically. That scene always made Margot laugh out loud, but this time her laughter turned quickly into tears. What Frances didn't know was that Marcello was going to move on to someone else soon. That's the way men worked! Margot squeezed Philippe tightly and cried, soaking her pillow in tears. She'd never meet anyone else, no one like Marcello, and even if she did, he'd leave her or cheat on her or lie to her. Just like Frances, right when she was getting back on top, someone would rip the rug right out from under her again.

As the movie wrapped up, Margot recited Frances's entire final monologue word-for-word. She could watch *Under the Tuscan Sun* every day the rest of her life. "It's never too late," she said out loud, hitting a pillow. "Never too late!"

She got out of bed and went to her closet. Before she could talk herself out of it, she took out her running clothes and set them on the bed. She pulled off her nightgown and looked at herself in the mirror. Aside from the last year of her marriage where she stopped eating, she'd always had a curvy body with love handles, but things were getting out of hand. Way out of hand. She touched her breasts. They'd grown at least another size. She'd been busting out of her bras lately.

She put on a tight t-shirt, stretch pants, and running shoes, and she and Philippe headed outside into the mid-seventies crisp air. She could still taste the gelato in her mouth. She strolled for a while, singing songs she'd performed in the past from *Guys and Dolls, The Sound of Music, My Fair Lady*. She eventually broke into a jog and instantly began to breathe heavily, craving oxygen. Her knees hurt too.

Margot and her dog ran up the steep part of Antinori Road. She didn't last long. Slowing back down to a brisk walk, reaching Col

Solare, she moved her arms with her stride, hoping her extra effort would burn a few extra calories.

Coming down the hill, they passed Hedges Family Estate, one of the first growers on Red Mountain. Tom Hedges had grown up only a short drive away in Richland, and his lovely wife, Anne-Marie, came from Champagne, France. Margot couldn't get enough of her French ways, and the two women had hit it off from the moment they'd met. The Hedges' son, Christophe, inherited the old world masonry skills of his Champenoise great-grandfather, and the awe-inspiring Hedges chateau was his playground. Their daughter, Sarah, had found her calling as head winemaker. Margot had also heard Sarah was a world-class bread baker, but Margot hadn't yet been fortunate enough to get her hands on a loaf.

Margot saw someone running toward her off in the distance and decided to pick up the pace again, as if she had something to prove. As they got closer, she recognized him and her heart pounded. She hadn't met Jake Forester, but of course she knew he lived on the mountain and had hoped she might meet him one day. Just not on a day when she was absurdly fat and bloated, without makeup, and covered in sweat.

Jake wore extremely short shorts that showed off unbearably sexy legs with well-formed calves. The perfect amount of curly dark hair ran from his ankles to his shorts, and his tank top revealed his muscles and tattoos, which were glistening in sweat. He stopped running and waved, slowing her down. As he got closer, she noticed the sharpness of his cheeks and jaws and his broad nose, a very refined look, like he should be on the cover of a cigar magazine. She also noticed hints of gray in his black hair, only enhancing his refinement. He absolutely radiated sex appeal. Margot's face flushed red, and she felt a warm pulse between her legs.

"You must be a neighbor I've never met." He reached out his hand. "I'm Jake."

"Margot." She worked hard to meet his handsome eyes.

"Oh, sure! You're building Épiphanie."

"At this rate, I'll be building it for the rest of my life."

"Oh, no. The same thing happened with Lacoda and our place. It never works out exactly as planned."

"Not even close." She shook her head.

"As soon as you do open, we'll do our best to support you. I can't tell you how happy I am to know there will finally be a place to stay around here."

"We need it, don't we?"

"Badly." He bent down to say hello to Philippe. "Who's this guy?"

"This is Philippe."

"Hi, Philippe," he said, running his hand through the dog's wiry hair. He stood back up and said, "I heard you have a musician in the family too. Right?"

"Yes, I do." Margot beamed. "My son, Jasper. He's a pianist. World-class, really."

"His teacher told me. Quentin and I are old friends. He told me Jasper was a prodigy. Do you think he'd like to play some time?"

"Oh, my gosh! He would love that."

"If I can keep up with him. Would you mind giving me his number? I'll call him."

Jake entered Jasper's number into his phone while Margot tried not to completely freak out. She couldn't wait to get home to tell Jasper. As they said goodbye, he took her hand in both of his. "It's really nice to meet you, Margot. I imagine we'll see much more of each other."

"I hope so." Again, she worked hard to meet his electrifying eyes.

Margot and Philippe cut through a vineyard to get back home, running faster than she'd run in years, the giant cheat grass mounds of the Horse Heaven Hills looking back at them. Once they reached her driveway, she slowed to a walk, her mind on Jake. What a man. His wife was the luckiest woman on earth. She looked at her hand, the one he'd touched, and she licked it, tasting him, tasting the salty ruggedness.

Margot left Philippe in the kitchen with his favorite stuffed tiger, and with a deep desire coursing through her, she climbed the stairs. Before she'd even made it to her room, she was pulling off her running clothes and touching herself. She'd always been a sexual woman but lately she'd been desperately thirsty for a lover. Reaching her bed, she ran her hands along her body, thinking of Jake, imagining his nakedness next to her, touching her.

She climaxed with a great moan that made her cover her mouth.

~

AFTER LUNCH, she worked through her e-mails and daily chores, the requirements of starting a new business. All she wanted to do, though, was drive to Jasper's school, pull him out of class, and tell him about Jake's interest in playing music with him. She'd decided it would be more fun if she waited until he got home. They could celebrate and cook together.

Jasper had played with some wonderful musicians over the years, but Jake was such a big force in music. Margot was sure that Jasper would be blown away; it could be the best news her son had ever heard.

About two o'clock, Margot went out to her garden in the back yard. Margot's mother had been a wonderful gardener, and Margot had grown up in Virginia with her hands in the dirt. Even when she was singing in New York, she tended to a petit garden on the top of her building in Chelsea where she grew some of the best tomatoes in Manhattan. For this past season, she'd built four large boxes, filled them with very healthy soil and organic goat manure, and planted the basics. She started out the year with kale and rainbow chard and carrots of all colors; then the summer brought onions, zucchini, eggplant, tomatoes, and herbs. Now, she was beginning to collect her fall harvest: some beautiful collards, a second round of kale, acorn and butternut squash, pie pumpkins. Margot couldn't believe how well vegetables grew in eastern Washington.

She'd built a small two-foot fence around her garden to deter the chickens. With a basket of crisp greens in her hand, she stepped over the fence and went to the coop. Margot could tell by the *bwaking* coming from inside that one of her girls was in a nest, laying. Margot entered the run to fill their water and feeder.

As with any animal she'd ever owned, Margot took great care of these chickens, spoiling them any way she could. Tanner, her devil contractor, had spent three weeks building her dream cedar coop. Her ex had never let her even speak of getting chickens, so it was one of the first projects she jumped on when she and Jasper moved out west. The coop could hold twenty-five chickens comfortably, but she only had five so far. Like the garden, she wanted to start slowly until she got the hang of things. She'd spared no expense on the coop, including a completely unnecessary tin roof, but the most absurd feature—and her favorite—was the crystal chandelier hanging inside, the one already coated with a layer of chicken poop. God, if anyone knew what she'd spent!

The other hens came running when they heard her filling the feeder. "Hey, girls. How are we today? I don't know about you, but I met a man. A beautiful rooster. Of course, he's married. They all are." The hens pecked at their food aggressively, as she addressed each one by name (all Broadway women), asking them questions they'd never answer.

She was lifting up the hatch to collect some eggs when Jasper's high school principal called. "Is everything okay?" she asked, already knowing it wasn't.

"Jasper's been hurt," the man said. "He's in the hospital."

9

HEARTBREAK LOVES THE LOVER

In between free period and physics class, Emilia Forester knocked on Joe Massey's open door. She'd spent the entire night thinking about him, especially as Tex was kissing her goodnight in her driveway.

She didn't know what to expect from Mr. Massey. Maybe his marriage was on the rocks. He and Emilia had a magic between them that couldn't be denied. She'd never imagined the possibility of them until the moment they kissed; but once their lips met, she was on fire. She could see herself falling in love with him; she could see a future between them. It's not like he was that much older than she was.

He waved her in but didn't say anything. He didn't even smile.

"What's wrong?" she asked, her insecurity welling up inside of her.

He took a deep breath and said, "I am so sorry for yesterday. I was wrong to do that."

Emilia felt an escalating sadness in her bones. Was this really happening? Was he really going to end it right now?

He pinched his chin. "You're so amazing. But I'm married. And you're my student. It's just not right. You're seventeen."

"I'm not just any seventeen-year-old," she said, feeling so used and worthless.

"No, you're not. And that's why I will not have a hand in hurting you or your life. Your future. You're confused enough as it is. It was a mistake."

Emilia looked down at the floor. She felt her body plummeting; tears were coming. She didn't want him to see her cry again—ever again—so she turned and walked toward the door. He called out as she left his office. She had nothing more to say to him. She wouldn't dare beg; that's not what a confident and strong woman would do. But inside, in the depths of the real Emilia, the one she'd never let him see again, she wanted to get down on her knees and beg, beg like she used to beg her mom to play with her, beg like she used to beg her dad not to go on tour.

Tex was waiting by her locker. It was class change and the hallways were bustling. Tex was about the same height as Joe Massey, six foot two or so, but Tex was much stronger, with rock solid abs and much thicker arms—hidden at the moment by his letter jacket, a huge white *B* for Belmont High on the left side. He had a swath of curly brown hair that all the cheerleaders loved to run their fingers through, a gesture that continually annoyed Emilia.

His legal name was Derrick, but he grew up in Texas to proud Texans (she'd never seen his dad without his slightly obnoxious *T* for Texas belt buckle fastened around his waist) who'd bestowed the nickname upon him at birth.

From the moment he could hold a ball, Tex's parents had demanded that he be the great Texas hope, and even though they'd left Texas for Washington, Tex was still making Texas and his parents proud. Senior year had barely started, and he'd already signed with the Texas Longhorns. The young athlete was one of the fastest players in the country, running a 40 in 4.4 seconds. The Longhorns were giving him a full ride to play wide receiver, and NFL coaches were already eyeing him. Tex wasn't all jock, though; he had some substance. Enough so that Emilia had put up with him for the past couple of months, letting their high school fling play out.

"What's wrong, baby?" he asked, biting his upper lip.

She ignored him and opened her locker. She stared blankly at a photograph she'd taped to the inside of her door of Joni Mitchell holding a Martin acoustic guitar.

"Hey, what did I do?" He put his hand on her shoulder.

She shook him off. "Nothing, I just don't want to talk right now." She filled her backpack with textbooks, knowing she wasn't going to be back to school for a few days.

Tex asked, "What's wrong with you?"

"Leave me alone!" she snapped, unintentionally drawing attention from the entire hall. The bustle of her classmates turned to a curious silence. The spotlight suddenly shined on her, giving the world a rare glimpse at the less-than-perfect side of Emilia Forester.

She took her purse, tossed her backpack over her shoulder, and made way to the exit, her footsteps echoing in the quiet hallway, every eye on her, curiosity as invasive as the paparazzi. She burst through the double doors and went straight for her car. Only once she was safely outside did she let herself cry. And cry she did, a tremendous bawl that stained her shirt with tears.

She got into her Subaru, a car she chose over the Porsche her dad had offered her, and covered her face with her hands. It wasn't a feeling she was used to, not getting what she wanted. No one had ever broken up with her.

Tex suddenly knocked on the door, scaring her out of her misery. She rolled down the window. "What?"

"What's going on with you?" he asked. "I just want to help. Tell me how."

"I'm having a bad day, that's all."

"Is it your time of the month? Is that what this is all about?"

That was the wrong thing to say. Emilia squinted her eyes at him, the football player chewing on his lip again. She said, "You're so small-minded, Tex. How dare you. How dare you!"

She rolled up the window. While Tex watched her with clueless eyes and his hands in the air, Emilia sped out of the parking lot. Today was the worst day of her life. How could she ever recover? The lonely and quiet drive back to Red Mountain tortured her, her mind conjuring up worse and worse thoughts by the minute, and the questions kept coming.

Arriving home, she ran up to her room. Her dad was probably out in his studio. She didn't know where her mom was, probably looking at herself in a mirror somewhere. Emilia changed into her pajamas and crawled into bed, pulling the covers up tight. No, she was never getting out of that bed again. Maybe they'd have to drag her dead body out; then everyone could finally know the truth. She spent the next hours flipping from one side of the bed to the other, Suzanne Vega playing through the speakers of her CD player.

Sadie, her best friend, had been blowing her up with text messages all day. Emilia was ignoring them, but she did read one that came over about 2 p.m. *Your beau and his posse just sent that new kid, Jasper Simpson, to the hospital :(*

Emilia sat up and typed back a long series of question marks.

Sadie replied: *In the parking lot after school. Tex was making fun of him. Jasper kept walking and ignoring him. Tex pushed him and Jasper hit him in the face!*

That's it, Emilia thought. *I'm so done with him.* Tex and his friends were complete idiots. She hoped he would lose his scholarship and finally learn a real lesson. Why had she ever thought he had substance?

10

YOU CAN'T RUN FROM DYING

Otis had survived almost twenty-four hours with Morgan, but she was the least of his worries now. He was in the back of the winery with a glass in his hand, about to taste through all the wines. His assistant, Elijah, his intern from WSU, was in the lab running numbers. It was seven in the morning, and they'd been there since 5:30 a.m.

His winery, like the house down the hill, was built of stone. By design, the building looked like it had been constructed long before he was born. Many wineries in Washington chased modernity with their architecture—and their wine; Otis on the other hand, chased antiquity. He'd maxed out the space with a production of three thousand cases; which was just fine, considering he and Elijah were overwhelmed already. He would never sacrifice quality for quantity.

Otis sold all his wine through his wine club, which had a five-year waiting list. If you weren't on that list, you had to get very lucky to enjoy a bottle of Till Vineyards. Though Otis didn't put effort into pleasing the critics, they had been kind to him over the years. But word of mouth was really what had lifted Till Vineyards into the stratosphere. Tourists, bloggers, friends, fellow winemakers; they had all supported his efforts to bottle Red Mountain.

Past the tasting room in the cellar, Otis had seventy-two American and French oak barrels stacked against the left wall. On the opposite wall stood a collection of stainless steel tanks, clay amphorae, and concrete eggs. Constantly in pursuit of making wines of soul and truth, Otis constantly toyed with winemaking techniques used thousands of years ago on the other side of the ocean; hence the amphorae and concrete.

Otis removed the steel lid off an amphora. Ninety-five gallons of syrah, halfway through fermentation, bubbled with gusto. He rolled up his sleeves and punched down the cap, mixing the skins back into the juice. After a couple of minutes, he took his wine glass and plunged it down into the young wine, then brought it back up to his nose.

He couldn't smell a thing. No fruit, no yeast, no sulfur dioxide, no aroma compounds. Zip, zilch, nada, not a damn thing. It was like he had a glass of water in his hand.

He buried his nose further into the glass, breathing in deeply, taking in as much as he could. Nothing. He swirled the wine aggressively, trying to stir up more aromas. He put his nose back in the glass. Nothing. He took a sip, and keeping the wine in his mouth, sucked in some oxygen through puckered lips. He chewed on the wine, desperate to pick up some flavor. Nothing.

Otis had already spent time on his computer trying to find an answer. According to Dr. Google, he could have cancer, Parkinson's, heart disease, Alzheimer's, or a hundred other things. He wasn't sure it was that serious—he felt pretty great otherwise—but something was definitely wrong, and that awareness was terrifying and depressing. Another punch in the gut by Life.

He spit the wine in a perfect stream into the floor drain. The irony was nearly too much: a winemaker who has lost his senses. What an evil joke this damn world was playing on him. What kind of god would chop off his nose and cut out his tongue?

The wines would start suffering soon if he didn't figure something out. Though he'd taught Elijah a lot over the past year, he still didn't trust Elijah's palate. Should his health continue to deteriorate, this vintage would be Otis's last; he could afford absolutely no mistakes.

Otis needed to call Brooks, the winemaker Otis believed would take Red Mountain to the next level. The man he considered his son.

"*El Jefe*," Brooks said, answering the phone.

"You mind coming down to the winery? I need you."

"I'll be there in fifteen minutes. Just need to be back here by ten for an interview."

Brooks Baker had a heart of gold. Sure, Otis had done a lot for him, but it wasn't about that any more. Their relationship was so much more than a debt or obligation. The two men saw wine the same way. Wine wasn't a product. It wasn't a way to make a living; it wasn't PowerPoints and Excel sheets. Growing and making wine was the purest of art forms: to work the land all year—to work *with* the land all year—to bleed and sweat and toil through the seasons, to bring in the harvest and guide the juice all the way to a bottle, and to share that bottle with the world. To share the fruit of a time and place. To help people smile.

Brooks stepped into the cellar. "Whose SUV is that out there? With the Montana tags. Is Morgan here?"

"Indeed."

"What! I can't believe you didn't tell me. She didn't want to see me?"

"Oh, she's going to be here a while. You're on her short list. She has other objectives at the moment."

"Must be important. I really thought she and I had something."

"She's trying to find me a wife."

Brooks snickered and patted Otis on the shoulder. "I bet you love that."

"Two or three more weeks of this nonsense."

"Maybe she's right. It's about time you find somebody."

"Brooks, don't start. I've got something else going on." Otis made sure Elijah was out of earshot and whispered, "This is between you and me. No one knows what I'm about to tell you. I don't want anyone to. Not even Morgan."

Brooks's smile faded, a man used to bad news. "You have my word."

"I can't smell or taste any more."

"What are you talking about?"

"Something's wrong with me. It's serious. I can't smell a goddamn thing. Can't taste a damn thing."

"I'm sure it's just a cold."

"No, it's not a cold. Been down that road."

"Have you been to the doc?"

"Not yet. I'll get over there eventually. In the meantime, I need you to help me run through these wines. Tell me what I need to be doing."

"Jesus, Otis. You okay?"

"Peachy."

"I can only imagine. You know I'm happy to help every single day of this harvest if you need me."

"Oh, come on. You have a winery to run."

"You call me when you need me. Seriously. I've always got time for you."

Otis got a glass for Brooks, and the men worked through each vessel of wine. Otis took notes while Brooks smelled, tasted, and spat. No big flaws to speak of. Only a couple of barrels showing reduction, an issue usually fixed with some air exposure. Brooks especially liked the sangiovese, a variety just coming into its own on Red Mountain. "You know how to do sangio, Otis. You've been right all along. We can't treat it like cabernet. We need to get the fruit off the vines way early and touch it with oak, no more than that. It's more gamay than Bordeaux. Great acid, lively and light, cinnamon and roses for days. I could live off this stuff."

"You know I'm not a fan of the Super Tuscan."

Even with his crippled senses, Otis could still detect acid, a component that on its own didn't offer much, but combined with the right amount of fruit and astringency and alcohol, made good wine. This year had been one of the hottest years on record, but thankfully, the wines retained their acidity, a result of Otis's picking earlier than

most. He could never tell young winemakers enough that the decision of when to harvest was the most crucial aspect of the job;
choosing the most perfect day and even hour to get the grapes off the
vines was the most crucial of human contributions to a wine.

Otis figured it was his British heritage that made him dislike huge
wines. Even though Red Mountain had the potential to produce big,
powerful wines, he preferred taming the beast, harnessing the enor-
mity of the fruit, capturing the intensity with elegance and finesse.
Brooks understood this concept as well as anybody. Red Mountain
was not the next Napa Valley. The wines of Red Mountain required a
gentle, feminine touch. That's why the extraordinarily talented Sarah
Goedhart up at Hedges Family Estate was having so much success.

After they wrapped up, Brooks asked if he could say hello to
Morgan. Otis lit his pipe and puffed it to life. Even the tobacco smoke
was dull. He said, "Sure, why not? Maybe it will take some attention
off me. I'm sure she'd be happy to set you up with someone."

"Not possible at the moment. Believe it or not, I think I might be
in a relationship. Hell, I honestly might be falling in love."

"What? Brooks Baker falling in love?" They started down the path
toward the house to find Morgan. "Do I know her?"

"You won't believe it."

"Try me.

"Abby."

"Abby Sinclaire?" Everybody knew everybody on Red Mountain.

"That's the one."

"Look at you. She's a big deal."

"I know she is."

"I'm happy for you, son."

Morgan was standing at her easel in the living room, painting the
view from the window. When she saw Brooks, she lit up. "Now, here
cometh the sunshine to dry away the rain and shoo away the devil."
She stood and kissed him on the mouth. She'd met Brooks last time
she visited, and they'd hit it off annoyingly well. "You know you're the
real reason I came back, don't you?"

"I figured. You look younger and younger."

"It's all in the mind. That's what I keep telling Otis. He's starting to look like a corpse." She set down her paintbrush and tapped her head. "It's all in the mind."

Brooks said, "Otis tells me you're still trying to pair him up with someone. It's needed. He tells me all the time how lonely he is."

"You're a damn liar," Otis said, Brooks smiling at him. "Don't get her started."

"Any leads?" Brooks asked Morgan, crossing his arms, ignoring Otis.

"He didn't tell you?"

"Tell me what?"

"I think we found a winner. She was over here last night."

Brooks looked at Otis. "What?"

Morgan continued, "Her name's Joan Tobey. Stunning woman. She's a life coach and a yoga teacher."

"That's exactly what Otis needs," Brooks said.

"Exactly what I said," Morgan agreed. "He's taking her out tonight."

Otis jumped in. "I don't think I can tonight. She's very nice. But I'm busy with the wines right now."

Morgan crossed the room and pinched Otis's ear, like he was a child. "Otis Pennington Till, you are going to take her out tonight or I'll never talk to you again."

"You promise?"

She twisted his ear harder. "You don't take her out, that's like burning a winning lottery ticket."

"Let go of my ear. You're ridiculous."

"You little shit. You're going."

"We'll see."

"Yes, we will."

Brooks was bent over in laughter. "You are my favorite two people on earth. I can't get enough."

"I'll bet," Otis said, finally escaping Morgan's grip.

"You're next, Morgan," Brooks said. "We have to find you a man."

"Oh, I have three in every town between here and New York. You don't worry about me. It's my nephew that needs to get laid."

Brooks covered his mouth, stifling an outburst.

Otis put his hands on his hips. "Morgan, why don't you shut your mouth? You're embarrassing our family name."

Brooks clapped his hands together. "Oh, it's okay. I could listen to this all day."

Otis started to the door. "You two get caught up. I'm getting the hell out of here."

"Go find a better attitude while you're at it, you ol' grump," Morgan said.

Otis flung open the door and stomped back to the winery.

11

A TALE OF TWO FATHERS

"Where were you born?" Ari Weinstein, the *Rolling Stone* writer, asked. Brooks guessed the man was in his late forties, maybe older. The balding on top could be deceiving. Ari dressed youthfully—skater shoes, a Cars t-shirt, several rings on his fingers. As Jake had mentioned, Ari had been in the biz a long time and had interviewed big names like Johnny Cash and Tom Petty. This article would be *Rolling Stone's* first wine piece.

"According to my birth records, I was born in San Bernardino," Brooks answered. They were sitting at a table outside of the tasting room at Lacoda. It was another perfect fall day, with the craziness of harvest all around them. Looking south and west over the vineyards of Red Mountain, amongst the thick canopies of leaves, you could see the colorful clothing of the harvesters moving in between the rows, racing to fill their bins with grapes.

A tasting room employee had brought out a bottle of in-house sparkling water with mint and lemons. Brooks squeezed a slice into his water and said, "I was put up for adoption and moved around a lot, so I wouldn't call that home."

"Okay, so take me from Southern Cali kid to making wines on Red Mountain. How does that happen?"

Brooks smiled at the complexity of the question, staring at Ari's recording device and noticing the anxiety that came with talking about himself. "A man from Red Mountain saved my life. I was down and out, barely hanging on, and Otis Till—from Till Vineyards down the mountain there," Brooks pointed, "stepped into my life and gave me a second chance. So you ask how am I here? That man and that man alone. He's the closest I'll ever have to a father." Brooks scratched his head. "And that's fine by me. He's the greatest man I've ever known. Best winemaker in the country. If you would even call him that. He's more philosopher than winemaker."

"I've heard his name tossed around the past couple of days."

"Yeah, he's the one you should be writing about."

Ari waved his hand in the air. "I'll certainly track him down...but let's go back. You said you were hanging on by a thread. What got you to the tipping point? Were you ever adopted?"

"Yeah. I bounced around foster homes until finally this young couple decided to take me home. I was seven or eight years old, something like that, and totally unfit for normal family life. They returned me two months later. I wasn't quite what they'd hoped for. I don't blame them, though. I was already so jaded and burnt by life. I didn't trust a soul. Back to the foster circuit I went. Quite the nasty run. Town to town, family to family, one bully to the next, one messed up situation to one twice as bad. As soon as I had the sense, I took off. Ran off one night and didn't come back. Finally escaped all the madness. I was fourteen."

Brooks remembered sneaking down those creaky stairs with a grocery bag full of his belongings, slipping out the door, and running, running like hell; as if anyone even cared he was running. He remembered feeling freedom and fear...freedom and fear.

"From there?" Ari said.

"L.A., San Fran. Kept running north. Five years later I was in Portland, then Seattle. Then I hitchhiked and jumped trains to New Orleans and Miami."

"How were you surviving? Eating?"

"Any way I could. Panhandling, stealing, lying, slinging drugs. A few honest gigs here and there. Washing dishes, building houses, bartending. But most of it I'd be smart not to talk about. Stuff I'm not proud of. I wasted most of my twenties, let's put it that way. A jaded runaway without a prayer. The crimes got deeper and deeper, and I got more and more lost in the maze." Brooks took a sip of water and wiped the sweat from his forehead. "It's funny. I haven't talked about this before. Jake and Otis are the only ones who know my story. Not that it's much of one. I just don't like telling it."

"It's time you share your tale. It's worth sharing."

"I don't want kids to read my story in *Rolling Stone* and think that going bad is good."

"I think they'll read it and be inspired. I hate to sound cliché, but this is the American fucking dream—the real one. Second chances, growing up. So how did Otis come into it?"

"Ten years ago, I was living in a cardboard box in New York. Waiting and wishing to die, living off whatever people put in my cup, you know...wasting away. Honestly, losing my mind. It was about this time of year. I remember the leaves were falling in Central Park. I was sitting on a bench sucking down the last of a cigarette I'd found on the ground, feeling sorry for myself. I remember being so damn angry. My thighs were the size of my arms now."

Brooks crossed his legs and took a breath before continuing. "Otis came out of nowhere and sat down on the bench next to me. He started making conversation. I ignored him at first, but he's got a way with words, makes you want to listen to him. He told me he wanted to help, simple as that. Later, I realized that I was about the same age as his son who passed away, so that's what had drawn him to me. He said he knew what it was like to be down and out. He told me some things about his life that made mine peachy in comparison. It was more than just a man who was talking to me; it felt like something big was happening, like he was something otherworldly, on earth to change my destiny. I don't even know how to describe it."

"I know what you mean," Ari said.

"It felt big, important. That moment. Like I needed to pay attention. He left me his card. Told me to get clean and call him. Said he'd fly me to this place I'd never heard of called Red Mountain in the desert of eastern Washington. He said he'd give me a place to stay and a job. A second chance, like you said. Then he walked away. I called him a month later on a borrowed cell phone. Not too long after that I was learning how to make wine on Red Mountain. Studied under him for eight years. Everything I am, everything I know, the way I experience wine, my respect for *terroir*, I owe to him."

Ari picked and pried for two more hours before Abby finally rescued Brooks. His life had been covered in extreme detail, something Brooks had never been comfortable with. But he knew he had to open up. He owed that to Jake and to the winery and to Otis and to Red Mountain. Press was a good thing, and the story probably was worth sharing. People liked a comeback kid.

"Hey you," Brooks said to Abby, her trucker hat hiding most of her hair.

"Hi, gentlemen. I don't mean to interrupt."

Ari crossed his arms. "I think I've gotten all I can out of him anyway."

"He looks like you beat him up."

"Bled me dry," Brooks admitted.

Abby said to Brooks. "I brought you lunch."

"That's really nice of you." He was thrilled to see her for many reasons. Brooks looked at Ari. "Can we call it?"

"I think I've got enough to work with. I'll run the story by you before we go to press. I might have some follow-up we can do by phone."

Abby and Brooks said goodbye to Ari and sat at the same table to enjoy lunch. Abby pulled out a thermos and poured the contents into their bowls. "Pumpkin curry soup from pumpkins I picked this morning. I hope you like it."

"Just pumpkin. The curry isn't from the garden? You're slacking."

"I'm terribly sorry to disappoint you. I bought the curry at the store."

"I guess it will suffice."

"Look who is humorous today. Aren't you cute?"

They smiled at each other, a very nice moment, a real connection.

She opened some foil to reveal a stack of homemade roti bread.

"This is going to require a nice glass of wine." He ran inside. Back at the table, he poured them glasses. "This is a new project, just bottled last week. A Red Mountain chenin blanc, indigenous fermentation, no RS, neutral barrel. I'm really excited about it. Great fruit from our lowest elevation planting."

Abby took a sip. "I'm embarrassed to say I don't understand half of what you said, but it's delicious."

"You don't have to be embarrassed. Let me tell you something. I spent the first five years with Otis learning to taste wine, learning all the flavors, the flaws, the aromas, the science. And here I am a few years after that trying to forget it all, trying to get back to where you are. We winemakers are cursed with being over-analytical. Now, all I want to do is experience a wine without thinking about the pH or the alcohol level or the wine's lack of, or overabundance of, fruit, or its viscosity—you know, the thickness of it."

She shook her head. "Exhausting."

"I want to taste a wine like you taste it. What does it say to me? Is it delicious? In the end, all that matters is one thing: does it get you off? That's why Otis is so damn good. He can analyze a wine with the best of them scientifically, but he can shut his left brain off in a second, and taste a wine like he's tasting wine for the first time."

Brooks hadn't been able to shake Otis from his mind all morning. He wanted to talk to Abby about Otis's plight, but he'd promised to keep it to himself. Brooks brushed the thoughts away and focused on this special woman in front of him.

"Enough about the wine. Let's talk about this lunch. Let's talk about you. You're such a good cook. You made this today?"

Abby wiped her mouth. "A little while ago. Jake and Carmen are down at their house eating the same thing."

"Will you be my assistant, please?"

"You couldn't afford me."

"That's probably true."

Abby dipped a piece of roti into the soup, asking, "So how'd the interview go?" before taking a bite of the dripping bread.

"I hate talking about myself. It's over."

"You're going to be in *Rolling Stone*. That's a huge deal."

"It is. I'm definitely excited and humbled and all that."

"I can't wait to read it."

"You're a much more interesting subject," Brooks said. "We've known each other for what? Two years now? But you've only lived here for half of it."

"Right. I think the first time we met—"

"Abby, I know the first time we met. I'll never forget it. You and the Foresters came over from Seattle for the Lacoda groundbreaking. You had longer hair then. You barely noticed me."

"I was playing it cool."

"If I would have asked you out that day, what would you have said?"

She smiled effortlessly. "I remember thinking you were gorgeous, and you looked like a lot of trouble...with your tattoos and your motorcycle. You were exactly my type."

Brooks laughed.

"I would have said yes," she admitted.

"So I've missed out on two years with you."

"Timing is everything, isn't it?"

Brooks figured that could mean many things. "You are the end of the rainbow to me, something I can never really reach. You kept your distance."

"That's my *modus operandi*," she said.

"We have a lot of catching up to do, don't we? I know you're a Vegas girl. How did you hook up with the Foresters?"

She nodded, while adjusting her orange-banded watch. "Grew up in Las Vegas, went to UNLV, and paid for it by nannying at the big casinos. That's where I met the Foresters. Jake was doing a run of shows at the MGM for a week, and Carmen hired me to help with Emilia. She was an adorable baby back then. After that week,

Carmen tried to hire me full-time. I wasn't ready to leave and turned her down. Had some family things going on. We ran into each other a few years later, and she asked me again, this time to be her personal assistant, help with the kids, cook some, whatever she needed. By then I was ready to get out of Vegas, so I took the job. That was five years ago. Luca was three."

"Where did you learn how to cook? I mean, who else in Washington knows how to make roti?"

"Carmen sent me to cooking classes while we were living in Seattle. Three days a week for a year."

"You may have the coolest job ever. Get to travel with the Foresters all over the world, learn to cook, backstage passes, movie premiers; you get to meet great people, live on a vineyard."

"I'm not complaining. You know as well as I do that working for the Foresters is pretty nice. Consumes your life, but that's not necessarily a bad thing."

"It's certainly a lifestyle, not a nine-to-five." Brooks had been trying to get up the nerve to kiss her the entire conversation and finally decided it was now or never. He stood and went to her side of the table. "Stand up. I want to tell you something." He took her hand and pulled her up. "I've wanted to do this for years."

"Years?"

"Well, too long." He leaned in. Their lips met, and it made up for the two years he'd wasted. How had a runt like him made it to this point, to be so lucky to kiss this woman so out of his league? All the broken roads of his life had finally led him somewhere worth being.

◇

AFTER A LONG DAY, Brooks rode his motorcycle through the vineyards, taking the off-road shortcut to Demoss Road, where he lived. He used the last of the daylight to navigate. Built ten years earlier, his home was right on the Yakima River, set on two acres of mostly scrubland, with a tiny patch of green grass he mowed when he had time. There was a deck out back that looked over the river.

The view, the entire home in general, was more than he ever thought he'd have.

He couldn't wait to bring Abby over and sit out back and light the grill and drink wine and do normal things, all the things that most humans took for granted. He'd bought this house—the first one he'd ever owned—with a signing bonus from Jake, and Abby would be the first woman other than Carmen to see it.

A man dressed in khakis and a white polo was waiting in his driveway, sitting on the hood of a sedan bearing a Hertz sticker on the windshield. As Brooks pulled in, the man hopped down and waved. Brooks didn't feel that much apprehension; he'd lived on the streets way too long to fear strangers.

"Can I help you?" Brooks asked, stepping off his bike. He hadn't bothered putting his helmet on for the short ride.

"Hello, Brooks." The man stepped closer.

Seeing the man's face, Brooks suddenly felt an overwhelming rush of emotion, nearly losing his balance, losing his breath.

"Look at ya. All grown up."

"Who are you?" Brooks asked, already knowing damn well.

"I wasn't sure until right this minute, but look at you. You're a spitting image. I'm your father, Son."

A punch in the gut, a clock-stopping, mind-numbing confusion, emptiness, blackness, a cold, swallowing, deafening, drowning fall.

The man grabbed his arm, catching him, pulling him back. "Brooks, you okay?"

Brooks found his footing and blinked his eyes several times, looking for clarity. As it came, the man was saying, "I know it's overwhelming. It was for me too."

The years of waiting and wondering and growing up alone had never quite prepared him for this moment. Brooks felt so terribly uneasy that he wanted an escape. He couldn't even look the man in the eyes. "Look," Brooks managed to say. "I can't do this right now."

"I understand."

"Let's talk in the morning. I've had a long day."

The man handed him a business card. "I'm here for a couple of days. Call me when you can. I just want to talk. I'm not looking for anything from you. I'm not looking to hurt you. I'm simply here to say hello, to say I'm sorry, and to see what happens."

Brooks nodded, and the man got back into his rental car and drove away.

12

MARGOT 2.0

Margot and Jasper left the hospital two hours after he'd been taken to the ER. No broken bones, no internal bleeding. Jasper's left eye had puffed up so badly he couldn't see through it. His sweater was torn from the struggle on the pavement. Margot couldn't bear to look at him without wanting to cry. He said his whole body hurt. They'd punched and kicked him until he'd nearly lost consciousness.

Margot had screamed at the principal in the hospital. Where the hell was the supervision? She was inclined to sue the school and the families of the three kids involved, but Jasper had been trying desperately to soothe her. He was right. If she started a war, it would only make things worse for him. Let the kids get their suspensions and get the principal to take steps to make sure it didn't happen again. Make sure the school paid the bills.

Margot drove slowly on the way home. As they pulled onto the highway, Jasper said, "If you keep driving this way, we're never going to get home."

"I don't want to hurt you."

"Mom, I'm a man. I'm not fragile."

"Look at you. You need to be taken care of."

"I really don't. I'm fine. This is part of growing up."

"Getting beat up isn't part of growing up, Jasper. What if they'd done worse? What if they'd hurt your hands?"

"They didn't."

Just then she remembered Jake. She couldn't believe she'd forgotten, but she'd been so caught up with worry. "Can I change the subject? I have some really wonderful news. I ran into another musician today who wants to play with you."

"Oh, that's cool. Who?"

"I think he's a guitar player mainly. Really nice guy. He lives on Red Mountain."

"Who?"

"Jake Forester."

There was silence.

"What are you talking about?" Jasper said, lighting up. "What do you mean you ran into him?"

"I was jogging and he was jogging, and he stopped to talk to me. I told him who I was, and he immediately asked about you, said he had heard a lot."

"You're kidding me. He's heard about me?"

"From your teacher. They supposedly go way back. Jake asked for your number. Says he'd like to play."

"That's insane. Quentin didn't even say anything. Do you think he'll really call?"

"I watched him enter your number into his phone. I'd say you've got a good chance."

～

JAKE CALLED THAT EVENING. Margot and Jasper were in the dining room eating squash casserole and giggling at "The Serenity Now" episode of *Seinfeld* when Jasper's phone rang. He answered and after a few seconds, he covered the mouthpiece of the phone and said, "It's Jake. Be right back."

Jasper ran upstairs to his room, and Margot followed him, doing

her best to be discreet. She stopped right outside his door and
listened to her son have a conversation with one of the most important musicians on the planet. She glowed with pride.

A few minutes later, Jasper opened the door to find Margot
standing there. "Really, Mom?"

"I couldn't help it. What did he say?"

"He wants to jam some. I'm going over there tomorrow after
school."

"What? Does he have a piano?"

"He's Jake Forester. I'm sure. I bet he has an entire recording
studio with every instrument you could think of. I would if I were
him."

"Oh, my god, this is a big deal."

After dinner, Jasper went to his piano, and Margot drew a bath
upstairs. In her velvet robe, she sat on the edge of the claw foot tub as
it filled, enjoying a salted caramel cupcake from the freezer. Once the
tub was full and steaming, she disrobed and slipped into the hot
water with her glass of wine. She was prepared to kill.

Closing her eyes, she traveled back in time, back to their home in
Burlington where her ex was probably still porking that whore.

*Margot had dressed in black for the occasion. She drank wine and
listened to Sarah Vaughn and waited for her victim. Rory came into the
kitchen smiling, pouring himself a scotch and kissing Margot on the cheek
dutifully. "How was your day, dear?"*

*Margot had no time for small talk. "Jasper's gone for the night. We have
the house to ourselves."*

*Her ex's eyes widened and his mouth opened as if someone had jammed
a carrot in there. She knew that look well. One of surprise and disinterest,
near disappointment. He had no desire for her. Margot didn't care. She let
her black blouse fall, revealing her lack of undergarments. She prowled
toward him and took his briefcase, dropping it to the floor. She grabbed him
by the tie and pulled him into a kiss, the last of his life.*

*Margot pushed him backward until he hit the counter. She undressed
him slowly, at last pulling down his boxers one creeping inch at a time. She
reached for the olive oil next to the stove and poured some on her hands. She*

gripped his penis and stroked him, taking him toward climax. He sloppily groped at her breasts. Just as he began to moan and quiver, Margot reached toward the stove once again, this time grabbing a garlic press. He was completely oblivious, his eyes closed. She lowered the press to his midsection while still pleasuring him with the other hand. She opened the press and clenched it around one of his testicles.

He screamed as he fell to the floor, writhing in pain. Still naked, Margot found her glass of wine and hopped up on the counter, admiring her work.

Margot opened her eyes. Wow, that got aggressive. It scared her to think about how much satisfaction she felt. What kind of person thinks these things? The affair was destroying her.

As she climbed out of the water, she saw herself in the mirror, and what she saw disgusted her even more. It wasn't her physical appearance. Sure, she had weight to lose. That was doable. But what she saw and what she didn't like was deeper, beyond the skin. She needed help.

Seeing Jake Forester had awakened something inside of her. He was so at peace with himself and so kind and endearing; he'd made her feel calm and happy. She wanted that of herself. She wanted to feel confident and whole again. The truth was that Margot was a complete boiling hot mess. She knew it. Jasper probably knew it. Her friends back home knew it, though she'd run most of them off in her depression.

From the moment she'd seen that woman's face in her husband's lap, Margot had begun a downward spiral. Overeating, overthinking, over-parenting. Dreaming up ways to kill her husband every day! What was wrong with her?

Whatever it was, seeing Jake had made her aware. She missed her old self, the person she was before her husband, and even in the early days of her marriage. She was a big deal in her own right—not just on the Broadway stage, but also in life. What happened to that woman? How could she be a great mother if she didn't have it together herself? How could she expect to run a successful inn and farm sanctuary? How could she give cooking classes? How would she ever meet a man again?

She needed change. She walked closer to the mirror and looked at herself in the eyes. She stuck a finger in the air and said, "You need to change, Margot Pierce. Not tomorrow. Right now. Enough of this crap." She lifted her arms in the air, liberating herself. "I am beautiful. I am sexy. I am smart. I am a supernova. A diva. I am Magic Mom." She lowered her arms, clenched her fists, and gazed even deeper into the eyes of her reflection. "I am Margot 2.0."

~

JASPER CAME into the kitchen the next morning, running late as usual. The swelling in his face had subsided, leaving a circle of black and blue around his eye. "Wow, Mom, look at you!"

Margot was dressed to kill. She'd been saving this red strapless dress for months (she looked best in red), and today was the day. Today was her day. She'd also spent a lot of time with her makeup, not overdoing it, but putting in more effort than usual. Margot 1.0 was all about the sweatpants and some blush. Maybe some lipstick if her lips were lucky. She smiled. "Not bad for an ol' bag, right?"

"Hot date?"

"No, sweetheart. I've decided it's time to start taking care of myself."

"Good for you."

She handed him a kale and green apple smoothie. "We're going to start doing a lot more of these."

He took a sip and wiped his mouth. "Yeah, I can do these for a while. Can I take it with me? I've got to get outta here."

"Don't speed and don't punch anyone."

He gave her a kiss and headed off to school. Margot left shortly after. No better way to begin a transformation than with some shopping.

Barnes & Noble was the first stop. She got a double espresso and spent an hour in the self-help section, then over to religion and then exercise. She didn't even care what the woman at the checkout thought. Margot 2.0 wasn't affected by what people thought.

She put a giant stack of books on the counter with pride. *Awaken the Giant Within by* Tony Robbins, *The Power of Now* by Eckhart Tolle, *Psycho-Cybernetics* by Maxwell Maltz, *You Are a Badass* by Jen Sincero, *The Power of Positive Thinking* by Dr. Norman Vincent Peale, *The Four Agreements* by Don Miguel Ruiz, *iWant* by Jane Velez-Mitchell. The list went on: books on Buddhism, Taoism, yoga, pilates. She even bought a book on learning French, a language she'd been toying with and butchering since high school. Well, now it was time to get serious.

She spent the next hour shopping for workout clothes— Lululemon and Spiritual Gangster. She spent another hour in the mall buying more clothes. She needed a few things until she got her new body, which she figured would take a couple of months. Finally, she joined a yoga studio. She'd messed around with yoga back in New York and in her early days in Vermont, but she hadn't been on a mat since Jasper was born. Way too long.

On the drive back, she called her contractor. "Tanner," she said, "aren't you supposed to be back today? I was hoping to see you this morning."

"Yeah, I'm sorry I didn't call. Picked up a bug while I was in Cancun. I'll be there first thing Monday."

"Tanner, I mean this with all the love in the world. I'm running out of patience...and money. It's inexcusable that you didn't have anyone lined up this week while you were gone. The inn is sitting there, nothing is happening. There's plywood and plastic in place of the back door. I don't know whether it's because I'm a woman or what, but I feel like I'm getting taken advantage of."

"Wait a minute," Tanner began.

"Let me finish. Then you can speak. I'm going to take a much more active role in managing this project. I want weekly reports of who is coming by and how much they are going to cost. I want a crystal clear breakdown of what you're doing, and I want to see workers every single day of the week. Weekends too. If you have a problem with that, it's best we cut ties now. I need people staying in this inn by March, and that means every detail needs to be taken care of by the end of January. I don't even want to be screwing in light bulbs in February. You understand?"

"Yes, ma'am."

"I've been pushed around too much lately and that's going to stop now. You want this job, you're going to have to earn it every day. Do you have anything to say?"

"Nope. We'll get it done."

Margot hung up and a grin slowly formed as she roared down the highway. She looked in the rearview mirror at herself. "Good for you," she said. "Margot 2.0 is here to stay."

Taking her eyes back to the road, she said, "Margot 2.0." Then again with more confidence, "Margot 2.0." She broke into song, her full Broadway voice improvising absurdities that made her even happier. "Margot 2.0 is here, she's here to stay, she's heeeeeere to stay. Everyone look out for Margot 2.0, she's the baddest woman, the finest woman, the sexiest woman on Red Mountain. She's a mother, she's a lover, she's a chef, she's the queeeeeeeeeeen."

13

THE MUSIC MAKER

The doorbell rang for a third time. Then a fourth. The dogs had left Emilia's bed and were at the front door barking incessantly. "Go away!" she screamed, pulling a pillow over her head. She'd skipped school, and still hadn't eaten a thing. She was still in her pajamas, still listening to Suzanne Vega. Emilia hadn't told anyone about Joe. Not Sadie. Not her parents. No one.

The doorbell wouldn't stop. And above the volume of Suzanne Vega and the barking and the doorbell, she could hear music coming from the studio out back past the pool. Her dad was playing electric guitar, and obviously couldn't hear a thing. Emilia finally got out of bed, yelling, "I'm coming!" She didn't care that she hadn't looked in the mirror today. She stomped down the stairs, calmed the dogs, and opened the door.

A kid from school was standing in front of her. The kid who got beat up, obviously. He had a black eye. There was a cut on his opposite cheek. He wore the same wool fedora he always wore.

"Hi," he said.

Pepper and Wilson barreled out and jumped on him. He knelt and petted them both until they calmed down. The dogs licked his face, and he laughed. He stood back up and said, "You probably don't know who I am." He stuck his hand out. "I'm Jasper."

Emilia shook his hand and looked him up and down. He was well put together with his t-shirt and blazer, his dark jeans and leather shoes, kind of dapper, the way a young Euro hipster might look. He was short, barely taller than she was. "I know who you are. I'm Emilia. My boyfriend, soon to be ex-boyfriend, did that to you yesterday, didn't he?"

Jasper nodded. "He's quite the charmer."

"I'm really sorry."

"It's not your fault. He has to do his thing, be the football player and all that. He needs to beat up someone."

She lifted the corner of her mouth. "I guess you're right. Well, for what it's worth, I'm not happy about it. He's not who he used to be."

He shrugged. "Don't worry about it. It's over. You didn't go to school?"

"No, I'm not feeling too well." She suddenly realized how disgusting she must look.

"I'm sorry to hear that. Anyway, I'm here to see your dad. Is he around?"

"My dad?"

"Yeah, he called yesterday. We were going to play some music."

"Oh, he's giving you a lesson?"

"I...I don't think so. I think we're just going to jam some."

"You play?"

Jasper fingered an imaginary piano. "I tickle the ivories from time to time."

"He called you?" she asked, a little shocked.

"Yeah, he called yesterday."

Emilia was upset she didn't know anything about it, but she tried not to be a bitch. Everything upset her right now. The poor guy had gotten enough hell for the week. "He's out back in his studio. Come on in."

Jasper followed her inside. She led him out the back door and past the pool to the studio, a separate building her dad called the ultimate man cave, complete with a recording booth, an arsenal of instruments, gold and platinum records on the walls, a full-sized bar and kitchen, a pool table, a dart board, a movie theater, a chess table. She opened the door and pointed. "He's in there. He'll be the guy destroying his hearing."

"Thanks," Jasper said. "It's nice to meet you, Emilia."

"You too. Again, I'm really sorry about Tex."

Emilia found a pint of Ben and Jerry's ice cream in the kitchen. She ate a few bites of Cherry Garcia while leaning against the counter. She poured herself some water and went back up to her room and got in bed to listen to more Suzanne Vega, her only hope of survival.

Joe still hadn't called. Probably never would again. She climbed back into bed and closed her eyes. How could she have done things differently? She shouldn't have gone into his office so much. She should have played hard to get. She made it too easy for him.

Curiosity brought her out of her mind games. Emilia went back down the stairs and outside, past the pool to the studio. She could hear the muffled sounds of piano and guitar as she got close. The studio leaked just enough sound to make out the instruments.

She went through the first door and took a seat in the hallway. The music was much louder there. She could see the back of the piano through the glass of the second door. Jasper sounded like a professional. Her dad was singing. They were playing a song Emilia had heard her dad messing with lately. The two musicians sounded like they'd been playing together for years.

They wrapped up the tune, and Jasper and Jake talked for a while; about his black eye, about school, about Red Mountain, and about music. Jasper talked about chord progressions and improvisation. Then her dad started to teach him a new song he'd written. Jasper picked it up with ease.

The music was gorgeous. By the second verse, Emilia was crying mightily, torn up by the beauty of her classmate's playing. This music, Jasper and her father's music, touched her deeply.

As they finished, her dad expressed his excitement. "Jasper, you're dangerous. We need to record. Let's do an album together."

"Really?"

"I'm serious. I've got a ton of new tunes and didn't know what to do with them. Now I know. For a classical musician, you have no trouble improvising. Would you be up for an album?"

"For real? Hell yes, I'm up for it!"

"Do you write at all?" Jake asked.

"Sure. I was trying to think what might work with the two of us."

"I could get a drummer and bassist to come in too, so think quartet. Not rock, not too poppy, something in a Billy Joel/Elton vein. Maybe even Bruce Hornsby. Do you listen to them much?"

"Sure, I know them. Great pianists."

"You're on their level, aren't you? You're that good. Or better."

Jasper laughed. "Oh, I don't know about that." Jasper tinkered around on the piano for a moment, toying with the notes, ending with a fast run. Emilia noticed how beautifully the melody continued even after he released the keys.

"Here's a tune I've been working on." Jasper played the opening chords, a slow yet heavy tune in a minor key. Emilia closed her eyes and listened intently. It was like she and her dad were experiencing some new force in music yet to be heard. Jasper began singing. He had a wonderful voice, extremely mature and perfectly in tune:

You can see right through the chords I'm playing,
    I know
You can hear through the lyrics I'm singing, I know
Hell, you pretty much wrote the words
If there's a way for us to make it
I don't see it
But that never stopped us before

JASPER HAMMERED louder on the keys and her dad followed with heavy bar chords, leading into the chorus:

> Caroline
> You're a heartbeat knocking down a door
> Caroline
> Haven't we been here before?
> Caroline
> I'll never be the one to say it's over
> That's in your hands
> So put down that lazy little frown,
> Caroline and come see me,
> Come see me...one more time

THEY HIT a big dark chord and let it ring for a few seconds; Jasper wrapped up the chorus with a whispered repeat of, "One more time..."

Emilia broke into a schoolgirl weep, the kind you only let your mother see, where the tears come with thunder and lightning like raindrops in a storm.

She listened to them play a few more songs but disappeared before they wrapped up, returning to her room. From her bedroom window, she watched Jasper and her dad leave the studio and walk by the pool into the house. She crept to the stairs and listened. Her dad thanked him, and they agreed to get together in a couple of days. Emilia returned to her room and got on her laptop. She wanted to know more about Jasper. She searched her social media pages but without a last name, it was hopeless. She texted Sadie to ask her. Her friend responded immediately, but didn't know.

After Jasper left, Emilia went downstairs. Her dad was leaning against the counter in the kitchen wearing a way-past-its-prime NPR t-shirt, dipping red radishes into a small metal tin of pink salt. With a mouthful, he said, "Well, look who decided to come out."

"Hi, Dad."

"How are you feeling, sweetheart?" He offered her a radish and she declined.

"Still lousy."

"You know, my daughter, I've been around a long time. I know the difference between heartache and the flu. Something go down with you and Tex?"

"Something like that. So why was Jasper here?" She sat on a metal stool that needed tightening.

"You know him?"

"Barely. Did he tell you Tex did that to his eye?"

"I put it together." Her dad shook his head in disgust. Jake was never the biggest Tex fan. Even Tex knew that. "You tell Tex I'm not happy. Tell him I'll find him if he touches Jasper again. What's he doing getting in fights anyway? No coach in the country wants a player they can't control."

"I'm not talking to him anyway. I'm over him." She could see the relief in his eyes.

"Between you and me, I thought you could do better." He stepped towards her. "What can I do for you? I can't stand seeing you heartbroken."

"I need time, that's all."

"Wanna go to a movie tonight? That might take your mind off things."

"What's Mom doing?"

"She's staying in Seattle one more night, a charity event. Abby is taking Luca to swimming. It's just you and me."

"Can I pick the movie?"

"Anything you'd like."

"Even a rom-com?"

"So long as you're not embarrassed when I start crying."

"I'll bring tissues."

They both smiled. Yeah, he was a pretty awesome dad.

14

THE COYOTE GETS CAUGHT

O tis was stoned and drunk and stumbling around his property at 2 a.m. He'd tried to sleep but realized he was wasting his time. He went down to the sheep pasture and through the gate. The sheep and Jonathan came running once they sensed him.

As usual, Otis had brought a bucket of grain. He sat cross-legged in the grass and scooped out a handful. The sheep fought each other to get to his hand, one braver than the next. Jonathan plopped down and buried his nose in Otis's lap. Otis stroked the dog's fur with his free hand, mumbling and smiling.

The Southdowns were a teddy-bearish English breed with short legs. Ideally, their stature kept them from munching on grapes and leaves when he let them trim the weeds in the vineyards. But lately Otis had caught them hopping up on their hind legs and chowing down. Until further notice, the sheep were not allowed in the vine-yard during the growing season. Maybe with his next planting, he'd train the vines another foot or two higher like he'd seen in Tuscany.

Otis pulled a black container closer and put some of the grain in there. The sheep dove in, pushing and shoving like he hadn't fed them in weeks. He ran his hands through their soft wool, like petting a cloud.

It was rather unusual to be able to pet sheep like dogs, but Otis had spent many hours befriending them. Coming down with delicious grain and graham crackers didn't hurt. His animals—the chickens, the sheep, the dogs—were the pulse of his farm, of his wines. There was a sense of nature in his wines, and it was because of all of the heartbeats. It all came together, it all made sense, because of Red Mountain.

He believed that the finest grapes in the country could be grown on Red Mountain. What he was trying to bring to the table was this sense of purpose in farming, this sense of truth. Connecting to the earth. Adding vitality to the grapes by adding vitality to the soil, the farm, and even the culture. Red Mountain had to become a place that visionaries and poets sought out, much like Haight-Ashbury, where he'd lived when he dropped out of college. Or Greenwich Village or Paris, decades ago. Only then would the wines reach their full potential.

Some of the hot winemakers in the press today had forgotten the true definition of *terroir*; they'd forgotten the concept of unity with nature and culture and community. Making good and honest wine wasn't about a name on a bottle; it wasn't about a brand. It was about committing to a piece of land, to an area; not simply by planting vines, but by building a community, an ecosystem where animals thrive, where healthy children are raised with great ambition; a place that people talk about all over the globe, a place chefs come to open restaurants in hopes of finding that perfect pairing or perhaps connecting with farmers to bring back an old heirloom grain. It was about creating a magical environment, so that when people tasted the wines at a later time in another place, they would be transported to Red Mountain and all its greatness.

That's what Otis wanted.

But it was going to pieces.

How could he possibly contribute if he couldn't smell? If he couldn't taste the damn wines? He had nothing to offer if he couldn't keep doing what he was doing. He was only sixty-four, by God! He had more to give. He still had twenty good vintages left in him, and he still hadn't had the vintage he'd been waiting for. The one he'd dreamed about. It was out there in the future somewhere.

Otis didn't know what was going on with his body, but he knew it wasn't good. And he knew it wasn't anything that was going to go away. This would be his last vintage.

"Fuck!" he screamed. "And it was brutally hot this year. I would rather have gone out on a cool vintage, where the bloody alcohols weren't so high."

He shook his head and lay back on the ground. He couldn't even smell the sheep, a smell he'd grown to love immensely. A smell he'd started to pick up in his wines, nothing too offensive but a seductive tertiary note that sang like a lone tenor off in the background, his flock of sheep somewhere deep inside his bottles, a collective *bah* rising up out of each glass.

"Ha, ha!" he said, drunkenly reflecting on that smell he could no longer perceive. "I should name my next wine 'Bah Bah Blackbird Syrah.'" Neither the dog nor the sheep got the joke, but that didn't keep Otis from enjoying his own humor, the reference to a tune from his youth. He belted out a long laugh that ignited with a Santa-like chuckle but soon turned into an hacking cough that left Otis flat on his back, sighing.

What could he do now for Red Mountain? He hadn't made enough of a difference yet. Brooks would carry his legacy, but would it be sufficient?

The forces weren't strong enough yet. Where were the other people they needed? Sure, there were other wineries, powerful ones, but did they understand the potential of Red Mountain? Were they bringing with them the right tools to help grow this region? And where were the restaurants and the hotels and bed and breakfasts? The live music and the artists? The poets! He needed to be there when they came; he needed to help draw them.

What kept running through Otis's mind wasn't just losing his winemaking ability. The other thought that poisoned his peace was his mortality. Maybe Red Mountain was already on the right track; but what if he wasn't there to see it? What if whatever was going on with his body was the beginning of his demise?

He stared at the stars, thousands of them like tiny holes in black paper. Jonathan lay next to him. The sheep had moved away, having emptied the grain bucket. He felt sad. His life had been so close to perfect so many times, only to have perfection stripped away. He'd fight back, then get knocked down again; a vicious cycle that seemed to define his life. How could he come back from this one, though? Perhaps this was his swan song.

Just then a coyote howled. And another. Jonathan dashed to the fence and growled, a deep dark growl that no coyote would dare challenge.

"They're not coming down here, dog. Especially now." Otis stood and wobbled over to this giant mass, petting him. "It's okay." Jonathan's 120 pounds looked even more daunting in the darkness, a ghost in the night.

Otis made way toward the coyotes. He entered the syrah vineyard, stumbling from time to time, chuckling again at his absurd idea of Bah Bah Blackbird Syrah. Reaching the center of a row, he pulled off his clothes. The coyotes were in full song now, calling out to their gods.

Naked, Otis went down on all fours and howled with them, half drunkard and half dog.

Ahhhhh-oooooo!

He gazed at the stars and found solace in the constellations, and he let another howl and then another go until he was in sync with the other desert dogs.

Ahhhhhhhh-oooooo!

"What in the hell are you doing, Otis?" a voice said, someone walking up the row with a flashlight, a voice sending him on the long journey back toward sobriety.

The marijuana and alcohol had slowed his reaction time tremendously, and it took him a moment to realize what was going on. "Hello?" he said. "Who's out there?"

"It's me, Morgan." Then there was a light in his face. "What are you doing?"

"Oh, shit," Otis mumbled. He covered his midsection. "Cut the damn light off. I'll be down soon."

"I will not cut this light off," she said. "I want to know what is going on with you. You're running around drunk in the middle of the night, barking like a dog. You refuse to call Joan. You were supposed to go out with her tonight and stood her up. You've been downright rude to me and everyone who gets near you." She shined the light on his clothes. "Now put your clothes on and get inside. We're going to have a heart-to-heart."

"Morgan, I am not your child. I'm sixty-four years old. I'm old enough to die."

Morgan approached and slapped him hard on the face. "You're the last bit of family I've got, and you're gonna have to clean up your act. Nobody is dying here." She picked up his pants and handed them to him. "Now come inside immediately. You stink like whisky and you are mumbling bat-shit nothings. I'm going to put on a pot of coffee."

Otis couldn't believe what was happening. He didn't care about being naked—not really. But it was a bit embarrassing and sobering to have been caught with his pants down, yelling with the wild dogs. He watched her walk back down the hill as he dressed. Then he slowly stumbled back to the house, his mind becoming uncluttered, his ego shattered, his world slowly going away. The coyotes had quieted and returned to their dens.

~

HE WAS IN THE KITCHEN, sitting at the counter with a cup of strong black coffee in his hand. Morgan sat facing him on the other side, dressed in a nightgown, a cup in her own hand.

"What are you doing up so late?" he asked.

"What am I doing up late? I should ask you."

"Lot on my mind," Otis admitted. "You have no idea."

"Give me an idea. I'm not going to be kept in the dark one more moment. I haven't seen you in a long while, but I know you, Otis Till. I know you're not yourself, and I want to know about it. I want to help."

He took a sip, and the warmth running down his throat felt nice. The burst of caffeine was waking him. "I'm not sure you can help."

"Let me try. At least I can listen."

Otis told her of his woes, and Morgan listened quietly, sipping her coffee, absorbing some of his pain. She finally asked the same questions Brooks had. Was it temporary? Had he been to the doctor? What could it be? Otis told her it could be many things and that he hadn't had it checked out yet.

Morgan said, "You're scared. I've been through it when I had cancer. I knew something was wrong. My body felt off. But I didn't want to go to the doctor and justify it. I felt like if I kept it to myself, it might go away. Or at least I could enjoy a few more days without having to deal with any bad news. But you know what? This could be a new chapter in your life, and if you're putting off finding out what's going on, you could be making it worse. Your body is asking for your help right now, and you're ignoring it."

"I'm not ignoring—"

"Shh, Otis. Can't you listen for once in your life? Let an old lady speak her mind."

"I know a thing or two about dying. Now, you might get it checked out, and it's nothing. A quick remedy and you're all fixed up. In that case, you're wasting a whole lot of good life, hell, this whole harvest, worrying for no reason. Let's say there is something wrong. What if it's one of those things better to catch early on? What if it's something treatable? What if you could be healing by now?"

She threw her finger in the air. "Okay, and worst-case. What if the doctor tells you you're dying? Don't you want to know that? Don't you have better things to do in your final days than running around naked barking like a dog?"

Otis laughed and his face reddened. "You wouldn't understand."

"You're probably right. Do you hear me, though? Go to the doctor. Find out what's going on. I can help take care of things around here."

Otis nodded and polished off his cup, feeling the grounds of her cowgirl coffee on his tongue. "I'll consider it."

Morgan leaned forward. "You're going to make an appointment in the morning, or I'm going to do it for you. There's no considering. Quit feeling sorry for yourself. You're drinking too much. Your belly's growing. Your wrinkles are showing. Your skin is sagging. You've still got Rebecca's ashes in your office. And you're crawling around on all fours in your birthday suit. Things are going to have to change. Don't make me set up an intervention. Because I've been thinking about it."

"You set up an intervention, and I'll chase your ass all the way back to Montana."

"Then I have your attention. I look forward to hearing you on that phone at 8 a.m., or whenever the doctor's office opens. I'm going to stay as long as I need to. You need me right now. Look at it this way. As soon as you're on the right track, I'll leave. That should be good enough incentive."

Otis didn't know a pushier woman in the world, but he also knew she loved him. Probably more than anyone else on earth. He took her hand. "Thank you. I'm not trying to get rid of you. I'm getting old and grumpy but I appreciate your being here. Maybe I needed it."

"I love you, Otis."

"Love you too."

"I can't hear you through all that mumbling."

"I love you, Morgan."

"I needed to hear that. Can you believe no one has told me that in fifteen years? Maybe twenty."

That saddened Otis, and he realized he'd been so caught up in his own crap that he hadn't even thought about the other people in his world. Morgan. Brooks. Chaco, his vineyard manager. Elijah. What about them?

Otis, you selfish bastard. Pull it together.

Pull it together.

15

FILLING IN THE MISSING YEARS

Brooks had a father. Of course, he had never considered the possibility of immaculate conception. Obviously some irresponsible flake had impregnated a woman, and had disappeared after that. But Brooks never thought about his parents any more.

Sure, when he was fifteen and jumping trains he used to close his eyes and, while the car shook and the land flew by, dream of a normal family. He would dream of his parents finding him and explaining it was all a mistake, giving him back the Christmases and birthdays and Halloweens that he'd missed.

That was a long time ago. For so many years he'd pushed away these thoughts, until they'd disappeared. He no longer wondered where they were or if they were alive; what life might have been like. So many people over the years had asked him if he'd tried to find his parents. No, he'd never tried. He didn't want to. They'd decided they didn't want him in his life. That decision lasts a lifetime.

Brooks sat across from his possible father at a booth in a dive breakfast joint in Benton City. A neon Corona sign hung on the wall to his right. Four different kinds of hot sauce, bottles of ketchup and mustard, and malt vinegar filled a metal basket in the middle of the table. The two men didn't shake hands.

"Good morning," the man said. "I'm glad you came." He was dressed like a golfer, with a V-neck sweater-vest over a stiff-collared polo shirt. Brooks thought about the age progression tools that the FBI used to catch their most wanted. The dude across from him was exactly what the FBI would come up with if they used Brooks as the starting point. His father didn't have the body art, and Brooks didn't have the preppie look—the marks of their life experiences—but nothing could hide their similarities.

"Good morning." Brooks removed his motorcycle jacket. Brooks had spent the previous evening staring at the wall, trying to understand what was happening, what this meant, what he was to do, how he was to handle this man coming into his life.

A freckled, red-haired waitress in an apron came over to fill up Brooks's coffee cup. He thanked her and looked across the booth. "How do you know for sure?"

"That I'm your father?"

Brooks analyzed the man again. It was an almost ridiculous question considering their likeness. They had the same dark brown hair, though Brooks didn't have the graying yet. The same rather deep-socketed brown eyes with bushy eyebrows, the same forgettable nose, the same slightly pointed ears. The man—Brooks still wasn't ready to call him his father—was almost twenty years older; the wrinkles and the gray made that clear. They had similar body types too: six feet tall and skinny, though the man was probably fifteen pounds lighter than Brooks—not weak, but aging. Had they run across each other under more random circumstances, say on the street, they would have come to the same conclusion quickly and stopped each other. There was no question that they shared family blood.

"We're obviously related in some way. What makes you say you're my father?"

"I'm pretty sure." The man offered his hand to Brooks. "Let's start here, though. I'm Charles Wildridge."

"Brooks Baker." Brooks shook his hand and gave a half-hearted smile.

"I've read you were put up for adoption. Is that right?"

"That's true."

"And you're thirty-six?"

"Yep."

Charles nodded. "Do you know your real birthday? My wife gave birth to a baby boy on July 5, 1980 in the Community Hospital in San Bernardino, California. A day later we put him up for adoption. Is that you, Brooks Baker?"

A tear rose from Brooks's left eye. He wiped it quickly.

The waitress appeared again. "Okay, you ready to order, boys?"

"Can you give us a minute?" Charles asked.

"Take your time." She went to her next table.

His father reached across the table and put his hand on top of Brooks's. "I'm sorry for leaving you, son."

Brooks bit his lip, fighting back emotions. Pulling his hand away, he tried to say something but didn't have the words. He took his first sip of coffee, noticing its burnt bitterness, like the pot had been on all night.

Charles said, "I've been looking for you since you were fifteen years old. All your paperwork was lost. Or in some cases, they wouldn't give it to me, not even when I offered money. A lot of money. My only hope was that you'd reach out to the CDSS."

"The CDSS?"

"California Department of Social Services. That was the first thing I did when trying to find you. I filled out a *Consent for Contact*. And then all I could do was wait. After a few years, I figured you'd decided you didn't want to see us." He shrugged. "To meet us, you know, your mom and me."

Brooks tried to picture his mom; he'd wondered about her all night. "So?"

"A month ago, I bought a bottle of wine from my local shop in San Diego where we live now. I'm not an expert by any means, but I love wine and try to drink good bottles. I don't know much about Washington wines, but the guy recommended a bottle of Till Vineyards syrah from Red Mountain. I really liked it. I went back asking for more a week later, and I went home with a bottle of Lacoda marsanne as well. It knocked my socks off, one of the best wines I've ever had."

The waitress came back, and they both ordered over-easy eggs and bacon and toast, yet another sign of their connection. Once she'd gone, Charles continued. "I went to Lacoda's website to see what it was all about. I read about Jake Forester and more about Red Mountain, and then I clicked on the winemaker tab. A younger version of myself was staring back at me. Well, a more handsome version, but there was no denying who you were. After digging for a while, I found an article on the Internet where they mentioned you'd been put up for adoption. So here I am."

"Where's my—where's your wife?"

His father took a deep breath, struggling with his answer. "She wasn't ready. I can only imagine how hard this is on you emotionally, and you would probably laugh if I told you how hard it is for us, but it is. I know it's our fault. That makes it worse. There's so much to say. The short of it is we weren't ready for a kid. We were eighteen, two lovebirds going to different colleges. Your mom gave birth to you the summer after we graduated high school. We were kids. I was a surf bum. Your mom was going into nursing."

"Why didn't she have an abortion?"

"It didn't feel right. We decided our child would find a great home and grow up to be someone special. To change lives. We knew there were so many parents eager to have children that weren't able. We believed in the adoption process."

Brooks chuckled. "Yeah, I guess it works out sometimes."

"I couldn't find much of your story. I take it your path wasn't picturesque?"

"I was adopted a couple of times and then given back. Spent most of my life in foster homes."

Charles straightened the paper placemat. "We signed you over to the adoption agency, and they said they had a list of parents waiting. I don't know what happened. I went back to them...you know, fifteen years later, and they wouldn't tell me anything. I did everything short of kidnapping some lawyer's kids trying to find you. But I finally realized that you had to want to find me too."

"I guess that changed."

"When I saw your face, there was nothing that was going to stop me from at least shaking your hand. I wanted you to know that we were out there. I've spent many years hurting, wondering; loving a kid that I didn't know a damn thing about. Your mom too."

Brooks found himself tapping his hand on his jeans. "It's a lot to take in. It's just a lot to take in."

"Yes, it is. I know you're right in the middle of harvest and deep in the weeds. I hope you'll forgive me for barging into your life like this. I didn't know how else to do it. I'd like to get to know you. I'm not looking for anything other than a second chance with my oldest son."

Brooks had wondered about siblings too, but he hadn't gotten around to asking yet. "I have a brother?"

"Yes, you do. Your mom broke up with me our freshman year of college, but I never stopped chasing her, and we eventually got married. That's when we had your brother, Seamus. We call him Shay. He's turning twenty-eight next month."

"Where is he?"

His father sat up straighter, eyes downcast. "Your mom and I haven't spoken to him in about a year. We don't know where he is."

Brooks braved another sip of the burnt coffee. "What happened?"

"I don't know. He's a smart kid. We raised him well. The best we could. But he wasn't happy. We'll have plenty of time to talk about all that. Look, Brooks, we're not perfect, but your mom and I are good people. Let's put this family back together. Let's all get to know each other. Maybe one day we can get your brother back."

Brooks didn't want to be a jerk. Part of him felt excited to have a family. Shit, he'd wanted that for so long. But the suddenness of it all was what had him so shaken up. "Look, Charles, I'm glad you're here. It's great to meet you. I wanted a family my whole life. But I can't...I can't," Brooks sighed, "I can't just jump into your family like I was always there. I'm not going to start calling you 'Dad.' I've had a hard life and I don't trust people. I'm not easy. I'm much better than I was when I was younger. I'm healthier. I'm not angry with you for what you've done. I'd like to get to know you. But if we're going to do this, we'll have to take it slowly."

His father smiled. Not a tiny smile, but a big grin showing off his slightly crooked bottom teeth, a grin that said a lot about the man, a lot about how long he'd waited to hear those words, to sit at this table, to find his lost son. "I'm glad to finally have met you. We can take it easy, whatever you want."

"How long are you here?" Brooks asked, wanting some more normal conversation. "Where are you staying?"

"I'm over in Richland at the Courtyard Marriott. I'm here as long as you want me. I've heard what harvest is like for a winemaker. You want me gone, I can take off today and come back in a few weeks, or months, or whatever. If you don't mind me staying, I can stay for a while. We can catch up when you're free. Get to know each other some. There's a lot we have to share. Probably a lot you want to know."

The waitress brought their food, and Brooks and his father reached for the Tapatío hot sauce at the same time. They smiled at each other and Brooks said, "You first."

As Charles dumped some hot sauce over his eggs, Brooks said, "Why don't you stay a few days? I'll make some time."

Charles handed his son the bottle without putting the top back on. "I'd love that."

❧

BROOKS ARRIVED at Lacoda a couple of hours late and jumped right into work. He said hello to his cellar workers and ambled into the lab. His assistant winemaker, Pak—short for his much longer Thai name, Pakkapong—was testing sulfur dioxide levels.

He had hired Pak two years earlier as an intern from Washington State University's wine program, one of the best in the country. Brooks had promoted him to assistant winemaker earlier that year, a

well-deserved position Pak had earned with hard work and a devotion to Red Môuntain. Pak grew up in Bangkok and moved with his
parents to Seattle in high school, where he washed dishes and was
eventually serving tables at several high-end Seattle restaurants,
including Marjorie and Tilth. That's where he'd caught the wine bug.

"Hey, boss," Pak said, a Nike visor resting on his head. He was
currently pouring some iodine into a pipette, preparing to run titra-
tions, looking for total sulfur dioxide levels. Brooks and his team kept
the sulfur dioxide additions to a minimum, but as Otis had taught
him, a small amount was crucial to protect the wine.

"Good morning," Brooks said. "What's going on today?"

"You're looking at it." Pak turned and gestured to the long line of
wine samples on the metal table, each labeled according to their
variety and barrel. "Everything's moving along. That CAB08 barrel
seems a tad reduced, might want to try it."

Brooks took a glass off the rack and filled it halfway with the
cabernet sauvignon. Sure enough, he smelled a fair amount of
hydrogen sulfide, the sulfur compound associated with the smell of
rotten eggs. Brooks remembered the first time he'd discovered that
smell, his second year working with Otis. Brooks put down the glass
and looked at Pak. "Yeah, that's not too good. Let's get the wine out of
the barrel and run some copper trials on it. See if we can clean it up a
bit."

"You got it. I marked the others you might want to try. Other than
that, the cab franc starter is rolling along. I think we're ready to drop
it into the concrete and let it go."

"Go for it. E-mail me those numbers when you can."

Brooks tasted the other problem samples and then went up to his
office, closed the door, and dialed Abby's number. He put his phone
on speaker and placed it in front of him on his desk. "There he is,"
she said. "I thought you might be playing hard to get."

He smiled. "No, not me. When it comes to you, I'm easy. What are
you up to?"

"Getting back from the gym."

"Good for you. Got time for a walk later?"

"You bet."

They arranged a time. Brooks worked through his e-mails and then went down to the crush pad, where the grapes came in and were processed. His guys were bringing in a few tons of syrah. Halfway through, the destemmer/crusher hung up on something, and he spent the next two hours taking apart and rebuilding it.

He met Abby in the parking lot. They kissed, a passionate one that spoke so much about how they felt about each other. Brooks sensed the wanting in her lips and her hands as she pulled him closer. His feelings toward her were testing the walls he'd spent so many years constructing.

"I'm so glad to see you," he said, leading her down the steps into the vineyard, passing a wooden sign that read "Marsanne" in a simple black font.

"Likewise. How's your day going?" She squeezed his hand, and he really felt like she was into him. Really into him. Was that possible?

"I met my dad last night," Brooks said, feeling the freedom of finally telling someone.

"Your dad? Like the man who adopted you?"

"No, I mean my biological father. The man who put me up for adoption when I was a day old."

"Oh, my god." She stopped and faced him, furrowing her brow. "Are you okay?"

"Yeah, I think so. I feel like I'm in some sort of daydream."

She reached up and touched his cheek, looking him in the eyes. "Is this a good thing? I can't imagine what you're going through."

Brooks raised his bushy eyebrows and held her gaze. "Once it all settles, I imagine it will be a good thing."

She stood on her toes and kissed him. "Tell me about it."

Brooks told her the story as they meandered through the vines, talking and connecting. After sharing, he felt much better about his father appearing out of the blue. She was right; it was okay to be scared and apprehensive. The alternative of still being fatherless was much less appealing.

16

THE CHALLENGES OF TRANSFORMATION

Day two of Margot 2.0 was off to a great start. Jasper was still asleep when she and Philippe walked out the door for a jog. The sun was coming up over the top of Red Mountain, lighting up the vines, warming up the air. It couldn't have been a more beautiful day, and she had a swagger today, a little extra kick. Halfway up Antinori Road, she started to slow, but she wouldn't let her body stop running. Sure enough, she made it all the way. When she reached the top, she slowed for a while, regaining her breath, allowing her heart rate to slow.

She looked around. "What a beautiful place," she said to Philippe, proud to call Red Mountain home. On this clear day, she could see the treeless hills, almost like waves, rolling west for many miles to Mount Adams. From her vantage point, looking down at all the vineyards surrounding her, she could see the harvesters' heads, in their hoodies and wide-brimmed hats, bobbing up and down as they moved from vine to vine collecting their bounty.

She hoped she might see Jake today; the possibility fueled her inspired run. She'd reveled in Jasper's joy when her son had returned from Jake's home the day before. In fact, Jake had asked Jasper if he was interested in cutting a record together. Margot was trying desperately not to get too excited. Jasper, on the other hand, was being way too cool about it, all "no big deal, Mom."

This Jake Forester was really becoming something special to Margot. He was the perfect guy, a complete dream. Here was the bottom line, though: Jake was married. Margot 2.0 doesn't sleep with married people. Even Margot 1.0 wouldn't do that. Not a chance. Not that she had a chance anyway. She enjoyed the fantasy, to think about a world where Jake was single and chasing her. What a dream! How ridiculous! Margot would be at the back of a long line of supermodels. Only if Margot was the last woman on earth would she have a chance.

"Margot, stop thinking that way," she said out loud. "I am a perfect woman. I love myself just the way I am. If Jake was single, I'd have as much of a chance as any woman out there. I might not look like a supermodel, but I am on the inside. There's more to being hot than size zeroes with long legs in stilettos on runways. Besides, what I lack in bodily perfection I certainly make up for in the kitchen." She grinned and added, "And in the bedroom."

That last thought made her cover her mouth. She instantly started running, thinking that her mind was taking her down a dangerous path. "I hope you can't understand what I say, Philippe. I'd be mortified."

When they got back, Jasper was gone. She couldn't suppress the urge another moment. Leaving Philippe with a handful of treats in the kitchen, Margot ran up the stairs to her room, touching herself while in stride, imagining Jake inside of her. She finished on the bed and lay on her back with a grand smile on her face.

She meditated on the floor of her office for ten minutes using the meditation app on her phone. Her mind was ablaze in thought but at least she was present enough to see the noise of her mental ticker tape. She sat at her computer and started on her belief statement, a document she would read out loud every day. A statement of everything she wanted to come true in life. She first wrote about how it was time to get back to taking care of herself, that she was entering a new phase in life. She wrote about Jasper and about being a great mother.

And she wrote about her success with Épiphanie and the farm sanctuary. She printed it and read her words out loud twice, believing the
statement with all her heart.

She reached for her journal. The last entry was three years
before. Back when their life in Vermont was a happy one. She wrote
the date and then: *I am back. Margot is back. He's not going to drain me
anymore. I am two days into a new me, and I'm already feeling a difference! See you tomorrow. I love you, Margot Pierce.*

Time to go see her contractor, Tanner. She meandered out the
side door and down the tiled path to what would one day be
Épiphanie. The front of the inn had giant wooden doors she'd found
at Second Use in Seattle. They were the perfect way to greet her
guests. She pushed the right one open and found Tanner sitting on
the steps, talking on the phone. Sawdust and nails covered the
floors, signs of many more months of work. But the reclaimed hand-
hewn beams running along the ceilings and the rough exposed
brick of the stairwell gave glimpses of the European atmosphere to
come.

Tanner Henderson wore the same thing every day: a pair of blue
Dickies, Red Wing work boots, and an undersized gray shirt. There
was an orange pencil stuck behind his ear. Margot at one time had
thought he was handsome with his slightly longer blond hair and
beard. Now, when she looked at him, she saw a man she couldn't
trust, a man in it for himself, a man she'd have to babysit all the way
to the end of the project. The problem with replacing him was she
was scared she'd do worse the next time around. Men loved to take
advantage of her.

He stuck his finger out, indicating for her to hold on, and he said
into the phone, "I'm going to have call you back." Hanging up, he
stood and said to Margot, "How's it going? You ready to get this thing
done?"

"I was ready months ago," she said firmly.

"I know," he said, clearly about to start one of his seemingly
bright diatribes, the ones that were charming at first, until you started
to see through all the BS. "These holdups are unbearable. You know

what it is? We're dealing with construction people. They're all unreliable."

Margot didn't disagree with that.

"They're all Budweiser-drinking rednecks who don't have any education, and they don't understand that building is an art. They don't have a passion for what they're doing. They're doing the only job they can, which no one else wants to do because it's freaking hot outside, and it's hard, physical work. They don't get what I'm trying to do here; they don't understand authenticity. But the main problem I'm having is finding the good ones. They're out there, but they're getting overpaid by the government and by these huge construction companies that are taking advantage of the real estate boom here in the Tri-Cities. So I'm trying to save you money. That's the bottom line. I don't want you overpaying just so you can meet your deadline."

Margot had grown so weary of these talks. She didn't believe a thing coming out of his mouth and didn't care for his elitist attitude. "So who have you lined up this week?" she asked. "Weren't you trying to get the plumber in to run lines?"

Tanner showed his teeth. "He says he's backed up for a couple of weeks. But don't worry; I've got calls in to a few others. I'll get somebody out here in the next few days."

"Who have you called? I'll follow up."

"Oh, don't bother. He won't call you back any faster than me. Hey, I'll keep this project going. You should focus on the fun stuff like finding the last of the fixtures, the furniture, the things that will complete your dream. It really is going to be a stunning place."

"Tanner, who is the plumber you contacted?"

He thought for a moment. "Triple A over in Kennewick. I'm telling you, don't waste your time calling."

She ignored him. "We're getting a plumber in here this week. I don't care if I have to bring someone over from Yakima. Let's sit down tomorrow morning first thing and look at numbers. I want to know exactly what I'm writing checks for over the next month, and I want to talk about a new timeline."

"Yeah, sure. Let me clean up my spreadsheet and we can definitely look at it. I know it seems like we're blowing money, but believe me, things are going to start flying. You've paid for the worst of it. I'd say you're 80% done with writing checks. We'll have you wrapped up in six weeks."

His spreadsheet talk was the worst. There was no spreadsheet. Stop lying! "Tanner, there is no way that we're going to be done in less than two months. You're out of your mind."

He ran his fingers through his hair and grinned again, showing even more teeth. "Trust me, I've been doing this a long time. You won't believe how fast things start to move. All the small stuff will happen before you know it, and you'll be scrambling for furniture. We're done, I'm telling you."

Margot resisted the urge to snap at him. Sure, he was talented. She'd seen some of the things he'd built. They were unlike much of the modern construction out there. They had a much more old-world feel, which is what most of the new architecture on Red Mountain was moving toward, mostly because the French and the Italians were taking over.

Back at her place, she called AAA Plumbing and left a message, then spent a couple of hours working on the marketing of Épiphanie, a job she hoped she'd be doing full-time by now. She had no time to manage Tanner.

Starved, she threw together a salad of butter lettuce, spinach, pine nuts, red onions, cherry tomatoes, white beans, and a homemade mustard vinaigrette she kept in the fridge. Afterwards, she caught herself sneaking into the pantry for a piece of chocolate and decided against it. At one o'clock, she went into town for a yoga class, her first in many years.

When she returned, still sweaty from the class, she found Jasper sitting at his piano playing Liszt from memory. Not wanting to disturb him, she sat down on a chair and listened. She could tell when he was sad. It was written all over his music. The left-hand chords had extra power and dissonance, and his dynamics and even his physical movements—the sway of his shoulders and the aggressive nodding of his head—were more dramatic. It was stunning to hear how much heart her son could put into his playing.

When he finished, Margot said, "That was gorgeous."

He turned on the bench, tears on his face. "Hey," he said, wiping his face. "I didn't know you were here."

"I could have come in banging pots and pans, and you wouldn't have noticed me. What's wrong?"

"Nothing."

"Jasper. Don't." She hated when he hid his troubles from her, protecting her.

"Just a rough day. That's all."

"Wanna talk about it?"

"Nah, Mom. Let's pretend everything is perfect."

"What is that supposed to mean?"

"I mean let's not talk about it."

"You and I, we have to stick together. I'm your friend. We're on a new adventure. You have to be honest with me."

"Where would I even begin?"

"How about we go out to the courtyard with some yummy food, put on Bill Evans, and drink a glass of wine? It's Friday night. We can talk for a while. I have some things to tell you about my life too."

Jasper nodded. "Yeah, okay. I'll meet you up there in ten."

Margot found a bottle of Lacoda single vineyard Marsanne, fitting for the occasion. She started to make a cheese plate but changed her mind. She was trying very hard to eat vegan for a while, something that was nearly impossible due to her love for dairy. But Margot 2.0 had found some new discipline, so today she put together a tray of vegetables.

Mother and son sat in the sun, and with Bill Evans playing his sweet piano in the background, they talked. "Enough skirting things, Jasper. Tell me what's going on."

Jasper took his first sip and took a moment to enjoy it, a connoisseur of all artistry stuck in a teenage body. Then, "Can I give it to you in list form?"

Margot laughed, thinking that was the cutest thing she'd ever heard. "Okay, bring on the list."

"One, I've been thinking about Dad lately. He keeps calling. Two, school is pretty hard. I have a lot of enemies. Three, I'm in love with a girl who doesn't even see me. Four, I'm not happy with my piano playing lately. I've hit the ultimate plateau. Five, I'm not sure I want to record an album with Jake. Six, I hate that I'm so short. Seven, I wish I could play football. Eight." He looked into the air. "Maybe there is no eight. That covers most of it. This world can be so painful, that's really what it is." He sighed. "So damn painful."

Margot finished chewing a purple carrot. "You have a lot going on. Should we address them in order?"

"Only if you don't treat me like I'm ten."

"Sweetheart, you're the most mature seventeen-year-old in the world. It's okay to have bad days." She sat up. "Okay, so one: Dad. Have you talked to him?"

"I haven't picked up. I've just listened to messages."

"What's he saying?"

"That he misses me. He wants me to come stay with him. Or at least come see him."

"What do you want to do?"

"Strangle him with piano wire."

"If you will promise to do just that, I'll buy you a plane ticket to leave tomorrow morning. First class. So long as you don't get caught, I think it's a great idea."

Jasper burst into a laugh and so did Margot. "I don't want to see him," he said. "He can call all he wants. It just makes me think about growing up with you two. Before he turned into an asshole. We had fun, you know? It was nice."

"I know. It *was* nice. I miss that sometimes too. I know it's hard not having a father around."

"It just makes me sad, that's all. It doesn't help that school is suck-ing. I feel like every person in the building wants me gone. I get pushed and shoved and laughed at daily. Everyone is laughing at me. I'm a joke. I'm this little, puny boy with nothing to offer."

"Jasper Simpson. You have more to offer than anyone I know. Forget about your piano playing, which is a talent no one else can touch in that school. Your heart, Jasper, your heart is so full of love, you brighten people's worlds."

"Oh, my god, you sound like a preacher."

"I'm serious. You're brilliant too. Jasper, you are one of a kind. You are destined to change this world. You're not some jock that's going to go toss around balls in college and go off to die in some wasteland job. You're going to be remembered. You're special."

"I'm special, all right."

"I want to skip down the list a few," Margot said. "You're in love? Who is she?"

He bit a slice of red pepper. "Jake Forester's daughter."

Margot's eyes blew up. "Oh! What's her name again?"

"Emilia."

"You met her yesterday?"

"We have some classes together, but she's never noticed me. We finally spoke yesterday at their house."

"We're drinking the right bottle of wine, then." She held up the bottle of Lacoda, which was in a very unique bottle shape, short and squatty, like all of their wines, reminding Margot of a Sicilian wine she knew. "Tell me about Emilia Forester."

"She's it. She's like some princess from a far-off land, like an exchange student studying in Washington for a year. She's not even human, Mom. She takes me away from anything that hurts. How awful this world is to put her on this planet with a sign on her forehead only I can see that says: *Don't bother.*"

"Who says she isn't the one for you?"

"Emilia Forester is the stuff of legend. She will go on to solve the world's problems, probably lead us into world peace, and she will marry either the President of the United States or some NASA guy."

"Well, if that's true, you have a pretty good chance, because you're the stuff of legend too."

Jasper rolled his eyes.

"Let me sum all this up for you. I've got a few years on you and my wisdom is sometimes valuable. I don't even think we need to go through the whole list. You're just having a bad day, and when you have a bad day, everything looks ugly. You're right; the world is painful. Who you are, the future, your chances with a girl, your looks, even your piano playing can seem awful sometimes. But that's your mind playing tricks on you. You can't think that way. You are a rock star, not just in music but in life."

"What mom doesn't tell her kid they are a rock star?"

"I'm not even playing that game. You're smarter than I am. You were born with gifts beyond most anyone in the world. Son, you are Superman. I hate to tell you, but you're going to have to accept your greatness and live up to it. Why don't you ask her out?"

"I'm trying not to get beat up at the moment."

"I will talk to the principal again."

"No, you will not. I can handle this crap. It will stop eventually."

"You say the word and I will do whatever you need."

"I know that."

"There's a book I had to read in college that I've just picked up again called *Psycho-Cybernetics*. It's all about having the right image of yourself, the correct one. The one that you truly are, the one that wants to be successful. If you see that true image of yourself, you will grow into it. If you see a negative image, that's what you'll grow into. It's time you accept that you're made for greatness, and you need to put on your seatbelt because your life is going to be one wild ride. One amazing storybook ride."

"You don't need to worry about me. I'm allowed to have down times. I know things are going to work out. I know what I'm doing. I'm still just a kid, though. I have a lot to learn."

"Don't we all?"

17

WHO ELSE KNOWS?

Emilia met Tex before school at a drive-up coffee stand that had become trendy with the seniors. Tex had been suspended for a week for fighting Jasper, but she'd asked him to meet her before she went to class. She climbed up into his oversized truck, trying not to spill her almond milk pumpkin latte. His football helmet, shoulder pads, and gym bag were in the back seat, giving off a faint locker room smell—one that she had previously found slightly appealing.

He turned down the modern country music pumping through his audio system and looked at her. She could tell by the lack of life in his face that he was well aware of what was coming.

She'd ignored his calls for a couple of days, so he'd have to be an idiot not to get the hint. Nevertheless, Emilia had finally contacted him, thinking it would be best if they actually spoke about their relationship. She never was one for the passive break up, one that fizzled into nothing, leaving both parties hoping not to run into one another ever again.

"So what's up?" he asked, his low voice not as confident as it usually was. Tex was undeniably handsome with his very broad and rugged features, in every way the alpha male. She'd felt safe with him. In fact, that might have been what drew her to him. Had they been in Rome two thousand years ago, he would be the top gladiator.

Now, though, thinking about how he'd sent Jasper to the hospital, she saw Tex simply as a mindless brute. "What got into you Wednesday? Why would you do that?"

He shook his head. "He pissed me off. He challenged me. I didn't have a choice."

"That's ridiculous. The guy's half your size. Was he really that threatening?"

"He made me look like an ass in front of everyone."

"He didn't take your bait."

"I was asking him a question and he was ignoring me."

"You were picking on him in front of the school because he's the new kid and he's not a giant football player. He didn't let you. Don't try to become some kind of victim."

"I'm not trying to be a victim. Shit, Emilia, I messed up, okay? He pissed me off and made me look like an idiot, and I lost my temper. I'm out of school for a week because of it. My parents are furious. The Longhorns will probably hear about it. I'm already being punished enough."

"My dad's pissed off too."

"What does your dad have to do with it?"

Emilia told him about Jasper and her dad playing music. "My dad says to stay away from Jasper or he'll come find you."

Tex didn't say anything.

"Anyway, I'm over this. You're not who you used to be. We need to stop seeing each other."

"What!"

"We had some good times, but it's time to move on. We have college coming soon. We're not going to last."

"How do you know? C'mon, Em. Don't do this."

"I'm sorry." What else could she say?

"What's wrong with you? What happened the other day?"

"What's that supposed to mean?"

"Is there someone else?"

"No."

He looked at the center of the steering wheel. "I'm going to ask you something, and I don't want you to lie to me. I'm not going to lose my cool, no matter what you say. But I want to know."

"What?"

"Is there something going on with you and Mr. Massey?"

"What?" Emilia did her best to look disgusted. "Where did you get that from?"

"You're in his office a lot."

"Because I love writing."

"You came storming out of his office the other day when you blew up at me."

"He had nothing to do with it."

"If he did, I will kill him."

Emilia searched for the best lie, completely caught off guard. "It was a phone call, and it's personal."

He slumped. "Since when do we not share everything with each other?"

"Since you started beating people up. I want nothing to do with that."

"That wasn't me." He took a deep breath. "Please, you know that wasn't me."

"It was you. It's not just that. We've been over for a while now. We both knew it was coming."

"I didn't."

"I'm sorry." She had nothing left to say. "I've gotta go." She stepped out of his truck for the last time. He wouldn't look at her as she closed the door.

Emilia spent the rest of the school day feeling like everyone was looking and talking about her. She did her best to seem proud and confident, even forcing a cunning smile from time to time, the one she'd perfected in the mirror, the one that said she was completely in control. If people only knew the truth.

∽

BACK HOME, Emilia put on her swimsuit and went out to the pool. She laid out a towel, put on her sunglasses, and stretched out in the afternoon sun. It was now October 2 and there weren't many good pool days left. With some electro music in her ears, she spent the time trying to make sense of what she'd gotten herself into.

A text about homework from Sadie interrupted her mind chatter. As she punched out her reply, her dad and Jasper appeared, heading toward the studio. Emilia got a quick glance of Jasper before twisting her head back toward the sun and closing her eyes, pretending not to have noticed. She didn't feel like talking to anyone.

Later, hearing some muffled music, she wrapped herself in a towel and walked over to the studio. As soon as she cracked the first door, the music came barreling out. Like last time, she crept into the hallway and sat out of sight. Jasper was singing a song she'd never heard before. His voice instantly affected her. She leaned back against the wall and wrapped her arms around her knees. Her dad sounded good too, as usual. But she did notice something different in his playing, in his approach to the guitar. Her dad's playing elevated when he was with someone who raised the musical stakes.

What Jasper and her dad were playing was something special. Something unique. They'd found a voice together after only two days. After only an hour. She suddenly felt a sense of profound jealousy. She wished she were that good at music—or anything, for that matter.

And she wished she could connect with her father like Jasper did. Music, despite his lies saying otherwise, was Jake Forester's first love. Before his wife or his children. He'd never admit it, but they were all aware of his priorities. Music made his world go 'round. It wasn't just his identity; it was his religion. Music was his reason to be on the planet.

And Jasper was right there, tapping into the deepest part of her dad. Emilia would never do that. Sure, they'd played music together a million times and she'd sung pretty well. But the music coming out of that room at that moment was something she'd never be a part of.

The relationship developing in there was something she would never know.

Her dad's other love was wine, a passion growing nearly as important to him as music. He'd loved wine for years; his band had played all over Europe, and they'd drunk some of the finest wines in the world. But once Jake decided to start a winery on Red Mountain, he became obsessed. For a while, Emilia thought perhaps she'd study under Brooks and Pak and learn how to make wine herself. That would make her dad proud...but would it make her happy?

She sneaked out of the studio before they finished, and when Jasper and her dad came out, Emilia was treading in the heated water.

"Hi, Emilia," Jasper said, walking past her, waving at her. "How's the water feel?"

"Relaxing. You two sound good in there."

He smiled. "Thanks. See you at school tomorrow."

Emilia smiled, unsure what to think of Jasper Simpson.

18

THE NOW GIRL AND THE FOREVER GIRL

Otis wandered out of the room at Kadlec Clinic on Monday morning feeling worse about his health. With his head down, he followed the lonely hallway to the counter and checked out. The nurse, who looked shockingly like Oprah Winfrey, handed him a piece of paper with appointment info for his MRI, which was scheduled with a Dr. Jezewski at the Kadlec Regional Medical Center.

Otis hated hospitals. He didn't blame Oprah for his troubles, though, and thanked her kindly before making way through the nearly full waiting room on his way out.

He liked his doctor for not beating around the bush, but for once, Otis wished the doctor had painted a prettier picture. Instead, they'd talked about all the potential brain issues that could be going on, tumors and strokes being the most obvious. Otis felt like he'd just been given an hourglass, and the last grain of sand would be his last breath.

"Otis," he heard a woman's voice say.

He turned. Joan Tobey sat in one of the chairs with a magazine on her lap.

"Hi," he said. "What are you...?" He stopped himself. He took a seat next to her. He whispered, "I was going to ask you what you were doing here but realized that wasn't a question to ask in the waiting room of a doctor's office. How are you?" He bit his lip. "Yet another question not fit for a doctor's office."

They smiled at each other, and he realized how much he'd missed her.

"I'm great," she said. "I'd rather be somewhere else at the moment, considering."

"I know what you mean. I apologize for not calling."

She closed a *National Geographic* and set it on the table. "Oh, you don't need to apologize."

"No, really. I have wanted to call. My life is tumultuous at the moment. I didn't want to bring you into it."

"Is there anything I can do?"

Otis sat back and took a breath. "I don't exactly know what's going on. I guess that's half the issue. I'll tell you this. Just scheduled the first MRI of my life."

Joan put her hand on top of his. "I'm so sorry."

"So please understand why I haven't been in touch."

"Otis, we're getting old. Did you just figure that out? That's more reason to call me. We don't have time to waste."

"I'm worried I'm taking my last lap."

She squeezed his hand. "You look like you've got thirty or forty years left. Whatever it is you're going through, I don't see you letting it get the best of you. I see a man with a lot of fight left."

"I want to be that man."

"You are that man."

He faked a smile. "Well, how about tonight? If my clock's ticking, I'd best make my move."

"Are you asking me out in a doctor's office?"

"The first of many terribly romantic gestures you can expect."

"How about you come by my house at four? You can get a glimpse into my world."

"It's a date," he said.

～

BACK HOME, Otis sat in his recliner and eyed Rebecca's urn. All their years together flashed before him.

"Rebecca, I've just asked a woman out. I think you'd like her, darling. I really do. I'm asking for your forgiveness. Something tells me you'd want this for me, a new breath of life. I'll always be yours, but I'm going to let her borrow me for a while. We still have eternity. You're my forever girl." With those words, he broke into tears, a good cry that soaked his hands.

Coming out of it, he reached up and took the urn by the dark blue handles. He crept past Morgan, who was painting in the living room, and went outside. He hiked up to his oldest vineyard of syrah, the one Otis and Rebecca had planted themselves. With a few words of prayer, he spread her ashes in the middle of two rows, the last of her gently falling like snowflakes to the ground. She would be a part of Red Mountain for eternity.

～

OTIS SHOWERED AND SHAVED. He combed his hair. Thank God he still had a full head of hair. He tossed his towel to the floor and looked at what the good Lord had given him. A few sags here and there, but working a farm and vineyard and winery for decades had kept him fit. It's what had kept him alive. He plucked a few stray hairs from his arm. He tried on four different shirts, checking in the mirror to see what color worked for him. Then he debated between khaki pants and khaki shorts.

He decided on the shorts and loafers without socks. A proper English look, he thought. Finally, he put on his pop's Rolex, a watch he hadn't worn in years. He combed a decisive part in the left side of his hair and smiled, thinking he still had just a bit of his good looks. He certainly wasn't Sean Connery, but he brought some charm to the table. He'd make the women at any nursing home run wild.

He found Morgan sipping a scotch, staring at her work, that same depiction of the view out of the window, the vines, the sheep, the Horse Heaven Hills, rising up behind. "Well, well!" she exclaimed. "Look at you, Handsome."

"Not bad for an old T-Rex."

"If I weren't related to you…"

"Morgan!"

"What?" she asked, innocently.

"You need to keep your Montana backwoods thinking to yourself."

"I'm simply saying Joan Tobey is one lucky woman."

"Do you have everything you need?" he asked. "I'm sure I'll be back by eight."

"Don't come home until morning. You're an adult; have some fun."

"Morgan, do you have to cross every line you come upon?"

"I do when it comes to you, my young nephew. I'm trying to lighten you up. You used to be way more fun."

"I'm getting back there. Give me time."

Otis used the GPS on his phone to lead him to Joan's home. He might be a dinosaur, but he did understand technology. Joan lived on the Columbia River in Richland in a home he definitely did not expect. Hidden down a long drive, it was one of the nicer homes in the Tri-Cities, almost palatial, compared to the others. The landscaping was very well done.

Joan answered the door in a purple and white sundress. She didn't have shoes on, and her toenails were painted a deep pink.

Otis put a hand to his chest. "Are you trying to give me a heart attack? You're gorgeous." They kissed cheeks and went inside.

Joan had tremendous taste, from the rugs to the furniture. Victorian and elegant, like the inside of Buckingham Palace. The art on the walls begged to be admired; she explained she'd been collecting since college.

She led him to the back porch, and they looked out past her giant lawn to the Columbia River slowly flowing toward Oregon. There was a substantial and very healthy looking garden about halfway down. And along the river there was a dock with two Jet Skis.

"This is absolutely beautiful," Otis said. "What a gem. You must have a team of landscapers."

"Just me."

"You do this yourself?"

"Every last blade. Do you care for some rosé?"

"Ah, yes. Rosé is the key to my wit."

She came back out a few moments later with a bottle of rosé resting in an ice bucket. "Let me do that," he said, taking the corkscrew from her. He poured them glasses and they sat back in rocking chairs. With little hope, he put the glass to his nose. Not a thing. All he could do was see the color and imagine the smell, the light pink indicating dried rose petals and strawberries. He took a sip, imagining a sharpness indicative of a lighter, less ripe color. Perhaps that was his life now, letting his other senses lead the way, allowing them to remind him of what he used to smell and taste.

Pushing these sad thoughts aside, he said, "I am so glad to see your world. I'm slowly unraveling the mystery. This is your view every morning. This is your garden. Your life. A very happy life."

She smiled. "I do have a happy life."

"I can feel your happiness every time I see you. Every time I'm around you. It's infectious."

She smiled brighter.

"And those Jet Skis...are they yours?"

"Of course."

"And you ride them?"

"Absolutely. All the time. Would you like to?"

"I...I don't know. I haven't ridden one in several thousand years."

"I think you've just signed yourself up," she said.

"I didn't bring a bathing suit."

"Ah, well you can go in your underwear."

Otis took a huge gulp of wine. It was the first time in many moons that his libido had been stirred, something he thought had shriveled up and run off.

"So how did you end up here?" he asked.

"He says, changing the subject."

Otis's face reddened. "Talk to me after this bottle is finished about Jet Skis and underwear. Deal?"

"Deal."

They talked for a while, and Joan got into her past. "As I've told you, my husband was a very bright, wealthy man, an engineer and entrepreneur. We bought this house thirty years ago. I thought for a while about selling it after he passed away, but once I'd found happiness again, I realized that was just the part of me trying to run away. I love this home."

"I do too. You've got one of the finest properties within fifty miles. Look at this view." The Columbia River was so vast there. You could feel its power. "Anyway, I want to know more about you. That's all I want right now. Start with when you were a child. You are the most intriguing woman I've ever met. I barely know you, and I get this feeling that I'm with someone great. Who are you, Joan Tobey?"

"Otis, I have the same feeling about you. You're the one with the beautifully powerful aura. You are a kind and wonderful man. I can see the years through your eyes. I can see greatness in your face and in every move you make. I'm craving you right now."

The hair on Otis's arms stood up. It was that kind of moment that was so strong and pure that he felt this marvelous connection to the universe. What had just happened?

They talked some and he topped off their glasses. "So about those Jet Skis?"

"You're interested now?" she asked.

"You've just made me feel like I was thirty again. The thirty-year-old in me would already be on the water."

"What are we going to do about a bathing suit?"

Otis stood and did something he wouldn't have done the day before. He wouldn't have done it the week before or even the year before. The old Otis, the one from years ago, the one when his entire family was still on the planet, came alive. He set his glass down, stood up, and pulled off his shirt. He dropped his pants, suddenly standing in his plaid boxers, exposed to the world. The coyote in him was breaking out, but this time, it was different. He wasn't awakening in the middle of the night under the cover of darkness. He was coming alive in front of another human, in front of a woman who was doing something to him.

Otis put his hands in the air and faced her. "I'm not scared."

"Look at you, Otis Till." She eyed him up and down. "What a man you are. What a great man."

Twenty minutes later, they were on the water, shooting up and down the Columbia River, smiling like school children, Otis in his underwear, and Joan in hers.

19

HOLDING HANDS AND STEPPING INTO THE DARKNESS

Saturday mornings and weekends mean nothing to winemakers at harvest. Each day runs into the next, like it does for the soldier, the jobless, the homeless, or the musician. There is no nine to five; there is no normalcy. There is no average day.

Brooks had been half of those things and had gotten pretty used to a job that didn't pay by the hour. One day, he might be fixing a broken bottling line; the next, he might be planting a new vineyard or running barrel trials or driving into town chasing down odd parts.

This particular Saturday morning stood out, though. He'd already been at the winery since dawn putting out fires and lining up work orders, but now it was time to go see Jake and Carmen. He and Abby had decided to tell them about their relationship—more like ambush them—the first official step at what would be his first official relationship of his entire life. Brooks had gone thirty-six years without love. Of course, he'd had run-ins or even what one would call a girlfriend, but this one was different. This girl, this relationship, had begun on the happier, healthier side of his life.

Not until lately was he truly ready to embrace a relationship, to hold a woman's hands and look her in the eyes with not just a craving, but true caring. It had only been a few days, but Brooks had a feeling he and Abby would last a long time.

Brooks walked down toward the Foresters' house. He found Jake in the corner of the vineyard, shirtless, digging a hole.

"Need some help?" Brooks asked.

"No, thank you." Jake's jeans were torn and his boots were dusty. He wore a straw cowboy hat that looked like it belonged there. He said, "If a man can't fix his own irrigation, then he has no business owning a vineyard."

Brooks admired that about Jake. This whole idea of Lacoda hadn't been some project to fill Jake's ego, some way to impress his peers. Brooks knew so many people with money who needed to have a winery or at least a bottle of wine with their names on the label to satisfy their ego. An attempt by the uber-rich to outdo each other. No, not Jake. Jake was a *terroir* man, a lover of the land, a damn passionate son of a bitch who not only had been a part of the building of the winery and the planting of the vineyard, but also had spent countless hours learning everyone's jobs, asking questions and studying wine books like he was in an Ivy League college.

Brooks was pretty sure that by now, Jake could come into the cellar and make his own vintage without assistance from Brooks or Pak. He had a feeling it was that same determination that had led Jake to success in the music world. The guy was unstoppable, a complete workaholic, an insomniac, and an artist of the highest caliber.

"You got a few minutes?" Brooks asked. "I've got some things on my mind."

"Yeah, sure. Can we talk while I'm shoveling?"

"Actually, you mind if we include Carmen? Is she down there?"

"I think so. I think she's with Abby, canning things. Everything all right?"

"All is good. Don't worry." Brooks already knew Abby was with Carmen, but didn't mention it.

They found the two women in the kitchen, both laughing uncontrollably. They were standing around the island, slicing cucumbers.

Boxes of Mason jars were stacked on the counter. "What's going on with you two?" Jake asked. He'd slipped a shirt on and kicked off his boots. "Hate to bust into your party."

The women looked at him, wiping tears from their faces, these two women that got along so well. Carmen looked awkward holding a knife, like she didn't belong in the kitchen. Abby, on the other hand, looked like a chef, her hair up in a ponytail, a flowery apron hanging around her neck, an enormous knife held comfortably in her hand.

They said their hellos and Carmen said, "We're discussing things you brutes would never understand."

"I have no doubt about that." Jake kissed her on the cheek and said, "Brooks wanted to chat with us." He looked at Abby. "Do you mind giving the three of us a few minutes?"

"Actually," Brooks said, "Abby and I wanted to talk to you." He strutted to Abby, and much like Jake had done to Carmen, whispered in her ear, "Hi," and then kissed her on the cheek. He took her hand and looked back at Jake and Carmen.

"I guess I should have seen it coming," Jake said. "Is this your way of telling us you're a couple?"

Abby said, "This is our way of asking you if it's all right. We've realized how much we like each other. Only a few days ago."

Carmen's smile had gone away. "And what happens if you break up? Am I going to be out of an assistant? Are we going to be out a winemaker?"

Brooks had known Carmen long enough to accept her somewhat harsh behavior, but this reaction seemed over the top, even for her.

"Carmen," Brooks started, squeezing Abby's hand tighter. "We're not going anywhere. We've already talked about it at length. We both love our jobs. Should it not work out, we'll put it behind us and move on, all the better for knowing we gave it a go. But there's no way we can't give it a chance. We really hope you can understand." Brooks hoped what he was saying was true, that they'd be able to put a failed attempt behind them.

Carmen nodded. She didn't look happy, but she wasn't about to press the subject. "I don't mean to act like I'm not happy for you."

"Thanks for saying that, Carmen," Jake said. "You certainly sounded like you weren't happy for them."

"I'm happy for you," she said. "You know me. I'm full of worry half the time. Forgive me for being such a bitch." She stuck her finger in the air. "I have an idea. Let's have some bubbles to celebrate." She approached Brooks and Abby with open arms. "I'm very happy for you both."

That was Carmen's way. Every time you were really starting to dislike her, she would redeem herself. She was the kind of person who had issues one could list for days, but she knew she had them and was doing her best to control them. Brooks supposed that was much of what Jake saw in her, almost like a beautiful, yet wounded bird that needed healing.

The four of them sat in the garden on the side of the house around an iron table, sipping sparkling wine. The cold nights were wilting the once lively flowers on the lattices.

This is what it was like to be normal, Brooks thought. This is what being in a real relationship feels like. For the first time he knew what it was like to be a "couple" and to do "couple" things. Such an insignificant concept in most people's worlds, but to Brooks at that moment, there was nothing more special. God, if she ever left him, it was going to hurt.

Brooks and Abby explained how their new relationship started. Brooks brought up the sudden appearance of his father, which floored the Foresters. Carmen, being a storm chaser and gossip lover, needed to know each and every detail. Brooks happily shared, feeling better every time a new person found out his secrets. Before long, he'd have no more secrets.

The women went back to their canning, and Jake and Brooks returned to a topic they'd virtually exhausted over the past year: turning the vineyard into more of a farm. Brooks had been insisting on bringing animals to the winery since he'd started, but Jake had delayed the idea. "Let's do one thing at a time," he had said. "Let's get the vineyard planted and the winery built, then get a vintage under our belt. Then I'll let you bring in your animals." That was back when Jake was really learning about wine. Jake wasn't exactly a novice, having experienced a lifetime of being wined and dined as a celebrity, but only once the musician had gotten his hands dirty had he started to understand the true meaning of what they were trying to achieve.

Otis had taught Brooks that making good wine meant taking care of the land and creating more of a permaculture. Otis told him that you can't just plant vines and plan to make good wine. You need to have a living farm, a place that encourages the circle of life. You need biodiversity, like gardens and trees and lavender. You need a place that feeds the cycle of life: chickens for eggs and pest control, sheep for weed control and manure and milk, bees to pollinate and to give honey, dogs to protect and entertain and, of course, to clean up your accidents in the kitchen.

Working at Till Vineyards over the years, Brooks had learned that there was a rhythm to be achieved in a farm, and once reached, the wines would begin to sing a much richer song.

"Okay, Brooks. You got your concrete tanks and amphorae, you got your custom squat bottles. It just takes me some time to digest things. Find me someone to manage your animals, and we'll get going with that."

"Including the horses for plowing?"

Jake smiled. "Yep."

"And the bees?"

"Yes, the bees."

"I won't disappoint you, Jake."

"I know you won't. Anything else you want to throw at me? Your world seems to be in some sort of hyper state at the moment. A new woman, a new dad, right in the middle of harvest. Stay in the moment. Enjoy it."

"What a whirlwind, huh?"

"Nothing you can't handle."

"I hope you're right about that."

～

RED MOUNTAIN WAS TOO FAR out in the country for delivery, so he'd driven into West Richland and gotten some Thai take-out.

About seven o'clock, he heard a knock on the door. The moment he opened it, Abby jumped him. She pulled him toward her, kissing him with a savage passion, running her hands along his body, pulling him into her, turning him wild. They spun from wall to wall, tearing at each other. The coat rack crashed to the floor, a painting dropped from the wall, and she didn't even appear to notice.

Abby unbuttoned and unzipped him with one hand and reached into his jeans. A moment later, she pushed him against the stairwell, forcing him to sit. Brooks grasped the railing with both hands as she tugged off his jeans and took him into her mouth.

As he surrendered, his head falling back onto one of the steps, she reached up under his shirt and clawed her way down across his chest. He tried to stop her, but she brushed away his arm and slapped his face. "Keep your hands on the railing," she commanded. Brooks did as he was told.

They moved from room to room, laughing and groaning and chasing after each other, like two animals in the wild. They ended on the couch, naked and exhausted. She lay with her head on his lap, and he was stroking her hair.

Catching his breath, Brooks said, "I have no idea what just happened, but that was..." He didn't even know what to say; he bit his lip and shook his head.

"That was what?" she asked, running a finger along the bloody scratches on his chest.

"What just happened?"

"It was nice."

He smiled. "Nice isn't the first word that comes to mind."

She sat up and straddled him. "You've just been properly fucked."

"That's more like what I was thinking. Any more of that to come?"

"Do you want there to be?" She stroked the skin between his nose and upper lip.

"As long as we can keep the bleeding to a minimum."

"I'll do my best." She patted him on the cheek. "For a guy who has never had a girlfriend, you're pretty good at getting a woman off. Where'd you learn that?"

"Some things you're just born with, you know?"

She reached down between his legs. "You were born with many great things."

Brooks got the shivers. "I hope you like Thai food."

"I love anything spicy."

"Clearly. I now see a whole new side of you, Abby Sinclaire. You are full of surprises."

"We're just getting started."

They ate spicy Thai and drank Kiona late harvest chenin blanc, and then climbed into bed to watch Anthony Bourdain. They didn't get ten minutes into the episode before she started causing more trouble.

20

MARGOT AND THE SHAMAN

Aman from AAA Plumbing finally returned Margot's call on Saturday morning. She was in the kitchen washing out a blueberry and spinach concoction from the Vitamix when the phone rang. She dried her hands on a white towel embroidered with a rooster and answered.

An older man with a Midwestern accent introduced himself and said, "I'm sorry it took me a day. I'm the only one who isn't sick at the office. I'm doing everything."

"It's going around," Margot said. "The drop in temperature this time of year does it. Thanks for getting back to me on a Saturday."

"Your message said your contractor had put in a couple of calls to us. Tanner Henderson? I talked to everybody at the office. We haven't heard from him. You say you're building an inn, though. We'd love to be involved."

Margot sat down and massaged her forehead, trying to think. Then, "I've got your number now. I'll have to get back to you. Right now, I'm trying to figure out what he's doing."

He laughed. "You and every other person in the world with a contractor."

Margot hung up and sat for a while, contemplating Tanner, this man who was starting to ruin her life. What could be worse? Paying him to continue to do the bare minimum, or going out to find someone else? She clutched her heart, feeling the anxiety burning inside of her chest.

Margot mustered up enough discipline to make the 11 a.m. yoga class. The studio was in a strip mall in Richland. She checked in and followed two other women into the room. A speaker system on the shelf of the back wall played some soft Hindi chanting. In the front, there was an altar with a singing bowl and several Buddhas and pictures of many famous spiritual leaders: Gandhi, Bob Marley, Nelson Mandela, Eckhart Tolle. Margot rolled out her mat in the back and sat down. Mimicking the others, Margot stretched her legs and back while people trickled in. She tried not to get upset with herself when she reached for her toes and couldn't get much past her knees.

Soon, a barefooted woman in white with short, silver hair came in the door and went to the stereo system. She changed the music to something that Margot could only figure as tribal drumming. The woman weaved through the crowded room to the front, taking a seat cross-legged on the floor. She closed her eyes for a moment and took a breath. When her eyes opened again, she was nearly glowing, her beautiful, kind eyes making Margot want to hug her; her smile so confident and peaceful that Margot felt welcome there, despite being out of her element. Who was this woman? Her hair was the only sign of age. Her skin and physique, even the way she moved, exuded youth.

The teacher struck the singing bowl, and a long high note reverberated through the room. Once the note had died down to nothing, she spoke. "My name's Joan. I'll be steering the voyage today. Let's let go together. Don't worry. All your troubles, all your to-do lists and chores, all your obligations will be there when you leave this place. I promise."

Unintentionally, Margot mentally listed all her troubles, a list not unlike Jasper's: ex-husband, Jasper's new school, Tanner Henderson, her weight, her inn, her finances. She could have kept going until nightfall.

"For now," Joan said, "for the next hour and a half, I want you to leave all those thoughts outside. Leave them in the parking lot. In this room, the present moment is all that matters. You are safe here. Let's close our eyes and reconnect with our inner child."

Margot closed her eyes and listened to Joan's calming tone.

"When your outside world starts to creep into your mind, don't fight it, don't let it start spinning your wheels. Don't judge. Simply observe. Notice what's going on in your body and mind. Let these thoughts run their course and work your way toward stillness. Toss those thoughts into your mind's river and let them move downstream."

Margot tried hard to work her way toward stillness, but it felt like a volcano had erupted between her ears. The thoughts flowed like an Ice Age event, a huge glacial flood of mind chatter. She did her best to observe and not judge as overwhelming thoughts came in and out of her mind. As soon as she'd let one thought about Tanner go, she'd start listing her Épiphanie chores, and then start thinking about how tight her new yoga pants felt, and about how she'd probably never have sex again; then those stupid annoyances like her dirty car.

As if reading her mind, Joan said, "If you're new to meditation, or if you haven't practiced in a while, you must know it's no different than other skills. It takes practice. Don't get discouraged if the stillness doesn't come immediately. You must take time every day to grow these muscles. I promise you, it's worth it."

Five minutes went by and Margot was trying desperately not to move. The rest of the class was in dead silence, complete stillness, but Margot's legs were asleep; she could barely take another moment. Finally, Joan hit the singing bowl again. Margot untangled her legs too quickly and sighed as she stretched and the blood flowed back into her extremities. She didn't realize how loud her sigh was until the whole class giggled. Joan looked directly at Margot and whispered, "Great job."

Margot spent the next hour doing her best to keep up with the rest of the class. She could not believe how these people were able to contort themselves. Joan twisted and bent her body in ways no human should ever be able to, and most of the class was not far behind. Margot wanted so badly to be part of this collective. As the class finished, and her sweat dripped onto the mat below, she felt a great high, and she felt determined to become one of them, to become a Yogi. Margot watched Joan leave the room, hoping she'd see much more of this teacher in the future.

As everyone rolled up their mats, the woman to Margot's right looked over. She had a long black ponytail and deep green eyes. Margot had been trying to emulate her, watching her so closely that she'd even noticed the mole on the woman's shoulder. "Was this your first time?" her neighbor asked.

"That obvious?"

"No, I haven't seen you before. That's all."

"It's the second time since I had my son. Seventeen years ago. I feel like a sticky bun surrounded by carrot sticks."

The woman let out a laugh. "You're beautiful just the way you are. I'd kill for your curves."

"I look around at everyone and realize how far behind I am. I think I'm too old to even try."

"Go tell Joan that. See what she says."

"Who is that woman?" Margot asked. "I've never been around someone like that in my life."

"She's marvelous, isn't she?"

"Completely marvelous. I need more of her."

"She's a shaman, really," the woman said. "We're lucky to have her. She does some private consulting, life coach kind of stuff. Physical and spiritual health. I have friends who swear she changed their lives."

"Really? I'm going to go ask her about it. That's exactly what I need. It's nice to talk to you." Margot went out into the main lobby, her mat folded up under her arm. Two other students were talking to Joan. Margot patiently waited and finally got her chance to say hello.

"Thanks for coming today," Joan said, moving her red messenger bag to the other shoulder.

"I'm surprised they let people like me in the door."

The shaman smiled. "You show promise. The good thing about yoga is that it isn't a competition. The only goal is to push harder and connect with yourself and the rest of the class a little deeper every session. And to have fun doing it."

"I want so badly to have fun doing it. Today, I felt like all I was doing was trying to keep up."

"You did just fine. And may I say? You're a truly beautiful person. I noticed earlier in class. You radiate this wonderful energy, a very soothing sort of presence. I'm glad you're here."

Margot was totally flattered. "Did my son pay you to say that?"

Joan laughed. "I'm good at reading people, though you don't have to be good to see your beauty. You must be a great mother."

"God, I'll come to every one of your classes. You're going to make me blush."

Joan gestured to the logo on Margot's shirt. "I recognize the triangle. That's Red Mountain, right?"

"It is! How'd you know?"

"I'm actually dating a man from Red Mountain."

"I live there! I bet I know him. Who is it?"

"Otis Till."

"What a great man. I've met him a few times. He's so nice. And handsome too. You're a lucky woman."

"I'm very lucky."

Margot suddenly felt like she was taking up too much of Joan's time. Another student was waiting to talk to her. Margot said quickly, "I heard you do some private consulting. Is that right?"

Joan nodded. "I do."

"I'd love to talk to you about it. I'm going through some big changes right now, some mostly good changes, and I need some direction. First of all, I need to get better on my mat. My Chaturanga looks like a hippo humping the floor."

Joan grinned. Margot was no stranger to saying inappropriate words. Nevertheless, that's who she was at times, a hippo in a china shop. Never a dull moment!

"But other than that," Margot continued, "I could really use some help with meditation and making the right decisions, taking care of myself. To be honest, I'm a train wreck."

"Sounds like you have the motivation to get better," Joan said.

"I do have that."

Joan reached into her bag and handed over a card. Margot looked at the piece of paper. Her name was Joan Tobey. There was a telephone number and a stencil of an elephant. "Call me. We'll talk more."

"I look fairly normal," Margot said, "but you'll be amazed what kind of drama is hidden in here." Margot pointed at her head. "I may not be fixable."

Joan reached out and put her hand on Margot's arm. "You're not broken."

Margot stopped by Starbucks on the way home. As she ordered her espresso, she eyed the samples of red velvet cake tempting her by the cash register. She hadn't had sugar in a few days and was nearly dying. What's wrong with grabbing one? She was going to start anew with a life coach soon. She could cheat once.

She took a piece of red heaven, looked around to see if anyone was watching, and crammed it in her mouth. The sugar hit her tongue like an explosion of joy and she swallowed, letting the taste linger like a lover who had recently left the bed. How could one more hurt? She looked around again and snatched another. The barista noticed, and Margot said with her mouth full, "I couldn't help myself."

"I don't blame you," the girl said, her braces glittering on her teeth.

The guilt that consumed Margot on the way home was overwhelming. Margot 2.0 had slipped in a big way. How was she going to lose weight if she couldn't have the discipline to avoid samples at Starbucks! She drove down Van Giesen trying to tap back into Margot 2.0. *I slipped up. Not a big deal. Nobody is perfect.*

She turned on the radio, and Cutting Crew was playing "(I Just) Died in Your Arms," one of her all-time favorite songs. She sang with the lead singer, Nick Van Eede, belting out the words loudly, rolling the windows down, letting Margot 2.0 take back over. She reached the last stop light before her house and slowed down, still singing her face off. She happened to turn to her left to see Jake Forester in his old Land Rover Defender waving at her. A small boy was in the passenger seat. She immediately stopped singing and froze.

He rolled his window down and she did the same. "You didn't see me singing, did you?"

He smiled. "Maybe."

"I'm so embarrassed. Is this your son?"

"Yes." He sat back and motioned to his son. "This is Luca. Luca, meet Margot."

"Hi." Luca waved. He resembled his dad.

"What were you singing?" Jake asked her.

Margot's face had turned white. She told him the song. "I'm an eighties freak."

"That's one of the best songs ever written."

"I agree!" Margot felt some color returning.

"Jasper said you used to sing on Broadway."

"A long, long time ago."

"I'd love to hear you."

"Maybe one day."

"Margot, I mentioned this to Jasper, but I wanted to see if I could come by and chat with you two soon."

"Yeah, Jasper mentioned recording some songs."

"I know I don't need to tell you, but he's really good. I feel like I've hit the jackpot living on the same mountain."

Margot felt butterflies in her stomach. Or was that the red velvet cake? "I'm sure we can squeeze you in."

Jake liked that. "I'd invite you over tonight, but my wife is gone and my cooking ability is absolutely embarrassing. And Abby has the night off. It's just the kids and me."

Margot jumped in. "Why don't you guys come over to our place?

I'll cook dinner." Margot almost let it slip that Jasper had a crush on his daughter, but she didn't want to betray her son's trust.

"Really?"

"Yeah, sure." Margot's face had opened up into a smile so wide she was going to be sore in the morning. Realizing it, she forced herself to relax her face. "Say six?"

"Can I bring anything?" he asked.

"Maybe a bottle of white."

"We can't wait. They say you're the best chef on the mountain."

Someone behind Margot beeped a horn. "Better go," she said.

"Okay, see you in a bit."

Margot drove home, wondering what she was going to cook and what she was going to wear.

21

EMILIA SHAVES HER HEAD

Four days in, Emilia was still battling the sharp pains of heartache. She felt wounded, like a broken heart drying up in the dust. It was only a kiss, but it was so much more at the same time. It was the first time she'd felt this way, an attraction so overwhelming that nothing else seemed to matter. And then he'd dismissed her without a care in the world. It was now Saturday afternoon, and she was still having a hard time getting out of bed.

Pepper and Wilson were curled up next to her. *Sex and the City* was on the television. The door was locked. She'd refused to let her dad in today, but she had promised him via texts that she was okay. Her mom was in Seattle doing whatever it was she did, promoting a new perfume, doing another shoot, everything but focusing on her family and taking care of her daughter in despair.

Another bout of crying came, and she hugged Pepper's neck. Wilson got jealous and got involved, burying his snout into her arm.

Her dad knocked on the door. "Em, I need you to open the door."

"Not right now."

"I can't let you go all day without coming out. Can we talk?"

"Later."

"Give me a break. Let me be your dad."

He pleaded until she finally opened the door. He took the chair from her desk and pulled it up close to the bed.

"Where's Luca?" she asked.

"In his room, working on special effects for his movie. Wondering what's going on with you."

"Tell him I'm sick."

"He's smarter than that. I told him the truth, or at least what I know."

Jake put his hand on her foot, which was sticking out of the covers. "You don't have to tell me what's going on. I know life's tough, but you won't hurt forever. Even though that's what it feels like. I promise it gets better."

His kindness made her tear up again. "I don't know if I love my life, Dad." She covered her face and sobbed. He left the chair and climbed onto the bed, pulling her toward him, comforting her.

"No one can love their life all the time, sweetheart. Especially when your heart hurts. I don't even know what's going on and I'm hurting with you."

His words and his fatherly touch made her feel slightly better. "I might be in this bed for a year or two."

"It might be a better idea to stay busy."

"I'm busy with *Sex and the City*. Carrie Bradshaw needs my undivided attention."

"I see." He stood up. "We've been invited by Jasper's mom to dinner."

Emilia sat up. "I'm definitely not going to dinner anywhere."

"You definitely are. You and Luca."

"You're crazy." No way she could deal with making conversation. Jasper seemed like a nice guy but she didn't want to be around anybody.

"I'm asking you a favor. I accepted her invitation; she's already cooking. This Jasper, he's given me some new angles in sound. I like him. And it sounds like he's going through some rough times. His dad's back in Vermont, and there's some pain there. He's obviously not having a good experience at school. I'd like to help him out."

"Why do you care?"

"Something brought us to this mountain, Em. No matter where you go the rest of your life, Red Mountain is going to be a part of you. The people on this mountain are going to be a part of you. We have to take care of each other. Do you know how cool it would be if you came? The coolest and prettiest girl in school hanging out with the new kid. Besides, I hear his mom can throw down in the kitchen."

Didn't her dad understand? She didn't want to be the prettiest girl in school. She wanted to be the most important. And yet. She was so far from it.

He took her hand. "Please, Em. I don't ask for much."

It was nearly impossible to feel depressed when he was holding her hand, talking to her the way only he could. "What do I get out of it?"

"Besides being a friendly neighbor and eating a good meal? How about making your dad and your brother happy? It's Saturday night. Let's party."

"Nice, dad. A party with my eight-year-old brother and my ancient dad."

"Did you just call me ancient?"

"Decaying, whatever." She smiled faintly, the first smile in days.

"Now you definitely owe me." He kissed her on the forehead. "We have to be there at six."

Fine. She'd go to dinner. But this overwhelming feeling of not knowing who she was creeped in as her dad closed the door and her room became, once again, her sanctuary. She was a complete disaster, a teenage ball of confusion.

Great. She was the "cool" and "pretty" girl, the one guys wanted to have on their arm as eye candy. No, she didn't want that! She wanted to be the most thought-provoking woman, the one people fought to sit next to, the woman people desperately wanted to understand. Why couldn't she be more like Abby? Why did she have to keep living these lies? Why had she even created this false exterior? Who even cared?

Finding a brief moment of courage and inspiration, Emilia got out of bed and went into the bathroom. She sat down at the antique vanity her mother had had flown in from Paris for her. She stared in the mirror, a mirror that had fed vanity for more than one hundred years. Who knows how many beautiful women had prettied themselves on the same bench? And who cared?

She took a pair of scissors out of the drawer. No, this wasn't the answer to being free, but it was a start. No more would she be the pretty girl. It was time to shed all that baggage that her mom had burned into her about what to look like, what to wear, how to own the room with the way you walk, the way you move. No, Emilia wanted to own the room with the way she talked, the way she listened, the way she challenged everyone's thoughts. The only way to do that was to get people to stop looking at her like they wanted to touch her. Oh, hell yes, she felt it. She knew that it wasn't just guys her age. Every guy, every man, young and old, in every room she entered was undressing her in their minds. Raping her. *Leave me alone!*

Emilia lost her breath, feeling a very deep sadness. She bit her lip and squeezed her eyes shut; tears slid out of the corners and dripped down her face. "Leave me alone," she whispered. "I just want to be left alone."

She gripped the scissors with her fingertips and gathered a handful of hair. She made the first cut. Then the second, sawing through years of growth. She cut every bit she could with the scissors, but it wasn't enough. She could still see her mom's beauty shining through.

She crept into her parent's bathroom, looking for her dad's electric razor.

~

"Oh, my," Jake said as Emilia came down the stairs. He was in the living room chasing Luca with a dustbuster.

Both of them stopped when they saw her. Luca turned to her, red-faced and happy. "Cool," he said. "You look like a warrior."

"You going for the Sinead O'Connor look?" her dad asked, out of breath.

"Just something different."

"I like it," Jake said.

"You're not supposed to like it."

"What are we supposed to do?" he said. "Luca and I think you look cool."

Emilia didn't know what reaction she was hoping for, but they'd certainly surprised her, making her decision feel childish, almost silly.

A few minutes later, they were knocking on the door at the Pierces' home. Ms. Pierce, who insisted on being called Margot, even by Luca, led them inside. Emilia thought she was a really nice woman, so much more motherly and normal than her own mom.

Margot took them outside to the back patio, where Jasper was stoking a crackling fire in the pit, smoke rising into the breezeless night. As he turned to say hello to everyone, Emilia noticed again how nicely he dressed, this time in a half-buttoned wool cardigan that fit like he had a tailor upstairs. The young pianist met her brother, Luca, for the first time and was very kind to him, shaking his hand and asking good questions, proving he knew how to connect with children.

There was a wooden table by the fire with a bottle of Red Mountain white wine and a delicious display of vegetables and cheese. Margot opened the bottle and said to Jake, "I let Jasper have a glass from time to time."

"We do the same with Emilia," Jake said.

"I want a glass too," Luca said.

"You're not quite ready, big boy," Jake said.

"Why not? I know all the varieties on Red Mountain."

Margot twisted her head toward him. "You do? Let's hear them."

"Cabernet sauvignon, syrah, merlot, chardonnay, chenin blanc, sangiovese (the only one he mispronounced), cabernet franc, malbec, and...well, that's all I can think of."

Margot clapped her hands together. "That's really impressive!"

"It is indeed," Jake said, "but you're still going to have to wait until you're a teenager to give it a try."

"Dad, that's not fair. I'm going to be one of the best winemakers in the world, and you're denying me my education. Abby says you learn much faster when you're young."

"She's right about that, but underage drinking is against the law."

"Why can Emilia break the law?"

Jake smiled, obviously trying to find a better argument. "I let Emilia slide because she's almost old enough. When you're her age, I'll let you have a glass of wine on occasion. But for now, you'll have to be satisfied just smelling it."

Emilia took a glass from Margot and went for a bite. She'd been starving herself and the sight of this tempting plate summoned her. She cut a piece of a slightly creamy cheese and ate it with a cracker. "That's so good."

"That one is a Reblochon made by monks in the French Alps," Margot said. "Do you like cheese?"

"Who doesn't?"

She pointed out the others. "This one is Fiore Sardo, a sheep's milk cheese from Sardinia. And this one is a cave-aged cheddar from Somerset, England."

Emilia was fascinated. "You really are a chef."

"Well, it's no secret that I love food." Margot touched her stomach and smiled, and everyone laughed. "I'm trying not to eat as much cheese, but some nights discipline is the last thing that should be on the table." Emilia thought Margot carried her extra pounds well, all adding to this very sweet, nice motherly character that Emilia felt attracted to.

Luca was chasing the chickens with his video camera, and Margot and her dad dove into a conversation, something about the inn she was building and a bad contractor. Emilia felt slightly awkward, but Jasper jumped in quickly. He approached her without hesitation, like they'd known each other a long time. "When I first saw you, earlier, I was thinking that I'd be a lot cooler if I didn't mention your hair. But now that I'm talking, I'm going straight to the hair."

"My dad did the same thing. It's kind of an easy target."

"So you woke up today thinking you'd chop it all off?"

"I don't know why. Kind of regretting it now, to be honest."

"I don't know why I do half the things I do," he said, sipping his wine. "But change is a good thing. Think how easy it will be now that you don't have to brush it."

She smiled and said, "Your face looks better."

"I'm back to normal and ready for another good beating." He put up a fist. "Does your boyfriend still want some of this?"

"He's not my boyfriend. Not any more." Emilia drank from her glass. She felt comfortable talking to Jasper. He was a nice guy, and she didn't feel like a sex target for once.

Later, they were all around the dining room table feasting on Margot's homemade tagliatelle with wild mushrooms and black truffles. There was also a delicious bowl of kale and bitter greens sautéed in olive oil, finished with a pinch of red pepper flakes and a squeeze of lemon. Emilia couldn't remember a better meal in her entire life; she'd already had three helpings, cleaning the plate with a piece of crusty sourdough. She was having a great time, and the conversation came easily. She asked, "Margot, do you teach cooking lessons?"

"I will be very soon. A few people have been asking."

"I'd love to be a part. When will you start?"

"Probably once the inn is up and running, perhaps March."

"Oh, no. I'll be so close to graduating. You have to start earlier. I really want to learn from you."

"I'd love to teach you. Tell me when you want to start."

"Tomorrow night?"

Margot laughed out loud. "I could do Tuesday. Would that work?"

Jake jumped in. "Em, it's not the most polite thing in the world to invite yourself over."

"Nonsense!" Margot exclaimed. "I really would love to. It's part of my master plan, my dream. I've always wanted to do cooking classes. We could make it a ladies' night. I don't know another woman in this state. I'd really be honored, Jake. She can be my guinea pig."

Emilia was thrilled and thanked her. "Tell us about your master plan," Jake said, cramming another bite of pasta into his mouth.

Margot sat back with her glass of red wine. "I want Épiphanie to become an important part of Red Mountain and this community. I want to encourage slow food and provide a place to stay for all these winos coming to taste Red Mountain wine. I'll provide meals, of course, and I want to offer wine classes and all kinds of food classes, from cheese and pasta making to soups and stews and pastries and desserts. That's my dream."

"How about phase two, Mom?" Jasper asked. "Tell them. I think it's cool."

Margot lowered her head, almost in defeat. "Phase two has been phased out due to my completely inept contractor who has blown all my money and wasted all my time."

"What's phase two?" Emilia asked.

"Oh, I had this dream of buying the ten acres behind us for a farm sanctuary, you know, a place where we can save animals that are being poorly treated. Or are about to be killed."

"That's a beautiful idea," Jake said. "I saw the For Sale sign next door. What a knockout piece of land."

"It is. And I think it's important that Red Mountain isn't only vineyards. I haven't been here long enough to be a local, but if we're to build a world-class growing region, like Barolo for example, then you have to have a little diversity, some culture."

"Totally agree," Jake said. "You sound just like my winemaker."

"Are you a vegetarian?" Emilia interrupted.

"Yes. I know it doesn't look like it, but I am. Jasper too."

Emilia said, "I've been thinking about going in that direction. Can I ask your reasons?"

"How about next time?" Margot said. "Discussing dietary beliefs isn't far from politics and religion, if you know what I mean. We're just getting to know each other."

"Fair enough."

Jake clinked his wine glass with his fork. "I want to say something. First off, thank you for welcoming us into your home. I have no idea how you put together one of the best meals we've ever had with such short notice."

"It's my pleasure," Margot said.

Jake continued. "As I mentioned, I have a few ideas I wanted to run by you and Jasper. I can't say enough about how much I'm enjoying playing music with him." He looked at Jasper. "You're way beyond your years. And your talent is not something your teacher or anyone else can teach. That's deep inside of you." He touched his heart. "That's a gift." He looked back at Margot. "The force is strong in this one."

"I know." Margot's eyes shone with pride.

Jake looked back to Jasper. "I told you I want to record an album with you, and I mean it. I'll bring in a drummer and bassist, maybe some strings here and there. But I want you to really think about it." He shifted to Margot. "You too. Should we do this, he's going to get some attention. I'm not looking to derail him from school." Back to Jasper. "I don't want to mess with your life at all. I have a lot of momentum pushing my career, and you'll likely catch some of that— deservedly so. It could be a great thing if you want it. Lots of fun. If you don't, though, you will not hurt my feelings. This isn't about pressure."

Jasper spoke up. "I'm on this planet to play music, Jake. Whatever you're proposing, I'm in."

"He's right," Margot said. "There's nothing I could ever do to slow him down."

Emilia started feeling jealous again. They were talking about Jasper like he was the most important person alive. Right in front of her!

Her dad continued, "I'm not talking about starting a touring band and all that. Age has gotten the better of me. I can barely handle my infrequent tours with Folkwhore. I'm talking about making this record and promoting it with a show. Here on Red Mountain. Just one show."

"Keep going," Jasper said, leaning forward, bouncing his leg under the table with excitement. Emilia was hearing this idea for the first time.

"I was just thinking we could make the show a fund-raiser. Of course, you as my bandmate would have to agree, but what if we took all the proceeds and put it into your mom's farm sanctuary? Sounds like a perfect cause. I'll help buy the land. We could even do the show there."

"What?" Margot said.

He looked at Margot. "I don't mean to butt into your dream. Please know that I get excited sometimes and have to be shut down. Emilia can tell you that."

Margot covered her eyes. "I don't even know what to say."

"Just say yes, Mom. And thank you."

"I could never let you do that," Margot said, looking at Jake much more seriously.

"Margot, like you, I believe in Red Mountain. I like that about you. I want to help you realize your dream. I want to help you save some animals. I want more people like you on this mountain."

Emilia looked at Margot and saw a face full of gratitude and inspiration and above all, complete shock. Like she wasn't used to being loved. She wondered: what was Margot's past like? What had brought her to Red Mountain?

Emilia let go of her jealous feelings, realizing her own life wasn't that bad. Sure, her mom was a pain in the ass, but her dad was awesome. Seeing Margot light up and touched in such a way struck a chord with Emilia. Something was starting to make sense inside of her, but she couldn't put her finger on it quite yet. Some inner voice was trying to speak, but Emilia's ears and heart weren't yet capable of interpreting the message.

22

CODY, THE AUSTRALIAN SHEPHERD

This time, their date involved paddleboarding. Otis and Joan dragged the boards along the grass down to the water behind her house. Joan said, "You start on your knees and we'll get your balance right. Once you're comfortable, you stand and start going."

"Just like that, huh? You realize this water is really cold. It's October 3rd."

"Then you'd better not fall in."

Otis shook his head, knowing he was going to fall.

"Now, follow me." Joan pushed her board into the water, gracefully climbed on and stood, paddling away from the shore like a seasoned Hawaiian. She turned back to him. "Your turn."

"Here goes nothing," he said, as he pushed his ten-foot board into the water. He climbed on with the grace of a dog. He couldn't find his balance and fell onto his stomach, trying desperately not to roll into the chilly water.

"You have to get to your knees," Joan said.

"You made that clear. This isn't easy."

"Oh, you'll get it in no time."

Otis finally pushed up to his knees. Two ski boats were

passing by.

"Now, try to paddle toward me. You're getting it."

Otis began to paddle. He felt the current pushing him west.

"Keep your eyes on me or the horizon. It helps. Don't watch the water."

"I've got this," he said, moving farther out. He finally felt comfortable enough to look around. There he was on the middle of the water with this woman, the gorgeous scenery and blue sky adding to the sheer joy of being in her company.

Joan paddled close to him. "You're doing good. Ready to get to your feet?"

Otis bit his upper lip. "I don't know."

"You can do it."

"What's the trick?"

"Don't fall." She smiled.

"I figured that much."

"Keep your eye on the horizon. Have confidence. It's all about confidence."

"If I fall in, I'm pulling you in too."

"You'll have to catch me first. Now, c'mon. Let's go."

Otis lifted one knee off the board and replaced it with a foot. "What do I do with my paddle?"

"Use it like a tightrope walker would...for balance."

That concept made sense to Otis. He held the paddle out in front of him and pushed up with his legs. The board began to slip out from underneath him and he started shaking. "Oh, no."

He heard Joan give some words of encouragement, but it was too late. He fell to the side, his feet flew up into the air, and he plunged into the cold water headfirst. The chill went right through him, freezing the marrow in his bones. He kicked up and pulled himself back onto the board in seconds. Shivering and breathing in quick bursts, he looked at Joan. She was laughing hysterically.

"As soon as I can ride this thing, I'm coming to get you."

"Just try again. You're close. Remember the confidence thing."

"The confidence thing. This is going to take twenty years to learn."

"You can do it."

Otis attempted again, and again fell into the cold water. After falling in four times, he finally made it to his feet. After eight more times, he got the hang of it. And he kept his word. He started after Joan.

She turned her board and paddled away. "If you push me in, you're in big trouble."

"I just want a kiss."

"Come plant one on me then! If you can catch me."

He chased after her like he was back in grade school. "I'm on my way."

He drew near, and their boards touched, knocking her off balance.

"I'll save you!" Otis assured her. He jumped toward her, and the two of them splashed into the water. He swam up next to her, ignoring the cold, and he felt her legs kicking as he put his hands on her waist and kissed her, the first time he'd kissed a woman other than Rebecca in more than forty years. All the cold of that Columbia River couldn't keep him from warming up.

They climbed back onto their boards and paddled around for an hour before ending up in the grass of her back yard, drying off in the sun.

"You know," Otis told Joan, "dates with you are more like adventures."

"I refuse to lie down and die," she said. "I'm still in my prime, as far as I am concerned. I'm still thirty-two."

"I like that about you. No wonder you and Morgan hit it off."

"You're the same way," she said. "Who else your age can run an entire farm virtually by himself?"

With a sudden urge to push the boundaries, Otis said, "I just want to know if you can make love like a thirty-two-year-old."

She put her hands on him. "I hope you brought your Viagra, young man."

~

Otis left Joan's home in the early afternoon, racing to meet Brooks and taste the wines. As he neared his home, Otis noticed Morgan in the neighbor's back yard, shaking her finger at his neighbor.

Red Mountain was in the midst of a renaissance. The first vineyards were planted in the seventies, the wineries came soon after that, and in 2001, Red Mountain was recognized as an official American Viticultural Area. Each year, Red Mountain gained more and more notoriety as a place for world-class wines. Its cultural uprising and gentrification was happening, each day bringing news of developments, wineries, outdoor markets, galleries—all the signs of the momentum Otis had been anticipating for years.

Before the wine days, no bank would give construction loans out in the middle of nowhere. The only way to get a loan to live in Benton City—or any country back road of Washington—was to buy a double-wide trailer and put it on your land. These eyesores were slowly going away, but they were still there. Many of the people who had no interest in wine, the ones who'd owned the land back when it was a couple of hundred bucks an acre, were holding out for the big money. They were waiting for the day some of the big Napa wineries came knocking on the door with their checkbooks, looking for land.

Otis's neighbor, Henry Davidson, was one of those, and Otis didn't like the man a bit. It wasn't that the man was poor and lived in one of the double-wides. Otis certainly wanted the trailers gone, but he had nothing against the poor or non-wine people in general. But Henry Davidson was a drunk, and oftentimes a complete idiot. He had five acres next to Otis, and Otis had to witness every time the man started a project and never finished it.

Henry would get drunk and motivated and show up with a truck bed full of materials. But within a week, he'd move on to something else. Henry had started a garden with hay bales that had turned into a weed forest. He'd started a shed that still didn't have a roof on it. A year earlier, he'd had a truckload of white rocks delivered; they were still in a pile in the front yard. The back yard was littered with kids' toys, six rusting cars, and a boat that hadn't seen water in ten years. Worst of all, the bastard kept his poor Australian Shepherd leashed to a pole all day amidst the mess.

Stopping his truck, Otis hopped down and made his way over to see what kind of trouble Morgan had instigated. Davidson, who was in his late forties, wore dark brown Carhartt overalls and had a head of hair that looked like it hadn't been combed in years.

"What is this?" Henry snarled, revealing a missing front tooth. "I'm not running a nursing home here. You two need to get the hell off my property."

Morgan turned to Otis. "Did you know you were living next door to the loony bin? I came over to tell Dumbo here that he needs to give his dog a better life."

Otis looked at the Australian Shepherd, a gorgeous young dog with black and copper streaks on his white face and more of those streaks on his gray and white back. He had a long tail stuck far between his legs, looking like it hadn't been wagged in a very long time.

"What I do with my dog is none of your business."

"You should be locked up!" Morgan yelled.

"She's right," Otis said. "I've been looking at your poor dog chained up for almost a year. You shouldn't have a dog if you don't have time to treat him like a companion."

"You probably shouldn't be coming on my property telling me how to do things."

Morgan chimed in. "It's obvious you didn't have parents worth a damn to teach you anything, so I'm going to step in where they left off."

"Now you're insulting my parents?" Henry said, blowing up like he was ready to attack.

"Morgan," Otis said, "let's get out of here. You're not going to talk sense into this moron."

"You're right about that," Henry said.

Morgan started toward the dog. "I'm taking him with me."

"The hell you are." Henry moved aggressively toward the dog.

"What you're doing is abuse. I'm not going to have it." The dog growled at her as she approached, showing his teeth. "See, look at him. You're making him turn angry. How about I hook you to this chain for a year?"

The man stepped toward Morgan. "I'm calling the police if you don't get off my property."

Morgan knelt down. "C'mere, little guy. I'm not going to hurt you. Not all humans are barbarians."

The dog stopped growling. Morgan patted her own leg and whistled.

Henry stepped directly between Morgan and the dog and looked down, pointing a finger at her. "Ma'am, you're going to want to get off my property right now."

Otis came up behind him. "You point a finger at her again and I'll make you eat that hand."

The man turned to Otis. "Old man, I'll kick your ass all over this mountain. Now take Great-Grandma here and start moving before I remove you both. You're on my property and you're trespassing, and I'm perfectly within my legal bounds if it gets uglier."

Otis wasn't scared, but the last thing he needed was to get into a fight with a man twenty years younger. Whether he won or lost, he'd be nursing some wounds and bruises for a few weeks if he chose to swing.

He turned to Morgan, who was still trying to call the dog. "Let's go. Right. Now."

Morgan stood and addressed Henry. "I'll be on the phone with the cops in five minutes."

"Go ahead and waste your time, old woman."

Otis and Morgan marched back to his truck and drove home. Otis's heart was beating with anger. Getting out, he said to Morgan, "I've got to meet Brooks up at the cellar. Promise me you'll stay out of trouble."

"I'm calling the police," she said. "That man has no right."

"That's fine. Just stay in the house. You can do whatever you want."

At the winery, Otis found Brooks with his nose in a glass of red wine. "The potential with these wines is epic, Otis. Without a doubt, your best vintage."

"My vineyard's best, you mean."

"Yes, of course. They're young, but they're already saying so much. There's a vibrancy to them, not fresh but lively, almost athletic. Take my word for it, this vintage is the best you've ever had here, and I've tasted them all. It was a wet spring; then ripening got off to a slow start. Maybe the vines liked that."

"Every once in a while, it all aligns. The right fruit set, the right amount of heat in August. The right picking date."

"This is your year, my friend."

"Well, I'm glad someone can enjoy them."

"No news yet on your end? I mean health-wise?"

"MRI is Wednesday, if Morgan doesn't get me killed before then." Otis told Brooks about his encounter with Henry Davidson.

"Morgan really brings some excitement to the mountain, doesn't she?"

Otis rolled his eyes. "You bringing your dad tomorrow night?" He was referring to his annual harvest party, a celebration very few on the mountain missed. "I'd like to meet him."

"I'm thinking about it."

"Can I give you some advice?" Otis asked.

"Shoot."

"Let us into your world. We all love you on this mountain, Brooks. Your father doesn't define who you are. Don't be scared about bringing him around. He doesn't have to be something special for us to welcome him. Relish the fact that you have family. If I were in his shoes, I'd be a nervous wreck. Take him in and give him a chance. If he turns out to be a liar and a thief, well hell, at least you tried. No one here will feel differently about you."

23

THE HARVEST PARTY

The morning after Abby had thrown him up against the wall, Brooks peeled his eyes open and found her lying next to him. He craved her touch and slid closer to her, pressing his body against her back. She woke and whispered, "Good morning." She took his hand and pressed it to her chest.

"Good morning," he said, kissing her back and neck.

They cuddled for another hour, both of them going in and out of sleep. Eventually, their hands wandered, and the passion grew to a mutual climax, this time much warmer and caring, more personal and loving.

With nothing to cook in Brooks's nearly barren fridge, they went out to breakfast, excited to be an official couple, no longer hiding from the world. They talked of their family and friends, of their pasts and futures, and they explored politics and religion. Their beliefs tended to parallel, at least enough to find common ground. Brooks knew very little of politics, having missed high school and college. Abby, on the other hand, was well-read and well-educated, and he enjoyed hearing her views.

Brooks left her with a kiss and a great feeling building inside: she liked him as much as he liked her. He hoped so, at least.

~

EVERY YEAR, Otis had a party in the middle of harvest. Most people did their parties before or after, but he liked to have his right smack in the middle, right when everyone had been working too damn hard for too many hours for too damn long, and everybody was starting to lose their minds. It was a time to let loose and forget about how much more work was yet to be done. Everyone was invited, even—and especially—the colorful ones.

No one would miss it for the world. The owners and employees of all the wineries and vineyards were there. Even the folks who lived in Walla Walla and Woodinville and bought Red Mountain fruit drove over for the good times.

Brooks sat in the middle of a long, crowded table with Abby, his father, and the Forester family, minus Emilia. She was at another table with some friends. He kept looking over there, wondering why she'd shaved her head, wondering if she was okay.

Close to a hundred and fifty people filled the lawn in front of the tasting room of Till Vineyards, celebrating. Long strings of lights hung above them; a stereo played Dixieland jazz from somewhere off in the dark. A group of children were playing with the chickens. Wide smiles and erupting laughter and boisterous stories—at least half of them true—energized the tables, encouraging those still standing to sit down and get busy. Bottles and bottles of wine were uncorked, and huge platters, all brought by the guests, spilled over with tri-tip and coleslaw, deviled eggs, smoked salmon, cheese and sausages, stacks of bread, Margot's vegetables, and fifteen of Aunt Morgan's famous apple pies—made from organic Red Mountain Honeycrisps and Granny Smiths.

Luca turned his video camera toward Brooks's father. "May I interview you?" the young boy asked. Those who could hear paid attention; people loved listening to Luca take on a conversation.

"Of course," Charles said, looking into the camera with a smile. Brooks was glad he'd invited his father. Charles had made friends with everyone.

"What's your name?" Luca asked, beginning the interrogation.

"Charles Wildridge."

"What do you do?"

"I'm an engineer."

"Be specific. What kind of engineer?" Everyone laughed at Luca, who never failed to sound much older than his eight years.

"I'm a civil engineer."

"And you are Brooks's father? Why did you give him away when he was young?"

The table went silent for a cold few seconds. Jake, sitting on the other side of Luca, came to the rescue. "Son, that's not polite."

"No, no," Charles said, waving his hand. "It's perfectly okay. And a good question, I have to say."

Brooks said, "Leave it to an eight-year-old to ask the tough ones." But inside, Brooks was thinking how uncomfortable he was, how this question could never really be answered, but how he had wanted that answer for thirty-plus years.

Charles stuck out his hand, a gold watch wrapped around his wrist with a leather band. "I'll make a deal with you. I'll answer your question *if* you invite me to the premier of your movie. I'd love to see it."

"I'm not sure about a release for humans yet. I'm making this film as part of a research project for the Moon People. But how about this? If I do a premier for humans, I'll invite you."

"Fair enough." Charles looked back at the camera and straightened his shirt collar. "We had Brooks when we were very young. His mom and I were graduating high school. We didn't have much money. We weren't married then. We thought Brooks might have a better life if we put him up for adoption."

"Where is his mom now? Are you still married?"

"She's back in California. Yes, we are."

"Why didn't she come? She didn't want to meet Brooks?"

Carmen jumped in this time. She was sitting next to Abby, and they'd been lost in their own conversation. "Luca. That's enough."

"It really is okay," Charles said. "It's good to get these things out in the open. Right, Brooks?" He glanced at his son.

Brooks put up his hands and attempted to hide the eruption of emotions inside of him: the sadness, the curiosity, the embarrassment, the anger, the rage, all results of this absurdly bizarre situation he'd been thrown into. "You can't have secrets on this mountain. Might as well share with the world." It was true. It was best to let everyone on Red Mountain in on your secrets; that's the only way they wouldn't come back to haunt you.

Charles turned to Luca. "Brooks's mom is overwhelmed, that's all. She feels like she abandoned her son, and she's been dealing with that all her life. Now that she knows he truly exists and what he looks like and what he's up to, it's all very scary for her. Very exciting but also very scary."

Luca pointed the camera at Brooks. "Are you happy you have a dad now?"

Brooks flushed red. He thought about the question and answered honestly. "I'm very happy."

"Okay," Jake said to Luca. "Enough of the inquisition. Let's turn the camera off for a while."

Luca said, "Yes, sir." He put the camera into his backpack. Brooks felt his heart finally slow down, the tension in his neck subside.

The guests moved through bottles of wine and jokes and all the latest gossip. Like a freight train colliding with a truck stuck on the tracks, the arguments became more animated and controversial, the conversations grew edgier, and the laughter poured out, a welcome release for everyone suffering from harvest syndrome. People shuffled from table to table, catching up with old friends. Brooks shared some good banter with most of the people he knew and introduced his new girlfriend and his new dad to everyone. He didn't like being in the spotlight, but he knew it came with the territory. And for an introverted winemaker, he was getting better at carrying a conversation.

Later in the night, Brooks and his father found themselves at the bar in the tasting room, sipping scotch. By the light of the huge bonfire outside, Brooks could see Abby and Carmen still chatting at the table.

The tasting room of Till Vineyards was built with walls of thick glass so perfectly clean that an FBI crime scene unit couldn't have found a smudge anywhere except on or around the door handles. The hanging Edison bulbs and lighted candles standing on old wine barrels were the only sources of light, so it felt like an underground tavern at night. Ten wooden stools were pushed up to the bar, which was nothing more than a slab of concrete.

Brooks sipped his whisky and spoke his mind. "Tell me more about my brother." Yes, it hurt that his mother wasn't ready to see him yet. He'd spent many hours thinking of her, wondering if they'd ever meet. But even heavier on his mind was this mysterious brother who'd run away from his life, much like Brooks had. Now that he knew Shay was out there, Brooks was desperate to know about his younger brother, what made him tick, and what he'd gotten himself into.

Charles put his elbows on the bar and clasped his hands together. "Shay looks much more like his mom. I can see him in your eyes but that's about it. Still, he's good-looking, like you. He's got this curly brown hair that he lets grow wild. He shaves once a month and dresses himself with whatever he can find at Goodwill, usually one of those western snap-button shirts. We had fun watching him grow up, though he was a bit of a troublemaker in school, even when he was young." Charles let out a burst of air. "I had to pick him up from school his first day of second grade for putting superglue in the teacher's chair."

Brooks grinned.

"It was all mostly harmless. Once he became a teenager, he got into riding horses. One of his friends had a ranch and would take him. Shay got really into it and spent his summers in New Mexico working at a dude ranch, taking care of the animals and leading tours. He was on top of the world. He loved New Mexico so much that he went to college at the university there in Albuquerque. Your mom and I would go see him. Things were good." A pause. "Then something happened."

Brooks crossed his arms and sat back against the stool. "What?"

Charles looked down at the concrete of the bar. "Shay had a thing for bad women. I mean the kind you don't want to bring home."

Right then, Abby came in the door with a mischievous smile, the one she took on after a few drinks. "I was wondering where all the good-looking men had gone."

Both men turned. Charles pointed toward the back and said, "I think they went that way."

She pulled a stool up, forming a triangle. "What are you two talking about? You both look guilty."

Brooks rubbed her back. "Of drinking way too much single malt."

Abby took a sip from his glass and licked her lips. "So Charles, what do you make of Red Mountain now?"

"I'm starting to get it. You're all on a deserted island. There might as well be oceans in between you and the rest of the world."

"It feels that way sometimes."

"I could get used to this sort of life," Charles admitted. "You can be who you want to be. Doesn't seem to be much judgment going on."

"Oh, there's plenty of judging, plenty of good drama. But I'd say for the most part we're all open-minded."

"That's true," said Brooks. "You can be whoever you want to be out here. Some might judge you and talk about you behind your back, but so long as you don't let that bother you too much, you're fine. No one is particularly being evil, they're just digging up entertainment where they can."

"Look at everyone," Abby said, looking out the window to the crowd of people, the enormous fire licking the air. "Sometimes you can't help but be curious. Fritz Becker, the only German on the mountain—"

"A great winemaker." Brooks interjected.

"And a great drinker too. He just fell out of a tree."

"Is he okay?" Charles asked.

"I think so. He won't feel great in the morning, but his hangover will probably be worse than the bruises."

"What was he doing up there?" Brooks asked.

"He said he was chasing a rare bird."

Otis came in to help them finish the bottle. He offered to give Charles a tour of the winery, and Brooks jumped at the chance to take a walk with Abby. They held hands, walking down toward the sheep. Fittingly, the moon was full. Brooks thought Otis probably had chosen the night by design. His mentor did have a fascination with the darkness and the moon.

Brooks filled a bucket with grain from the metal trash can near the fence. Hearing the noise, the sheep came running, the flock moving as one, the genteel patter of hooves signaling the oncoming assault. Brooks climbed over the fence. He helped Abby over too. She'd never spent time with Otis's sheep. They both sat on the grass. "Now hold out your hand," Brooks said. The Southdowns tested the danger of the situation, moving closer, darting away, then moving closer again.

"I'm scared," Abby said.

"They won't bite, I promise."

Abby closed her eyes and held out her hand. One brave ewe dove in, taking every last bit of grain. "I can't believe how gentle they are. Do they have teeth?"

"Only on the bottom. Don't worry, they're not aggressive. Everything about them is peaceful. They're like little wooly Buddhas. This is what I want up at Lacoda. Sheep add good vibrations."

"Jake's told me all about your crazy ideas. Horses and sheep and chickens and ducks and goats." Abby took another handful of grain, desperate to feed another one.

"It really isn't crazy. Every time I drink Otis's wines I can taste so much more than grapes. There are these immeasurable dimensions that can only come from a farm singing in perfect harmony."

"I don't think you're crazy. And Jake thinks you're some sort of vine whisperer. He loves you."

"It's mutual; he's one of the best. Speaking of the Foresters, what's going on with Emilia? Why'd she shave her head? She seems out of it."

"I think love life problems. Jake said she and Tex broke up. We haven't gotten a chance to talk."

Brooks was now petting one of the sheep. "She can do better than Tex anyway."

"Jake says the same thing."

He said, "She's got it tough, you know? She's a really, really good person. I think people often judge her prematurely. Once you get to know her, you see how real she is."

"I love her to death. And she's breaking out of her shell." Abby petted another of the sheep thoughtfully. "What were you and your dad talking about up there? Seemed kind of serious."

"My brother, Shay."

"What's he up to? I know you've been curious."

Brooks told her what he knew. "I have this strange need to find him."

"Then let's find him," she said. "We can do it together."

Brooks shook his head. "I wouldn't know how."

"We'll hire a private investigator. It's not like he's hiding, is he?"

"I don't know."

They said goodbye to the sheep and strolled back up the hill alongside the sangiovese vineyard. Abby had her arm in his, and Brooks felt so proud leading her. She was his girl.

His girl.

He was her guy. Her guy.

Even when they weren't speaking, it felt wonderful. Neither of them felt a need to fill the silence. There were moments when Brooks felt her hand on his arm and heard her breathe. His senses felt so alive, like he'd awakened for the first time in his life.

The feeling scared him. There was still some inner voice that told him it was too good to be true. That's the way his world worked. How could she be different?

But the more rational part of him knew that he had to let that fear go if they were to ever truly become something. He needed to jump in with everything he had. What he needed to do was buy a ring and put it on her finger. Enough of all this worry, and trust issues and baggage. He'd never grow if he didn't take a leap of faith from time to time. That's what had gotten him out of the abyss. That's what had brought him to Red Mountain.

The sound of an ATV bouncing up the hill startled them. It came on so quickly that they both darted to their right, into the protection of the vines. Just in time.

A four-seater Polaris, more dune buggy than four-wheeler, zoomed by them. Brooks caught just enough of a view to see a man and a woman, buck naked, in the seats. Their laughter and some Top 40 Country blared as loud as the engine.

"Slow the fuck down!" Brooks yelled, his very rare temper flaring, no doubt easily accessed from the raw emotions of earlier in the night: the camera, the interrogation.

Brooks's anger did have justification. Someone could get hurt. He felt his heart start kicking his rib cage. The vehicle hung a hard left down into the valley. Brooks and Abby gasped.

The vehicle's headlights lit up the irrigation pond directly in front of them. It was too late to stop. The driver didn't even try, probably didn't even see the water. Brooks and Abby watched in horror as the Polaris plowed full-speed into the pond with a splash and a thud. Both of the passengers flew forward into the darkness. Brooks started running.

Yes, another full moon on Red Mountain.

24

A WOMAN ON THE MEND

Earlier on Sunday, before Otis's party, Margot had sat down in her favorite chair in the living room and called Joan Tobey. "I really need your help," Margot confessed, curling her legs up under her torso. "Could we meet this week?"

"I've been thinking about you, Margot."

"Really?"

"Yes. It's funny that we've met. It's difficult for me to agree to accept payment and take you on as a client professionally."

Margot immediately sunk her head, thinking Joan believed Margot could not be fixed. The Margot 2.0 day she was having, one full of positivity and hope, quickly disappeared into the abyss. "I'm that bad?"

"No. You're not bad at all; I think you're wonderful. First off, I'm spending more and more time on Red Mountain, and we know the same people, so it wouldn't be right for me to enter into this kind of relationship. Our worlds are too close for ethical comfort. I've done it before and regretted it mightily. But Margot, I think we could be friends. I love your energy, your sense of humor, and your humility. And really, your deep desire to better yourself. We only briefly met, but I do think we could be spiritual friends. And as a friend, I'd like to offer to help you. For no fee."

Margot's eyes widened. "How would I pay you back?"

"Friends do things for each other. I'm sure you'll be there for me one day. But I'm not worried about it. I love what I do and I'd love to share with you. Otis constantly talks of the community growing on Red Mountain and how everyone looks out for each other. This is me looking out for you."

"I could really use a spiritual friend."

"Why don't you come over tomorrow? We can talk and I can show you what I do."

Margot felt her eyes watering. Who was this woman? "I'd love to." She ended the call and sat in complete silence for a while, wondering what had brought her to this mountain, what had brought Joan and Jake into her life.

~

A DAY LATER, Margot walked into Joan Tobey's living room, a slight hangover from Otis Till's harvest party still lingering like ears ringing after a rock concert. The entire house was well-appointed and clean and peaceful, but the living room was clearly the life of the house, with its stunning view over a giant lawn and the Columbia River.

Opposite the windows, a bust of a smiling Buddha rested on the mantel; below it a gas fireplace waited a few more days for the cold weather. To the right was a wet bar with a nearly full wine rack. Music, the origin of which Margot couldn't even begin to guess, danced from a speaker system in the corner, bells chiming foreign melodies in strange modes. A faint smell of incense lingered—not the cheap hippie kind, but something you might smell in a temple in Tibet: waves of sandalwood and nutmeg and jasmine.

Teacher and student sat cross-legged on floor cushions facing each other. Joan poured them each a cup of tea, returning the teapot to the coffee table next to her.

"Are you ready?" Joan asked.

"I think so." Margot bit her lip and lifted her brow.

"Don't be nervous."

"I don't know what to expect."

"Trust me for a while, let go a little. We're going to have fun."

Margot took a deep breath and settled down. "Okay."

"Tell me, have you ever seen a therapist?"

"Are you kidding me? I have four of them on speed dial." Margot laughed nervously.

Joan burst into honest laughter. "I'm assuming that's a joke."

Margot smiled and covered her mouth, wishing she could keep her mouth shut when she felt uneasy. "I don't have them on speed dial, but I have seen plenty of therapists over the years, especially since my life fell to pieces."

"Okay, so I'm going to be the opposite of what you're used to. For the next twenty minutes, I want you to tell me all your woes. Everything that even slightly bothers you. Let's visit your past. For twenty minutes. And then, I don't want to talk about it again. Forever. Ever. Ever. And I don't want you to think about it again. Forever. Ever. Ever."

Margot thought dropping fifty pounds and becoming a super-model would probably be easier.

Joan said, "We'll talk about your past this one time so that I can get to know you. When your time is up, I want you to be in the present. Instead of your old therapists, who dove into and dissected every thought you've ever had, analyzing your past a million ways to Sunday and finding hidden meanings, I'm going to teach you to stop thinking about history and stop worrying about your future. I believe there's no good to be found in reliving memories, especially those times that hurt. And there's certainly no sense in dreading things that might not ever happen."

Joan sat up straighter and put her hands on her thighs, continuing. "You can talk about that time you got your pants pulled down in middle school to exhaustion; how you could have prevented it, who remembers it, what the implications truly were—and this over-thinking is never going to help you get over the experience. The only solution is to move on and be in this moment. Your pants aren't down now. That was a long time ago. It's all about this moment. Not the future, either. Who knows if your pants are going to get pulled down again? We can certainly plan for the future and steer our boat in the direction we want—for example, you can wear a belt—but no one can truly know what is to come. Does that make sense?"

"When you say it, of course." Margot had learned about the present moment and its benefits during college and the decade of her twenties, when she had enough time to look out for herself. She'd been refreshing that knowledge with the stack of books she'd purchased recently. She wanted to return to that woman of her past. Was it possible? Seeing and listening to this magic woman made her believe so.

Joan looked at her watch. "Okay, twenty minutes. Go."

"Twenty minutes might only touch the surface."

"Then you'd better get going. Speak your mind."

"Every afternoon," Margot started, "until a few days ago, I get in the bath with a glass of wine, close my eyes, and imagine ways of killing my ex-husband. I somehow justify this madness by making it a game, with the rule that I can only murder him using kitchen tools."

Joan smiled. "Now, that's a good place to start."

Margot ate up every bit of the twenty minutes like she was devouring a *pain au chocolat* from a Paris bakery. She talked of Jasper's father and of Tanner Henderson and the inn, and her worries about Jasper and her weight. Margot could have kept going, but on the mark, Joan said, "Stop. I get the picture."

"Am I crazy?"

"Not at all. You're normal. Actually, normal isn't the right word. Your problems are normal but you, Margot, are a vibrant and exciting woman."

"That's good, I guess."

"Now. Close your eyes. All that is gone now."

Margot noticed her legs falling asleep. "Could I stretch for a minute? My legs are killing me."

"Let's stand up and take a walk. You'll get used to the sitting soon."

Joan led Margot out the back door toward the river. "For the next five minutes, let's walk in silence. Imagine everything you just told me drifting along the grass to the river and then floating away toward Portland."

Margot let her thoughts go, and for short blocks of time, she felt completely aware of herself and her surroundings. It was almost scary being naked of thought, completely present, unconcerned of the past or future.

After a while, as they were watching the river flow, Joan interrupted the silence. "How was Otis's party last night?"

"Crazy, as usual." Margot felt much more peaceful than she'd felt in a long time.

"I was so sorry I couldn't make it. I had an emergency with a friend. Did you have fun?"

"It lived up to its billing. Did Otis tell you about the naked couple who drove into the irrigation pond on an ATV?"

"He did. I'm glad they're okay."

"I don't think they'll be invited back. Even for his harvest party, that got dangerous. Otis was furious."

"I know. He said he let them have it."

"In front of everyone, while they were still toweling off."

They watched the river flow for a while. Margot was fascinated by Joan. The woman could have found joy staring at the water for hours.

Margot told Joan about her plans for the inn. When she mentioned cooking classes, Joan said, "I'm a terrible cook, but I'm dying to get better. Otis can't stand that I can't cook. I love food and wine, but I've never spent the time to learn how. My husband did the cooking and ever since he died, I've kept it very simple."

"I'd love to teach you," Margot said, an idea coming to her. "That's how I could return the favor! Everyone is on me to teach classes. I just promised a young lady on Red Mountain that I'd begin teaching her. Tomorrow night, actually. If you'd like to join us, we could start a thing. Once a week or so. This girl is adorable. She's my son's age, seventeen, and she's very sweet, fun to be around. I think you'd like her a lot."

"Sign me up."

"Seriously?"

"Yes, seriously."

"Isn't it funny how the stars align sometimes? I know I don't look it but I'm going to focus on healthy stuff. Believe it or not, I'm a vegetarian. We're going to do spanakopita tomorrow."

"Love, love, love spanakopita. Oh, I'm delighted. I've been encouraging Otis to eat more vegetables anyway. Something about his English blood, he absolutely adores red meat and potato chips and French fries and all the deadly sins."

"My weakness is sugar. Sadly, I am really good at making desserts."

"We share this weakness."

Margot said, "I'd say you have it under control."

"It's a constant battle."

"Yes, and I'm losing the war. Sugar is winning."

"It's about being mindful, enjoying the bites more, savoring them, and stopping before you overeat. Presence and mindfulness can really help you in countless ways. Your eating, your moods, your troubles. You will notice great changes over the next few months."

Soon, they were back in the living room on their cushions.

"Close your eyes," Joan said, speaking slowly and quietly. "Pretend there's a string attached to the top of your head, pulling you up toward the sky. Let your back straighten. Breathe through your nose. Feel your body. Feel the life force surging through you."

The only life force Margot felt was her hunger pangs. All the talk of dessert had made her crave a pastry: maybe a hot and sticky cinnamon bun or even an éclair.

Joan stood. "I'm going to light some sage to help clear any negativity traveling with you. When you breathe out, breathe out any anxiety or nerves that you may notice, anything that doesn't feel good. Imagine tying kites to each negative thought or feeling and letting them float up into the air, letting them burn up in the atmosphere. Let go of possible tension in your jaw and your back and your stomach. Breathe it out. Let it go."

Margot heard a match strike and opened her eyes. Joan lit a bundle of sage. The shaman let the herb burn for a moment and blew it out. The bundle began to smoke, and a pleasant yet pungent smell took over the air. Joan performed a smudging ritual, circling the smoking sage around Margot's head and body, cleansing and replenishing her energy.

Feeling a lovely peacefulness, Margot closed her eyes and focused on her task. The next few minutes were incredible. Having Joan present helped Margot achieve a sensation she'd never known before. When Joan told her to start coming out of it and open her eyes, Margot didn't want to. She could have stayed there for hours.

~

MARGOT LOST track of time and had to rush back to meet a new contractor Jake had recommended. They had agreed on one o'clock. She'd firmly decided that she needed to explore her options. Tanner wasn't cutting it, and she was pretty sure he was ripping her off.

The man was standing in her driveway when she arrived. *A prompt contractor!* she thought. *He's off to a good start. And he's handsome.* He had shaggy hair and a thick blond mustache; his face showed a shadow of beard. A deep tan still lingered from the summer sun. His wide-brimmed khaki hat and eighties sunglasses dangling around his neck made him look more Florida or even Bahamas than Pacific Northwest. He was rugged and broad. More man than she'd know what to do with, she thought.

"I'm Ron Sallee," he said, extending his hand. She accepted, noticing the rough spots, the calluses, the leathered hands of a man who'd been working with hammer and nail for many years. She also noticed his wedding ring.

"It's a beautiful start," he said, speaking louder than normal, maybe brought on by a slight loss of hearing from running equipment for years. "Who drew up the plans?" She told him the name of the architectural firm. He said, "And then your contractor took it from there?"

"Yes, exactly. His name's Tanner Henderson. I gave him the plans and the green light in June of last year. He said he'd have it done by September. We're not even close."

She pushed open the large wooden door and led him in. Ron looked around, nodding his head. He left the foyer and walked into the reception area. There was still plywood showing on the walls, way too much work left. Ron was meticulous, pulling back layers when he could, peeking behind walls. They went into the dining room and the kitchen, which still lacked the marble countertops and appliances. Then they toured the upstairs.

Ron was being too quiet.

"How bad is it?" she asked as they got back to the top of the stairs.

"This is pretty shoddy work, Ms. Pierce."

"Please call me Margot."

"Doesn't look like he knows how to use a level. The cabinets and shelving are way off. And these claw foot tubs you have up here, they're heavy. I didn't see enough structural support downstairs to hold them. I wouldn't want to stand under one for long after it's filled. Might drop on your head."

He asked more questions and brought up more concerns. She told him of Tanner's lie about the plumber.

Ron pulled at his mustache. "Where is he today? It *is* Monday."

"He had to go to Seattle for something. At least, that's what he said. I don't know what to believe anymore."

"You want my honest opinion?"

"Of course. Jake says I can trust you."

"You tell this Tanner not to come back. I don't know how much of the carpentry he's doing himself, but it's terrible. He can't use a level and he sure as hell doesn't know how to cut wood to the right measurements."

"I'm paying him sixty an hour, and you're telling me he doesn't know what he's doing?"

"Sixty dollars an hour!"

Margot threw up her hands. "This is all new to me. He said sixty was a friendly rate."

"He's not worth minimum wage. He couldn't build a sandbox, and it sounds like he's no better at managing his people. Are you all settled up with him?"

Margot wiped a tear from her eye. "I owe him a couple thousand dollars right now."

"Don't pay him. Fire him today and tell him you know how much he's taken advantage of you. Tell him that I'm taking over and if he's got a problem, he can come to me."

Margot was heartbroken. She'd really messed up. Ron read her sadness and put a respectful hand on her upper arm. "We can fix this. It's not too late at all."

Margot lifted one side of her lips, trying to smile. "If I can afford to fix it."

He moved his hand. "I'll do the best I can."

"And you're available?"

"I will be in about a week. I'll make the time. Jake has been good to me. He asked me to take care of you."

"How long will the whole project take from here?" Margot asked, not really wanting to know the answer.

"I'll have to spend some more time out here and get a better idea of what you're trying to do, see the plans and all that. I don't want to guess right now. As you've learned, putting an end date in stone can be suicide. I can come back next Wednesday to get started. We'll get it done as quickly as we can."

"Thank you," she said.

"You just tell this Tanner Henderson to come pick up his tools and get out of here. And watch him when he comes. Make sure he doesn't take anything you own."

Once he was gone, she sat down on the steps and sobbed. *What kind of world is this? Why would Tanner take my money and lie to me? I was so stupid to trust him. So stupid to even try to make this dream come true.* She crossed her arms and let her head drop, and she wept until she had no more tears to cry. When Jasper pulled into the driveway, she hid in the inn, not wanting him to see her this way. She had to be strong. Back in the old days, when she was weak, her husband could be the strong one. And vice versa. Now, she had both roles. She had to be mother and father.

25

THE COOKING CLUB

Emilia moseyed along to Margot's house, shortcutting through the dusty, rocky tractor paths that defined the vineyard block boundaries. She spoke to the vineyard workers she passed along the way, testing the Spanish she'd been learning for years.

Reaching a quiet stretch, she ran her fingers along the leaves of a row of vines and plucked some grapes from a cluster. She tasted them and spat out the seeds. It was a beautiful life here on Red Mountain, this wine life. She understood why her dad had been so caught up. He had seen and done it all, and very little excited him any more. All he could do to find satisfaction was to go back to the basics. To agriculture and winemaking. Nothing made him happier now than playing music and working outside during the day, then sitting at a dinner table drinking a good bottle of wine and sharing conversation with his loved ones. It was a beautiful life.

Jasper answered the door, and in a convincing British accent, one she would hear often in the future, he said, "Good evening, miss. Have ya come for the tea and crumpets?"

Caught off guard yet slightly intrigued, Emilia jumped into her own best British. "I've come 'round to study the art of cooking with your mum." Her accent wasn't as convincing, but surprisingly, she didn't care.

"Ah, yes. You are one of her new pupils." Jasper reached out his hand. "I am Jasper, her bastard son."

"She's told tales. She keeps you locked in the basement. The accordion player, right?"

"Yes, of course. I've just escaped and now I'm on my way to Scotland to learn the bagpipes. May I take you away with me?"

"Oh, please."

"Give me your hand, my lady."

He took her hand, and a wonderful moment passed between them. Jasper smiled. "Come on in, my fellow thespian."

Emilia followed him in, but he didn't let go of her hand for another few seconds. She said, "So you're as weird as I am, I see."

"Weirder. Hence my popularity at school. My mom and Joan are in here." He swung the kitchen door open and held it for her. Aretha Franklin was singing "I Never Loved a Man," and Margot and Joan were singing along.

"Have fun," Jasper said.

"You're not cooking with us?"

Jasper rolled his eyes. "Too much estrogen in here for me." He touched his ear. "My mom's already got Aretha going. Soon you'll be sipping apple martinis and making fun of the dresses in *People*. Try to have fun without me."

"We'll do our best." She smiled and stepped into the kitchen. Margot and Joan were busily preparing food, both in flowery aprons. They stopped singing to welcome her. Margot turned down the music and said, "We were getting our rhythm and blues on."

"I love it." Emilia had a feeling she was going to like these women.

They made introductions. Joan wore a hemp shirt with baggy black pants and sandals. A simple chain necklace with a gorgeous blue crystal hung around her neck. "Oh, my god, I love your style," Emilia told her. "Where did you get your necklace?"

"This was a gift from an old friend when I was living in London ages ago. Somehow I still have it."

"What's the stone?"

"Jeremejevite."

"I've never heard of it." Emilia thought for a moment that her mom probably had one bigger, and the thought amused her.

Joan said, "A mineralogist discovered the stone in Siberia in the late 1800s. This one came from an antique shop in Notting Hill."

"It's gorgeous."

"I like you already, young lady. Now come join us."

"She needs an apron first." Margot handed her a yellow apron with white daisies on the front, and Emilia slipped it over her head. Margot said, "Is Abby coming?"

"No, she and my mom are hanging out. She promised next time, though."

Margot led them through the preparation, making the phyllo dough, dicing onions and garlic, chopping the spinach and fresh herbs, crumbling the feta. Once everything was ready, Margot turned on the stove and went to work, detailing her actions and walking through the thought process for her students.

Watching her cook was beautiful. Her timing was spot on, and she made cooking look fun and easy. Her knives and bowls and each of her gadgets were top of the line, and Emilia compared Margot's cooking arsenal with her dad's guitars. Margot was as proud of her Shun knives as her dad was of his 1972 Les Paul. And Margot's ingredients were all the best: fresh, bright vegetables from the garden and farmers' market and green and blue eggs from her Easter Egger chickens.

Once the spanakopita was in the oven, they went into the living room. While cooking, they'd covered all the getting-to-know-you topics, and now they were getting along like old friends. Emilia felt the wonderful bond of common ground with Margot and Joan, though they were both older. The two women treated Emilia like she was a friend; age didn't matter. Truthfully, Emilia preferred the company of people at least a few years older.

Like Joe Massey. With a start, Emilia realized she'd been having so much fun that she hadn't thought about him the entire night. What a relief.

"Emilia," Margot said, "your dad is such a gentleman that he probably didn't tell you how much I embarrassed myself the other day. Just before you guys came over." Margot was sitting on the other side of a long mustard-colored couch with a pillow on her lap. Joan was sitting across from them in a plush chair, her feet on the ottoman.

"He didn't mention anything."

"I was coming home Saturday from yoga and feeling really good, thanks to Joan. And you know that song, 'I Just Died in Your Arms Tonight?'"

"Of course."

"I was singing my heart out at the light in West Richland and looked over to find your dad and brother staring at me like I was some lunatic. I was mortified."

Emilia laughed out loud. "He didn't tell me."

Margot said, "I could write a book on all my embarrassing moments. I'm like a magnet for them."

"What's your worst?" Emilia asked.

"Oh, gosh," Margot said, looking up to the ceiling, thinking for a moment. "Other than learning of my husband's affair on CNN, along with every other person in the world, I guess I'd have to say it was my senior year of high school, back in Virginia. There was this girl in my grade, Mindy Sabien. She was such a bully—you know, we were all scared of her. You'd call her 'goth' these days. She wore black lipstick and dark mascara and combat boots and had piercings in strange places. There were rumors that she dabbled in Wicca. And she was big, not fat, just a big girl. Not someone you wanted to mess with. Oh, my gosh, you two can't tell anyone this."

Margot lowered her voice. "I was on my period and went into the bathroom, into one of the stalls. I was changing my tampon when Mindy came in. She sat down in the stall next to me. I saw her combat boots, and it must have made me really nervous. I accidentally dropped the tampon, and it rolled over—blood trail and all—and it hit her foot."

"Oh, no!" Emilia said, giggling.

"I've never been so scared in my life. She started screaming, 'What the!' You know."

"What did you do?"

"I got out of there so quickly. I remember running out into the hall still pulling my pants up."

By then, Emilia and Joan were laughing hysterically.

"Did she ever figure out that it was you?" Joan asked.

"Never. How about you, Joan? You're so perfect, I bet you've never been embarrassed in your life."

"*Au contraire.* I could tell you stories all night."

"Let's hear your best," Margot said.

"That's easy. I'm still horrified thinking of it."

"This was 1981, a couple of years after my husband and I were married. We were living in Manhattan in a lovely two-floor apartment on the Upper East Side. Where he grew up, actually. It was my birthday and he was taking me out to dinner. A Saturday night. I was getting ready and George was downstairs watching a game. I had the sudden urge for some birthday nooky." Joan looked at Emilia, "Forgive me, darling."

"Keep going," Emilia giggled.

"Wearing absolutely nothing but some very high heels—which I rarely wear, by the way—I walked down the stairs."

Emilia and Margot were sitting on the edges of their seats, ears perked.

"I went down the stairs and called for him, speaking very naughtily, I should add."

"Oh, God," Margot said. "What were you saying?"

"Something like, 'George, you know what I really want for my birthday? I want you. Right now.' That sort of thing. It was oddly quiet down there. I was mid-sentence when I came around the corner into the living room."

"Who was there?" Emilia asked.

"Who wasn't there, my dear? I came around that corner stark naked except for the stilettos, only to find out he'd organized a huge surprise party. While I was upstairs showering, he'd ushered in every friend and family member within fifty miles. We'd never had so many people squeezed in there before, even at our Christmas parties."

The women roared.

Joan shook her head. "And the worst of it: George's parents, who were the straightest two people I've ever met, upper-class New Yorkers, the whole bit, were sitting on the couch front and center."

"I would have died!" Margot said. "What did you do?"

"I cursed and nearly flew back up the stairs. Didn't come out of my bedroom for three days. I've never heard the end of it. To this day, people bring it up."

"At least you have a gorgeous body," Margot said. "I bet everyone was jealous, the women and the men."

"I don't know about that." She clapped her hands. "Okay, Emilia. Your turn."

Emilia wiped the tears from her eyes and composed herself. "I can't imagine how humiliated you were."

"Still. I'm *still* humiliated. Imagine every single person you know seeing you naked. C'mon, let's have it, Emilia."

Emilia already knew the story she was going to tell. "I've never told anyone this in my life. Two summers ago, we were staying at Le Meurice in Paris, one of my mom's favorite hotels. While I was in the elevator, I accidently broke wind in front of, um, Elton John."

Margot and Joan laughed loudly, and it made Emilia laugh too.

"You farted in front of Sir Elton?" Margot asked.

Emilia nodded. "It was just the two of us. I was completely starstruck; I'm a huge fan."

"Who isn't?" Margot asked.

"We said hello to each other on the first floor and then there was silence. About halfway up, I accidentally tooted. Thank God it didn't smell. I was so mortified! He was so kind to say goodbye when we reached the top. *That* is the worst thing that ever happened to me."

⤳

WHEN JOAN DROPPED her off later, Emilia said, "That was the best night I've had all year. Thanks for including me."

"No. Thanks for including me. I can't wait for next Tuesday."

"Me either."

Emilia entered the living room where her mother was watching a reality show. Carmen was lying on the couch in her standard loungewear, a silk robe and thick socks, and drinking a martini.

"Hey, sweetie. You're getting home late."

"Sorry, we were having so much fun. They're really great people." Emilia sat down next to her, immediately smelling the gin on her mother's breath. Carmen had clearly over-imbibed. Of course, she ate like a bird and weighed next to nothing, so even the smallest amount of alcohol would send her into orbit. Her mom was staring off into space.

"You okay, Mom?"

"Yeah, just had a few too many."

"Did you have fun with Abby?"

"We had a nice time. It was good to catch up."

"You should come to Margot's next time." Emilia told her about Margot and Joan.

"Maybe I will. Sounds like fun."

Emilia knew she probably wouldn't come. Carmen was very social but tended to be selective about the people with whom she spent her time. Emilia knew that hesitancy came from a lifetime of being famous. Carmen didn't like to put herself in situations where people were pulling at her, faking their way into friendship. Emilia didn't blame her, though of course Margot and Joan were far from being stalkers. It was okay, though. If Emilia was going to bring someone else, she'd rather bring Abby. Her mom might be too uptight.

What sucked about her mom was that she didn't even ask what the women had done, what they cooked, what they talked about. Instead, her mom opened her arms and said, "I still can't get used to your hair. Don't worry; it will grow back in no time. You're still beautiful. Come cuddle with me."

Emilia went into her mother's arms.

LETTING GO OF REBECCA

O tis howled with the coyotes again. Dreading the MRI the next morning, he'd been unable to sleep in his chair. He was in the middle of the vines, stripped naked, down on his knees, howling with everything he had. It felt so damn good.

After a while, he dressed and made his way back to the house. Sitting in his recliner, he closed his eyes. A strange feeling came to him. For the first time since Rebecca had died, he had an urge to get into their bed. No, not their bed. His bed. She wasn't around any more. It wasn't her bed any more.

Otis opened the bedroom door. He dressed daily in there, but entering now was different. The desk where she used to write in her diary, the closet door where she hung her vast collection of bathrobes, the bedside table where she kept a stack of trashy romance novels. All memories moving to a different spot in his heart. He looked at the bed, the beige duvet cover, the white shams, the blue blanket folded at the edge. Rebecca had passed away five years earlier, and he hadn't slept in there once, hadn't even stretched out on the bed. He'd only changed the sheets every few months.

He closed the door and undressed. He set the shams on the chair next to the bed, the one where she used to place what she planned to wear the next day. He folded the blanket back, revealing stark white sheets. He peeled back the sheet, noticing its satiny feel, remembering how obsessed Rebecca was with having nice sheets. He climbed inside.

So many memories flooded through him. He didn't know whether to welcome them or shy away. Was it okay to think about her naked body curled up against him? Though he couldn't smell, lying in the bed and feeling the sheets on his body reminded Otis of what Rebecca had smelled like. She'd never worn perfume. It would have only masked the very delicate smell he could detect when they cuddled together. Even when she would sweat in the garden, she smelled delightful. It was her scent, and he loved it so much.

They'd conceived their children in this bed, back in Sonoma. They'd cried so many tears in this bed when their first son died. There were months when they couldn't get out of this bed, nearly imprisoned in it, wallowing in agony and loss. They'd made love the night before her car slid into the river, killing her and their last living son. The night Otis had lost it all.

Was it okay? No, none of it was okay. That was the damn point! Time to get over it. Time to move on. It will never be okay. If he was going to make room for Joan in his heart, he had to move on. At least for this life. The memories would be his forever. There was nothing wrong with remembering their love. But what he'd been doing was holding on to it with too tight a grasp—red, bloodied knuckles clenching their love as though letting go would end his life.

All thoughts drifted away as he finally found room for both Rebecca and Joan in his heart, in his life. What came was the finest sleep he'd had in years.

~

HE WOKE with a wonderful feeling of not wanting to get out of bed, and he let himself doze off a couple more times. Then the reality of the MRI hit him, and all the glory of that slumber dissipated.

He went to brush his teeth and noticed his right hand shaking. He set down his toothbrush and grabbed his right wrist with his left hand. Not a good sign. He'd never seen his hand shake before. Was this shaking another symptom of this unknown illness?

He found Morgan in the kitchen, standing over a bubbling and greasy pan of bacon on the stove.

"Good morning, good lookin'," Otis said, kissing her on the forehead.

"Someone got a good night's rest. You hungry?"

"Always." Otis sat on a stool at the counter. "I'd say it smells good in here but I can't smell a thing."

"Did you sleep in your bedroom last night?"

"I did."

"What's that about?"

"I have no idea. It felt good, though."

"Well, yes. There's a reason the majority of the world sleeps in beds. That recliner is for reading and watching TV. The bed, the mattress, is for sleeping."

"I forgot what I was missing."

"Would this new move have something to do with Joan Tobey?"

"Perhaps."

Morgan raised her eyes to the heavens. "I feel like my life has been fulfilled and I can finally meet my maker. I helped you find a new woman and led you out of this dreadful depression."

"The way my luck is, the depression will come around again."

"If you keep talking like that, it will."

"I'm speaking from experience. The sun doesn't shine on me for very long."

"The more reason to enjoy the sunshine when it comes." Morgan put a plate of bacon and eggs and smashed potatoes in front of him. "Enjoy."

"You not eating?" he asked.

"No, I'm not hungry."

"You cooked all this for me?"

"Otis Till, why is it so hard for you to understand that people love you? I cooked breakfast for you because I love you, and I want to take care of you. You work hard and you deserve a break."

"Well, if we were in Montana, I might just marry you."

"You couldn't keep up with me."

"Now you've crossed every line there is to cross."

"Eat up and hit the road," she said. "Isn't your appointment at nine?"

"Nine or ten or so."

"No, Otis. It's nine o'clock. Don't play around. You're not getting out of it."

"I don't like hospitals."

"Find me one person who does."

"Doctors. Nurses. Pharmaceutical reps. Developers."

Morgan shook her head. "You're such a pain in my ass. But I love you."

She cleaned dishes as Otis ate his breakfast, letting the warmth and the textures stimulate his memories of when breakfast was delicious.

With a mouthful, he said, "What are you doing today?"

"I'm going to paint all day," she said with determination.

"Good for you." He cut the beautiful orange yolk of the egg and it ran into the potatoes. "So now that you've done your duty, you heading back to Montana?"

She spoke over the sound of the water hitting the dishes. "Still trying to get rid of me? That hurts my feelings."

"I'm just joking, Morgan. You know, to be honest, I like having you here. If you ever want to sell your place, you can move in here. I need somebody to take care of me anyway."

"Take care of you? I'm twenty years older!"

"Then we can take care of each other."

She shut off the water and turned to him, leaning a hand on the counter. "Right here and now, after sixty years of trying, I have cracked through the hard shell wrapped around my little nephew. You're a doll, Otis." She stepped to the table and pinched him on the cheek. "Everything's going to be all right. You and I are made of strong stuff. We might just live forever."

He nodded his head, thinking about those shaking fingers and thinking he might already have one foot in the grave.

~

OTIS RIPPED the white bracelet off his arm as he slogged out of the hospital, focusing on his day ahead with Joan. He didn't want to be a downer. If the scan showed he was going to die, he'd better enjoy these last few days.

Driving over the bridge to Joan's house, he kept telling himself that he didn't want to dwell on what could happen. He didn't want to dwell on himself at all. He wanted to focus on her. If he was going to die, he wanted to take in every last moment he had with her.

Dying would be okay. Rebecca was somewhere on the other side waiting for him. He didn't know how the science or the religion of it would go, but he knew they'd have their reunion.

But it wasn't quite time yet. He and Joan had crossed paths for a reason, and he intended to hang around a while longer and love her like she deserved to be loved.

Joan welcomed him at the door with a great big hug that warmed his heart. "Was it scary?"

"No."

"Are you afraid?"

Otis didn't answer. How could he ever really explain to her that yes, he was afraid to die because he couldn't stand the thought of losing her. But at the same time, he wasn't afraid to die because Rebecca was waiting.

She took his hand. "Why don't we go have a long lunch and not talk about it?"

"This is exactly why I like you, Joan Tobey. That's what I need."

They sat on the patio of Anthony's, drinking wine and talking non-stop. Otis barely thought about the results of his MRI, and he did his best not to let his concern get him down. He bathed in the warmth of Joan's beauty and presence. Never would he have imagined that it was possible to love a woman again.

~

HE FOUND her face down on the rug on the living room floor. Her body lay there amongst her paints and brushes. She'd knocked over the easel on her way down. The palette had fallen and painted a section of the rug a rainbow of colors.

Otis ran to her and knelt. He put his cheek to her mouth, trying to feel her breath. He put his hand to her heart and felt futilely for a beat. He began to weep. "Why did you leave me?" he asked out loud. "Where did you go, Morgan? Come back to me."

He dug the phone out of his pocket and called 911. Then he sat down on the floor and pulled her head up to his lap, stroking her forehead until the ambulance came.

After they took her away, Otis picked up the easel and her paints. Only then did he notice what she'd been working on. He would cherish it forever.

The painting depicted a side view of Otis naked on all fours in his vineyard. A full moon and bright stars shined down on him. He was howling.

27

GO GET HIM, BROOKS

"I can't believe I'm leaving Red Mountain right now," Brooks told Abby as they hung a right in the winery truck onto Highway 14, the road that ran west along the Columbia River toward Portland. "Smack in the middle of harvest."

"It's a worthy mission. We're like bounty hunters."

"Off to find the brother I've never met. Sounds crazy. I don't know how he's going to take it. I'm nervous."

She adjusted her bracelets. "You should be excited. You have this family that has risen out of nowhere and keeps growing. How cool is that!"

"It's the unknowns that scare me. My dad seems pretty cool. But is he? I bet Bernie Madoff seemed pretty cool. What if Charles turns out to be a creep?"

"You know as well as I do you can't live in a world of 'what if's.' You've spent more time with him than I have, but I think Charles is a nice guy. Very normal. You got lucky, if you ask me."

"For some reason, I don't think my brother is going to be that normal. Who knows what he's going to think?"

"Why wouldn't he be happy to see you? You have this deep need to meet him. I'm sure he feels the same way. You two have a bond that no one else can ever share. Even though you haven't met, it's there. He's known that bond since he was a kid. I bet he thinks of you often. I bet he's always had a hole in his heart."

Brooks shrugged. Maybe she was right.

"You can't not go," Abby reasoned. "What's the worst that can happen?"

Brooks was too ashamed to say what he was thinking. The "worst" was that his brother could tell him to get the hell out of his face. And Brooks couldn't handle rejection. That's why it had taken so long for him to connect with Abby. "I don't know," he finally said. "I really hope he's receptive."

While Abby kept on with her encouragement, Brooks's mind was drifting toward another possible rejection. He was thinking about the diamond ring in his backpack, the one he'd impulsively bought the day before. The one he intended to use tonight to propose to Abby. What if his brother and Abby both shut him down?

Abby took his hand, taking him out of his tailspin. "I'm going to be right next to you. If he tells you to go away, we'll walk away knowing we tried. That's the best we can do."

"It's ridiculous how nerve-racking this is for me. It shouldn't be that big a deal. I feel like... like a baby."

"Brooks, you're human. You grew up without a family. Having feelings doesn't mean you're a baby. It means you're able to connect to yourself. You're such a man to me. You're more man than anyone I've ever met. It's okay to have feelings. Don't ever stop."

He squeezed her hand. "Thank you."

She patted his leg. "I have an idea."

"What?"

"You need to let all this go for a while. Let's enjoy the drive, enjoy being together. This is our first road trip."

He turned to her. "It is our first road trip, isn't it? I like all these firsts."

"You want to do something stupid? Let's stick our heads out the window. Fresh air will do wonders."

"Let's do it." He liked to say yes to her, to go with her ideas. It fed the awe of their relationship.

They rolled down their windows and stuck out their heads. Brooks was driving close to eighty miles an hour, and force of the wind made his cheeks stretch backwards and his eyes water. He heard Abby yell and he yelled too. She yelled again and he mimicked her, a big fat smile taking over his face, the cold wind hitting him and revitalizing him, taking him away from the dark places.

He rolled the window back up and looked at Abby. "That worked."

"I feel way better," she said.

They giggled together and kissed. His first road trip with a woman. A really great woman. How cool was that?

Eventually, they crossed the river into Oregon. "So when are you asking me to marry you?" Abby asked, once again penetrating into his deepest thoughts, a step ahead of him.

Brooks wasn't exactly sure how to answer the question. He switched hands on the wheel and glanced over. "We'd be good together, wouldn't we?"

"We *are* good together."

He said, "Is this your roundabout way of asking me to marry you?"

"This is my roundabout way of asking *you* to ask me."

Brooks grinned. "You know, I come off strong but fade fast. I'm more sprint; marriage is more marathon. We're only a few weeks in. What happens when you start getting tired of me?"

"You're more marathon than you think. You're actually growing on me." She put her hand in between his legs. "See?"

"I will pull over right this minute if you are going to get me started."

She withdrew her hand. "Save it for the hotel, gorgeous."

Brooks shook his head. "I'm going to bring in the big guns tonight."

"You are, are you?"

"Prepare for battle."

A few minutes later, Abby said, "I love you, Brooks Baker. So you know, should you decide to ask me to marry you, I'd probably say yes."

"I love you too." And those words—his first time saying them—made him dizzy with confidence and delight.

～

BROOKS KNEW PORTLAND WELL. He'd spent a year living on the streets there when he was younger. To be accurate, he knew back-alley Portland well: the dumpster-diving homeless, the meth addicts, the jobless anarchists, the hard-core punk scene. He'd had only glimpses of the brighter sides of Portland: the farm-to-table restaurants, fleets of food trucks, affluent brownstone neighborhoods, pinot noir bars, the Trail Blazers, and Stumptown coffee.

He'd visited a few times since Otis had rescued him, mostly to taste the good pinot noirs. Portland and the Willamette Valley was an easy trip from Red Mountain. From time to time, a man can get tired of hot climate grapes like cabernet sauvignon and merlot, so Brooks would hop on his bike and ride over for a long weekend.

But this time they were on a mission. A private investigator Abby found online had tracked down Shay in two days. Brooks and Abby now had home and work addresses.

The couple checked into The Nines, the nicest hotel Brooks had ever stayed in. He was happy he could finally afford this kind of place; but at the same time, he felt like an impostor, like a peasant trying on a crown.

While they unpacked, Brooks said, "I'd like to go by myself. Does that hurt your feelings?"

"Don't worry about me. Today is about you and your brother." She grinned. "I'm sure there's some thrift store shopping to be done. I'll have my phone."

～

BROOKS AMBLED down Morrison Street and caught the trail that ran along the Willamette River. The liberal nature of the inhabitants of Portland had created a very hospitable place for the homeless, and they were scattered about the grass—some napping, some smoking and staring off to nowhere, some chatting with friends, some chatting with themselves—perhaps fueled by heroin or methadone.

A few hundred yards down, Brooks found the bench where he used to sit for hours every day, panhandling and pondering his existence. A filthy man about his own age was sitting there shaking an old coffee cup. "Can you spare a dollar or two?" he asked through crooked brown teeth. Brooks had a deep insecurity about his own teeth. He'd spent a fortune repairing the effects of years without dental care. He took two twenties out of his wallet and dropped them into the cup.

"Thank you, sir. Thank you."

Brooks smiled and moved on. He emptied the rest of his wallet helping a few others before continuing his mission.

The address the P.I. had found led him across the river to an apartment complex adorned with clothes hanging on balconies and trash littering the hallways. It was the kind of place you could find heroin in great abundance.

There was no elevator. Brooks climbed to the fourth floor and found the correct door. An empty planter sat neglected on the floor, the remnants of something long dead withered away in the dry soil.

He took a deep breath and held it for a moment, not quite ready for this encounter. But he never would be, would he? He breathed out and knocked.

A shoeless man who was definitely not his brother answered the door. The man's muscles burst out of his sleeveless shirt, almost pulsing as he stood there, like he was in between sets at the gym, steroids firing through his veins. A few other guys were talking inside.

"What?" the guy said.

"I'm looking for Shay Wildridge. Does he live here?"

"Yeah, but he's not here. He's working."

"At Colson's?"

"That's the last I heard. Who's asking?"

"An old friend." Brooks retreated and threw up a wave.

He found Colson's a few blocks away. The restaurant was nothing special; it looked like a mediocre steak house from the outside.

Brooks entered under a green canopy with the Colson's logo. The place was about half-full and smelled like fried shrimp. People stood in a line at the salad bar on the right. Straight ahead, an open slot window showed the kitchen. A young girl with pigtails offered him a table. "No, thanks. I'm looking for Shay Wildridge. Is he in the back?"

"He should be," she said warmly.

She couldn't have any idea how big this moment was for Brooks Baker. He had thought about this meeting a million times, how Shay would take the news. Would he even believe him?

Time to find out.

Brooks made his way to the back of the restaurant. Several servers were going in and out of the swinging door. He waited for the right moment and pushed it open. A black guy with a net holding down a huge head of hair said in a deep Motown voice, "Can I help you?"

"Looking for Shay."

The man gestured to his right. "Over there."

Brooks had already seen him. Shay stood in front of a deep fryer, shaking the oil off a batch of French fries. Brooks couldn't see his brother's face yet but he could tell just by looking at the man's back and his neckline and his hair that they were related.

"Hey, Shay," the Motown guy said. "This guy's looking for you."

Shay emptied out the fries on the table and turned his head, wiping his hands on his apron.

Brooks strolled past another cook chopping giant heads of broccoli and approached Shay. He had rehearsed this moment twenty times while walking over, but all of that preparation had gone out the window.

He and Shay had similar features, but weren't spitting images like Brooks and his father. Charles had said Shay was twenty-eight, but he looked older than Brooks in a way. He had wrinkles around his eyes that shouldn't have come for another ten years. He wore a blue bandana wrapped around his head and he had a big beard hiding rosy cheeks. Brooks thought he'd be the perfect character for a box of pancake mix, a more modern, Portlandized Aunt Jemima.

Silence filled the space as Brooks searched for words. What he realized, though, was that Shay was coming around to the truth on his own. Shay's look changed from *Who the fuck are you?* to *You look a lot like my father.*

"Goddamn," he said.

Brooks stretched his mouth at the corners, not really smiling, just a nervous reaction. "You know who I am?"

Shay looked his face up and down, up and down. He crossed his arms. "So I do have a brother."

"That's what I've been told," Brooks said.

"Just like that, it happens, right?"

Brooks shook his head slowly. "Can you take five?"

Shay yelled for another guy to man the fry station. He led Brooks out the back door near the dumpster, where the air smelled of used cooking oil and rotting food. Shay lit up a cigarette immediately and took a few drags before looking back at Brooks.

"How'd you find me? Did Charles finally find you?"

Brooks nodded his head. "Last week."

"Where is he?"

"At my house in eastern Washington. A small town called Benton City. You weren't hard to find. We hired a P.I. to track you down."

Shay blew out smoke. "Well, you found me. Am I everything you hoped for?"

"I don't know yet. I don't know you at all. I can tell you're a smart-ass, just like me. I know where you work and where you live, that's about it."

"Yep, almost thirty and frying food and washing dishes for a living. Turns out no one likes to hire felons. I live with three other dudes in a small apartment. Charles would say I have failed at life. In fact, he has said that."

"Hey, a few years ago I was living in a cardboard box in Central Park. Don't start crying to me about your lot in life. At least you had parents that gave a shit about you. That same couple left me on a doorstep."

Shay rolled his eyes. "Why are you here? Are we supposed to hang out and go get beers and pretend like we have a normal family?"

"I guess we could. I'd like to get to know you. Until last week, I didn't have any family. Now I have a brother and a father. Our mom doesn't want to see me. Not yet, anyway. I don't want to pretend we have a normal family. We don't. But I do want to tell you a story and make you a proposition. If you'll hear me out, you can decide what we do from here. My girlfriend and I drove over for the night and we're heading back tomorrow morning. I'm a winemaker and we're picking grapes, so I'm short on time."

"A winemaker?"

"I wasn't always a winemaker." Brooks told his story in brief, from bouncing around orphanages to hitting the streets to meeting Otis and how things had changed. "I could never repay Otis for what he did for me. But I figure I can pay it forward. Abby and I are getting breakfast at eight in our hotel and then taking off. Come have breakfast with us and ride to Red Mountain. I've got a place for you to live for a while, and I've got a job for you. Leave this place behind. Start over."

"What makes you think I'm looking to start over?"

"You're my brother. I don't know you but I am you. If you're like me, you need a break in life. This is your break. You think I haven't committed felonies? I just wasn't caught. I'm saying that you're made of the same stuff I am and maybe you could use a new shot."

His brother was sucking on that cigarette like he'd never have another one.

Brooks threw up his hands. "Or maybe you don't. I'm not making you get in a truck with me. You're my brother. I have a fucking brother. That might not be much to you, but it's a hell of a lot to me. I want family in my life. Someone gave me a second chance, and I was led to this place four hours east of here. There are good people there. There are opportunities. I am your ticket in. You won't owe me anything. The only thing I ask is that you come with a good attitude and some serious work ethic. Like Otis told me, I'm not giving you a handout. I'm offering to put you in a place where you can succeed. You deserve that as my brother."

"What does Charles say?"

"He's got one son back. He wants his other son. He's praying that you're going to come back with me. We didn't have a normal childhood, but maybe we could get normal for a while."

"It's that easy, huh?"

"Nope. Nothing about it was easy for me, and it won't be easy for you. Especially with that attitude. But if you want it bad enough, you can turn things around. I don't know if you're doing drugs, but there will be no place for that. I'll fire you and kick your ass out of my house in one second. If you come ready to start again, Red Mountain might just save you. It saved me."

Brooks stood up. "Now I'm going to go propose to my girlfriend. So, eight o'clock. The Nines."

Shay's exterior softened some. "Good luck."

Brooks nodded.

Shay rubbed his beard. "And hey, thanks for the offer."

"That's what family's for. No hard feelings if you aren't there. I'd still love to catch up sometime." Brooks handed his brother his card. "You know where to find me."

~

AFTER DINNER in the Pearl District, Brooks took Abby to the hotel bar. They drank a bottle of pinot noir from Beckham Estate Vineyard.

Brooks knew the wines well. "This guy, Andrew Beckham, built a few of my amphorae, the clay pots I use to ferment and age my wine. He's got a beautiful estate down in Sherwood. Ages all his wines in his amphorae. Has Southdown sheep like Otis too."

"So what's the deal with these amphorae? I keep hearing that word."

"Some of us are trying to get back to the way things used to be done. Amphorae are great because the wines still breathe some through the clay, and once they're broken in, the clay doesn't impart much flavor into the wines. It's like an older barrel, but they're much easier to maintain, so you can make them last forever. Barrels can turn into a science experiment after a while and they can ruin your wine if you're not careful. Wines in clay also develop more quickly; and to me, have a rounder palate feel, a very different texture." He realized he was rambling and abruptly closed his mouth.

She put a hand on his face. "You have a beautiful mind."

Unable to wait another moment, he said, "I want to marry you."

Abby pulled her head back. "Are you proposing to me right now?"

Brooks knelt. *Here I go.* His whole body was tingling.

"Abby Sinclaire, you are the best thing that ever happened to me. Every day gets better and better." His hands were as shaky as his words. "We've only been together a couple of weeks, but it's all I need to know that we're meant for each other." He opened the box from his pocket, revealing the ring, and she gasped. Oval cut; antique band. Brooks had learned everything about diamond rings the past week.

"You're serious?"

"Will you marry me?" he asked.

She pulled him up by the collar and kissed him. "Yes. Of course I will."

Without a doubt in the world, he put the ring on her finger as she gushed over it, kissing and hugging him through tears of joy.

Within minutes Brooks was fumbling to open the door of their room. He picked his fiancée up and laid her on the bed. "Let me stand here for a moment and take this in, almost-Mrs. Baker." He looked at her, bathing in the idea that he'd be looking at her for the rest of their lives. Her smile. Her beauty. Her energy.

She reached for his belt. "I want you to tie me up."

He nodded, liking where things were headed, once again going where Brooks Baker had never gone before.

He unzipped her dress, touching her back and kissing her on the neck. He unclasped her bra and put his arms around her, feeling her ample breasts, feeling her nipples harden in his fingers. They both breathed heavily as she turned around to undress him. She unbuttoned his shirt and ran her fingers along his chest, down to his abdomen, and to the button of his jeans.

She pulled his jeans down and he kicked them off. She knelt and took him in her mouth; Brooks let his eyes close. She stood again and kissed him.

She caught him off guard with a playful slap to the face. "Now tie me up."

He grinned as his temptress climbed onto the bed, looking back at him with her sexy eyes, inviting him to follow. He crawled to her and reached for her hands, pulling them up to the bed frame, binding them together with the belt, Abby kissing and playfully biting his chest.

"Take me," she whispered.

And he did just that, slipping off her underwear, pleasuring her with his mouth and fingers and finally pushing himself into her, Abby letting out a gasp as he entered, pulling at her bound hands, her moans growing louder and louder until she convulsed in climax, filling the room and the hallway and perhaps the entire hotel with the joy and craving of their union.

～

ABBY FINISHED up a bowl of blueberries and yogurt while Brooks signed the check, his hopes of seeing his brother waning. Brooks drained the last of a pulpy glass of orange juice.

"I guess he decided not to come."

"Are you sad?"

"A little. All I can do is offer to help. I can't grab him by the ear and push him into the truck."

"He didn't have much notice. I wouldn't give up. I'm sure you'll see him again."

Brooks looked to the elevator one more time. "I'll be damned."

This time he had a pink bandana wrapped around his head and an Army duffle thrown over his back. The guy would be a great cartoon character. Brooks waved him over.

"I'm full of surprises," Shay said, as he dropped his bag next to the table.

The two brothers looked at each other for a moment, understanding one another. Brooks stuck out his hand. "I'm glad you came."

Shay shook his older brother's hand and looked him in the eyes. "I'm thankful."

Brooks eyed the bag. "Is that all you have?"

"All that's worth keeping."

Brooks nodded. "Let me introduce you to Abby, my fiancée. Last night I somehow managed to talk her into marrying me."

Abby finished chewing her fruit and stood. She pushed away Shay's outstretched hand. "You're my brother too, now." She opened her arms.

Shay embraced her. "Well then, it's nice to meet you, sis."

∽

Shay sat behind Abby in the Lacoda truck. They spent most of the drive along the Columbia River getting to know each other.

And yet, Brooks sensed that Shay was hiding. He had secrets, many secrets, perhaps darker than Brooks's secrets, and he wasn't keen to share too quickly. Only after they'd turned onto 221, running north from Oregon up to Red Mountain, did Brooks feel like bringing up their father.

"So you and Dad. I still don't know where you stand. How's this gonna go?"

"Is he at your place now?"

"He's staying there. I'm assuming so. I texted him earlier and said we were on the way. You two going to be okay?"

"I don't know." Shay let the words hang.

"Can I ask what happened?"

"Charles didn't tell you?"

"I don't think he really knows."

Shay shook his head. "When your son goes to prison, he becomes something you didn't dream about." He made an awkward laugh. "They came to see me behind bars. I'll never forget their faces, the disappointment of many years doing their best to raise a child and knowing that they failed, their worst fears realized. It hurt. Mom came once. That was the last time I saw her. Dad came three times, and I told him to stop coming."

"Why?"

"Doin' time changes you, bro. I'm still changed. I don't know how anybody can walk out of prison and not hate the world. I couldn't look at his damn brokenhearted face again."

"That's the last time you saw him?"

"Yeah. We've spoken a few times. You know, a holiday call, that kind of thing. I tried. They did too. But still, I'm a disappointment. We bring out the hurt in each other. It was best I stay away."

"Then what are you doing now?"

"I have no clue." They were all silent for a minute. "But I will tell you this: I somehow knew you were coming. Mom and Dad told me about you when I was a kid, you know, once I could understand. I've been thinking more about you lately, wondering where you were."

Abby spoke for the first time in a while, clutching Brooks's arm. "That's exactly what I told Brooks, that you were probably wondering about him, just like he was wondering about you."

Brooks said, "Dad said it all started with a girl."

Another awkward laugh. "I guess it did. They didn't like her from the beginning. That's where our relationship started to come apart. That's when the disappointment started coming. And I couldn't fucking take it. Prison sealed the deal. They were right, and I was wrong. Or so they had decided. Dad took every chance to say, "I told you so." I can't stand 'I told you so's.' Can't stand 'em."

"I don't see Charles being like that."

"You don't know him like I do." Shay added, "And they never knew the whole truth."

"What's the truth?" Brooks asked.

"Doesn't matter anymore. The truth won't set me free."

~

BROOKS TURNED down Demoss Road and drove along the Yakima River, the agony of the last mile like a pot of hot water seconds away from boiling. They were all silent, knowing Shay and Charles were about to see each other for the first time in seven years—since Charles had looked at his son through an inch of glass in Albuquerque, and his son had told him to leave and not come back.

Charles's rental car was parked in the driveway. Brooks had thought for a bleak minute that his father had taken off, deciding that this instant family was too much for him. But before they'd even gotten out of the truck, Charles opened the front door and came out to greet them. His chest was puffed up and his smile somewhat forced, the tension revealing how much he wanted this to work and how heavy the prospect of seeing Shay again had weighed on him for the past few hours.

Brooks and Abby watched Shay and Charles walk toward each other, then stop a few feet away, like two men in a duel. Charles made the first move. He opened his arms but didn't take a step forward. "I missed you, son," he said, instantly tearing up. Brooks felt those same tears rise in his own eyes.

The leaves of fall fell and the birds went on chirping, but the rest of the world stopped for Shay, as Charles stood with those open arms and moist eyes. Seven years of pain frozen in the air.

Finally, Shay took a step and then another step and opened his arms and they embraced. Brooks felt the pain melt away and he took what felt like his first breath in a long while.

28

MARGOT 2.0 SLIPS BACK INTO THE TUB

Margot was having one of those days. After losing six pounds, she'd somehow gained back four. And she was starving herself! She was trying to be calm and tap into her inner warrior, as Joan had taught her. She had even tried tapping into Frances from *Under the Tuscan Sun*, thinking *what would Frances do?* Well, the real answer was Frances wouldn't be this fat!

Margot somehow found enough discipline to make it to Joan's 10 a.m. yoga class. At the moment, she was dripping in sweat, and the class was moving into the Crow position, an inversion where the student has knees resting on elbows, feet off the ground. Margot had a very good idea of what would happen if she tried this, so she took the easy way out and got into Child's Pose, the pose suggested for rest, and the pose Margot loved most. But as she sat there with her face against the mat and her arms extended, she felt guilty. She knew everyone was watching her, judging her, laughing at her lack of athleticism.

Margot rose from the mat, suddenly deciding this would be her day. It couldn't get worse, could it? Margot 2.0 was going to take on Crow. With a deep breath and a determined mind, she squatted. Her knees creaked like trees snapping in a lightning storm. She leaned forward and put her hands on the mat. She put her knees on her elbows and tilted forward, letting her feet rise off the ground. Only an inch off, she began to wobble and returned to her feet. She went back to a squat and tried again. This time, she decided to fully commit. Joan had said something once about Crow, how you had to make the firm decision and go for it. Margot did just that and pushed forward with her legs, putting her eyes a few inches forward, a full-on commitment, believing she could do it in her heart, letting the warrior lead the way.

For a second or two, she had it. Owning Crow! Her inner warrior wanted to scream victory. And then...she lost her balance. What started as a wobble in her elbows crept into her legs and suddenly she was kicking her feet up in the air trying not to lose her balance. "Oh, no!" she said out loud. Her legs and right arm slapped the hard floor, missing the mat entirely.

Joan came rushing over. "Are you okay?"

"I think so." Margot couldn't sense any pain over the embarrassment.

"Don't worry. We've all been there. Let's try again."

Margot thought that was the worst idea she'd ever heard.

Joan whispered, "Trust me."

Margot nodded, trying to push away the fear.

This time, Joan led her through it, holding her by the shins. For a moment, Margot felt she understood Crow. Joan let go of her, and Margot lasted longer this time. As she fell, Joan caught her, guiding her to the ground.

Joan said, "I'm proud of you for committing. At some point, each of us in this class made the same decision and hit the floor."

Afterward, as everyone rolled up their mats, a gorgeous man sat down next to Margot and stuck his hand out. "I'm Jay." Jay had jet-black hair and radiant green eyes that were so stunning Margot had to look away for a moment. His face glistened with sweat.

She finally spit out, "Hi, I'm Margot." Margot couldn't believe it. She was being hit on in a yoga class. By a beautiful, beautiful man. And she was wearing very tight clothes, which meant he'd seen exactly what she had—all the goods. Margot 2.0 did not yet have the 2.0 body she desired. But this man didn't seem to care. Was he about to ask her out? The warrior inside began to beat her drum.

"Are you new?"

"Yeah. Well, this is my fourth class. How about you?" She sat up, tightening her belly, trying to look proud and confident.

"No, no." He turned more towards her. "My wife and I have been coming here for about four years now."

Margot's shoulders slumped as she glanced at his left hand. "Gotcha."

"Anyway, I wanted to welcome you. It's great to see fresh faces. I hope you stick around." He stood up and walked toward the exit. "'Bye, Margot."

Margot quickly rolled up her mat and ducked out the door. Once she was in her car, she bawled. Tears rolled down her cheeks and dropped onto her lap. She put her face in her hands and let go, crying harder than she could ever remember. She had a vision of her inner warrior curling into the fetal position, rotting away into nothing.

Someone knocked. Wiping away the tears, she looked up to see Joan. Margot rolled down the window.

"What's going on, sweetie?" Joan asked.

Margot could barely get the words out. "All the good men are married. I'm old. Old, old, old. Who would ever love me? There's no man out there for me. Who wants a forty-something washed-up divorcée?"

"You have to love *you*. And as soon as you do, the men will come running. You are a very special, talented, amazing woman. You will have your pick soon. What are you? Two weeks in? It's going to take longer than that. Remember what I told you. The ego is going to fight back, but you can't let it win. Trust in who you really are."

Margot nodded, still mopping away tears. "Maybe I'm too old to change."

"If you're old, what am I? Quit talking like that. Go do something for yourself today. Go pamper yourself. Love yourself. That's what you should be doing. Reminding yourself that you're perfect just the way you are."

"Right. I'd be the perfect plus-sized model."

Joan cracked a smile. "You don't have that much weight to lose to hit your goal. And even if you didn't lose a pound, you're still perfect. What I would do for your curves! Now go take care of yourself. Make it your day."

"Thank you." Margot attempted a smile, and then rolled up the window and pulled away.

She knew it wasn't a good time to go to the grocery store but she did anyway. The ensuing shopping spree was not something Joan would have approved of as a way to pamper herself. She tore into the overflowing grocery bags as soon as she got home. She didn't even take the time to use the oven to heat up her Beecher's Mac and Cheese. She heated up the huge tray in the microwave, an epic sacrilege, and got into her comfy bed. Cramming forkfuls of creamy, cheesy goodness into her mouth, she found a movie on the Hallmark Channel, the only place where good men could be found.

Twenty minutes into the movie, one of the characters committed adultery, and Margot's thoughts went to her husband. She still couldn't shake him. The bastard. Her thoughts turned evil, and against her better judgment, she got out of bed and ran the bath.

She noticed herself as she climbed in, her fat ass and this darn gut that wasn't shrinking, and stretch marks that seemed to be getting worse. God, she hated herself sometimes. But the warm water brought her comfort and she laid back, closed her eyes, and saw her husband, a very real vision of him coming out of their master bathroom in Vermont. She could even see the piece of toilet paper he'd used to stop the bleeding from a shaving nick.

"Hey, Marge," he said, "did you get more dental floss?"

"I forgot. Sorry. I'll do it today."

"How many times do I have to ask? I'm at work all day; your job is managing the house. I really need to be able to count on you."

"It's dental floss. My number one priority is our son. Don't use this to jump on me."

"You're lazy sometimes, Margot."

"Lazy?" she asked. "You son of a bitch."

She shot out of bed, a butane torch in her right hand, a lighter in her left. Jumping toward him, she pressed the button. He raised his hands and covered his face, leaving his torso exposed. She burned a hole right in his chest, the stench of seared hair and flesh filling the air. When he screamed and attempted to push her away, she moved sideways and put the flame to his ear. He fell and she went to her knees, lighting his robe on fire, screaming, "You evil bastard!"

Back in the bathtub on Red Mountain, Margot came to, realizing what she'd done, knowing Joan would be disgusted with her. She felt a terrible satisfaction that made her realize how sick she was, how addicted she'd become to this behavior. This time *had* to be the last.

She climbed back into bed and didn't get out until she had to, an hour later. Ron, her new contractor, would be arriving at one to take over the project. She took the empty tray of Beecher's Mac and Cheese to the outside trash can, hiding the evidence.

~

RON STEPPED out of his truck. He was on time. What a different experience from Tanner. Thank God that bastard was never coming back!

Ron buckled his tool belt as he walked confidently toward her. She met him in the middle of the driveway. He removed his Panama Jack hat and stuck out his hand. She took it, revisiting the calluses of his fingers and palm—those extremely manly hands, one with a wedding ring. Margot imagined Ron's wife as a blond, skinny goddess who he brought flowers to every night, their marriage as perfect as the day they wed.

"How's your day going, Mrs. Pierce?"

"First of all, it's 'Miss.' My ex-husband is shacked up in my ex-house with some hussy..." Hearing the misery in her voice, Margot stopped talking. *Oh, my god. Listen to you, Margot.* She was sounding completely crazy. Composing herself, she said, "Sorry. I'm having a day. Let's try this again. I'm no longer married. And you couldn't be that much younger. Please call me Margot."

"Don't be offended. I call all my bosses 'Mr.' and 'Mrs.' It's been a habit since I took my first job in high school. I imagine I'm a few years older than you anyway."

"I highly doubt it."

"I'm assuming you spoke with Tanner?" he asked.

"I called him and let him know."

"How'd he take it?"

"He got all defensive and started spitting excuses."

Ron shook his head. "I'm sorry he took advantage of you. I'm going to do the best I can to make things right and get you up and running."

"I'd really appreciate that."

"Give me an hour to poke around and get an idea where we stand, see where we are and where we need to be. Perhaps we can talk again later this afternoon, and I'll tell you what I'm thinking. We're going to have some fun. You really are off to a rocking head start."

As she went back around the house to spoil the chickens with some dried bugs, she looked over at the property next door, the parcel she'd wanted to buy for her farm sanctuary. The For Sale sign was gone.

∾

RON KNOCKED on her door an hour later, and Margot invited him inside. He removed his hat and followed her in. "Smells good in here."

"Thank you. I'm making a quiche for dinner. Can I get you a glass of wine or something? I think I'm going to need one."

"Do you have a beer by chance? I'm not much of a wine guy."

Margot thought that was adorable.

"Of course." Margot was an entertainer; she always had an assortment of alcohol. She took two local beers from the fridge, trying not to think about calories as she popped the tops.

They sat across from each other at the table. Ron set his hat in front of him. "How bad is it?" she asked.

He rubbed his mustache. "You want the good news first?"

"No. Give me the worst."

He took a sip of his beer. "Tanner Henderson should be shot. They should pull his license and lock him up. He cut every corner he could, and it's going to take some work to fix. Whoever he hired to do the electrical is an idiot. We're going to have to get a good electrician out here to clean it up. None of it is to code. The breakers aren't even labeled."

"I spent probably twenty thousand on the last one."

"We'll get it straightened out. I've got a guy who will treat you well. So, I already told you about adding some additional load-bearing support below the tubs. We don't want your guests to fall through the floor."

"I would rather not have that happen."

"Right. And he's got your main plumbing lines under two feet of concrete. That's going to be one hell of a headache some day. He should have left some access. I think we should fix it now, before we lay down tile. There's a list of things like that. His finish work so far is atrocious. Little things that you might not notice now, but they'll stand out later. I think the worst of it, though, considering how much you're telling me you've paid him, is that you should be moving in by now. I don't know what he's been doing, but if he's billed you for that many hours, then he's been sitting on his butt."

Margot drank her beer and felt the rage. If she were one level crazier, she'd go find Tanner Henderson and cut his balls off with a sushi knife.

"There is some good news, though. I can fix everything, and I'll save you a lot of money. We can get the stucco slapped up and get all the carpentry finished. And you'll be in. We'll have you done by early spring, if not before."

"Thank you. You're a godsend." She felt she could trust Ron. But she had also trusted Tanner...

"I'll manage the project and bring in my own guys, who are darn good at what they do. And fast. I've spent ten years putting my team together. They're some of the best in the state. My standard rate is 15% but I'm going to charge you half."

"Why would you do that for me?"

"I don't like seeing people get taken advantage of."

"You have no idea how badly I need you in my life right now. Why can't the world be full of people like you, Ron Sallee?"

"I'm glad we caught it when we did, and I'm happy to help."

Margot took another sip of her beer. "On this team of yours," she said, "do you happen to have a hitman?"

"A hitman?"

"Yeah, you know, an assassin. I need to get rid of Tanner Henderson."

Ron looked at her for a moment, taking her way more seriously than she intended. But she couldn't resist keeping it going.

"I'm going to get my checkbook. You tell me how much you would require to kill Tanner Henderson."

"Margot."

She put her hands up. "I'm totally joking."

He smiled. "I thought you were serious."

"Only halfway."

He put his fist on the table. "He'll get what's coming to him."

"I hope you're right. So seriously, how much?"

29

LOOK WHO'S BACK

Aften the last class of the day, Emilia bumped into Jasper. "Did you read *To Kill a Mockingbird* yet?" he asked. "I can see you being huge into the classics."

She liked seeing him and talking to him. He was becoming a friend. And the jealousy she'd felt toward him was going away. Who cared if he had a deeper relationship than she did with her dad? At least her dad was happy.

"I thought it was really good. Not Jane Austen good, but still brilliant."

"I think they're all bad. I don't understand why we have to keep reading these dinosaur books that are supposed to be the best, but they're kind of sloppy. Maybe they were good when there was no such thing as television. Writers could crap out any legible fiction, and it would blow people's minds. Back when people were desperate for any sort of escape."

"Did you just insinuate that *Pride and Prejudice* was crapped out one sentence at a time?"

"A complete literary bowel movement."

"What if I said Beethoven spent his life crapping out notes that don't deserve to be played ever again?" She ran her hands through her very short hair.

"I'd feel sorry for you."

"'Für Elise' is the worst thing I've ever heard."

"I'm going to pretend you didn't say that." And then, "Aren't books supposed to take you away somewhere? Half of these novels we read are worthless. I'm sure Harper Lee is a genius, but I honestly don't feel pulled to get back to reading her book. Great sentences are one thing but a compelling story is more important. No wonder education is taking a nosedive in the U.S. They're not teaching people to love to read. They're cramming a stone-age curriculum down our throats. I think it's because our archaic school system has grown so large that no one can steer it, no one can change the way things are done. It's this giant boat we can't turn. Know what I mean? I think they're doing a good job of making sure that half of us will never read again."

Talking to Jasper sometimes felt like she was talking to someone much older, and Emilia enjoyed the challenge. Raising her eyebrow, she said, "The government is trying to destroy the book industry. I think you're onto something. I had no idea you were so opinionated."

"I'm just getting started."

"Well, you've disappointed me for the first time. Not liking Jane Austen is close to a crime."

"Then put me behind bars. And if you really want to punish me, make me read her trash all day long for the rest of my life."

"You're a dog, Jasper."

Tex appeared from around the corner. He looked pissed.

Emilia nodded to her right. "Jasper, look out behind you."

Before Jasper could turn, Tex slammed him up against a locker. Emilia yelled, "Tex!"

"What do you think you're doing?" Tex said into Jasper's face.

"This is called human interaction," Jasper said. "We're speaking. Talking. Chatting. Conversing. I don't know what your people call it."

"My people?" Tex said.

"Yeah, you know, your tribe. You and your backwoods Texas cavemen."

"Shut the fuck up." Tex pulled Jasper away from the locker and threw him to the ground. Jasper dropped onto his back, losing his breath, his fedora falling next to him. Tex put a foot on him. "I don't want you talking to her again."

"Tex!" Emilia screamed again. "Get off him." She grabbed his arm. He pushed her away and she fell backwards, catching herself on the lockers. Tex knelt, digging a knee into Jasper's chest, and pushed the side of his head into the floor with his hand. "Are you ever going to talk to her again, you prick?"

"You push her again," Jasper said, "and I'll ruin your life."

Tex laughed loudly, obnoxiously. "Ruin my life?"

Emilia went for him again. "Tex, stop!" she screamed, trying to push him over. He was too big.

Jasper was drooling on the ground as Tex pushed the side of his head harder. Jasper mumbled, "You're so insignificant in this world. Such a small thing. I would pity you if I had the time to waste."

In desperation, Emilia pulled her history book out of her locker. Winding back, she hit Tex in the back of the head. Tex fell off Jasper and hit the ground with a thud. Emilia heard gasps all around her.

Jasper slowly pushed himself up, straightening out his blazer. "You okay?" he asked her.

"I'm fine."

Jasper reared a smile. "You didn't have to do that."

"Oh. Did you have it under control?" she asked.

"I was about to unleash hell."

"I'll bet."

Jasper looked down at a fuzzy-eyed Tex. "Remember what I said," he whispered. "You're insignificant."

Tex was starting to get up. "I'm going to kill you."

Emilia said, "He's ten times the man you'll ever be. And he's right. You're insignificant."

With that, she put her arm in Jasper's and they strode down the hall. "I actually haven't read *Pride and Prejudice*," she said.

"You were pulling my leg?"

"Just a little."

"And Beethoven."

"Who doesn't love Beethoven?"

"I've underestimated you, Emilia Forester. Well played. Fifteen-love, as they say on the courts. Although I must admit that I haven't read any Jane Austen either."

Emilia's mouth fell agape.

~

THAT EVENING, Emilia went over to Margot's for ladies' night. Jasper answered the door wearing a frown.

She said, "I'm so sorry. Tex is a jerk. I don't know what else to say."

"Yeah, you know how to pick 'em."

"He wasn't always this way. I broke his heart and he was jealous."

Jasper nodded. "My mom and Joan are out in the courtyard."

"Are you mad at me?" she asked. He wasn't his typical self.

"No. Why?"

"You're being very short."

"I had a long day. Some stupid stuff with my dad came up. He keeps calling, wanting to come see me."

She'd never spoken with him about his father. "What did you say? Do you want him to come?"

"I don't return his calls. I don't ever text him back. We haven't spoken in forever."

Emilia nodded. "If you ever want to talk about it, I'm a good listener. My mom and dad are fighting like crazy right now, so I kind of understand what you feel."

Jasper escorted her to the courtyard, where Joan and Margot were sitting at a table next to the fire pit, a roaring fire keeping them warm. "I hope you don't mind my coming early," she said to them. "I had to get out of the house."

"You all right?" Margot asked.

"Yeah, my parents are just fighting. A lot lately."

"I think it's great you came early," Joan said. "Some of what I'm showing Margot could be good for you too."

"I don't want to interrupt."

"Don't say another word. Just sit down," Margot said. "I think you'll love it."

Joan reached out her hands. "Let's hold hands." The three women formed a circle. "We hold hands to strengthen our connection with the universe and with life. Close your eyes. Now, take in a huge breath through your nose. Fill your abdomen. And hold it. For ten heartbeats. Feel the life pulse inside of you. Then blow out."

Emilia loved this. Joan was such a deeply spiritual woman, more so than anyone she'd ever met. Emilia wanted that for herself. Was Joan holding the key to what she'd been missing?

"Do this four more times," Joan said. "You're signaling to your mind and body that you're ready to go deeper into the present moment. You're ready to let go."

Emilia opened her eyes for a moment to see that both women were taking this very seriously; their eyes were closed, and their hearts were open. She thought she could see a glow around them. Emilia closed her eyes again, noticing the crackle from the fire pit and the smell of burning wood.

"Now let's all sit here for a while," Joan continued. "Don't try to breathe. Let your body do what it needs to take in air. All you have to do is observe. Watch your breath. Watch your thoughts. Notice the fire; notice the chill in the air. Open up. If a thought comes by, don't analyze it. Let it be. It's okay. Watch it all go by."

Then silence.

A few minutes later, Joan spoke again. Emilia felt very comfortable with these women, still holding their hands. She'd meditated before in some Seattle yoga classes with her mom, but this experience was different. This time it felt real. Her mom's version of yoga was more about sculpting her abs and tightening up the curves, and less about tapping into the universe.

"Now," Joan said, "we're going to practice some visualization. If you can create something in your mind, you can create it in your physical world as well. I want you to picture yourself on this day a year from now. Picture where you are. Where you want to be. Picture what you're wearing. All the way to your socks and shoes. What are you doing? Who are you with? What do you smell? What do you feel like? Every detail. That's you. That can be your reality. I practice this every day. I create my own reality. We all do."

Joan squeezed Emilia's hand, sending Emilia her energy, her force, a very powerful sensation nearly unexplainable. Emilia felt an ineffable energy in her whole body. Who—what—was this Joan?

"One year from today," Joan said, "I'm with Otis Till. We love each other desperately, like all we know is how to love each other. We work hard at loving each other. We still have the magic of when we first met. We might even be married. He's cooking vegetables on the grill at his place. The sunset is one of those Red Mountain sunsets that you never forget and you know you'll never see again. We're happy and healthy."

Emilia had no idea where she herself wanted to be, so how could she possibly envision her future? She knew where she was supposed to be. At a good school getting good grades preparing for a good job. Vanilla, vanilla, vanilla, vanilla. Was that really what she—the *real* Emilia—wanted, deep down? She tried to come up with some images, tried to see herself in the future, hoping the real Emilia would show herself. Nothing came, though. Her future was blank. And that was scary. If she wasn't able to picture something, something or someone else would draw her destiny.

~

LATER, the three women were in the kitchen cooking and laughing. Emilia couldn't stop smiling. Sure, her future wasn't clear, but she'd found a part of who she wanted to be with these women. Maybe she'd finally found her real self.

This time, they started with a beetroot carpaccio with pomegranate and microgreens; then for the main course, they prepared a raw spinach lasagna with walnut meat and homemade pesto. Emilia savored each bite, thinking she'd never had better food in her life. What an odd friendship these three had created around food and spirituality. Emilia had never felt better and more satisfied in her life.

Toward the end of the night, Emilia excused herself and went to the restroom. She checked her phone. To her complete astonishment, Joe Massey had texted her. After all her worry, all her sadness, wondering if he even cared, her English teacher had finally resurfaced. But she knew better this time. Through all the pain, she'd finally realized how wrong she'd been to let him touch her.

30

THE DAYS AFTER LOSING

Otis spent three days in Bozeman, Montana attending Morgan's funeral and visiting with her friends. He also met with her lawyer, who brought one last surprise. Morgan had left Otis everything: the ranch, all her money, and even her animals. But that wasn't the surprise.

Reclined in a brown leather chair that nearly swallowed him, the lawyer, a bow-tied Seventh Day Adventist who kept a Bible on his desk, handed Otis a handwritten letter from Morgan. He recognized the large scrawl all too easily. What had she done this time? She wrote:

OTIS,

I told you you'd outlive me. You've still got a long way to go. Hopefully this letter finds you in a good place: steamy in love, I hope. I know how badly your heart hurt when you lost Rebecca. Mine did too. I truly hope you're able to find love again. You've got a lot of love to give. I know that.

And in the meantime, I have a favor to ask. There were so many places I didn't get to visit in my life. There was never enough time. Oh, how I wish there had been more hours in a day, more days in a month, more years in a life. But I have no regrets; I had a rich life.

I've left you everything, including a lot of money. Some of which you're going to need for this final request. I'd like to be cremated, and I'd like you to spread my ashes in the places I never was able to see. Yes, you're going to have to travel the world and leave your farm for a little while. But there's plenty of money for you to travel in style, and even to take a woman, should there be one by now. I truly hope this isn't a burden to you. In fact, I hope it might prove to be a wonderful journey. I've left these ten locations somewhat vague. The specific location is in your hands, though I swear I will come back to haunt you if you scatter my darn ashes in airports. Here's my list, my dearest nephew, in no particular order:

Prague, Czech Republic
Cape Town, South Africa
Dublin, Ireland
Hanoi, Vietnam
Kauai, USA
Papeete, Tahiti
Galapagos Islands, Ecuador
Machu Picchu, Peru
Reykjavik, Iceland
Red Mountain, Washington—So I can keep a close eye on you.

Goodbye for now,
Morgan

OTIS PUT down the letter and looked back at the lawyer, who had probably known about this "little" request for a long time. "You're kidding me."

"I told her it was a lot to ask."

Otis nodded. "She can't even die half-ass."

"As I said, you'll have to go on this journey before I can sign over her estate to you." The bow-tied lawyer put an elbow on his desk and rested his chin in his hand. "Are you up for it?"

Otis shook his head and blew out a blast of air. "If I don't do it, she'll figure out a way to come after me. I don't see anything keeping her down. Not even a cremator."

"She was a spry one, wasn't she?"

"Oh, quite. I'd like to think on it some. Can you give me a few days? Taking off right now isn't the most ideal."

"You have one year to complete your journey. I'll need a photograph taken with the current local newspaper in each location."

"Jesus, she really didn't trust me."

"She told me she might have to give you an extra nudge, that's all. Sounds like fun, if you ask me."

"How about you go, and no one will ever know?"

The man offered a closed-lip smile.

Otis drove back to Red Mountain, initially furious about the demand. But by the time he hit Washington, he realized what a gift she'd given him.

Did he have a woman who might be interested in going? Damn right he did. But it would take him a few days to run it by her. The results of his MRI took precedence.

~

A WEEK after Morgan's death, Otis left Kadlec Hospital in Richland and stepped into his truck. He put the keys in the ignition, but didn't start the engine. He put his hand to his mouth, curling his index finger around his upper lip, and he stared out into nothing, not seeing the cars passing by, not seeing the people, the trees, the sidewalk. The thoughts were pouring in so quickly that he couldn't even follow them. He heard the phone ring a few times but couldn't bear to look at it.

He finally glanced at the clock. Almost eleven. He needed to see Joan. She'd called five times. Brooks had called too. The two most important people in his world, now that Morgan was gone. It was better that he didn't have to share this news with his aunt anyway.

When Joan opened her door, Otis's lips quivered.

"Oh, baby." Joan took him in his arms. He hugged her like he was losing her.

He didn't cry, though. He bit his bottom lip and drew in a breath. He had to be strong. This news wouldn't be easy for her.

"Come inside," she whispered into his neck. "Tell me."

They sat down next to each other on the couch. Joan took his hand, running her thumb over his knuckles.

"I've got an aneurysm in my brain and they think it burst and bled. They think I had a minor hemorrhagic stroke and didn't realize it."

Joan squeezed his hand. "Is it still bleeding?"

"No. But they're worried. It's big. And it could happen again. Joan, they said it's too dangerous to operate on. In most cases, with an aneurysm of this size that's already ruptured at least once, there's a good chance I won't survive surgery." He breathed out. "The doctor said I might have three or four years if I'm lucky. And it really comes down to statistics and luck."

He was having a hard time looking at her. They sat there for a while in silence, absorbing the verdict that had been dealt to both of them.

"I guess old age has to get you one way or another," Otis finally said.

"I think you know me enough to know I don't believe we have to surrender so easily. What did he say you could do?"

"Oh, you know, the same old bullshit. Quit smoking my pipe. Eat healthy. Stop drinking. Exercise."

"Otis Till, that's not the same old bull." She put a hand on his knee. "You know what?"

"What?"

"You're going to beat this thing."

"There's no beating this. You know me by now. I'm not the guy who beats things. I'm the guy who gets defeated. Good luck doesn't come my way."

"I came your way, didn't I? We're going to beat this together, darling. You're going to change today."

"Let's go get a bone-in grass-fed rib eye and talk about it."

"Don't start your humor thing to push this aside. You've got many years left. We're going to fight it with everything we have. You're going to get healthy. I do know you, and I know you're a fighter. And I'm not talking tomorrow. I'm talking today. Today, you're a new man."

Otis wasn't convinced that he'd beat this thing; in fact, he knew he wouldn't. But he also knew his last days on this earth would be lived for Joan Tobey. So he said, "Then show me to your Downward Dog."

"Oh, my god. Only you can make light of this, Otis."

"Welcome to my coping mechanism."

"I guess there are unhealthier ways to deal."

"We could start with a bottle of whisky."

~

OTIS LEFT Joan with many hugs and kisses and went to catch up with work. He didn't have time to sit around and wait for the Grim Reaper. If this was going to be his last vintage, he was going to make sure it was his finest. Mother Nature had given him plenty to work with; he just needed extra assistance from Brooks.

As he pulled down his driveway, he saw Elijah, his intern, and Esteban, his vineyard guy, waiting for him on the crush pad. They'd let Jonathan out; the animal was sprawled on the concrete next to a huge stack of yellow picking bins full of sangiovese that Esteban's crew had picked that morning. Otis had asked them to wait until he got home to start crushing. He liked being there; it was the control freak in him.

"How's the fruit looking?" he asked, rubbing Jonathan's ears.

"*Muy bueno*," Elijah said. It was the language of the vineyards, and it came out from time to time, even among the English speakers.

Elijah wore the same over-sized dark blue Till Vineyards fleece vest every day. He was a little guy with a big heart and even bigger devotion to Red Mountain. Otis loved the kid and planned to hire him after graduation. He might even leave him a chunk of land.

Elijah said, "We got just under a ton."

Otis took a cluster and tasted them. He could sense some acid but the particulars were missing. "Let's start crushing."

Within minutes, they were dumping the yellow lugs into the destemmer/crusher. The machine would separate the grapes and stems into two different buckets. Once the grape bucket was full, one of them would dump it into the larger fermenter, where the juice would stay for most of the fermentation. They'd cast the stems into a wheelbarrow, eventually to be added to the compost pile on the other side of the vineyard.

Brooks arrived later in the afternoon. Otis was moving one of the tanks on the forklift. He immediately hopped off and shook Brooks's hand. "Look who it is."

"How'd it go with the doctor?"

Otis ignored the question. "You look like you're in a good mood."

"I got engaged last night."

"What? I didn't know that was coming."

"I barely did myself." Brooks told Otis the story.

"And what about your brother?"

"We brought him back. Must be in the blood. We have this subconscious pull to Red Mountain. And against all odds, he and Charles haven't killed each other yet."

"They're probably happy to see each other."

"I think so. I left them this morning cleaning out my garage. Get this. My bro rides bikes. Knows how to fix 'em. We're the same person."

"Well, then the mountain just got lucky. Bring him over before too long. And you let me know if he needs some work. I'm happy to help."

"Thank you. I'm going to feel him out first. Make sure he wants it.

Just like you did with me, I'm going to put him out in the vineyard and let him pick grapes for a while. See if he breaks."

"You get along with him?"

"He's pissed off at the world. Like I was. Nothing I can't handle. He'll come around."

"Instant family. Now all you need is your mom and some ankle biters."

"I've got my hands full with harvest right now," Brooks said. "Anyway, what went down with the doctor? Any news yet?"

"I saw you called. Thank you." Otis ran a hand through his hair. "Not good, Brooks. Not good."

"Oh, shit. Here I was doing the talking. What is it?"

Otis told him and finished with, "I don't want you telling anyone that I'm on my deathbed just yet."

Brooks put an arm on Otis's shoulder and turned that into a hug. He squeezed him tight, patting him on the back. "You listen to what they say. You'll be okay. No one can knock you down."

"That's what Joan says. You two must have gotten me confused with someone else." He pulled off his tweed cap. "We'll see. If not, we'd better make sure this vintage is memorable. Could be my last."

"You're too tough for that. But we'll make sure it's a good one. I'm serious when I tell you your wines are going to be top-notch this year."

"That gives me reason to fight. Hey, why don't you and your family come by tonight? I want you to meet Joan anyway."

"The whole family?"

"Yep, everyone."

"We'll do that. Assuming we're still intact by then."

"Quit your worrying, boy. Long as you don't expect everyone to be perfect, the more the merrier. Only a month ago, all you and I had was making wine. Now our lives are getting richer."

"I feel that. But I also feel like I'm playing Jenga, with the pieces made of new family members and good luck. I've been playing Jenga since I moved here. How high can I keep stacking before it all comes crumbling down?"

"You've been around me too long. That's something I would say."

"That's a compliment. You're the wisest man I know."

"If you're ever going to take advice from me, hear this now: don't listen to a word I say." They both chuckled as they entered the cellar. Otis thought how odd it was to be able to laugh on the day you find out how you're going to die.

31

THE JENGA TOWER

Making up for lost time with his family was hard to do with Otis's health weighing heavy on Brooks's mind. Otis Till still had much to give to this world, to give to Red Mountain.

Brooks had gone out to put a bag of trash in the can. His brother, father, and fiancée (that's right, fiancée!) were inside prepping dinner and making what seemed like fairly friendly conversation. No doubt Abby's presence encouraged the good behavior.

He took a detour before returning. He meandered along Demoss Road, along the river, watching the ripples as the water wound through the bends, and thinking about Otis. Specifically, he was trying to imagine 1969, the year Otis had moved to San Francisco and met Rebecca. Otis had only been living in California a month when he was talked into hopping a bus to Woodstock. Rebecca was on that bus too, and they'd fallen in love by the time the bus had crossed into Utah. Then, a week later, Otis proposed to Rebecca with a ring made of a small birch branch, one knee in the mud and the rain pouring down, listening to Crosby, Stills, Nash, and Young.

What a beautiful story, Brooks thought, and how ugly it turned. Otis and Rebecca had lost their first son in a fishing accident; their second son and Rebecca perished a few years later, sliding on an icy road into the very river Brooks was standing next to. Otis now faced the end. At least he wasn't alone any more. This Joan woman sounded like she'd turned Otis's world upside down, or rather, upside right.

Brooks stopped to watch as several beavers, noticing him, high-tailed it toward the faster moving water. He saw the shreds of a fallen tree where they'd been sharpening their teeth.

What a hell of a day it was for Brooks otherwise. His instant family had grown to four. Better get in there and manage it before something went awry. Truthfully, Charles and Shay were getting along fine. They hadn't gotten into any meaty discussions, both treading lightly, but there was nothing wrong with that. They'd have to ease into the emotions of one another.

Eventually, Brooks returned to the kitchen. Abby had the men working, helping her make chili. His dad, in a Pebble Beach sweater-vest and loafers, was opening cans of tomatoes while Shay, the white male Aunt Jemima dressed in Goodwill's finest, ran vegetables through a food processor. Ground bison and venison sizzled in a large pan in front of Abby. The smells of chili powder and cumin and grease made Brooks's mouth water.

When Shay stopped the food processor, finishing up the celery, Abby said, "So Shay, have you thought more about taking care of the animals up at Lacoda?"

"Don't need to think about it. It beats standing in front of a fryer all night. Actually, I think it's a good opportunity. I'm appreciative." He went into the refrigerator for a beer. "Brooks says I have to earn my street cred first and pick some fruit, scrub some floors, that kind of thing."

"The initiation," Brooks smiled, appreciating his brother's atti-tude. It was clear everyone was trying. They'd all missed this sense of family, simple evenings of loved ones cooking together and catching up.

"It must feel somewhat nice being able to walk away so easily," Abby said. "You're like DeNiro in *Heat*."

Shay smiled, popped the top and took a sip. In a very good Robert DeNiro voice, he quoted a line from *Heat*.

"No way!" Abby giggled. "You're really good."

"I watch a lot of movies."

"Always has," Charles said. "Since he was a kid. He would get up on the table and do scenes for his mom and me."

"How old was he?" Abby asked, still tending to the meat.

"Shoot, since he could speak. He had an uncanny ability to remember dialogue. Still does, clearly!"

"Let's hear another," Abby said to Shay.

Shay thought about it for a moment and then spat out a nearly spot-on Russell Crowe.

"*Gladiator!*" Abby said. "Unbelievable."

Shay looked at Brooks, grinning, a real smile that reddened the rounds of his rosy cheeks even more. "She's a good one, man. Any woman who knows *Gladiator*."

"The layers keep on peeling back," Brooks replied.

"One more," Abby said.

Brooks saw how genuine Shay's smile was and realized that the four of them were connecting. They were actually having fun. Brooks, for God's sake, was having fun, though deep down, he couldn't shake his fear of it all coming down.

"Okay, one more," Shay said and took a moment to compose himself. "This one's gonna be kind of silly." He broke into another impressive accent, delivering a monologue Brooks didn't recognize.

When he finished, Abby said, "I know it's Christopher Walken, but I don't know the movie."

"Anyone?" Shay said, looking at his dad and Brooks.

Brooks didn't see many movies growing up. He still hadn't seen *Star Wars* or *The Godfather* or all those movies people referred to at dinner parties. So he shook his head.

"Walken in *True Romance*, one of Quentin Tarantino's early movies. 1993. That movie was a big part of my growing up."

"Oh, I do know that one," Abby said. "Brad Pitt was in that too."

"And Christian Slater. Dennis Hopper. Val Kilmer. Gary Oldman.

Samuel L. Jackson. Shoot, Gandolfini, pre-*Sopranos*, God rest his soul."

"You should go to Hollywood," Abby said. "You're good."

"I was good back in San Bernardino. Everyone's good in Hollywood." He smiled and started on a red pepper.

~

Brooks drove them to Otis's after dinner and met Joan for the first time. Otis was in a surprisingly good mood, bouncing around, telling jokes and giving out hugs. And Brooks knew why. This woman was special.

Joan Tobey had this way about her, this soothing vibe. She'd caught Brooks off guard when he'd first shaken her hand. He'd been so in his own head about his brother and father and Otis's aneurysm; just her touch and voice centered him. Good for Otis, he thought. His mentor had finally found someone.

They drank grower Champagne and filled the living room with their storytelling and laughter as they got to know each other.

Joan, sitting next to Otis on the couch, said, "Brooks, Otis speaks so highly of you."

"Then I'm sure he's told you how much I owe him."

"He told me you showed up just when he needed you."

"Not now," Brooks said, "but I'll tell you the whole story one day. He's the one who showed up at the right time, before I was too far gone. I'm sure his version takes away his glory. He's never one for self-praise."

"I'd be great at self-praise if I had anything to brag about," Otis said.

Brooks rolled his eyes. "For this woman to even give you the time of day, you must be all right. You know she's way out of your league."

"I keep wondering when I'm going to wake up and realize she was just a dream."

Brooks knew that feeling too well. He'd spent the entire day and night with thoughts like *this is too good to be true* running through him. He'd never known family, but suddenly, he had everything he'd ever dreamed of. When was Abby going to leave him? When was Shay going to stand up and start yelling at Charles? The Jenga blocks will eventually fall.

Otis put his arm around Joan, and Brooks loved seeing it. He'd never known Rebecca, so he'd never seen Otis with a woman. Otis was a different guy now. The dark cloud that had hovered over him had gone west with the wind, revealing clear blue skies.

32

THE BATTLE INSIDE

Margot was back on top of the world. She knew a few slip-ups here and there were inevitable. As Joan had told her, she was shedding the old Margot. There would be resistance, a pulling and stretching battle of ego and true self. There would be a few gelato and Hallmark binging breakdowns. But Margot 2.0 was now seventeen days old. She'd lost a few pounds; but more importantly, she felt better.

She woke up on Friday, meditated, then stood up and crept barefoot onto the cold tile of the bathroom. Following Joan's instructions, she looked into the mirror and said, "I love you, Margot. I love you. Just the way you are. You are perfect just the way you are." She even lifted up her shirt and said, "I love you, stomach. You're perfect just the way you are." And she worked hard to say it with conviction. She went on like that for a while, talking to her saggy arms and her white legs and her bra-bursting breasts and the rest of the body parts Margot 1.0 had hated; then she went back into her bedroom.

She took her journal out and read her belief statement out loud, though not loud enough for Jasper to hear in his room, where he was preparing for school. She finished, repeating several times, "Every day in every way, I am getting better and better." She scribbled with a ballpoint pen a new entry about renewing herself and not killing her husband anymore; being healthy inside and out.

She dressed with care, trying on several outfits before deciding on a revealing white blouse and a more conservative green skirt. Joan told her that dressing well, even if she wasn't going out, was a way to build self-esteem. It was part of the Margot 2.0 recipe. *Love yourself, Margot.* But there was another reason. Jake Forester was coming over to talk about the concert with Jasper and to discuss the farm sanctuary. Jake had confirmed through texts that he had, in fact, bought the property next to her and that he would sell it to her when she was ready. She wasn't after him, of course, but she sure as hell was going to look good.

First things first, though. As Joan had taught her, Margot had to stop living through Jasper. Margot's life was her own, and to truly be a good mother, she had to find her own health, build her own life. So she was back with full focus on Épiphanie. Ron, her gift from the gods, had only been on the project for three days, but things were moving along. He'd given her some hope. She crossed the property to the construction zone. Four trucks filled the drive in zigzags, and several gorgeously rugged men were entering with huge planks and sheets of plywood.

Ron stood over a big black bucket of crème stucco holding a mixing drill, the trigger down, the machine roaring, the paddle spinning. The two stucco guys he'd hired stood a safe distance away, studying his technique, waiting for Ron to get them the perfect mixture.

Standing where the driveway met the brick walkway, Margot looked at the building and tried to see the future, tried to imagine what it would look like, what she wanted it to look like, tried to imagine the bustle of a busy inn, a place where people drove up and couldn't wait to get out of their cars, dragging their bags in to get their vacations started.

She looked at the glistening new windows, stickers still showing, and knew the pastel yellow she'd chosen for the shutters was indeed the right call, a perfect accent to the stucco. And she wanted to do flower boxes at the base of the windows. That wouldn't be too difficult.

She lowered her gaze to the big beautiful wooden doors. What about some tall lattices on either side, where she could grow short-rooted honeysuckles? Margot remembered honeysuckles from her childhood in Charlottesville. She and her mother used to go on walks and suck the honey from the insides. She could still taste the sweet nectar.

She turned her attention to the empty flower beds. She needed to get a landscaper in soon. It was too cold to plant anything, but they could start planning. She adored roses and wanted them everywhere, every color she could find.

Her mind drifted to lighting. Torches came to mind, but she thought they might be too Hawaiian. Perhaps strands of giant globe lights would be more fitting, long lines of lights on metal poles like Otis had done for his harvest party.

She dodged one of the carpenters and went inside, taking out her phone to make notes of what she needed: desks, chairs, side tables, lamps, rugs, candles, more artwork. She'd been collecting things here and there, but had put off the bulk of buying because she didn't have a place for storage. Though it would hurt to burn up her credit card, she was going to have a ball finishing up. She figured a week or two in Seattle bouncing from the used places to the wonderful furniture stores and art galleries, and she'd be set.

All she really had so far, which was in storage in West Richland, was her new kitchen stuff, none of which had been cheap. All of the appliances were there, including the best refrigerator and stove and food processor she could find. She'd bought her wine glasses from Gabriel Glas, an Austrian producer of the highest quality. When her guests dropped a glass, it would be sad, but Margot believed too much in good glassware. How could you be in a world-class grape growing region and not have the best stemware?

The only real good Tanner had done was building her several extra-long dining room tables from reclaimed wood. He'd done an amazing job. She had stained them herself in a very dark espresso.

She hoped one day she'd be able to look at those tables and not think of him.

She'd also begun putting together a wild collection of dining chairs, none of which matched. Her dining room would seat sixty, though she only had eight bedrooms. She wanted to be prepared for weddings and other large events.

Upstairs, Margot thought about the bedrooms. She had already decided the rooms would have the most comfortable mattresses she could afford, and she'd finish them with fluffy and luxurious bedding, all in white. Beds no one would ever want to leave. Half of the bedrooms had gas fireplaces, and she was reminded to make sure Ron knew they needed gas lines. Tanner might have made yet another mistake. Those same rooms also had huge claw-foot tubs, and she needed to find bath caddies and shower curtains.

She made a note to start figuring out toiletries. Several companies had sent samples, but nothing had worked quite yet. She hated shampoos with fake scents. She wanted something natural and local. In fact, anything that she could do in an organic version would be perfect. The cost was higher, but that didn't matter. Quality had to be her number one priority.

She caught up with Ron for a while, answering questions about the locations of outlets and appliances, her plans for the patio out back, and her vision for the stairway railing. He even had a few ideas of his own, including a dumbwaiter—a tiny elevator for food—to help her with room service. He thought he could squeeze one in near the stairs.

Margot spent the rest of the day on the computer and phone, talking with suppliers, booking services, her accountant, and several PR firms. She spent some time on social media, posting pictures on Instagram and Facebook. After an exhausting day, she finally sat down to read *The Power of Now* for a few moments before Jake and Jasper arrived.

The first thing she said to Jake when she answered the door was, "I can't believe you bought the property."

Jake, who looked as manly and attractive as ever, said, "I got excited." He made a face that longed for approval more than thanks. Almost as though he was more interested in making her happy than receiving gratitude.

"Yes you did." Margot didn't have to fake her excitement. "I couldn't be more thrilled. To think you can actually still live your dream in this world!"

"Of course you can."

"Sometimes it takes help along the way."

"I've never done anything great without a little help from my friends."

"What good friends you must have, then."

"The best and the worst, and I can't live without them."

She liked how Jake sometimes spoke with philosophical undertones that left several options for deciphering. He delighted her by asking for a tour of Épiphanie, and she gladly led him through the site, pointing out her favorite parts, the kitchen, of course, taking up half the tour.

Back outside, they strolled over to the back of her house, near the chicken coop, where they could take a look at the plot for the farm sanctuary. Margot crossed her arms as they gazed over the property, wondering how she'd been so lucky to end up here. The ten acres reached toward 224 to the south; to the north, it ran right up to where the slope of Red Mountain began, a perfect plot of flat desert with nothing but sagebrush and a dusty dirt road running down the middle of it. One day, she'd have wonderfully happy animals of every kind running around playing with each other there.

"I want to give you the land," Jake said, turning to her.

"You can't do that."

"Why not?"

"Because that's not the way the world works."

"Don't we decide how the world works?"

"Jake, you just can't. I don't want your charity."

"What you're doing is a charity. You can't fund it yourself, you have to raise money."

He was right about that.

He said, "I'm not throwing money at you because you need it. You didn't even ask me. I want to help a great cause. I think you're a good person and you've got a great idea here. It's good for you and me and for the animals and for Red Mountain. What kind of animals are you thinking, by the way?"

"Oh, gosh. Horses, sheep, goats, chickens, turkeys, ducks, alpacas, lions, tigers. I basically want Noah's Ark."

He chuckled.

"So you're really going to give me ten acres of Red Mountain land? Just like that?"

"Just like that."

Margot felt the tears coming and worked desperately to hide them from him. She wanted to say, "Things don't happen to me this way. My husband cheated on me in front of the entire world. I lost everything. I blew up to fat and ugly. Now, I'm friendless, husband-less, and utterly alone." But she didn't say that. She caught herself. Margot 2.0 said something much better, much stronger: "Thank you, Jake. You're a good man."

"You're welcome."

Margot 2.0 strikes again! She smiled, a big smile that was almost embarrassing. "I'm so happy," she said.

"You've got the world by a string," Jake said. "An inn under construction and a farm sanctuary on the horizon."

"It's going to be fun." Frances from *Under the Tuscan Sun* would be so proud of her.

"One more thing," he said. "I really don't want to pry too much, and if you think I'm overstepping my bounds, tell me now. But have you met my winemaker, Brooks?"

"Yes, we've caught up a couple of times." She instantly was worried Jake was going to try to set them up, but that wasn't the case.

"He has a brother named Shay who's moved to the mountain. From what Brooks says, he's handy with animals. Used to work at a ranch in New Mexico. Brooks has been on me for a while about bringing in some sheep and goats and chickens and the whole bit. I was thinking maybe we could give Shay some work if he decides to stick around."

"Sounds too good to be true."

Jake smiled and flashed his eyebrows. "I don't believe in such things."

Jasper approached. He and Jake shook hands, and Jasper gave his mother a kiss. They caught Jasper up on the plans, and Jake said, "I've been doing some homework about this gig I mentioned." He looked straight at Jasper. "What do you think of this? We bring a big tent and put it right there." He pointed out to the middle of the ten acres. "I'm talking about a huge tent, a big stage with my lighting and sound guys. We could squeeze eight or nine hundred people in there. Charge a lot of money."

"You're shitting me," Jasper said.

"That's the kind of money your mom needs to get the sanctuary going. It's a small venue, brand-new album. People will come from all over. Trust me. We'll cut this album quickly and have it ready before then. I'll get us worldwide distribution for the album. That's where you'll see some good cash, Jasper. We split it down the middle. It'll help with college, though I'm sure they're throwing scholarships at you. If not college, you'll need some dough after school. What do you think?"

Jasper looked at Margot and Jake. He grinned. "We need to find a band."

33

THE UGLINESS OF INFIDELITY

"**W**ake up, sis!" Luca screamed.

Emilia pulled the covers over her head. "How did you get in here?"

"Easy. I invented a new device that opens all doors."

She pulled down the covers. "That's a neat device but not very fair to use. People need their privacy. People lock doors for a reason."

"Locked doors are there to be unlocked. Talk to Houdini about that." Luca wore robot pajamas and oversized slippers that their mom had brought back from a Four Seasons somewhere.

"No, my door is locked to stay locked. It's Saturday morning, Luca. What time is it?" Emilia looked at her phone. "Luca! It's 6:09 a.m."

"Yeah, it's already way past my deadline with the Moon People. You don't understand. I know you want to sleep in, but I'm on a mission of the highest importance. I told them we'd beam the video up by this afternoon. They're sending a special convoy all the way back to our solar system just to get the video. The world is now in your hands."

"Luca, I don't know if I have time today."

"You don't have time to save the world?" He climbed onto the bed. "Please tell me what you're doing today that's more important than a top secret mission to save our planet. Hanging out with Tex. Let me be the only one brave enough to tell you that he's a loser. Everybody knows it."

She laughed. "I know that. Actually, I was going to go see my new friend, Joan, today."

Luca put his hand on his forehead. "Oh, my gosh. Don't you realize? No one will even have friends if we don't get this video out. I need you to get up and get dressed and start immediately."

Emilia knew she wasn't going to win this one. She sat up. "Bring me your camera."

He jumped off the bed and reached into his backpack. "I need you to make this two hours max. I'm not sure how many hours of video I have, but it's a lot."

"Then I'd better get started."

"Cool. You know, I'll probably be awarded the Medal of Honor and the Pulitzer and the Nobel Peace Prize. I'll see if I can get you an Oscar for your editing work. Maybe an honorable mention or something from the President of the United States."

"That would be great."

Emilia set a few firm pillows behind her and sat up. She opened iMovie, the Apple moviemaking software, and imported all the video, almost five hours of footage. She said, "Okay, Luca. What's the name of the video?"

"I'm calling it *Red Mountain: A Study in Human Behavior.*"

Emilia laughed. "That sounds like a blockbuster to me."

"Well, it's only for the Moon People for now. They wanted me to craft my film after one of those shows we watch on National Geographic. Something very cerebral."

"Cerebral? How do you know that word?"

"I know almost all words. I study the dictionary when I go poop."

Fully entertained, she said, "You have to tell me what footage you want to keep."

He cuddled up next to her and watched her work. She played his raw footage. The first scene was their dad playing his acoustic guitar on the patio. On the screen, Jake stopped to say hi to Luca and went back to playing. Emilia dragged the clip to her live reel. Cut to Emilia in boxers and a t-shirt putting on makeup. "Get out of here!" she screamed. Emilia quickly deleted that part.

"What are you doing?" Luca said. "I decide what stays and goes."

"Luca, nothing of me in my bathroom or bedroom is staying. You have to understand privacy."

"Privacy *shmivacy*."

They kept going, rolling through the video. Luca led Emilia through the edits, keeping only his favorite parts. There was footage of a butterfly fluttering its wings near the pool; vineyard workers harvesting grapes; Abby driving him to school; his classmates making funny faces; their mom and dad together in the kitchen; a dinner party; and a highly entertaining scene in Luca's room where he sat down and described a new invention involving space travel.

Emilia enjoyed seeing the world through her brother's eyes. Some of what he had captured was absolutely beautiful. He had this unique way of looking at even the most mundane parts of life and finding beauty in them.

They'd worked through an hour of footage when someone knocked on the door. It was their mom. "Hi, Mom," they said together.

"Good morning. You're up early for a Saturday morning." Carmen looked like she'd just woken up, her hair all over the place.

Emilia said, "We're saving the world, Mom. I'm helping him with this documentary. The Moon People need it by the end of the day."

"That's ambitious," Carmen replied.

"That's what I said."

Luca said, "You can't be lazy when the entire universe is counting on you."

Carmen sat on the edge of the bed, cinching the belt of her robe tighter. "What are they going to do with the video?"

"Mom, I can't even tell my contact at the U.N. that information right now. If the Moon People knew I was discussing classified material with you, they'd have to beam you up to their ship and erase your memory."

"Oh. Then I'd better go downstairs."

"Probably a good idea."

"You two hungry?"

"Yes!" Luca said.

"Okay, how about I bring up some fruit?"

"Yes. Now go, Mom. Emilia is getting distracted. She's an artist. You can't interrupt

artists while they're working."

"Um, yes, your dad taught me that lesson long ago." With that, she closed the door.

They kept editing for another twenty minutes and had an hour of good footage. They were about to take a break when she got to a part where Luca was outside at night. She kept watching because he wasn't ever supposed to be outside at night. "This is kind of scary," she said.

"Yeah, I'm about to spy on Abby. And I'm trying out some narration."

"Luca, I'm serious. You can't go sneaking around on people with a video camera. You're going to get in trouble."

He put a finger to his mouth. "Shh, watch. This is so funny."

Back to the footage. Luca pointed the camera and a flashlight at his own face. He whispered, "I'm about to infiltrate Abby's house. I see a light on. Let's go." With that, he crept through sagebrush in the dark to the other side of the property where Abby's guesthouse was located. He put the camera against the window, looking in.

There were two figures, hugging and kissing. Emilia saw a naked Abby. The other person had to be Brooks. "Luca!" Emilia yelled. "You can't film this. It's private." Emilia had no interest in watching further. She moved her finger to the keyboard to fast-forward but one last glimpse stopped her short.

It wasn't Brooks. She closed the laptop quickly.

"What's wrong?" Luca asked.

Emilia didn't know what to say. "We're going to have to finish your video later, okay?"

"Why?"

"I need to take a break."

"Why?"

Emilia had no intention of explaining. "I need to take a break, that's all."

"Sis!"

"Luca, get out of my room. I need a break."

Emilia pushed Luca out of her room and locked the door. She cried for a few minutes and the sadness turned to anger. Nearly shattered, Emilia went down the stairs. Her mom was coming up with a big tray of fruit and water.

"I was bringing you breakfast in bed."

Emilia raised her hands and brought them down hard. The tray crashed to the stairs, spilling the water and strawberries and blueberries and peaches; the fruit rolled down the stairs.

"What the hell, young lady?" Her mom had a temper that was easily ignited.

Emilia could care less. "You and Abby?"

"What are you talking about?" her mom asked.

"You know what I'm talking about. How could you do that to Dad? To us?"

"Emilia."

Emilia started walking down the rest of the stairs. "You're such a selfish bitch. You tell Dad or I will."

"You have no idea what you're talking about."

"I saw you on film. Your son just saw you on film getting naked with another woman. A hundred yards from this house! Our nanny! That's so messed up!" She spat out, "What's wrong with you?"

Carmen followed her daughter down the stairs.

Emilia kept walking to the front door. "You tell Dad or I will. I'm leaving."

"Em!"

"No!" Emilia left the house, ignoring her mother's begging.

Once she got into her car, Emilia texted Joe Massey: *I need to see you.*

34

A MAN ON THE MEND

"What do you do with the rest of your life when you're dying?" Otis asked Joan. Otis was on his third cup of coffee, trying to put off the bike ride he'd somehow agreed to.

He wore sweatpants and a t-shirt. Otis couldn't remember the last time he'd worn sweatpants. He felt like an idiot.

"First of all," Joan said. "I don't want to ever hear you say that again. If you decide you're dying, then you're dying. I heard Morgan say that more than once."

"She said many things."

"She was a wise woman."

"All I'm saying is that if I only have a couple of years left, I'll be damned if I'm going to spend it avoiding everything I love—scotch, tri-tip, a good steak, smoking my pipe, bacon. For God's sake, bacon! Bacon is my religion."

"Do you really think doctors are always right? Don't you want to be the guy who experiences a miracle? Don't you want to live more than a couple of years? I don't know about you, but I think you and I have crossed paths for a reason. How about we see where it goes?"

"You know I care deeply about you. You woke me up from a bad dream."

"Then let me do what I do. Let me lead you. Let me restore your belief in miracles. Let me love you. Open up your heart."

Otis felt a great moment of weakness, an overwhelming sense of vulnerability, and he slowly raised his head, looking into her eyes. "I'm scared. I don't want to die."

She took him in her arms. "You don't have to die." She touched his face. "But you must decide to live."

Could she be right? He wanted so much to believe her, to believe that he could be that guy who beats the odds. But his past begged to differ.

"You ready?" she asked. "I know you keep filling your cup trying to procrastinate. I wasn't born yesterday."

"I don't know what you're talking about." They left their cups on the table.

Joan had surprised him the night before with a brand-new road bike. As she helped him adjust his seat, he said, "This could be dangerous. I haven't pedaled a bike in thirty years."

"It's like riding a bike," she said, smirking. "You'll pick it back up quickly."

"Right."

They pedaled up the driveway and onto Sunset Road. Otis wasn't about to admit it, but riding was fun. They worked their way to 224 and rode east, circling around Red Mountain. Reaching Demoss Road on the other side, Otis pointed out Brooks's house. They rode along the river side by side. By then, Otis was covered in sweat and breathing heavily. "You're trying to kill me, aren't you? I'm literally having a heart attack."

He looked over at her. Not a drop of sweat. She said, "That's not a heart attack. That's your body saying, 'Hello. I've missed you.'"

"It misses a bacon sandwich and a Guinness. "

"Somehow I doubt that. If you're good and do what I say for a week, you can have one piece of bacon and a big ol' pint of Guinness."

"One piece of bacon? That's a teaser. I'll need a whole hog after a week."

"You're going to be a vegan for a week."

Otis laughed. "Now that is funny. A vegan. I'm going to *eat* a vegan after this ride."

"I'm serious. You'd be amazed how great vegetarian food is."

"For a rabbit."

Returning, they drank ice water in the kitchen. Joan took a big sip and pulled Otis by the shirt toward her. She kissed him and pulled him closer. "Come take a shower with me."

"Sign me up," he said.

They undressed each other and stepped into the shower, the warm water splashing against them as they explored each other's bodies. Otis felt ashamed at first, as he hadn't taken his blue pill. But Joan reassured and comforted him. She didn't care. She liked him just the way he was. "You never know, I might wake him up one day."

"He's awake. He just doesn't want to get out of bed."

"Let's get your heart working. You never know."

They dressed and Joan pulled out a grocery bag from the refrigerator. She blended a smoothie with peaches, blueberries, Maca powder, cocoa nibs, banana, homemade almond milk, and bee pollen. They sat down at the kitchen table. Otis looked doubtfully at the concoction.

"Give it a try," Joan said.

Reluctantly, Otis put his lips to the glass.

"You're like a five year old," she said. "Just drink it."

He took a sip. "I can tell it's cold, that's about it. I can't taste a thing."

"Then who cares what you put in your mouth? Bacon or spinach?"

"Nice try. What do I get if I do this for a month?"

"What do you get? How about a healthy heart? You'll lose a few pounds. You'll be on your way to building some good habits."

"Yahoo."

"It's all about attitude."

"Might as well bury me now, then."

"Not funny, Otis."

"I thought it was funny. So what's for lunch? Daffodils?" He smiled. "With a side of grass? An *amuse-bouche* of dirt?"

"Actually, you're close. Leafy greens, hemp hearts, and quinoa salad."

"I'm going to disintegrate."

"Oh, hush."

Otis looked at the clock. "I've got to get over to the winery soon. What's the rest of your day look like?"

"I'm not sure yet."

"Then I'm going to hold you hostage," Otis said. "If you leave my side for one minute the rest of the day, I'll gorge myself on barbecued ribs."

"That's a nice way to hold a woman hostage."

"I'm simply using the tools at my disposal."

"I think in Otis language, that's you trying to say you don't want me to go."

They drank their smoothies and Joan took Otis's hand. "Before we go up to the winery, we have something else we need to do." She led him to the living room, and they sat together on the rug facing each other.

"Put your hands on your knees," she said. "I want to teach you about visualization and neuroplasticity."

"The who and the what?"

"I want to teach you how you can heal yourself. Along with following a healthier lifestyle, you need to work on encouraging your brain to heal. Before you start saying this is mumbo jumbo, listen to me. I can give you endless scientific documentation proving the efficacy of visualization and belief and the ability of the brain and the body to heal itself. So don't start blabbing the classic Otis skepticism at me. The key to what I'm going to show you is belief. You have to believe. I will tell you beautiful stories of people I've seen heal themselves, and I will share stacks of books with you, but for now, I'm going to teach you how it works. You're going to have to trust me."

She was right; Otis immediately reacted skeptically, but he loved and respected her so much that he wanted to believe her. Perhaps that was a start.

She asked him to close his eyes and relax for a moment. Otis obeyed, and the light disappeared. She said, "You have an aneurysm located at the base of your brain. At the center of a collection of arteries. I want you to imagine this area, imagine this vital network of arteries running from your heart up through your neck and into your brain. Now locate the aneurysm in the Circle of Willis at the base. There's one artery with a weak spot. You can see that spot, you can see where it ruptured, and you can see the clot. Try to remember what your MRI scan looked like. Do you see it?"

Otis found one of the images in his memory and said, "Yes."

"Now look clearly at the clot itself and at the damaged area. Breathe in deeply and send this area a ray of golden light. Send it your healing power. Repair the clot. Picture the cells regenerating, forming a strong artery, as good as new."

Otis did as directed while Joan continued helping him visualize. Though he had his doubts, Joan's unswayable belief was infectious.

After a few more minutes, she redirected his attention. "Now, Otis, let's focus on your sense of taste. Your parietal lobe is located just under your skull at the top of your head. Take your attention there. Picture the neurons that process flavors. Try to remember what it was like to taste. Reawaken those little guys. Encourage those neurons to start firing together again. Bring back your lovely taste buds. Remember what your favorite wine was like. What did it taste like? Get specific. What wine? What year? Where were you? Taste in your mind and your body will follow. You have to do this every day, Otis. And every day, you'll get better. Practice makes perfect.

"Now," she said, "let's go visit your frontal lobe, where you process your smells. Just behind your forehead. Go there. Envision those tiny neurons. Find the ones that don't speak to each other any more, the ones that were damaged. Ignite them. It doesn't matter that they can't smell through your nose and mouth right now. Give them smells through your imagination. Remind them of the experience of processing odorants."

She put a hand on his knee. "Repeat the following to yourself three times: neurons that fire together, wire together. Never forget those words. Let the neurons fire. Give them your favorite smells, your Burgundy or your bacon, if you have to. Whatever is going to get them excited. You have to do this every day. Every single day. And you have to believe with every cell in your body."

They finished by sitting in silence. She ended the session by moving to Otis and hugging him around the neck and kissing his forehead, cheeks and mouth.

He thanked her and said, "How do you possibly know all this?"

"You have your wine. And your animals. And your farm. This is what I do. I believe in the power of love and the power of the human spirit. And I believe that there's no greater conduit for healing than belief. I've seen it in action so many times. I've seen the great sufferers of the world come back to life. We can do anything we put our minds to. It's the most beautiful component of life."

"You are truly the most amazing woman I've ever met."

Joan smiled. "I love you too, Otis Till."

He kissed her again and said, "I need to tell you something about Morgan's will. She left me everything. Not a big surprise. I'm all she had left. But there was a condition. She wrote me a letter asking that I spread her ashes in a few places around the world."

"I *love* this idea. Why haven't you told me?"

He looked at her. "I guess I had other things on my mind."

"Where does she want you to go?"

"Ten places." He told her the details of the letter. "And I have to provide a photo in each spot with a current newspaper."

"You have to do it."

"I think I want to. You know why? Because she said I should bring someone along. She left enough cash for a first rate trip. I was thinking maybe you'd come with me."

35

SHOT TO THE HEART

Brooks, Charles, and Shay were in the driveway playing H.O.R.S.E. The falling sun shot splinters of light through the trees onto the pavement and the backboard. Shay, with his purple headband, was schooling them, dropping three pointers with ease and dribbling to the net like a pro. He said he'd spent a lot of time playing street ball, but Brooks hadn't expected Aunt Jemima to have such grace. Charles's regular squash games back home had kept him in great shape, and he was nimble for a guy his age. He was having no problem throwing up some winners.

Abby pulled into the driveway, and Brooks stepped away from the game to say hello. She returned his kiss, but it wasn't much of an effort. "Can you hop in? I need to tell you something."

He looked at her frown and his heart sank, noticing more and more how he couldn't stand to see her hurting. That's what love was, he was learning. Putting her before himself.

Brooks looked back at Charles and Shay. "Be right back." As she reversed onto Demoss Road, her silence turned uncomfortable and the seriousness of the moment gained intensity. He felt his Jenga tower starting to lean.

She pulled onto the side of the road by the river at Margaritaville

Beach, a name completely at odds with reality. The spot was nothing more than a small parking area with a picnic table and a clearing that led to the Yakima River. A large painted sign read *Margaritaville Beach* with a palm tree for the *i*. The truth was that you couldn't be any farther from a place tropical enough to be deemed as such. A classic touch of eastern Washington rodeo country.

She parked and got out. "Let's go sit down."

They sat at the table and Brooks studied her face. He saw weakness in her exterior like a castle under attack. His fear twisted tighter.

She opened her mouth several times before actually getting words out. She finally shook her head and let it go. "I cheated on you."

Those words hit hard. A tension in his bones seemed to paralyze him.

"It was a while ago. And I probably wasn't going to tell you."

Short shallow breaths. "Why are you?"

"Because you were going to find out anyway."

Who could it be? he wondered. *Jake? Pak? No, it couldn't. They wouldn't do that to him. Shay?*

She said, "With a woman. Not that it matters, I guess."

Another shocker that left Brooks dumbfounded.

"You know her."

Truthfully, the sting of her words subsided when she admitted it was with a woman, but the fact that he knew her brought back the pain and even fear. "Who was it?" He didn't want to ask, didn't even know who to guess, but he had to know.

Abby scratched at the worn wood of the table and her lower jaw and neck tightened. "Carmen."

Brooks crossed his arms and stared, feeling the blocks of his life crashing to the floor—boom, boom, boom.

"It was a drunken thing a little while ago. It happened one time. I was drunk. She was too. And it happened."

"Who found out?"

"Emilia. You know that movie Luca is working on? The Moon People thing? He snuck out that night and happened to catch us on film through a window. He didn't even know what he was recording, but Emilia saw it while editing the movie yesterday."

Brooks immediately felt Emilia's pain. "Where's Emilia?"

"We don't know. She blew up at Carmen and took off. She's not answering her phone."

"Does Jake know?"

"Probably by now."

"Why wouldn't you have told me?"

"I don't know. I'd like to say I was going to. It was eating me up. But what good would it have accomplished? It's not like I love her. It's not like I was going to run away with her. It was just a stupid thing that happened; something that's been building for a long time."

"What are you doing with me if you like women?"

"No, Brooks. I love you. I want to be with you." She looked out to the river and sighed. "I'm just sexual. You know that about me. But this was all before you asked me to marry you. How could I know you really felt this way about me?"

"Um, because I've told you from the beginning how I felt?"

"You think you're the first guy to tell me how much they loved me? How many of those guys were telling the truth? I've been lied to all my life, Brooks. How was I to know you were different?"

"You were going to bury this?"

"You mean by not telling you?"

Brooks lowered his chin.

"What good would have come from telling you? Tell me that. You would end it. We don't get to live our lives together. We both walk away from the love of our life. Just for one stupid mistake. For one drunken night with my boss, before you and I were even serious."

"Your boss? She's my boss too."

"That's another reason I didn't want to say anything. You're doing what you love. You have the job of a lifetime. A dream job. I didn't want to ruin that. Ruin you."

"That's the kind of thing you think about before you fuck her. Or whatever it is you two did. Whatever you call it. Jesus Christ."

Brooks took a deep breath and looked at the river. A pelican floated by. The bird looked out of place, a long way from home. What was a pelican doing in a river in the desert? *What am I doing here? What I am trying to do, pretending to be something I'm not?*

Brooks could imagine what Jake and the kids were feeling. He felt like driving to the Foresters' house and screaming at Carmen. He felt like diving into the river and drifting away.

"So here we are," he said finally. "I had to know Red Mountain was too good to be true. It was too much of a dream." He smiled cynically. "I should have known."

"Brooks, you can look at it that way. Or we can work it out. Let's all sit down and talk about it and find a way to get past it. You can't run from everything."

"I can't? That's what I've been doing my whole life. Finally I decide not to and my whole world comes crashing down." He burst into a nervous, awkward, angry laugh.

She said, "That's not what you want to do. Let's fix this. Let's sit down with Jake and Carmen and figure out a way to get past it. I'm not saying it would be easy but it's doable. It happened a while ago, early in our relationship. C'mon, Brooks. I love you. That's what I've been trying to say. You are everything to me. I want to marry you. I want to spend the rest of my life with you. I want to find life with you. I want to tell you all the things I've never told anyone."

"Yeah, but what do I want? I spent my whole life running from shit. Running from people I can't trust. Running from the law. Running from people trying to take advantage of me. From a system that keeps stomping on me." He looked her right in the eyes, and he saw big targets with bull's-eyes. "You know what I want?"

"What?"

"I want someone I can trust. I want—wanted—to know that I'd found someone in this bitch of a world—other than Otis—who wouldn't abandon me. Leave me on a porch stoop. Now I'm right back on that goddamn porch stoop, left again by the one who is supposed to love me. I'm a fucking idiot."

Abby had started crying but by now her tears wouldn't stop.

Brooks didn't feel bad for her. The Jenga blocks had fallen; now he used them to build a wall around himself. He felt nothing.

He stuck out his hand. "May I have that ring back, please?"

She looked at him with red eyes. "You don't mean that."

"Keep it if you want. Pawn it for all I care. Put it on Carmen's finger." He stood up and started to walk away.

Abby came chasing after him. "Here's the ring. It's your ring. Please, Brooks. Don't let us go this quickly."

"I didn't. You did."

Brooks tossed the ring into the river and it disappeared, leaving a ripple that he knew would start small and swell for days, maybe forever.

36

THE LAWS OF GRAVITY

"How many women do you have joining us tonight?" Joan asked, as they wrapped up their weekly session at Margot's house.

"Nine," Margot said.

"Nine!"

"I know. As long as this nasty weather doesn't discourage them."

"I'm so proud of you. Really. Do you see how much you're changing your world? Do you see what you're creating?"

"Not bad, right?" Margot beamed. She couldn't believe it herself. Word had traveled about the cooking classes, and all of a sudden every woman on Red Mountain wanted to join. Their excitement proved what Margot had thought. Red Mountain was so up and coming that the right people were there, but the elements for getting people together were still desperately needed. That's exactly why her inn was going to work. People needed a place to stay, a place to eat, a place to spend time.

Joan asked, "Should we be worried about Emilia?"

"I don't know. It's not like her. She loves coming over here. Maybe she's just studying and forgot to call." They'd both texted her.

"Yeah, I hope everything's okay."

"Maybe she's coming later." Margot asked, "How's Otis?"

"He's adjusting. It's really scary to be in his shoes right now."

"It puts things into perspective, doesn't it? We have all these worries in life, but then you hear about someone else's troubles that are so much worse."

"Death is the ultimate wake-up call."

The other women arrived shortly after, and Margot led them in making paella—sans meat, of course. It was a full-blown evening of fun. Nancy Corell got too drunk and told the entire class about her yeast infection. Jane Sensky told everyone about her husband's giant member. Louisa Peterson broke into tears and admitted that she and her husband hadn't had sex in seventeen years, but that she had a growing collection of dildos to keep her busy. It was a night to remember: a collection of women who all needed to release some tension, but had only tonight found out how.

They talked about Jake and how they loved to see him running on Red Mountain with his shirt off. They talked clothes and shopping and gossip. The women had needed this outlet for too long. They had moved with anticipation to the excitement of wine country, only to be let down by the fact that Red Mountain was in the middle of nowhere. More and more, Margot realized she'd found her calling on Red Mountain: to bring people together.

Jasper had gone to Seattle for a long weekend to see Chick Corea at Jazz Alley. Though tomorrow was a school day, Margot was letting him skip. His grades were great and he rarely missed a day. He was the kind of kid you could let manage himself. She'd even paid for his hotel in Seattle, encouraging him to explore and have some fun. He needed to get to know the Pacific Northwest more anyway. Perhaps he would even meet a girl.

Margot went upstairs, put on her robe, and poured a nightcap. She sat down in her chair and couldn't stop smiling. Everything was wonderful. "Every day," she said, "in every way, I'm getting better and better." She repeated it again with conviction. Just when she thought she might climb in bed, the doorbell rang. *One of the women must have forgotten her jacket or purse*, she thought.

She opened the door to find Jake Forester standing in the rain, one of the first rains of the fall, with giant drops that were pelting the dusty driveway. Margot immediately felt for the top of her robe, making sure it was closed properly. She crossed her arms to cover her nipples that were poking at the fabric. "I can't believe I answered the door in my robe. Please excuse me."

"Oh, no. It's late. I'm sorry to bother you." He held up a hand, protecting his eyes from the raindrops.

"You're not bothering me. Come in. Please."

He took a step in and stayed on the welcome mat, kicking water off his tennis shoes.

"I'm looking for Emilia. Did she come by tonight?"

Margot could smell liquor on his breath. "No, I haven't seen her. I was worried. She comes over on Sundays for class."

"Yeah, that's what I thought."

"Is everything okay? No offense, but you look awful." He had bags under his eyes, and the beauty she was used to was all but gone.

He put his head down. "Long couple of days."

"You want to sit down? I'm a good listener."

"I don't want to take up your time."

"Do I look busy? C'mon. What are neighbors for? Have a seat. I don't know about you, but I've already had too much to drink tonight. Let's have a pot of tea,"

"That's a really good idea. I've definitely had enough to drink tonight."

Margot put on a copper pot of water and sat down across from him.

"How are your cooking classes going?" he asked. "Emilia seems to love them."

"Growing in numbers."

"Good for you."

"Your daughter is one of my favorite people ever. You guys did such a good job raising her."

He lifted his eyebrows. "I wish I could take all the credit. She came out perfect." He dropped his head. Clearly, his mind was on other things.

"What's wrong, Jake?" she asked.

"It's a long story."

"I have all night. Sometimes it's good to talk it out."

"Why do I feel so comfortable when I'm around you? You really want to hear what's going on?"

"We all need people we can share with. Let it out."

"My poor daughter. She found out yesterday that my wife cheated on me."

"Oh, God." Margot instantly felt for him. She'd been there. "I'm so sorry. Did you know?"

"Carmen told me last night. Emilia found out and we haven't seen her or heard from her since. She's not answering her phone."

"Have you thought about calling the police?"

"We will tomorrow. She never gets into trouble. I'm sure she's just confused. Sad. Furious at her mother."

"Poor girl."

"I know. And you. How are you?"

"Jake, who cares how I am? Your wife cheated on you. It's okay to talk about you for once."

"I don't know what's worse. That my wife cheated on me. That my daughter is the one who found out. Or the person she cheated on me with. It's been a pretty bad 24 hours."

"What can I do? Your daughter means a lot to me. You have been so good to me. Maybe she wants to stay here for a while."

"I'll talk to her. I don't know what we're going to do." His eyes watered and he rubbed them. "You got anything stronger than tea while we wait for the water to boil?"

Margot smiled. "Of course." She came back a couple of minutes later with a bottle of scotch. They clinked glasses.

"Do you know our assistant? My wife's assistant? Abby?"

"Sure. Emilia was going to bring her tonight. I've run into her on the mountain. A really nice girl."

"Yep. She's amazing. So amazing my wife slept with her."

"That's who Carmen cheated on you with?"

Jake slowly nodded his head. "A really nice girl."

"Well, I would say I can't imagine what you're going through, but actually, I know exactly what you're going through."

"I can't wait for a reporter to get hold of this one. The one thing I've learned being in this business... this business of fame... is they always find out. Especially the stuff that you don't want them to."

"Do you think you'll ever be able to forgive her?"

He looked at Margot. He'd clearly been pondering that question for a while.

She said, "That's none of my business, sorry."

"I thought I'd leave her if something like this happened." He polished off his glass. "It destroys the trust. How do I know if she's done it before? How can I really believe her, no matter what comes out of her mouth? The only reason I know about this one is that my daughter made her tell me. I don't know what I'll do."

Margot replenished the scotch. He took a huge gulp, enjoying the burn, and then looked at her. "You left your husband immediately?"

She nodded her head. "I found out about it on the national news. He was the mayor of our town."

"Jasper told me. Burlington?"

"Yep. I was ironing the bastard's shirts and watching the news. Next thing I know I'm looking at a woman with her head in his lap. Yeah, I left him that second. I hated him that second. Love to hate, just like that, like turning a key. But I'm better now. I've moved on. It's taken me almost two years, but I'm getting stronger." Margot couldn't believe she was saying those words. Funny thing, they were actually true.

Jake said, "Carmen is such a handful anyway. Part of me is so used to putting up with her that I'm not surprised. You know, it would be so much worse if it had been a man. I feel like such a sexist or something saying it, but for some reason, I keep thinking about that. I knew she'd had some sexual tendencies toward women before we met. I really didn't mind that. So it doesn't hurt quite as bad as if it was a man."

"I don't think you're being sexist. You're being honest with yourself. I see where you're coming from." Margot walked to his side of the table to refill his glass.

As she poured, he said, "It feels so good to talk to someone who understands." He put a gentle hand on her arm. He didn't need to say a word. She knew what he wanted. She stopped pouring prematurely.

They looked into each other's eyes for a moment. His eyes had gained back some of their color, calling to her, making her feel so beautiful, so worthy, so special. A chill ran through her. She felt moist between her legs. If he wanted this, he was going to get it.

He said, "I'm so attracted to you. I can't think of a reason not to kiss you right now."

Margot was so worked up herself she had no intention of rationalizing. Sometimes, the laws of attraction must be followed. She gave a green light with her whole body, welcoming him into her world. "Me either," she whispered.

His kiss was as full of passion and manhood as she could have ever imagined. She tasted the whisky on his breath, but he brought her down to his chair with absolute control. She sat on his lap, facing him. They were both buzzed but not drunk enough to use that as an excuse. She liked that. This would have happened with or without alcohol. This was two sexual beings looking for satisfaction, something that, at least from Margot's perspective, was premeditated.

He pulled the belt of her robe and it came undone. She had a moment of modesty, an insecurity about her appearance. But he didn't let her sink into her own thoughts for very long. He touched ever so gently yet firmly, dancing in between the savage and the artistic. She pulled his shirt off, exposing his cut abs and tattoos.

She was wet and wanting as he kissed her stomach and breasts, and she stood from his lap and pulled him up to his feet. She pulled down his pants and worked him with her hands and in moments they were on the floor, and he was inside her. They both giggled as the pot of water started to boil, the high pitch of the whistle whining like the freight train they were currently occupying.

They moved from the floor to the couch and, finally, to the bed, an hour of passion that left them both high from the experience.

Margot's mind had been blown; she'd finally met her match in the bedroom. He knew just how fast to go, when to slow down, when to speed up. When to go deeper. He looked equally satisfied. A man who'd probably been with so many women. But tonight only she existed.

Later, they were both in robes on her private patio. He offered her a smoke, and she accepted. They spent another hour talking and smoking. He left her with a kiss. No talk about tomorrow. No worries about what they'd just done. Just two comets colliding in one of those rare moments, an explosion so bright and beautiful that both of them were sure to be forever changed. That's what Margot hoped, at least. She finally closed her eyes that night, wondering what Frances would have said.

～

WHEN MARGOT WOKE the next morning, her first thoughts were of Emilia. Now, both her parents had cheated. And it was Margot's fault. She could have said no. She *should* have said no.

Despite the wonderful evening she'd had with Jake, it wasn't worth it. Emilia was like her daughter and her friend at the same time.

Margot rolled over and noticed Philippe staring at her from the floor. "What?" she asked. "Don't judge me. You would have done the same thing." She buried her head in the pillow.

37

REGRET IS A DANGEROUS BEDFELLOW

E milia woke up next to Joe Massey. They were covered by an awful 1970s brown and orange bedspread that had provided fodder for a litany of jokes the night before. Joe slept on his back with a mummified smile on his face.

They were at the Best Western right off the highway in Prosser, about twenty miles west of Red Mountain and forty miles from Belmont High School. Far enough to stay away from prying eyes. Prosser was an old western town reinvigorated by the world-class grapes grown near there, and the hotel shared a highway exit with a host of wineries strategically positioned to take advantage of the traffic.

Emilia sat up, her eyes on her teacher. She leaned over and kissed his dry lips. Joe opened his eyes to a squint and reached for his glasses on the bedside table.

"Good morning," she said, helping him adjust his glasses on his nose and pushing his hair back on his forehead. She kissed him again. This time, he kissed her back. She could smell his stale morning breath and it didn't bother her at all. In fact, she kind of liked it; she liked the manliness of it.

She'd stopped short of having sex; she wasn't ready. He'd been respectful and backed off, and they'd spent most of the night holding each other. He was so different from Tex. Joe Massey knew how to treat a woman.

He ran his fingers through her hair. "I'm getting used to this new look. You're beautiful in the morning. How'd you sleep?"

"It's not the Ritz, but I slept okay."

"Yeah, teachers and Ritz-Carltons are like rock stars and Best Westerns. Know what I mean?"

Emilia smiled. "Can I ask you something?" she said. "Why did you end things after we kissed? We hadn't even gotten started."

He stroked her hair. "Because this isn't easy for me. I'm married. Tara and I go through our rough patches, but we still made a commitment to each other. I was trying to abide by that."

"And now?" Emilia suddenly felt used again. Something about hearing his wife's name. *Tara.* What was Emilia doing in bed with this guy? It wasn't right; it wasn't going to last. No, she wasn't the married one, but Emilia realized that she had a responsibility too. Why was she getting in the way of a couple's marriage? Why would she want to have a hand in hurting another woman?

"I couldn't stop thinking about you." He touched her under the covers.

"Will you stay with her?"

"Of course I'm going to stay with her. She's my wife."

Emilia nodded, finally seeing how stupid she'd been. He attempted to kiss her but she sat up, avoiding his approach. "I'm hungry," she said, thinking how she'd never make this mistake again.

~

HER CLASSMATES WERE STARING at Emilia when she pulled into the parking lot. As she parked, she looked at a photo Sadie had texted her. Emilia immediately felt sick. It was a picture of Emilia and Joe coming out of their motel room earlier that morning. After the picture, the text read: *You may not want to go to school today. Like thirty people have already sent this to me. Call me!!! WTF??*

Emilia drove back out of the parking lot, careful not to make eye contact with anyone. Her life was over. Just like that. She could barely hold herself together enough to drive. Her hands shook and her cry was loud and wet and devastating. "Oh, my god," she moaned. "Oh, my god. Please don't let this be happening."

She needed someone to talk to, desperately. But she had no one. She didn't want to call Sadie. Definitely not her mom. Her dad was already destroyed inside. She had nowhere to go. She thought of Joan and Margot.

She called Margot, who said, "We've been trying to find you. Are you okay?"

"I'm not good."

"I'm sure you're not. I heard."

"You heard?"

"About your mom. Yeah. Your dad was looking for you last night."

Emilia had been ignoring everyone's calls, even her dad's, which she knew wasn't right. What had he done to hurt her? "You don't understand." Emilia could hear herself stuttering. "My life's over."

"Where are you?" Margot asked. "Why don't you come over?"

"Will you call Joan too?" Emilia needed them both.

"We'll be waiting for you. It's going to be okay."

"You don't understand. No, it's not."

Emilia hung up the phone and couldn't stop crying. She screamed at the top of her lungs, scaring herself with her own ferocity.

She answered a call from Joe, knowing they needed to talk. "You saw the pic? I was just asked to leave the property," he said.

His words drove the reality of their predicament home, and she felt an incredible sense of worry. "I don't know what to do."

"It's my fault," he said. "It's going to get really ugly for both of us, but it's my fault. You need to know that. I am older than you and I started this thing. Please know this wasn't your fault."

"What's going to happen?"

"I don't know." His fear was audible. "We need to have our story straight. We need to decide what our story is right now and stick to it forever."

"Okay," she said, hoping he could fix all this, desperate to hear his plan.

"We're friends, that's all we have to say. We got to know each other through class and decided to meet at the hotel last night just to talk. We never kissed."

Emilia nodded silently, knowing how much of a lie that would be.

"Emilia? Are we on the same page?"

"Yes. We never kissed."

"Look, I'm so sorry. Go find your dad now."

"How about you?" she asked, turning right onto the highway toward Red Mountain.

"Don't worry about me. I deserve what's coming."

"Why aren't you worried, Joe?"

It took him a while to answer. "I am."

"What are you going to do?"

"I don't know. Don't worry. I'll survive. Just don't let this get to you. All I ask, Emilia, is don't let this knock you down. You're a shooting star."

Emilia cried again. He'd been so kind to her. "What's going to happen?"

"I don't know. I just don't know."

～

EMILIA FOUND Margot and Joan in the kitchen at Margot's house. The three of them embraced. Margot handed Emilia a glass of water, and they sat down around the dining room table, the same table where Margot and Jake had exchanged their first touches. Margot moved a vase of lilies out of the way.

Emilia wiped her eyes. "Something else has happened."

"What?" Joan said, touching her back.

Emilia told them about Joe Massey and the photograph.

"You need to tell your parents," Joan said. "I'm sure you already know, but this could be bad, my dear. He could go to prison. The media may get involved."

"Of course the media will get involved." Emilia said. "They always do; I spend my life under a microscope." She rubbed her red eyes. "I'm not talking to my mom. I'll tell my dad. My mom can go jump off a cliff as far as I am concerned."

The women discussed what could and probably would happen to Joe Massey, and both Margot and Joan gave their best advice, both encouraging her to tell her father immediately. Emilia didn't want to, but she knew he'd find out soon. There was no way around it.

Emilia just wanted to run. To leave Red Mountain. To leave Washington. To escape. She'd never be able to get past this day. Even as Margot and Joan hugged her and tried so desperately to comfort her, they couldn't hide their fear of what could happen to her. Their deep sympathy only reinforced her fear that what was to come would be very bad.

Jasper came in the door and set his backpack down on the floor. Margot said, "Aren't you supposed to be in school?"

"Yeah, but I wanted to check on Emilia." He approached her. "I'm so sorry."

Emilia couldn't smile. "Thanks."

He approached her and she twisted toward him in her chair and they hugged. "You want to take a walk?" he asked.

"She needs to call her dad," Margot said.

"No," Emilia said. "I'd like to take a walk. I'll go see him soon. Promise. I could use a walk."

Jasper took her hand and they strode out the front door. Cutting through a vineyard, they made their way through a maze of vines, hidden from the horrors of the outside world. He didn't let go of her hand, and it was a gesture of such great power that Emilia felt a sense of calm come over her.

"Do you want to talk about it?" he said.

"I don't know." Emilia sighed and bit her lip. "Does everyone know?"

"Yep. I'd say so. Mr. Massey is gone. I think the teachers know too. He's going to get in some trouble. How long's this been going on?"

"Not long."

Jasper nodded his head. "You know I'm your friend, right?"

Emilia smiled. "Jasper, you're maybe my only real friend. We don't even know each other that well, but I like you so much. I feel connected to you." This realization only came to her as the words were coming out of her mouth. He was such a good guy, a great friend. Other than Joe, he was the only one who could see the real Emilia. And not only could he see her, he was okay with it.

"Then know that I'm here for you," Jasper said. "If I can do anything, tell me. Okay? Everything is going to be all right. We both want to think we're adults, but we're not. We're just dumb kids with a lot to learn. You made a mistake. We all do. Look at my dad. He got caught on national television getting a blow job from his secretary."

"You probably haven't even heard yet," she said, "but I found out yesterday that my mom was cheating on my dad with Abby."

"What? Your mom and Abby?"

"I know."

He let that sink in. "Jake knows?"

She nodded and she could tell by his silence and the way that he looked down at the dirt that Jasper felt bad for her dad. He finally said, "See? How are we supposed to be more grown up than our parents? Everybody makes mistakes," he said.

"Is this when you tell me that it's what you do after the mistake that defines you?"

Jasper grinned. "No, I wasn't going to say that, but it does seem like a good bit of wisdom. I'm not a girl, but Mr. Massey is kind of good-looking. I don't think you did that much wrong. What's the worst thing you did? Hook up with an older guy? He's not even that old. What is he? Twenty-eight?"

"Twenty-six."

"That's nothing. So you cheated on Tex? Is that the worst? If you were seeing Massey while you were with Tex, that makes me happy. Tex is a chump. He doesn't deserve to breathe the same air as you."

"He is kind of a chump, isn't he? I'm sure he's found out by now. Wonder what's going through his mind."

"I don't think anything goes through his mind except how to pull up a jock strap and how to catch a ball. It's pretty empty up there."

She smiled. "Well, I wasn't doing anything with Mr. Massey. We were just friends."

Jasper nodded and she didn't pick up any skepticism in his face. "Seriously, Emilia. This isn't the end of the world. You're still the best thing that ever came to this place. You're smart. You're interesting. And you're deep. You have this desire, this craving for life that everybody wants to be a part of."

How much of that part of me is even real? she wondered. *Maybe he doesn't know the real me.*

He put his hand in the air and continued. "But with all that comes a lot of heaviness. I know that. Everyone expects so much of you. You're Jake and Carmen Forester's daughter. You're supposed to be perfect. You're supposed to change the world, like your parents did. Everyone expects you to leave this great big mark on the world."

"Maybe I don't want to leave a great mark," she said.

"I don't think you have to. No, that's not what I mean. I think you, just by being you, are leaving a great mark on the world. You don't have to go out and do something, play in a band or make a magazine cover. Just Emilia, the Emilia I know. You're already leaving a great mark on this world. My life is better with you in it. That's worth something."

She turned and gave him a hug. "I love you, Jasper Simpson. You're the most wonderful man. You deserve so much. You're so good to me."

"I mean every word."

Maybe he did understand her after all.

38

RED MOUNTAIN, THE TINY ISLAND

B rooks walked into Jake's house, recognizing the look his boss had when he was hung over: the drowsy eyes, the sweatpants, the moccasins, that "average human" thing that he rarely showed. Brooks leaned over and massaged Pepper and Wilson for a moment.

"What a mess," Jake said.

Brooks stood tall again. They faced each other in the foyer. Pepper and Wilson took the hint and backed away, both plopping down on the hardwood floor. Brooks said, "How's Emilia doing?"

"She won't talk to me."

"And Luca?"

"He has no idea what's going on. He's the one who saw them together, but he doesn't understand it. He keeps asking where his sister is and keeps talking about how he has to finish this video. Jake rubbed his forehead and eyes. "I told Carmen to stay in Seattle for a couple of days. What are you going to do?"

"To be honest, part of me wants to run as far as I can away from here. How the hell can we all live on this mountain together? How messed up can one group of people be? How can a place so beautiful with such epic wines breed such bad things?"

"This stuff goes on everywhere, man. Red Mountain is just smaller than most places, so word travels easier. And I think something about the people here... we don't feel like hiding any more. Sometimes to a fault, we do and say what we please and really no longer care what others think. That's why we're here. We're just an island in a hurricane right now. It will pass. Storms move along. The blue skies will return."

Jake usually did have a different way to look at things. He was able to navigate to the bright side. "You could be cool not firing Abby and letting everything get back to normal?"

"I'm not pissed at Abby," Jake said. "Not at all, really. Shit, she's so good with the kids. She's great at her job. She's a great person. I need her. I don't want to fire her. She's back in Vegas for a bit, until the storm blows over, but I can't live without her. My wife's the one who caused it to go down. You and I both know that."

Brooks shook his head. "This mountain."

"Will you marry her?" Jake asked.

"I threw the ring in the water. How can I still work for you? How can I work for Carmen after all this? How can Abby and I be on the same mountain?"

"You're not going anywhere. You can't even think about leaving me, man. We're in this together. Lacoda is as much your winery as it is mine. You know that. Red Mountain is nothing without you."

"Red Mountain is just a place."

"It's more than a place. Don't give me that. So what? My wife slept with your fiancée. Weirder things have happened." Jake waved his hand in the air. "This mountain... all of us... sure, we all have our personal drama. At least we know what we're getting with the people here. You know where you stand. We have to stick together. I've never been more connected to a place, and half of that is because of all the people. They might stab you in the back, but they'll love you more than you've ever been loved."

Jake punched his fist into his opposite palm. "What's stopping us from letting this one go? Two beautiful women slept together. So what? I have to repair some trust issues. You do too. And I have to figure out my daughter. But I can promise you this. No matter where you go, no matter where I go, something won't be right. At some point in your life you have to decide to throw the anchor and accept that your home isn't perfect, but it's home. And your friends and lovers aren't perfect either, but they're what you've got, and you damn well better love them. I've been in a band for more than thirty years. We love each other but we hate each other too. We've done things to each other that are unforgivable. But if I left them and found another band, the same thing would happen. There would be times we'd want to kill each other. We're humans. No one is ever going to be perfect."

Brooks knew Jake was making sense but there was still the issue of deceit. Abby had covered up something. Not every human was a liar. She'd intentionally decided not to tell him. It was the lie, more than the act of getting naked with Carmen, that bugged him. Where does one lie start and another end? When will the next one be? When will the next time be? "I've got to do some thinking," he finally said.

"Brooks Baker, you're not leaving your job. You leave, I'm leaving. Lacoda goes up for sale. I can't do it without you. You and Abby have to work it out."

"You can find another winemaker in ten minutes."

"I can't find another you. I'm telling you the truth. You quit and I'll sell this winery and this house. I'm living in a dream, and that dream takes place on Red Mountain. And you're part of it. A big part." Jake took several big breaths and knelt down to rub Pepper's back. "How are your dad and your brother? You can't let them go."

"I'm sure all of my other relationships are destined for failure too."

Still running his hand along his dog's back, Jake stared at Brooks. "C'mon. Not everything is destined for failure. This mountain brought you your family. How can you walk away from that?"

"We'll see how long it lasts." Brooks smiled, the kind of smile that lacked happiness. "You're a hell of a salesman, you know that?"

"What is it you think I do on stage?"

"Fair enough."

"But I'm not trying to sell you on something I don't believe in. That's not who I am."

"I know that. I have to figure out how much of this dream we have in common. I can't be here for your dream, as much as I like you. This has to be for me."

Jake nodded. "You're right."

Jasper and Emilia showed up at the door; Jake let them in. "What are you doing home? I thought you were going back to school today."

"Something bad has happened," she said.

"What, baby?"

Emilia started crying and Jake pulled her in and squeezed her tight. Brooks thought it best to take off, and Jasper followed.

39

THE POLICE STATION

Jake sat Emilia down on the stool at the counter in the kitchen. "Daddy," she said, resting her feet on the rung. "I'm scared to tell you. You're going to lose your temper."

"It's okay. You can tell me." It was times like these that her dad was such a great father.

She didn't want to break his heart but she had to tell him. "I was hanging out with my teacher last night. And it had nothing to do with school."

"What do you mean?"

"His name's Mr. Massey. Joe Massey." Emilia watched him try to tame the rage building inside of him, verifying that it was best for everyone if she didn't tell the whole truth. So she told a lie that she'd only get away with if she believed it herself. "Don't worry. We didn't do anything. It wasn't like that. We're friends. He's young, anyway. He's only twenty-six."

"You're *friends* with a male teacher?"

"I'm serious. Just friends."

"What's going on, Em?"

"We stayed at the Best Western in Prosser last night. I was so upset, and I felt like he was the only one who could understand.

Someone saw us leaving this morning and took pictures. Now the entire school knows. Joe was just sent home by the principal. I'm sure the cops have been called." Emilia felt the tension leave her body as each word left her mouth, and she suddenly felt like collapsing. She brought her hands to her face, breaking into yet another cry. It was amazing she still had tears.

Her dad surprised her. Without a trace of anger, he moved to her and wrapped his arms around her. "We're going to figure this out, honey. We're going to figure this out."

She believed him; it was going to be okay. He held her for a while. She felt safe and wanted him to keep holding her forever. But she knew he was thinking about what steps he was going to take.

"Dad?" she said.

"Yeah?"

"He's a good guy. I don't want this to ruin his life."

Jake didn't say anything. After another minute, he let go of her. "I need to make a few phone calls. Figure out exactly how to handle it." He touched her cheek. "It's going to be all right. Trust me. Why don't you watch some TV for a few minutes? I'll be back."

She went into the living room, but didn't watch TV. Instead, she tugged the folded quilt from the back of the couch and wrapped herself in it, curling up, finding comfort in disappearing.

Her father returned twenty minutes later. She was still curled up, engulfed in a black hole of emptiness. "We've got to go down to the police station."

She poked her head up in alarm. "You called the police?"

"No, they called me. They were with your principal at school. It's okay. They have to get involved. You're not in trouble."

"But he is?"

"He could be. You have to understand, sweetheart. It's illegal for a teacher to have a relationship outside of class with a student. It doesn't matter how old he is. And no matter what you or anyone else tells me, the fact that you were photographed outside of a motel room is a real problem. I don't know if you and this guy have worked out some story, but if they can prove that you two even kissed, he's going to jail. Either way, even if you are just friends, he's losing his job. It has nothing to do with you. It was his responsibility not to let it happen. Did you sleep with him?"

"No, Daddy."

"Did he touch you?"

"No."

"Emilia, you tell me right now if he touched you."

"He didn't."

"Look. Maybe you feel like you're protecting him by lying. Or maybe you're telling the truth. I've been around long enough to know that I can't exactly believe you right now. No grown man goes to a hotel with a woman of any age and doesn't get something out of it. Or at least try to. So I'll tell you this: don't cover for him. We're going down to the police station for an interview. You need to tell the truth. If you lie to protect him, it might happen again with someone else. I need you to tell the truth."

The idea of having to walk into the police station terrified Emilia. "I don't want to go."

"You have to. If we don't go there right now, it will turn into a bigger deal. They'll drag you out of here with a subpoena. I don't know; they might even force you to be tested for rape. I've talked to our lawyer. We need to go downtown right now. You're in a mess and I'm going to help you clean it up, but you have to listen to me. Let's get in the car."

They drove for a while in silence, making their way from their home in the middle of nowhere into civilization. On the highway, she asked, "Are you pissed?"

"I'm pissed at this guy, yes."

"He didn't do anything wrong."

"He did. You might not be able to understand it, but he did."

"He's a great guy. He was there for me when no one else was."

"That's how these people do it. That's how they take advantage of you."

"He didn't take advantage of me. I told you that."

"I'm going to ask you again. Did he touch you?"

"No."

Her dad nodded. She didn't think he believed her, but she wasn't about to change her story. She'd promised Joe. They reached the police station and parked close to the front. Jake escorted her in with his arm around her. She watched her feet, ashamed of the circumstances, knowing people recognized her father, knowing they loved these kinds of stories. She and her father checked in at a window.

Eventually, a detective led them into the interview room. Gino Corelli, an overweight Italian, had a strong New York accent and his breath reeked of cigarettes.

"You guys sit here. I'm going to make sure the recording gear is on, and we'll get started."

He returned several minutes later and sat on the opposite side of the table. Tiny beads of sweat collected on his forehead. "This interview is being recorded. That okay with you? I need a verbal response."

"Yes," she said.

He asked her to state her name and date of birth. Then, "Can you tell me what you did last night?"

"I met Mr. Massey in Prosser."

"You spent the night with him?"

"We stayed in a motel together."

"What motel?"

"The Best Western."

Corelli nodded like a Bobblehead, his entire jiggly body getting into it. "How long have you been seeing him?"

"I haven't been seeing him."

He nodded again, knowing damn well she was beginning to tell him lies. "Ms. Forester, you should know that we will be pursuing a case against Joe Massey. We will subpoena phone records. We will see every text that's been sent. We will find security cameras, we will find witnesses. Whatever it takes to get to the truth. So the more you tell us now, the easier it will be on everyone. Including you and Massey. Do you understand?"

"Yes, sir."

He took out a handkerchief from his back pocket and dabbed his brow. "Now, how long have you had a relationship with him outside of class?"

"Just the one time last night. He was helping me get through some things."

"Did you have sexual intercourse with Joe Massey?"

"No."

Detective Corelli didn't say anything for a while, almost like he was waiting for her to correct herself. "Have the two of you had sexual contact? In the state of Washington, and in this case, that would include kissing."

"No." Emilia realized as Corelli spoke that Joe Massey had done his homework. That's why he'd said not to mention kissing earlier. It creeped her out, like he wasn't as innocent as he let on.

"Not even a peck on the cheek?" the Italian man said with a strong confidence in his interrogation abilities.

"No."

Corelli looked at her dad for a moment and back to her. "You sure?"

"Yes, I'm sure. I was there. We're just friends."

He hammered her with more questions, asking how their friendship had begun. He wanted specifics.

As she was talking about the details of their dinner the night before—the pepperoni pizza, and the Caesar salad they'd shared with one fork because the restaurant had forgotten to provide two—another police officer entered and asked to speak to Corelli. Both men left the room.

When Corelli returned, he took his time sitting down. "Do you know Tex Gentry?"

"Yes, he's my ex-boyfriend." Emilia wondered what Tex had to do with anything.

Corelli bounced his eyes back and forth between Emilia and her dad. "I sent two officers to pick up Joe Massey for questioning. Tex Gentry was there."

"What?" Emilia said.

"There was an altercation in the house. Joe Massey's been hurt pretty badly."

"What? Where is he?"

"The hospital. And Tex is here at the station getting booked."

The rest of the interview was a complete blur. As her dad led her back to the parking lot, she realized today would be a defining day in her life. Today, she had been introduced to the evil of this world. The innocence of childhood, the beauty of the kind world, no longer existed. In its place came reality, the bleak, desolate, dangerous and selfish real world, her rite of passage come and gone.

For the rest of her life, Emilia would try to reconnect with the inner child that left her that day.

40
OTIS AND THE ANGRY NEIGHBOR

Otis opened his eyes and rolled over to see his queen lying next to him. They were at Joan's house, where he'd spent many nights lately. They'd spent nearly every minute together for a week straight, and he was on top of the world. He felt like a new man.

As he looked at Joan sleeping, her beauty, her light, he thought of how lucky he was to be next to her, to have the great honor of sharing a bed with her, to be the man with the pleasure of waking up next to her. To watch her sleeping might be one of the most beautiful sights he'd ever seen.

She smiled before she opened her eyes. "Are you watching me?"

"Guilty."

She opened her eyes and he saw what he saw every morning. She looked refreshed, ready to seize the day. "I slept so well."

He found her hand under the sheets. "I have this great need to tell you how I feel. Right now."

"Right now?"

"Yes. I'm obsessed with you, Joan. I love you. I love you and I never want to lose you. This feeling I have inside is so real, so genuine. So... so... true. I don't know what brought us together, but I know that I've lived my life and walked my path to reach this moment right now. You're changing me. You're waking me up."

"All right, that's enough. You're very sweet, Otis. But I'm not changing you. You're changing yourself."

"I mean it. Now don't think you're going to hear this from me all the time. You're not. So soak it up!"

"Oh, I know," she said. "You're going to have to go back to being Otis the Tough."

"That's exactly right. So soak this in and know that I mean it. I never thought I'd feel this way again." He thought for a moment. "But it's not the same way I felt about Rebecca. It's not better or worse, it's just new and different. It's a feeling just for us, something no one else could ever know. I love you, Joan Tobey, with all I have. You're my dream come true."

Joan turned on her side and faced him. "I love you too."

"I think you must be crazy."

"Despite all your faults, the ones we don't have time to count right now, you're something special." She smiled. "The things that you don't like about you are what I love best. I love your grumpy moods. I love your smelly feet."

"Smelly feet? That's the smell of a real man."

"I love how you can't sit still for a minute. I love how you're always trying to clean. I love your road rage."

"Now I understand you. You're slightly deranged. You love things that no one else loves. I'm surprised this house isn't covered in pound puppies."

"You're my little mutt." She kissed him on the cheek and ran her fingers down his belly and below. She took hold of him. "Did someone take a pill this morning?"

"No, I didn't."

She smiled. "Then let's not waste this wonderful moment."

~

ON HIS WAY HOME, Otis caught himself whistling a Sidney Bichet tune. He couldn't remember being so carefree in his entire life. Maybe since that bus to Woodstock so many years ago when he met Rebecca. What a strange feeling to be in his sixties and feel so free. He shook his head in disbelief. He was in love. It had been a long time since he'd felt that wondrous feeling.

Whatever was going on, he wanted more of it. To feel young at sixty-four was something he never thought he'd know.

For exactly ten days (damn right he knew how many days), he'd been eating healthy and practicing what Joan had taught him, the whole meditation and visualization thing, the healthy lifestyle. No, nothing had happened, no big miracles, but he was still being diligent. He hadn't lit up his pipe and he hadn't touched red meat, save a beef jerky breakdown two days earlier. He was indeed working his ass off.

Pulling onto the gravel drive leading home, he passed his neighbor, Henry Davidson, walking around in the back yard calling for his Australian Shepherd. "Cody! Cody!" For the first time in a while, Otis didn't see Cody chained to that pole. Maybe the poor thing had finally got away.

Otis pulled into his own driveway and stepped out of his truck. The dog came out of nowhere and ran up to him, jumping on his leg.

"Down, buddy. Down." Otis knelt and petted him and rubbed his muzzle. "What're you doing over here?"

The dog barked.

"I can only imagine. How'd you end up with such a shithead owner, huh? Luck of the draw?" Otis stroked the dog's head. "I wish I could take you inside, my friend. I really do. But this day and age, you get shot for stealing dogs. Your owner isn't the nicest guy in the world."

"Cody!" came a voice from far off. "Get your ass over here, Cody!"

"Speaking of," Otis said. "I think he found you."

Henry came stomping toward them. Otis said, "Looks like he's getting tired of being chained up."

"He's begging to be whipped." The dog moved away from his owner, hiding behind Otis.

Otis was reminded of how big Davidson was as he came for his dog. Otis didn't care, though. "No dog in this world deserves to be whipped."

"Cody! You get your ass to me right now!"

The dog didn't obey.

"Cody!" Henry dashed after the dog. "You sit, you fucking bastard. I will beat the shit out of you if you don't sit your ass down."

"Now, c'mon," Otis said, speaking with more authority. "Don't speak to a dog like that. Didn't you learn anything about animals growing up?"

"It's none of your business what I do with my dog."

"On my property, it is all my business, son. You don't treat an animal that way."

Henry darted toward the dog, moving past Otis. The dog capitulated in fear and rolled onto his back, closing his eyes, knowing he was about to be hit.

Henry grabbed Cody's collar and reared back and slapped the dog hard on the muzzle; Cody yelped. The bastard reared back and hit Cody again.

Otis stopped him from swinging a third time. Otis threw his arm around the guy's neck and jerked him up to his feet, cutting off his oxygen. "I told you that's not how you treat an animal."

Henry made an attempt to twist out of Otis's lock, but he held strong. "Calm down," Otis said. "I'm not looking for a fight, but we're not going to have this kind of behavior here. Not for another damn minute. Now I'm going to let go. You go walk on home. The dog can stay with me until you calm down. Can I let you go?"

When Otis finally let him go, Henry quickly swung that thick right arm at Otis's face. He missed but ran at Otis and knocked him to the ground. Otis hit his back hard and felt a searing pain shoot up his spine—from the same spot he had damaged lifting the barrel. Otis rolled the man over and punched him in the face, knocking him dizzy.

Henry swung back and Otis deflected it. Otis elbowed him and punched him in the stomach, knocking his breath away. Otis punched him again and again, in the stomach and the face. It went back and forth for a while and Otis took a few good hits. They were both covered in blood and bruises, but in the end, Otis was the only one who could get up.

Ignoring the spasms in his back, Otis lifted Henry into the bed of the truck and drove him back to his own property. Limping, Otis pulled him out by the leg, and he fell to the ground, stirring dazedly, confusion turning to anger.

"You son of a bitch," he breathed.

Otis pointed a finger at him. "That dog of yours belongs to me now. I suggest you stay off my property and out of my life. You don't deserve a dog. You keep it up and I'll chain you to that pole, you son of a bitch."

41

STUCK IN THE MIDDLE OF YOU

Once again, Emilia found herself spending her days in bed, skipping meals and skipping school. An agonizing week went by. The principal was being lenient, and her teachers were helping her stay caught up via email, but too many more days and she'd be in danger of not graduating.

As expected, news of her relationship with Joe Massey had hit the papers hard, and all sorts of rumors that began in her small-town high school had spread across the country and the world—anywhere her parents' fans could be found. Thankfully, because of her age, her name had not seen print, so only the rumors existed.

She didn't have to talk to Detective Corelli to keep up with the latest Joe Massey news. The *Tri-City Herald* and *The Seattle Times* didn't stop reporting on him. Because there was no proof of sexual contact, Joe was not arrested. But he'd been fired from his job and would have a hard time ever finding work as a teacher again.

Joe hadn't made any comments to the media and was doing his best to stay out of the public eye. They'd shown a few pictures of him coming and going from his house, but that's it. Emilia assumed his wife had left him. Joe would certainly suffer the rest of his life for what he and Emilia had done.

She knew she had to go back to school, but she wasn't ready. She didn't want to see Tex or Sadie. She didn't want all the attention, all the stares, the laughing, the talking behind her back. But she'd go back. She wanted to graduate.

Her dad checked in on her from time to time, but she kept asking him for space. She felt so bad for him, but she couldn't help snapping at him. So he spent his days in his studio, playing music with the drummer and bassist he'd brought over from Seattle. Jasper would come over after school, and they'd play into the night, prepping for the new album. If all went well, they were going to start recording the next week.

She hadn't returned Jasper's texts, so he hadn't bothered coming up to talk to her. She felt too much shame to look anyone in the eyes.

But she had spent hours in the hallway entrance of the studio—the same place where she'd heard Jasper play for the first time—listening to their practices. She loved the music, and most of all, she loved what Jasper was doing with his voice and piano. Once again, she was finding comfort in his talents while she suffered so deeply inside.

All this pain on top of the true catalyst of her grief: the fact that her mom had had an affair with Abby, one of her favorite people on earth. It was wrong for so many reasons. Abby had practically raised her. Abby was her good friend. She had gotten the sense that Abby liked women as well as men (she'd heard Abby comment from time to time on a sexy or hot woman), but she didn't know that about her mom. The worst of it all was what both of them had done to her dad. Other than Emilia, they were the two most important, most trusted women in his life. They'd totally stabbed him in the back.

She hadn't spoken to either one since the day she'd seen Luca's video. Her mom was at their condo in Seattle, exiled until they could all figure out the next course of action. She didn't know if her dad had talked to her or not. Abby had gone back to Las Vegas.

Wednesday morning, Margot and Joan came by and left a care package. Her dad delivered the wicker basket to Emilia's door. There was a very sweet note that they both signed, a copy of *Under the*

Tuscan Sun, a CD of guided meditations, some bath salts (which made Emilia smile because Margot had brought Joan and Emilia to tears telling them about how she frequently 'murdered' her ex while in the bathtub), some chamomile tea from Oregon, and a beautiful singing bowl. It felt good to know she had friends who were thinking about her.

Emilia spent the morning watching *Under the Tuscan Sun.* She couldn't remember laughing and crying so much in her life. She knew exactly what Frances was going through.

With disturbingly perfect timing, as the credits rolled, her mom knocked on the door. She must have just returned from Seattle. "Em, could I come in?"

Emilia had a sudden flood of anger, wanting to start screaming obscenities and throwing things. That feeling was quickly replaced by sadness, a desperate need to hug and cuddle with her mother. But her mom was the center of the problem. How could Emilia be blamed for spending time with Joe Massey, an older teacher, if her mom was breaking the law by cheating on her husband with her assistant and nanny? These opposing feelings tore at her as her mom kept calling her name from the other side of the door. *I hate you, but I need you,* she thought. *I am so angry with you, but I love you.*

"I'd really like a chance to speak with you," Carmen was saying.

Emilia knew she'd have to give in eventually. What was she going to do, never speak to her mom again? She slipped out of bed, pulled on some sweatpants and a sweatshirt, and went to the door.

She twisted the lock and pulled the knob toward her. Carmen and Abby were standing next to each other, both looking at Emilia with sad, pleading eyes.

"You've got to be kidding me."

"Can we talk?" Carmen asked. Her mom wasn't wearing makeup, and looked like she still had on what she'd worn the day before. She was clearly a woman torn apart by the past week of pain.

"If you tell me you two are getting married and you're leaving Dad, I'll never talk to you again." Emilia offered a venomous smile. "You still want to talk?"

"I'm not leaving your father. Can we come in?"

Emilia got back under the covers. Carmen and Abby sat on the beige rug, cross-legged, looking up at her.

Carmen was the first to speak. "We've just talked with your dad for a while. We wanted to talk to him before talking to you."

"Please stop saying 'we' like you're some kind of couple."

"I don't mean to say it that way, darling."

"And definitely don't call me darling."

"Sorry." Carmen collected herself. "I'm sorry. That's the most important thing I want to say. I'm sorry. You and your father and Luca mean everything to me, and what I did was awful."

"And I'm sorry too, Em," Abby said, finally chiming in. She didn't look much better than Carmen.

So many questions hovered in the room that no one knew where to start. Emilia didn't want to speak, but at the same time, there was so much she wanted to know. What was going to happen? How long had they been having this egregious affair? Where was Abby going to go?

Emilia didn't look at Abby but asked her, "How's Brooks?"

"We haven't spoken since I told him. He's furious."

"So you're calling off the wedding?"

"I don't know."

Emilia looked at Abby and her mom. "Is this over or is it just beginning?"

"It's over. It was a one-time thing. It was my fault. I was drunk."

"Surprise there," Emilia said.

"I know," Carmen said. "There's nothing like losing your family to finally wake you up to the fact that you're drinking too much. But I'm going to change. I'm going to be the mom you used to know. I'm going to get help. Your dad and I are going to try to make it work."

"Dad forgave you? Shocker." Emilia wasn't surprised. Her mom had been walking all over her dad for years. He had too much love and forgiveness in his heart, probably his greatest fault.

"And how about you?" Emilia asked Abby.

Abby took a breath and kicked her legs out to her side. "Your parents want me to stay, but of course it's not that easy. There's a lot to figure out. The most important is what you want. If you'd like me to stay. And I have to figure out what's going on with Brooks. How could we continue to all live here and work together? I don't know what will become of us yet. If he never speaks to me again, how could I still work for your family?"

Shouldn't you have thought of that before? she wanted to say. Brooks was a great guy and he was in love. She knew Abby was too. Emilia felt sorry for Brooks. She wished everything could just go back to the way it was. But could it? She'd never trust Abby or her mom again. Neither could her dad.

Carmen stood and sat on the bed. "Can we talk about you?"

"What about me?"

"You and Joe Massey. I've called you a hundred times a day, and I wanted to come home, but I knew you needed some space. Your father said you needed some space. But I'm home now and I want to help you. I can't imagine what you're going through."

"The thing is...you're not really a mom, so I don't need you. As usual, Dad was there for me."

The words cut Carmen deeply. She hunched over, aging years in seconds. Emilia instantly regretted what she'd said, but she wasn't about to apologize. If her dad wasn't going to punish Carmen, then Emilia was.

Her face wet with tears, Carmen put her hand on Emilia's leg over the sheets. "I'm going to change. I swear to you, I'm going to change. It's going to get so much better."

"How is that, Mom? You're going to sober up and stop obsessing over your degenerating body. You're going to stop cheating on your husband? That still won't fix my life. I'm screwed either way. You might as well keep being the way you are. I'm still unhappy. This whole time we've talked about you, not a mention of how destroyed I am. How my life will never be the same, because every person I know knows that I hooked up with my teacher."

"I wanted to be here for you," Carmen said. "I've called and called. You didn't want me to come home. Your dad wouldn't let me. Abby and I both were worried to death."

"As you should be. My life's over. I don't know where I want to go to school. I don't have friends any more. My whole life is a lie. And it doesn't help that because of you and Dad and your fame, the whole world analyzes every move I make. I just want to be left alone. I'm not great. Nothing about me is great. I'm a lie. I'm a lie, Mom!"

"You're not!" her mom screamed back, going for her, throwing her arms around her. Abby stood and went to her too, and they held her.

"You're the best of all of us," Abby said, crying. "Don't ever think otherwise."

Carmen was crying too. All three of them were bawling. "She's right," Carmen said, "you've always been the best of all of us."

Emilia had nothing left in her, no fight, no energy reserve. She settled into their arms and wept, letting it all out, more emotions than should ever be fair for a seventeen-year-old to experience.

42

FORGIVENESS IS A BLACK HOLE

Brooks was standing at his office window looking down at the cellar. He spent all his time working now, staying occupied, trying to put off making the big decisions he knew were coming. His guys were shuffling around tanks and barrels, pumping over all the fermenting lots, and doing a good job of keeping everything clean. Pak was down there taking samples, running more numbers. Brooks's eyes went to Shay, who was still there after two weeks and working as hard as anyone there—maybe harder. His brother was on the forklift moving some empty barrels outside to clean.

Brooks had to give the guy credit. Shay had completely changed his attitude and had accepted his new job with eagerness and humility. He couldn't understand how Shay had gone down a path dark enough to end up in jail. He was a good guy, and the two brothers and their father were actually living under the same roof in relative harmony. They'd had a few disagreements here and there, but nothing out of the ordinary.

It didn't look like Shay was going anywhere. He'd picked rows and rows of grapes with seasoned Mexicans and kept up okay. He hadn't complained once. Then when the picking was done, he'd jumped right into the cellar, doing whatever people asked. It was starting to look like the wine bug had bitten him, and like some sort of beneficial leech, sucked the poison from his blood.

Brooks stepped onto the catwalk and yelled for Shay to come up. Shay closed the door behind him, pulling the blue bandana off his head and wiping his grape-stained face.

"How's it going down there?" Brooks asked, sitting back in his swivel chair.

"We're making progress. To be honest, I love this stuff. Beats anything else I've ever done."

"We have a good time around here."

"I love learning the process. You've got a cool job, Bro."

"Wine heals all," Brooks said, wishing that was true.

"You called Abby yet?" Shay wasn't one for small talk.

Brooks shook his head. She'd called him several times a day since their last day together.

"Not to get into your business, but you've got to talk to her."

"I know."

"She still loves you. You know that."

"I know."

"Then what's wrong with you? Give her another shot. You'll never find a woman like that again."

Brooks let out a subtle laugh. He didn't have any intention of finding another woman.

Shay moved over to the bookshelf and fingered the lineup of wine books. "At least call her. Give her some closure. Give her something other than throwing her ring in the river. Show her some compassion."

"You preaching now?"

"No. I'm giving some brotherly advice. I think she's a good person."

"Anyway," Brooks said. "Jake gave me full approval for the animals. You want this project, it's yours. You build the barn, build the lean-tos, build the fence, find the hay. And then you bring in the animals. You'll manage them, run them through the vineyards, all that. You'll be full time with us and that will include the farm sanctuary down at Margot's. Payment for your work there will come through the Lacoda paycheck."

"Does Jake own the sanctuary?" Shay asked.

"No. But this is his contribution. Margot owns it, but he's going to pay for your services."

"You know I'm in," Shay said. "Red Mountain's the place to be. Can't get a good bite to eat for forty miles unless it's at one of our houses or a winery. There's not a single woman for sixty miles, except for rodeo chicks; takes thirty minutes to get to the bank or a movie. But there's something about it."

"I know. That's why I'm here." For now, Brooks thought.

"I'm all in," Shay said. "I appreciate the opportunity, and I'll make you proud."

Brooks believed that.

"Can I borrow your phone for a second?" Shay asked. "Left mine at the house."

"Yeah, sure." Brooks took his phone off the desk and handed it to him.

Shay dialed a number and held the phone to his ear—only for a moment. He tossed it back to Brooks.

"It's for you," Shay said.

Brooks looked at the screen. Shay had dialed her number and the phone was ringing. Brooks stared at his brother and shook his head. Nothing he could do now. He could hear her voice as she answered. "Hello? Hello?"

Brooks put the phone to his ear. "It's me," he said.

"Hi," Abby said.

Brooks extended his middle finger. Shay flicked his eyebrows and grinned, then darted out the door.

Brooks took a while to say anything else, listening to her breathing. He hadn't prepared. Finally, "I feel broken."

"Me too."

"I've never been here. I don't know what to do."

"Give me another chance, Brooks. I don't deserve it, but give me one anyway."

"I really wish it was that simple."

"It is! There's no one else involved in the decision. Just you. I still want to marry you. Give me another chance."

"Abs, I'm... I'm not able to handle betrayal. I got messed up growing up, and I've been lied to and kicked around way too long. I need people in my life who I can trust. Otherwise, I'm too vulnerable. My whole world can fall apart. Look at me."

"I'm not perfect. I messed up. But I can tell you this. I love you with all my heart. I want to be with you and only you. I want to be faithful to you. I want to show you what trust really is."

"Then why did you fuck it up!"

"Because it was too good to be true and the awful part of me came out and decided to ruin it. You're not the only one with a screwed-up past. I'm as messed up as you are. Or worse. I have a hard time trusting people. I have a hard time seeing the beauty in things. I fight it every day. What you and I had and what we were promising each other, it was so wonderful, too wonderful, and I expected it to crash to pieces. I didn't want it to, but I knew it would. Maybe all that fear brought it to reality. Look, if you want someone perfect, you're right not to call again. But if you can handle someone who's not a perfect ten but is working hard every day to be better, then I'm your girl."

"What is this supposed to mean? You can slip and slide all over our relationship, and I'll just sit back and say, 'Oh, she's trying. It's fine.'"

"No, that's not what I mean. I'm asking you to see the good part of me, not the bad. I'm asking you to give the good part of me a chance. What I did with Carmen, that's the messed up girl still stuck inside that I'm trying to purge. I'll go see someone. I'll get help. Whatever it takes to keep you. I believe we are meant for each other. I will never lie to you or cheat on you again. I swear on everything that I am."

"That's exactly what anyone would say when they're in your shoes. You may even mean it. But what's going to stop you next time?"

"Next time I'm going to be stronger."

"I can't make these kinds of decisions in a week. Sure, I still love you, but I've learned that love can only go so far. For now, all I can say is don't leave the mountain. Don't leave your job. Let's not let this destroy what everyone here has created. Emilia and Luca need you. Carmen and Jake need you. Don't leave the mountain. Maybe we can see each other again. I don't know right now. But don't leave the mountain, okay?"

After a long pause and some audible whimpers, she said, "I'll be here. Waiting for you."

"Goodbye, Abby."

"Goodbye."

Brooks ended the call and set the phone on the desk. He sat back. The stillness revealed a boiling anger. Not at Abby particularly, but at the world.

He burst out of his chair and ripped his laptop from the cords, hurling the computer with all his might at the giant window looking down at the cellar. The laptop spun in the air and crashed through the glass, a detonating shatter scattering glass shards in every direction, then continued on through the opening. He heard it smack the concrete below, a momentary sanity leaving him thankful that it hadn't hit someone.

43

THE STORM IS OVER, RIGHT?

Margot took Philippe jogging every day in hopes of running into Jake. Though she'd enjoyed that evening immensely—in fact it was some of the best sex of her life—she'd not been able to relish the memory because of her guilt. Of course, it was wrong that he was married, and she desperately hoped Carmen didn't find out, but her regret was mostly due to Jasper and Emilia. If either of them knew what Margot and Jake had done, they'd be devastated.

She would have called Jake so that they might talk it out, but she knew he had much heavier things on his mind. Between Carmen's infidelity with Abby and Emilia's issues at school with Joe Massey, she knew he was drowning in sorrow.

On the tenth day, she finally recognized his exquisite physique running along Sunset Road at a near sprint. She wasn't moving nearly as fast, though she did feel lighter and her knees felt stronger now. He reached Margot and Philippe quickly and only slowed his pace directly in front of them.

Jake bent over, sucking in the late October air. He was shirtless and sweaty, and he wore very short yellow shorts and brand-new running shoes. They smiled at each other and she said, "Are you training for something?"

"Not particularly. I'm finding this a much healthier coping mechanism than copious bottles of wine." He rubbed Philippe's neck.

She asked about Emilia and Luca, and of his marriage, and then got to the point. "We should speak about what happened."

He nodded, pulling his left foot up behind him into a stretch. "I'm sorry for doing that. Showing up at your door, drunk."

"You don't have to apologize. It happened. It was fun."

"A little too fun." She could tell he really meant it.

"But," she said, "it's important that we put that behind us. I've been plagued with guilt. This mountain has seen enough trouble lately. It's time someone steps up and becomes a role model."

"It was a lovely night, wasn't it? I just have to say it. I don't regret it for a moment. You are something special." He took a deep breath. "You're right, though, I know. This mountain has seen enough."

"Have you told Carmen?" she asked.

"Yeah. I had to."

Margot had a bad feeling that he might; he was that kind of guy. "She probably wants to kill me."

"No, not at all. She doesn't blame you a bit. I showed up at your door. You didn't do anything wrong."

Still, Margot certainly felt intimidated by Carmen. That woman wasn't one you wanted on your bad side. "You're not going to tell Emilia, are you?"

"No, of course not. It's none of her business. It's time we move on. The storm is over. We need to take care of each other now."

"Well, then," she said, "I'm glad we've sorted it out. Jasper says you're starting the recording Friday."

"I think we're ready. I haven't had this much fun in a long time."

"He's pretty excited himself."

"He's going to explode onto the scene. You know that, right?"

She nodded her head. "I've known for a long time." She walked away, pulling Philippe's leash gently. "We'll see you soon, Jake."

He waved at her. "See you soon."

44

HOLIDAYS AND MISGIVINGS

Thanksgiving day in eastern Washington brought a radiant blue sky and crisp, clean and cool air, the kind of day that defines fall, though everyone knew winter was only days away. Soon, there would be no more dressing in a sweater and hat and going for a hike through the vines or to the top of Badger or Red Mountain. When winter hit, at the end of November or early December, it brought weather that kept you inside by the fire, gazing out the window at the snowfall, reading books and watching the Seahawks until February, when temperatures crept back up toward sixty.

Today was certainly one of the last decent days for a while, and Otis was indeed thankful on Thanksgiving. He had spent the night with Joan, and they were drinking coffee and watching the Columbia River run. It had been six weeks now since the doctor had told him about the inoperable aneurysm. His senses were still rubbish and his hand was still shaking, but a deep transformation had occurred over those weeks; and none of it had to do with surrender. He'd followed Joan's instructions to a *T*, changing his eating habits, exercising, meditating, visualizing, the whole damn bit. And he hadn't done it because she'd been all over him like some kind of drill sergeant. No, she'd simply set him on the path and walked away.

She'd put all the responsibility on him, which is exactly as it should have been. They were spending most nights together, switching between places every few days. She'd learned a great deal about winemaking, assisting Elijah in the lab and doing anything she could to be a part of it. He'd taught her how to recognize flavors and flaws and about the even more important aspect of understanding wine: the contextual importance.

As far as trying to bring his own senses back to life, Otis was sticking to his practice. Most days he found the courage and hope and belief that if he kept at it, maybe he'd smell again. Maybe he'd taste again. Every day, sometimes a few times a day, he'd sit or lie down and visit his brain, trying to ignite the neurons, working toward positive neuroplasticity, allowing his brain to heal itself. The idea made sense. Connect with the body. Eat healthy. Exercise. Stop smoking his pipe. Find some peace and presence. And prepare his brain for rewiring the neurons that would hopefully one day return his senses to him.

Other days, he'd get so angry that he'd curse and scream and punch walls and throw tantrums. Who the hell did he think he was trying to fix his brain, fix this aneurysm? But he kept at it anyway. He held on to enough hope to keep him going.

He hadn't bothered telling his doctor what Joan had him doing. Not because he didn't believe in it, but because he didn't want a doctor telling him that his girlfriend was crazy.

She wasn't, though. He knew that. Joan Tobey was a shaman, a wonder woman, a mystic who could touch people profoundly, a healer who could help people in ways not many other humans could.

There she was now, dressed in her robe, sipping her coffee, brightening his morning without even saying a word. He wondered what was going on in that head of hers. But really, he knew. She wasn't thinking at all. She was being. That's what she'd taught him so much about.

She was so good at stopping to notice life. At any given moment, she'd say, "Do you smell that?" Or, "Do you hear that?" Or, "Do you see that?" They'd go for a walk and she'd see a dog she'd never seen before and be totally captivated. She could watch this dog forever, it seemed. Or she could pick a flower and hold it in her hands for an hour. She found magic in the littlest things: the sound of her chimes on the deck blowing in the wind, the shapes of the clouds, the shimmer of the morning.

Despite her tutelage, Otis had not yet mastered the art of simply *being*. He was trying, and he loved the pursuit of quietness, but his mind was as active as his beehives. He'd spent so many years juggling all of his projects that he'd mastered multitasking. What he had to do that afternoon, what he forgot at the store, what chores there were at the farm, how his wines were selling in Seattle, and on and on and on.

But every once in a while he'd get a glimpse of where he wanted to be. It had only happened a few times, but on occasion over the past month, he'd be sitting on the floor with her, his eyes closed, his hands on his knees, and he'd find some space in his hectic world. He'd get so comfortable in the quiet that he felt like he could stay there forever. It was those glimpses that gave him the strength to believe. She'd opened up the door to spirituality for him, showing him that the magic of this world was in breathing and coming alive and being in the present moment, each cell in his body lighting up and glowing.

If the old Otis could hear his thoughts now! That pipe-smoking, to-do listing, bacon-eater would strike him in the face.

He started to say something to her and stopped himself. What words were necessary on this beautiful Thanksgiving Day? He did indeed have so much to be thankful for. Sure, he might be dying, but he'd found Joan and he'd gotten a taste of youth again. An absurd thought came to him and he pushed it away. It came back and he let it process. How about spending the rest of the day in silence? *Why not?* They were going over to Margot Pierce's for a Thanksgiving meal, but that shouldn't stop them. Staying silent during the festivities might be enjoyable. Perhaps a little weird, but after all, it was Red Mountain. Maybe others would join.

He scribbled on a piece of paper that he found in a drawer and handed it to her. *Let's go the entire day without saying a word. It could be our way of saying thanks to the universe.*

She read it quickly and let out a short burst of laughter. The second her lips curved he knew she liked the idea. Really, it was an idea that she might have had. She looked at him, put her left hand on her heart and raised her right finger to her mouth. He did the same and blew her a kiss. She caught it and stuck it in her pocket.

He wrote: *I won't break my vow for anything in the world. This is my gift to you.*

Their day of silence began. How could they have known what was to come?

~

DUTY DID CALL a couple of hours later, and he wrote her another note saying he had to run home and check on the animals.

Though he had wanted to, he didn't keep his neighbor's dog. After one night, he came to the reality that he didn't need trouble with Henry Davidson. You can't take a man's dog. Otis had led Cody back over the next day and found Davidson chopping wood. His neighbor gave him the evil eye but knew damn well he didn't want any more old-man ass-whuppings. Otis made a point of saying that if he ever saw him beating Cody again, he'd make sure it would be the last time. Henry replied by telling him to get off his property. The feud would continue.

Today, Otis had to feed Jonathan, the chickens, and the sheep. The sheep had eaten most of the grass in the pasture, and since grass growth had stopped for the year, he'd begun supplementing with hay. He stopped at Yoke's, the local supermarket, to get a few things for their big Thanksgiving dinner. If only Aunt Morgan could see him now, walking up to the counter with a pile of Swiss chard and a box of tofu. When the lady checking him out said, "Happy Thanksgiving," he smiled and put a finger to his mouth and his hand on his heart.

There were a few cars at his neighbor's house. Otis figured Henry was having friends over. What a league of idiots that would be. Poor Cody was chained up in the back again.

Otis pulled into his driveway and rushed down the hill. He went to the coop first and then headed over to the sheep. They all came running as he slung a block of hay over the fence. He knelt and gave Jonathan some attention. The dog quickly rolled onto his back, inviting more of Otis's love. Once the animals were satisfied, Otis went up to the winery. He intended to take a few samples of the new vintage to Margot's house.

He entered the front of the tasting room and saw that the glass door had been smashed and was wide open. Crime was rare on Red Mountain, so rare that most people didn't lock their doors. The tasting room was untouched. No bottles were missing from the back bar.

He went into the cellar and flipped on the overhead lights. The entire concrete floor was wet with wine, and a steady flow was running toward the drain in the center. He instantly felt a pain in his stomach and a deep feeling of loss. He looked around. Someone had destroyed his entire vintage. They'd pushed over the amphorae along the west wall. They'd taken a hammer to the ones that were too heavy to push over, and the last of the wine slowly dripped from the giant cracks. They'd pushed over the barrel stacks and the barrels lay like fallen soldiers on the floor, now empty. They'd also opened the levers on the fermentation bins, emptying everything. His stomach grew worse and his back immediately throbbed, and he gasped for air.

Ignoring the pain, he rushed to the closest barrel. The rubber bung had been pulled out. He rolled the barrel a couple of inches; it was mostly empty. There were bungs all over the floor. He righted a few barrels that were still slowly leaking and then went to the fermentation bins. With a burning in his back, he lifted them up, trying to save every last drop. But he'd lost nearly everything.

A new wave of back pain dropped him to the floor, and his knees hit the concrete. His trousers instantly soaked up the wine. Another sharp pain went through him as he began to cry.

His world went black.

45

BROTHERS IN ARMS

Brooks and Shay spent Thanksgiving morning on motorcycles riding down to the Columbia River and back. It was a chilly day to ride, but much colder days were coming. This was one of the last rides of the year. On the way back, they stopped at the Conoco at the bottom of the hill to fill up. "Let's ride up to see Otis," Brooks said to Shay. "I'd like to check in on him. You mind?"

Shay removed his helmet. "Yeah, sure."

After filling up and getting a drink, they rode up the hill and pulled into the driveway, standing their bikes next to Otis's truck. After trying the house, they walked up to the winery.

Reaching the tasting room, Brooks saw broken glass and the wide open door. He ran inside, yelling, "Otis! You in here?" Shay was right behind him. Hearing something, Brooks went back into the cellar. He saw the damage. Then he saw a figure on the ground. He moved closer. Otis lay on his back in a pool of wine.

He knelt beside his mentor and put his hand on him. "You okay?"

Otis opened his eyes.

"Who did this?"

Otis shook his head and put his hand on his heart.

"Can you stand?" Brooks asked, offering his hand. Shay and

Brooks lifted Otis up, guiding him to one of the tipped-over barrels where he could sit. "Who did this?"

Otis winced, a hand on his back.

Brooks knew about the altercation he'd had with Henry. "Was it your neighbor?"

Otis shook his head.

"Can you talk, Otis? Give me something to work with."

Otis reached into his shirt pocket and pulled out a notebook. He wrote: *I can't talk. I made a vow to Joan.*

"What? This is a big deal. Who did this?"

I don't know.

Brooks felt the rage building. "I'm going over there. We both know it was Henry."

"I'm coming with you," Shay said.

Before Otis could write the next note, they'd left the cellar. Brooks could feel the tension straining in his fists. This vintage meant everything to Otis. They'd spent every day on these wines for months, hell, the whole year. How could someone be that evil?

Brooks and Shay stormed out of the cellar before Otis could protest further. "I can't believe this," Brooks said to his brother as they crossed over into the neighbor's property. Henry's dog barked and pulled at his chain in the back yard. They passed the dog and the half-built shed and the stacks of rocks and the graveyard of toys and went to the front door. Brooks knocked, feeling like a boxer waiting for a bell.

Henry answered, wearing the same Carhartt overalls he wore every day, swaying some, a can of Budweiser in his hand. The sounds of holiday partying came from deeper in the house—some laughing, some sixties rock 'n' roll. "How can I help you?" Henry asked, revealing the missing tooth up front.

"Did you pour all of Otis's wine out?"

Henry looked him dead in the eyes and put on an evil grin. His speech was half confident and half drunk. "No idea what you're talking about."

That guilty grin was enough for Brooks. He charged Henry and tackled him onto the floor of his own house. "You fucking bastard!" Brooks said, punching his face. Henry's nose cracked and spattered blood, and the man squealed in pain.

Two men came from another room ready to fight and went after Brooks, pulling him off Henry. Shay jumped in and knocked them both down. Henry and Brooks went at it, while Shay did his best with the other two. It was a street brawl sort of fight, the kind where sharp angles and heavy objects came in handy, and nuts and eyes were fair game. Brooks was rusty when he threw the first punch, but the old feeling returned quickly, and the two brothers put up a hell of a fight.

About the time they were all bleeding and breathing heavily and running on empty, a woman came in holding a handgun. "Hey!" she yelled. "The hell you think you are?" Though their swings and kicks had lost some of their fury, the men kept at it. She pulled back the hammer and pointed the gun at Brooks's temple. "You touch my husband one more time and I'll kill you."

The fighting stopped quickly. Brooks let go of Henry. Shay rolled over, exhausted, and spat some blood on the floor. The woman wore an apron with a bikini body painted on it. Her own body wasn't quite as svelte. She had that look of having spent forty years on earth with a cigarette in her mouth and a drink in her hand, ignoring the gym and avoiding the outdoors all together. She told one of the men to get up and call the cops. He obeyed, like she wasn't the kind of woman you argued with.

Brooks stood and said to the lady, "Your husband poured out my friend's entire production of wine."

"Now, how the hell do you know that?" she asked, pointing the gun at his chest.

"Cause I know it, goddamn it."

"You're trespassing. The cops are on the way. Get your ass into the front yard, and we'll wait on 'em."

Henry got up, and Brooks could see they'd both taken a pretty good beating. Henry's nose was cracked and leaking blood. His eyes were leaking tears. Limping over to his wife, he reached for the gun. He pointed it at Brooks and Shay, licking the blood from his upper lip. "You heard her. Head out to the front yard. We'll let the cops sort things out. You're lucky I'm not shooting you right now, you sons of bitches."

Brooks and Shay followed Henry's orders, sitting on the ground. They weren't about to try running from a trigger-happy maniac.

〜

BROOKS AND SHAY were strip-searched and forced to dress in orange jumpsuits and Velcro sneakers, then put in a cell in the Benton County Jail in Kennewick, twenty-five minutes from Red Mountain. A smear of something that looked like shit striped the once-white wall next to the toilet. Brooks was sitting against the opposite wall, and Shay lay on the paper-thin mattress of the bottom bunk with his head on the rock-hard pillow. His feet were crossed, as if he couldn't be more relaxed.

"You did this for two years?" Brooks asked his brother.

"Two years and three days. This is jail, though. Different than prison."

Brooks nodded. He knew that. He'd never been busted, but he'd known plenty of people who had. "Dad said you stole a car."

Shay smiled. "Yeah. That's what they got me for."

"Why the hell did you steal a car?"

"I didn't. My girlfriend did. I'm the one that did the time."

"What do you mean?"

"You ever been so in love that you'd do anything for her?"

"Yeah." Brooks saw Abby's face for a moment.

"Her name was Julia. Julia Lam. A knockout. Curly brown hair, big thick eyebrows. A real woman, wide hips, curves for days. A real attitude. Man, she could piss me off. She wouldn't let me get away with anything. 'Quit chewing with your mouth open, get off your ass, quit leaving the seat up,' that kind of shit. But we had it. We had that once in a lifetime fire. We'd tear each other's clothes off and go at for days. We could lie in bed all damn weekend and have fun. Julia fucking Lam."

"Sounds like your type. You're saying you both stole the car?"

"She stole the car. Julia was a waitress in a bar in downtown Albuquerque. Said some guy didn't leave a tip after putting her through hell, talking shit to her, you know, hitting on her. She said he spent half the night talking about his new Mustang, flashing the keys, telling anybody that would listen how fast it was. A week later, she saw him at another place down the road and decided it would be a good idea to take his prized Mustang. Her dad was a car thief, so she had it in her blood, I guess. He'd taught her how to jimmy open a door and hot-wire the steering column and break the steering lock."

"Where were *you*?"

"At home watching *Golden Girls* or some shit. Studying for a chem final. I don't know. Not with her. She rolled in with the Mustang well past midnight. I was sleeping in her bed. She crawled in without waking me. I didn't know about her new toy until the next day. I told her we were going to take it back, that I didn't want her getting busted. She said, 'Let's take it for one last ride.' We did. Cops got us twenty minutes down the highway. She already had a record for slinging some coke, so she'd done some time. This would have been bad on her, so I took the blame. Told the cops that it was mine."

"You never told Dad this?"

"Shit, man. Everybody's innocent in prison. What do you say?"

Brooks nodded, knowing he was right. "She just let you do the time?"

"She wanted to take the blame but I wouldn't let her. She came to see me in prison a couple of times. Then she fell in love with a furniture salesman and moved to Alaska, and I got out with a felony record, no woman to go home to, and nowhere to go."

"You should tell Dad this."

"What difference does it make? I stole a car; I didn't steal a car. Dad cut me loose the day they found out. Mom took his side, being the obedient wife. They gave up on me. Came to see me but they'd given up on me. It's taken me many years to work it out."

"Dad seems all right to me. He's got his flaws. His dad was a hard-ass. You know that generation. Forgiveness didn't come as easily. You're expected to do your part."

"Sure, but this isn't Roman times. You don't throw away your problem children."

"Ah, give him a break. I bet he was just pissed he gave me away and kept you. Had he done the opposite, his life would have been easier."

Shay couldn't help cracking a grin with that one. "Maybe that's true. He gave away the wrong kid, didn't he?"

"Well, I didn't know him then, but he seems all right now. I can tell you this. He's happy to be with us both. Maybe he's changed."

"We both have. I'm trying to move past it. He seems better now." He shrugged. "What do you do?"

"He's all we got. That's for sure. I wonder what's going through our mom's head."

Shay sighed. "I bet she's thinking she gave away the wrong baby too. Had she kept you, she'd have this famous winemaker. But instead, she got a felon. Shit, I bet that's why she won't come up."

"Hey, I'll take my life over abortion any day. I haven't always felt that way, but I'll say that today. Even with all this crap with Abby going on. Life's all right. Having a family all of a sudden feels good. You have no idea."

"I kind of do, man. I haven't had one for a while either. It does feel good."

"We need to get Mom up here."

"How do we do that?"

"We buy her a ticket."

They shot the shit for another hour. Brooks found it amazing how bonding jail time could be. You run out of things to talk about, you just keep getting deeper. Letting it all out. The food sucked, but jail was way cheaper than family therapy.

Finally, the door popped open and a deputy said, "You two are out of here."

Brooks said, "I'm surprised he got us both out. I figured he'd leave you in here a while."

"You *are* his favorite."

Brooks patted Shay on the back. "One of us has to be."

They were processed and given back their belongings; and then escorted out to the lobby, where Charles was sitting reading the newspaper. He lowered the paper and asked Brooks, "Did Shay show you the ropes?"

"Fuck you, Dad."

"Aw, c'mon. What's Thanksgiving without bailing family out of jail? Lighten up." He stood and headed to the door. "Let's go eat turkey, boys."

46

ALL TOGETHER NOW, A.K.A. THE THANKSGIVING SPECTACULAR

Margot had her hands full. Not only, was she showing off her inn, her dream come true (or at least a closer-to-finished version) for the first time, she was also hosting a whole cast of Red Mountain characters, some of whom were already having a very hectic and drama-filled day.

Emilia, who had come earlier in the day and was in the kitchen with Jasper, had warned Margot that Brooks and Shay had just gotten out of jail for attacking a man they believed had destroyed Otis's wine.

This news was stacked on top of the typical holiday get-together, which Margot knew dragged long-hidden skeletons out of the closets. She and her ex-husband hosted the big family dinners back in Vermont, and half of them ended in too much drinking and arguing, and not enough love and forgiveness.

Perhaps equally as nerve-racking as showing off Épiphanie for the first time was the fact that she'd invited the Foresters, including Carmen, whom she hadn't seen since before sleeping with Jake. He had told Carmen about his infidelity, so seeing her could be awkward. She had to invite them, though, for Emilia's sake—and because Red Mountain was too small to let tiny tiffs turn into full-on feuds.

Otis and Joan arrived at Épiphanie first, ringing the doorbell exactly at five and setting Philippe into a tantrum of barking. Margot opened the giant wooden door and said, "Welcome, welcome." Philippe darted out the door and demanded attention before the guests could go further. Joan had a flower tucked behind her ear, no doubt a gift from Otis. He was carrying a black wine bag with offerings from his cellar.

Neither Otis nor Joan said anything to Margot as she hugged and wished them a happy Thanksgiving. As Margot wondered why they were silent, Joan handed Margot a note. *In honor of Thanksgiving, Otis and I have chosen to spend the day in silence. Please know that we are grateful to be here and we look forward to being with so many people we love.*

Margot thought the idea was more cute than anything else, though she thought the timing a little off, with all of them about to spend several hours together at the dinner table.

She handed the note back to Joan and said to Otis, "I'm so sorry about your wine."

He gave her a hug.

"Did they find out who did it?"

He scribbled a quick note in a notepad from his jacket pocket. *They're investigating.*

"I can't believe you're not talking after something like this has happened. It really speaks to your character."

I'm happy to be alive.

Margot led them on a tour of the inn, which was getting closer and closer to completion. Ron still had a good bit of finish work left, and Margot still had a ton of furniture and art to bring in, but for the first time, the construction hell she'd been living in was showing glimpses of a finished project. She'd turned every light on downstairs and there were candles in each room, creating an elegant European feel that she'd only been dreaming of until now.

She led them to the dining room, where two of her large oak

tables had been pushed together and covered with a giant white table linen. Delicious aromas of food she'd been cooking for several days wafted in from the kitchen. She'd set the table with her finest silverware and china, sets she'd inherited from her French grandmother.

Joan gasped as she took in the beauty of it all, and she gasped again when she saw the towering limoncello cake with mascarpone frosting on another table. Margot beamed with pride. Even at the worst of her depression, she had never stopped believing that she had gifts when it came to the culinary arts.

Though the rest of the inn wasn't quite ready, she'd made sure the dining room was perfect in every way. Her passion was not only cooking great food but also in providing everything surrounding the experience, from the place settings to the serving dishes and the presentation as a whole. Her cake was one of those delicacies so beautiful that pushing a knife into it for the first slice would feel like a crime.

They went in through the swinging door to the kitchen and found Jasper and Emilia scrubbing a stack of pots and pans and having fun doing it. Emilia's hair had grown out quite a bit, and now she looked less like she needed tattoos and piercings and more like she'd easily get cast as Tinkerbell. Margot loved that Emilia and Jasper had become such great friends. She kind of wished their friendship would turn into more, but she also knew she could never force that.

Jasper read Joan's piece of paper regarding their vow of silence out loud and said, "That's cool. Great idea. You're not talking until tomorrow?"

Joan shook her head and Emilia said, "I love it. My dad says you never learn anything by talking."

Brooks, his brother, and his dad arrived shortly after, followed by the Foresters. Margot hugged necks and kissed cheeks and soon got to Carmen. Margot felt intimidated and nervous, not knowing what to expect. They looked at each other—these two women who had shared a man—and Carmen said, "Happy Thanksgiving, Margot."

"Thank you. You too."

Carmen opened her arms and they hugged, and it wasn't a small hug. Carmen wrapped her long arms around Margot's whole body and pulled her tight and said into her ear, "I hope you enjoyed him." She stepped away with a wink. Margot smiled awkwardly and led everyone on a tour that ended up in the dining room.

They showered Margot with compliments on her new inn, the table settings, and the cake. It made her feel so good that she ran into the kitchen to bring out the rest of the dishes, assisted by Emilia and Jasper.

Margot had always wanted to serve something other than turkey on Thanksgiving, but her ex had never let her. This was her place, though, and today would be fully vegetarian.

They filled the table with Margot's famous broccoli casserole, her naughty mashed potatoes and even naughtier mac and cheese, piles of purple and white asparagus and Brussels sprouts, a giant salad of leafy greens from the garden, freshly shelled green peas, homemade relishes, and crusty bread from Walla Walla with butter from a local dairy.

Dinner began with a raised glass and cheers to Red Mountain before the group moved in on the food like a Roman army taking over a small village.

Halfway through the meal, Margot looked across the table at Jasper talking endlessly with Emilia; at Jake hugging on Carmen; at Brooks kissing Abby even after all they'd been through; at Charles and Shay laughing together; at Joan and Otis flirting—silently, of course; at Luca playing with his mashed potatoes; at everyone filling their stomachs and smiling. Despite all the craziness and drama that had hovered over them, they beamed with life and energy, and Margot knew she'd found home. Not *a* home. Home.

It was in that elation that Margot had a revelation: she and Jasper needed to call his father. Margot signaled her son, and they walked outside, finding their way along the pathway lit up by the lanterns, passing the fountain Margot had imported from France that she hoped Ron would have working soon.

"I think we should call your dad," Margot said. "I think we should invite him to your concert."

"Really? I was thinking about the same thing the other day. You sure, Mom?"

"I'm positive." She pulled her phone from the pocket of her apron and without another thought, she dialed his number. Though she'd deleted him from her contacts long ago, she'd probably never forget those digits, beginning with the Vermont area code.

When he answered, she said, "Rory."

"Margot?" He was shocked.

"Happy Thanksgiving."

"You too. I can't believe I'm hearing from you. How are you two? It's been so long."

"We're really good," she said. "We're finally feeling like we're home."

He was quiet for a moment, and she knew he might have been thinking she was calling to say they were coming home. "That's... that's good."

"I don't want you to take this the wrong way, but I want you to know that I forgive you. We made the right decision to divorce, and I'm not looking to rekindle our relationship in any way, but I want you to know that I forgive you and I only wish the best for you."

His voice had a gracious tone. "Do you know how badly I needed to hear that? I've been beating myself up since you left. I've lost thirty pounds. I'm a freaking mess."

She wasn't about to feel sorry for him. "Maybe this will help."

"I'm sorry. I deserve every bit of it. How is our son? I miss him so much, Margot."

"He wants to talk to you."

"Really?"

Margot handed Jasper the phone.

"Dad?" Then, "Yeah, I'm okay." Jasper answered his dad's questions and said, "Ever heard of Folkwhore? That's the one. I've been playing a lot with their lead singer, Jake Forester. Yeah, he lives here. We're doing a concert Saturday night here. Mom and I thought you might want to come." Jasper was ecstatic to be speaking with his father, nearly jumping up and down as he shared the news. No matter how bad a father is, he's still your father and he still has a great power over you.

They spoke for a while longer and Jasper said, "Goodnight, Dad. See you soon."

Margot and Jasper sauntered back to the inn, both glowing. Not because Rory made them glow, but because the dark past was quietly put to bed that night. Mother and child knew that from that moment forward, they would no longer carry Rory's public infidelity around like a ball and chain. Instead it would be a distant memory.

Back in the dining room, the wine had worked quickly. Someone had turned up the stereo a few notches, and some early forties Glenn Miller swing was forcing everyone but Otis and Joan to speak much louder. The cliques of the table had faded, and now the entire table was in on one discussion, a conversation magnetic enough to pull them all together.

"I'm just amazed, Otis," Brooks was saying, "that you're still not talking. I know we don't want to relive today too much, but I'm trying to imagine you writing notes on your pad to the cops. They must have thought you were crazy."

Otis smiled. He wrote in big letters: *Or mute.*

The entire table broke into the biggest laughter of the night, imagining the absurdity of it all, a thing that could only happen on Red Mountain. It was in those very difficult times on the mountain that the biggest smiles appeared.

"I don't understand why you didn't try this quiet game another day."

I made a vow to Joan. He was writing big enough for the table to read.

"I'm sure she would have forgiven you, considering the circumstances."

Of course.

"Then it's a testament to what you feel for this woman." Brooks turned to Joan. "He loves you more than his wine. I never thought I'd see the day."

Joan rubbed Otis's back as he wrote: *She's in a different league, my boy.*

Margot wondered if a man would ever truly love her that way. She felt happy for Joan, though, happy that her friend had found such a wonderful man, such a wonderful love.

Otis wrote another note. *I appreciate you standing up for me, going after him, going to jail. You didn't have to do that.*

"I'd do it again and again," Brooks said.

"I would too," Shay agreed.

Charles laughed. It was the first time Brooks's father had spoken in a while. The table turned their attention to him and he said, "Yes, he would. Shay will do anything to go back to jail. He must love the food." Margot felt the cold of his voice, a side she had never seen from Charles.

The table fell silent.

"Aww, c'mon, Dad," Brooks finally said. "Give him a break."

Charles looked down at the table and shook his head, trying to restrain his own mouth, letting another sly grin arise.

"What do you have to say, Charles?" Shay asked. "You have more to say, you might as well get it all out. Let this table be your pulpit and this group your congregation. Let's hear the words of your almighty God. Let's hear your thoughts on your son, the sinner."

Charles kept his eyes on his half-eaten plate.

"Come on, old man, let's hear the real Charles. I'm sure we all could use a lesson on this lovely Thanksgiving Day." Shay filled his glass with a nearby bottle of red and took a big gulp.

"Always so damn dramatic," Charles said, lifting his eyes and looking upon his son.

"That's right, Pop. So damn dramatic. As if I'm the one that can't let go of something that happened eight years ago. Keep holding on to it with everything you have. It's definitely helping. Great for the family."

"All right, guys," Brooks said. "Let's move on."

Shay crossed his arms and sat back against the chair. "Exactly what I've been saying for a long time. That's one thing this man can't do is move on."

"Tell him what you told me today," Brooks said. "He might as well know the truth."

"Like it would make a difference."

"Oh, the truth," Charles said. "What kind of truths shall we make up today?" He poured himself another glass.

Brooks said, "You remember that girl you didn't like? What was her name?"

"Leave it alone," Shay said.

"What was her name?"

"Julia Lam."

"Julia Lam!" Brooks said. "Your son didn't even steal that car. It was Julia. Shay covered for her."

"Oh, Jesus Christ," Charles said.

"No, really. Tell him, Shay."

Shay said, "Like it makes a difference."

"For once your brother is right," Charles said. "Like it makes a difference. And if that is true, then he's dumber than I thought. You went to jail for her? Didn't I teach you anything?"

"Charles," Brooks said, seeing the break in Shay's confidence, "now you're crossing lines. Leave it alone. I think it takes quite a man to love a woman that much."

Charles laughed. "No one but a fool could have loved that woman. But now it all makes sense. His whole life ruined, all that promise down the drain, because he thought his heart was in his pants." Charles looked at Shay. "That's your dick down there, son."

Shay pointed a finger at his dad. "There's the Charles I know. Where's he been hiding? You've put on a pretty good show since you've been here, haven't you? Even I was convinced. Proves the words you burned into me: nobody really changes. You're right about that."

Brooks smashed his fists on the table and screamed, "That's enough!" His crystal glass tipped over and cracked on his plate, spilling wine onto his lap. Brooks jumped up and tried to catch the wine with his napkin before it dripped to the floor.

He looked at the broken glass and then Margot. "I'm so sorry. I'll replace it."

"It's fine," Margot whispered. "Please don't worry about it." She could see the pain in his eyes. He'd been so proud of his family and now they'd let him down in front of everyone. The shame on his red face broke her heart. She wanted to hug him, but didn't dare move. The dining room became a tomb, with an empty silence no one dared to fill, all eyes on plates.

Moments went by. Slowly, one after another, the guests picked up their silverware, and the ping of forks and knives hitting her grandmother's china chipped away at the quiet.

As people started to breathe again, Carmen, while swirling her glass of Sauvignon Blanc more out of habit than intent, said, "Margot, you're a wonderful cook."

"Thank you so much," Margot said, from the other end of the table. Still the pings of the silverware and little else.

"You're a real talent. Now I see what my husband sees in you."

Jake twisted his head to his wife and said, "That's enough, Carmen."

"I can't help but wonder if you are as good in the bedroom as you are in the kitchen."

"Carmen!" Jake snapped.

Forks and knives crashed to their plates. Glasses floated to their owners' lips almost in unison. And then an agonizing silence swallowed Épiphanie whole, eating up every bit of good energy that had ever been there.

"Everyone lighten up," Carmen said. "We're all family here."

Margot immediately thought of Jasper and how awful this news would be for him. She turned to her son sitting next to her, expecting him to ask if it was true, knowing that this truth would break him apart, break his dream of playing music with Jake apart. She knew Jasper would never forgive her. He'd never forgive Jake either, this man who'd stepped in and nearly become a father to him—betraying him just like his own father.

Jasper looked up at his mom and shrugged. "I knew."

"What?" Margot said in shock.

Jasper looked at Emilia and then back at his mom. "We knew."

"And it's okay," Emilia said. "We're cool with it. I can't say I've done much better."

Jake jumped in. "Why didn't you say anything, honey?"

"I don't know. What were we supposed to say?"

"It was a one-time thing," Margot said. "Really."

"Mom, it doesn't matter. We all mess up. Don't worry about it."

How many nights had Margot spent sleepless in regret? "How did you know?"

"I was in Seattle that night, remember? I couldn't sleep after seeing Chick Corea, so I drove back home in the middle of the night. I saw Jake leaving and kind of figured it out."

"And you told Emilia?" Margot said, putting it all together.

"And I told Emilia the other day. Had to tell someone."

"You kids are too much."

Carmen, the great storm chaser, the woman most drawn to the drama of it all, the one more comfortable in this kind of chaos, said in her slightly drunk voice, "Honestly, Margot. Look at my husband." She pointed her hands at Jake as if showing him off like Vanna White would. "You would have been crazy not to take a bite out of this beautiful chunk of man. It wouldn't be right for me not to share."

At most dinner tables around the world, that comment might have stirred different emotions, but on Red Mountain that night, one grin turned to two, and a smile turned to two and three, and in seconds the entire table was laughing out loud.

Carmen's words had crossed every line left to cross, and the silence no longer had a place at the table. Like any good holiday meal on Red Mountain, the commencing laughter led to hugs, and the pain and guilt and sorrow left each of them, and all that was left was the love and camaraderie of these unique souls that belonged nowhere else. This group could not be brought down; their spirits had already been rubbed raw. And as it was on Red Mountain, no matter what you did, the others wouldn't stop loving you. They might not talk to you for a while, but they'd always love you to the core.

47

HOPE LIKE A LIGHT AT THE END OF THE TUNNEL

Later in the evening, Emilia, Abby, Carmen, and Margot were sitting together on one end of the dining room table talking girl stuff. Everyone had left but Jake and Jasper, who were playing music together in the foyer, their acoustic guitar and piano sounds creeping back into the dining room.

Emilia was surprised by her ability to have forgiven her mother and Abby for their affair and to even have forgiven her mother for the outburst at the table. She liked sitting there with all of them.

Abby talked about Brooks for a while, how they'd come a long way in repairing their relationship. She turned to Emilia.

"Why aren't you and Jasper dating?" Abby asked. "I didn't even realize it, but you two make such a cute couple."

Emilia was caught off guard and embarrassed, especially since Margot was sitting there. She didn't know what to say.

"He really is adorable," Carmen said.

Emilia looked up to the ceiling. "Jasper is...I don't know...in a different dimension. While all of us regular kids are going around dating each other and getting into trouble, Jasper is focused on his music. We're good friends."

Then Margot dropped a bomb. "You know he's obsessed with you, right?"

"What?" Emilia asked.

Margot put her hand to her mouth for a moment and then removed it. "I can't believe I just told you that. He would absolutely murder me if he knew."

"What did he say?"

"He thinks you're the greatest woman on earth."

"Why hasn't he ever asked me out?"

"Look at you, Emilia," Margot said. "You're one of the most beautiful young women in the world. You're intimidating."

"She's right," Carmen said. "Guys get scared."

"He likes me as a friend. We're great friends."

"Look, Emilia," Margot said. "Let me be very clear. He likes you. He'd probably marry you tomorrow morning. But I'm not supposed to say that, so you can't know how he feels."

"I guess I'll have to wait for him to tell me."

They left it at that, though Emilia spent the rest of the conversation wondering how she had totally missed seeing signs that Jasper was interested in her. She still didn't believe it. He was such an honest guy and such an adult. Why hadn't he said anything?

48

A REVELATION OF THE SENSES

On Saturday, Joan arrived at Otis's house and delighted him with a kiss fit for a teenager but more than welcome by an old man. They were dining together before the charity concert. Otis had made a very colorful stir-fry and intended to pair it with a riesling from the Mosel in Germany.

He wanted to grow riesling, but he didn't feel like he'd ever do justice to the variety like the Germans. Riesling was indeed his favorite grape, and in a way, it was nice that he didn't make his own. Better to leave some things to the imagination. He didn't want to know the growth cycles and ripening patterns and other intricacies of growing riesling, like he did of syrah and cabernet sauvignon and marsanne and viognier. He needed riesling to continue on its own mysterious path, only gracing him with its majestic qualities by way of a good German producer's hands.

He and Joan sat at the dining room table. He lit two candles and set the dish of stir-fry between them, an array of vegetables in his soy and ginger concoction resting on some basmati rice, a sprinkle of black and white sesame seeds on top. He served their plates and uncorked and poured the riesling. He loved sharing with her his fascination with wine from around the world, and he had a lot of it in his cellar. He'd be damned if his dead senses were going to prevent him from getting through every last bottle before the funeral home cooked him in a crematorium.

"I first visited the Mosel back in the early seventies, and I've been going back almost every other year. It's the kind of place that takes you back in time, ancient and beautiful, a culture very much still in touch with itself. Aside from this giant bridge they're constructing, which may bring some modernization one day, the region is untouched. The wines are cheap and real, and they come from vineyards that were planted hundreds of years ago by the Romans."

He threw his hands up. "I wouldn't dare plant riesling here in Washington. A lot of people do, but I wouldn't dare. Riesling belongs on the Mosel River, where it's steep and cold and wet. Riesling can grow with the ease of roses and make bad wine anywhere, but there are only a few places where it belongs, and that's when the wine is true and right."

Joan smiled. "When are we going? Sounds lovely."

"I'm going to take you there right now, my dear. Put the glass to your nose. Riesling changes in the bottle more than any variety I know. When it's only just been fermented, sometimes it can be uninteresting or average; then you visit that wine a year later and something beautiful has happened. It begins to show its character."

"Like a child," she said.

"Exactly. Like a child. And once these wines come alive they evolve every month. Sometimes every week or every day. That's why you have to buy cases of a single wine to experience the change. After several years the classic diesel aromas of riesling become quite obvious, but beyond that, the specific vineyards start to speak, the variety of slate and mineral, the specific slope, its direction in relation to the sun. The vineyards in the Mosel are the steepest I've seen in the world. Imagine slopes so steep the harvesters have to use harnesses so they don't slip and roll down to the road below. It can be so cold there that the grapes barely ripen, and the acidity can sometimes be absolutely racy." He pointed at the wine. "This is a 1995. I took my sons there, our first real boys' trip. Michael was barely eighteen. We shipped back five cases. This is my last bottle."

"Thank you for sharing it with me. It really does smell gorgeous."

"You're my queen. We'll drink every bottle in my cellar together. Now take a sip."

She closed her eyes and put the glass to her mouth, letting the wine flow gracefully. He raised his own glass to his nose. He wanted to follow the ritual and let his mind guide his senses and let his imagination take off. The Mosel riesling wafted up through his senses and struck his brain, intoxicating him with its beauty.

Wait a minute.

He could smell!

Otis smelled the wine again, taking in golden apples and nuances of citrus; and beyond that he smelled the diesel, and beyond that he smelled the Mosel, that minerality that could only come from those south German slopes. It was a wine of such great sophistication and precision that he nearly forgot to take a sip.

He was simply in the moment, experiencing wine the way he had at the peak of his career. Then he drank. The taste came to him in waves as well, bits of cinnamon and citrus and slate, perfect balance, a steely brightness that didn't overbear but simply elevated, and a finish that he wouldn't even bother describing—even later—some kind of ineffable taste subtleties that reminded him why he'd been on this wine journey for so long.

It hit him. "Joan," he said.

"That's a lovely wine," she said.

"I know. I can smell it. I can taste it!" He smacked the table. "Like when I was thirty-five." He stood from his chair and went to her. He planted a huge kiss on her lips. "I don't know what you've done, woman, but I'm back. I can taste this wine."

"I haven't done a thing," she said, running her hand through her hair.

"You've done everything."

Otis returned to his chair and picked up the glass of riesling. He smelled again and took a bite of the stir-fry. Flavors of sesame, soy, and ginger danced on his tongue. He put a water chestnut in his mouth. Instead of just a crisp crunch, he could taste his seasoning and sauce and even the very mild, slightly sweet, nuttiness of the water chestnut. "This is the best food I've ever had in my life." He stabbed at a carrot and a red pepper and crammed them in his mouth and then drank another sip of the riesling.

Joan put a hand on his arm, smiling. "Slow down, for heaven's sake!"

"You're not surprised, are you? I don't think you believe me."

"Oh, I believe you. But no, I'm not surprised. I knew you had it in you."

"Who are you, Joan Tobey?"

"I'm nobody, Otis Till."

He took another sip of wine and let the flavors blast his soul into the universe.

~

OTIS CAME BACK DOWN to earth a short time later, still on top of the world, but not quite dancing in the cosmos. He could now have a conversation without looking at his girlfriend like she was some kind of messiah.

"Now that you're back with us," Joan said, "Can we talk about Morgan's request? I think we should buy plane tickets."

"I do too," Otis said, feeling more carefree than he ever remembered. He'd been excited about the trip, but life had gotten in the way.

"So you do want to go?"

"I'd like to sit down with you tomorrow morning and buy all the plane tickets and book every hotel room. I can't wait."

"Really?" Joan was shocked.

"Don't ever let me forget how I feel at this moment," he said. "For the first time in my life, I get it. It's taken me sixty-four years, but today I have awakened."

49

TOO MANY PASSENGERS ON BOARD

Brooks stopped by Abby's villa Saturday afternoon. As usual, her place was very clean. She had the taste of an island artist, with an overabundance of bright and colorful paintings on the walls. He took his shoes off per protocol and stepped onto the Native American wool rug covering the pine floor.

"That was a heavy Thanksgiving, wasn't it?" she said, both of them taking a seat on her comfy leather couch.

"A little rough." He sank into the cushions, sitting dangerously close to her, too close for the current state of their relationship, but too far away to have once been engaged.

"Did Shay and your dad work it out?"

"I'm not sure. My dad headed back south."

"And Shay?"

"I don't know. Heard he's crashing with one of the cellar guys."

"I guess you're not going to the concert, are you?"

Brooks shook his head, knowing he wasn't in the right head space for a show.

"Bummer. I was hoping you were going to ask me to go. It's none of my business, but don't let one night ruin what you three have built. You have a terrible tendency to let tiny things grow into these huge devastating life blows. You know I love you, but I don't love that about you."

"Everyone has different concepts of tiny and devastating."

"You can't expect everybody to be perfect."

"I don't expect perfection, but I expect decency. They embarrassed me in front of everyone I know."

"Do you think you are the only ones who have it bad and get in fights? Go ask Otis. I bet he and his sons got in plenty. Look at what's going on with Jake and Carmen. Look at poor Margot and what happened with her husband. Look at what Emilia's going through. Nobody is going to judge you because of a small fight. People have their own problems. And that's okay."

"I guess." He threw his right leg over his left, eyeing a travel magazine on the coffee table, wondering if she was going somewhere. "Look, Abby. I'm not like other people. I can't let myself be vulnerable. I'm barely holding on, and all this frailty around me—it's not good."

"I wish you would listen to yourself."

He moved his chin up and down and left and right, confused. Yes, he could hear himself; yes, he knew he wasn't right in his thinking; yes, he was messed up. But he was a long way from changing. "I will always care about you, but we're not going to work. I wanted to try, but every moment we're together lately I feel this great resentment building. To the point where I know one day it's going to turn to hate. You hurt me so badly, but I don't want to hate you. I want you to be happy. I want you to stay on Red Mountain and continue working here. I don't want to get in the way of your future. But I can't be with you. Trust me, you don't want to be with me."

"That's exactly what I want."

Brooks looked at her and could see her jaw tensing and the tendons of her neck straining.

His next words were a whisper in a dark cave. "It's not what I want."

"This is the biggest mistake you will ever make, and you're going to hate yourself for ending what we have."

"I hate myself now. Don't you see that? I've somehow managed to make it look on the outside like I'm normal, but I'm not. Not even close. I don't love who I am. Shit, I don't know who I am. The only thing I do know is that I was a lot happier before you and Shay and Charles were in my life. As soon as I let myself start feeling something, then I set myself up to fall."

"That's what love is, you fool. To love is to open yourself up and to be vulnerable. But to love and to be loved is worth all the pain that comes with it."

Brooks gave a half-smile. "For some people. I don't buy into every cliché."

"Can we keep taking it slow?" she asked. "I won't leave the mountain, but I can't have you tell me right now that there's no chance for us. Let me win you back. Let me prove to you that you can trust me. Let me show you that love is better than what you'll find without it."

"No," he said. "We can't take it slow. I've made up my mind and there's no changing. It's not going to work between us, Abby. I'm sorry."

"But we were back; everything was getting better." She twisted her head away from him. Eventually, she said, "You're not even saying that you want to be friends."

"I don't know. Seems like a good idea, but I don't even think it's a conversation right now. I still love you, so I can't just turn a friend switch on."

"If you're still in love with me, fucking love me!" There was that F-word she so rarely used.

"I'm sorry," he said, standing. "The only thing I can say right now is that I hope you stay on the mountain. Red Mountain is better with you on it."

"Why the hell would I stay here? Do you really think I could go to work every day knowing you're right up the hill making wine? The man I love is a few feet away. And even though he loves me, he doesn't want to be with me. How could I ever stay here?"

"Then I'll leave. Luca and Emilia need you more than ever."

"You can't leave. That would break Jake's heart."

"If it comes down to one of us leaving, it's going to be me."

She cracked into a grin that was full of sarcasm and heartache. "This fucking mountain," she said.

"Tell me about it." Brooks went to the door and put his hand on the brass knob. "I'm sure we'll see each other around."

"Don't be so sure," she said.

"Take care, Abby." He navigated the steps as the door swung closed behind him.

50

THE CONCERT FOR ÉPIPHANIE

Tonight was a big night. Her son was about to take the stage with Jake Forester. He and Jake had finished their album but hadn't shared it with anyone outside of the recording studio. Tonight, they were giving away CDs and playing all the tunes in front of 994 people who'd paid a fortune to see the band and to contribute to the second phase of Épiphanie.

Margot had performed on Broadway for several years and had always been calm pre-show. But something about this evening made her desperately nervous for Jasper. It made no sense: he wasn't at all shaken up. In fact, he was in his room watching HBO, not a care in the world. That was, perhaps, why he was going to do so well. Sitting at a piano and dancing on the keys was easier to him than anything in the world, way easier than asking a girl out or even walking into a classroom.

She checked herself out in the long mirror hanging on the bathroom door. Margot wore a long yellow dress with three-quarter-length sleeves and a slit on the side that would have made Margot 1.0 uncomfortable. But she'd lost twenty-four pounds in just over two months, and she felt pretty great wearing it. "Look at those stems, girl," she said to herself, eyeing her legs. "Good for you."

What a long way she'd come. It was only a couple of months ago that she was a complete wreck. Sure, she had work to do, but that was okay. She was finally aware of herself, aware of how crazy she'd been. That was the most important part, to be able to see the sickness.

Look at her now. She looked better and felt better, and she'd been able to forgive the man who had single-handedly destroyed her life. Ever since Thanksgiving when they'd invited Rory, she'd felt more alive. She wasn't excited to see him, but she had come to the realization that she didn't need to expend more energy hating him or anyone else. Life was too short.

The only bit of sadness she had was that she didn't have a man to take her to this concert, someone to walk her across the field and into that tent. It was okay, though. She wasn't as sad as Margot 1.0 would have been. Two months before, she never thought she'd meet anyone again. Now, she knew she would eventually. And even if it took years —or even if she didn't, she'd be happy. It was just tonight that she wanted someone to share such a proud moment. Jasper was about to cross over into the real world. He'd never again be the sweet boy she once knew. And it would have been nice to have a man's arm to hold on to as she entered that tent. It was okay, though. It really was okay.

Her son came out of his room as she was going down the stairs. "Wow, Mom. Look at you. You look hot!"

"Thank you. And you look hot yourself." Jasper wore brand-new dark jeans, blue loafers, a white shirt, and a blue blazer. He'd slicked his hair back too—a new look that fit him well, one only a musician could get away with.

"Excited?" she asked.

"I feel like the clock stopped. I just want us to be on stage already."

"What time are you heading over?" They'd done a sound check earlier in the day.

"Meeting at 6:30 backstage." It was about 5:30 now.

"Have you talked to your dad?"

"We were texting earlier. I left a ticket for him at will call. I'll catch up with him after the show."

She strutted over and hugged him. "I'm really proud of you."

"You too, Mom! Look at all you've done, what you've created here."

She put her hand on his cheek. "Thanks for noticing."

"Can I escort you to the concert?" he asked. "I need a date."

Those words nearly brought her to her knees. Without warning, her eyes watered and she did her best to stifle a cry.

"Hey, what's going on? You okay?"

She wiped her eyes with her index fingers, trying hard not to ruin her mascara. "It would be my great honor to walk over with you."

~

HE WAS the best date she could ever ask for. Cars were already lining up along the gravel road leading past the inn, and people were making their way to the show. She'd turned on every light—inside and out—of Épiphanie, and her dream shined in the night like an *agriturismo* in Tuscany.

The evening was cool, and Margot was glad she'd worn a wrap. They'd lucked out on the weather. The past few days had been gray, but tonight was cloudless and full of stars.

She and Jasper talked and laughed as they strolled. He made her feel like a lady, and this walk felt very much to her like she was escorting her son to manhood. She knew he'd make such a fine husband one day, and a fine father. Somehow, despite the hardships of the past couple of years, Jasper had only become stronger and more resilient; and at the same time, more gentle and kind.

The gigantic white tent came into view, and Margot thought of her childhood and going to the circus. According to Jasper, the last time they'd used this particular tent was for a Cirque du Soleil event in Seattle. Lights lit the pathways and the grounds, and stronger lights pointed up from the ground to the tent, creating a wonderful glow that the people walking along the road headed toward.

It was chilly enough that not many people were standing outside of the tent. The elegant patrons rushed in, making for the open bar on the left near the heaters. Margot marveled at what Jake's team had done, especially with the stage. Spanish acoustic guitar music came from the stage speakers, increasing the anticipation of the concert to come, drawing attention to the instruments waiting for their masters.

Jasper's black Steinway shone bright in the lights stage left. They'd set Jake up in the middle, his four guitars propped up on stands. A sound tech was speaking into Jake's microphone, making last minute adjustments with a man behind the soundboard. Behind Jake's setup, there was a very simple drum kit with brushes resting on the snare. A lone electric bass waited stage right.

Above, a massive screen displayed a beautiful collage of farm animal photos with Épiphanie's logo—a simple affair with an old-fashioned font—hovering front and center. She never could have imagined the day, a complete dream come true. An inn, the sanctuary, and her son there to bring it all to reality using a talent so few could ever be blessed with.

Rows of chairs already more than half-full ran from the back bar all the way to the stage. Reporters from *Rolling Stone* and *The Seattle Times* were somewhere in that crowd. The bartenders wore black ties and were serving top-shelf liquor and Red Mountain wines; a gorgeous display of appetizers graced another table. Jasper got Margot a glass of wine. "Okay, Mom. I'm going to head back and get focused."

She balled her fist in the air. "Tear 'em up, kiddo."

"We will." He kissed her and headed to the stage, disappearing around the side. Margot sipped her wine and looked around. She didn't see anyone she knew.

Rory was suddenly standing next to her. "Hi, Margot."

She turned and looked at her ex-husband. He still dressed like he was only a moment away from his next speech, with his heavily starched shirt and perfectly pressed pants. He'd certainly aged some. That handsome, schoolboy face that had earned him the mayoral election had withered away, replaced by the figurative scarlet letter the public had burned onto his forehead. His smile looked foreign on him, like it was the first one in a while.

She was actually shocked by her own reaction. She had been worried that all of the old emotions would erupt upon seeing him, and she'd suddenly produce a filet knife from her purse and carve up his face.

Instead, what she felt first was pity. Rory was serving a life sentence, forced to live with his mistakes, forced to live without his wife and son. Perhaps he didn't care about her anymore, but he loved Jasper. He'd been a good father, had never missed a recital or a chance to visit his school, and he'd been nearly obsessed with their son since he'd been born. Then *whoosh*. Gone. No more son.

Margot saw the pain in him, and it was through that lens she found forgiveness. He'd been swept up in a stupid affair, and he'd been paying for it. He'd always pay for it. Forever and ever.

She didn't feel like hugging him; she wasn't quite that much of a Buddha. But she managed a smile. "I'm glad you came."

"Thanks for letting me. I miss him, Marge. I miss hearing him play."

"I know." She put some substance into the smile. "I know."

"You look great," he said. "Like, really great."

"Thank you."

"This is for you?" he asked. "This whole farm sanctuary?"

"It's not for me. It's for the animals. And for Red Mountain."

"It was your dream. Good for you."

"I can't believe it," she confessed.

"Well," he said, shrugging his shoulders. "I'm going to take a seat. If I don't see you again, please know how thankful I am. I know I don't deserve it."

"No, you don't. But he deserves a dad."

"He deserves better than me."

"Sometimes, we have to do the best with what we have."

He waved his hand. "Good to see you, Margot."

"You too."

51

STAGE PRESENTS

T he seats were about half-taken when Emilia and her mom arrived. They bumped into Margot, and the three ended up sitting together among a very mixed-age crowd. Jake's fans had always been that way: a mix of the people who had followed Folkwhore since their start in the Seattle grunge bars and the younger kids late to the discovery.

The chatter turned to heavy applause as Jake took the stage. The house lights dimmed, making it fairly dark inside the tent. He stepped up to the mike, into the spotlight. The crowd stood and cheered. The cameramen who were broadcasting the concert live over the Internet began shuffling back and forth.

Jake looked like he belonged. He wore jeans and cowboy boots and a black t-shirt, and he stuffed his hands into his back pockets and let the applause die down. When everything quieted, he smirked. "This is going to be fun!"

People clapped again. He asked everyone to sit, and they listened well.

"Tonight, I'm going to introduce you to someone I think you're going to like. A couple of months ago, I found out one of my neighbors here on Red Mountain plays the piano. Well, I shouldn't say 'plays.' This young man doesn't play the piano. He *is* the piano. His name is Jasper Simpson, and we've been playing music together nearly every day since we met. In only a month, we put together an album's worth of material; then we brought in Jay and Willy on bass and drums and cut this new record in four days. That doesn't happen." He smiled. "It's been way too much fun for an old codger like me, so I thought I'd ask you guys to come out and share with us. And there was an even better reason that brought us together."

He looked out to the crowd, past the light shining in his face. "Where's Margot Pierce?"

Emilia took Margot's arm. "Stand up!"

Margot stood and waved at Jake. "This woman is the reason we're all here," Jake said. "They say your mom makes you who you are. Well, this is Jasper's mom and he's a lucky guy. All of the proceeds tonight go to Épiphanie, the farm sanctuary Margot has started right on this very property. Your money tonight is going to help create a home for misplaced farm animals that deserve a better life than what they're getting."

He looked at Margot again and smiled. Margot blushed, feeling uncomfortable sitting so close to Carmen. Jake continued, "That's the kind of person Margot is, and we're happy to have her on Red Mountain. I'm sure you'll see her website all around tonight, in your booklet, on the bottles, behind us on the projector. We welcome you to donate more. We still have a long way to go, but tonight is a big jumpstart. It's a cool thing to have a farm sanctuary here on Red Mountain. This world would be a lot less wonderful without animals, and we need to take care of them.

"Also on this website, you'll see Margot is a couple of months away from opening an inn right down that road you came in on. She's a hell of a cook and host, and she's the first to give people a place to stay on this great mountain. So come stay at the inn and taste the wines and live the Red Mountain life for a few days. There's no place like it on earth, I promise you. Please give Margot a hand."

Margot waved to the crowd and sat down as the audience

continued a long applause. Jake made eye contact with Emilia and waved to her. She waved back.

"You guys ready to hear some music?"

The audience roared as the house lights dimmed. The band took the stage, and four bright lights hit the musicians. Emilia watched Jasper. He made an adorable wave to the crowd as he sat at the piano bench. He looked at the keys for a moment and took a deep breath. Then he turned back to Jake. They nodded at each other, and Jasper faced his piano again. He placed his fingers on the keys and waited a moment. The crowd quieted.

He began to play, tearing right into what Emilia thought was a fast and difficult passage. She recognized the tune from rehearsals. Emilia felt the whole crowd being blown away by Jasper's effortless virtuosity. The rest of the band joined in, and Jake started to sing. Her dad looked so happy, and they sounded like a band that had been playing together their whole lives.

The night flew by. Emilia realized she hadn't taken her eyes off Jasper the entire show. Jake spoke again before their last song, and he introduced the band and thanked everyone for coming. As the four men left the stage, the crowd screamed for an encore. Obligingly, the band came back for one more.

For the first time other than singing and saying "thank you," Jasper spoke. He took the mic off its stand and turned to the crowd. "Thanks for coming tonight. I hope you enjoy our new album, and I really hope I can talk Jake into another one of these gigs. This has been the highlight of my life. We're going to do one more."

Jasper spoke to the crowd like he'd been doing it his whole life. He glanced over at Emilia for a second, then turned back. "This one's for the girl whose light blinds all my darkness. And she doesn't even know it."

He turned back to the piano, raising his hand to count off. The band came in together, a groovy, almost R&B bass line leading the way. Jake and Jasper sang beautifully together, and Emilia broke into chill bumps. As they brought the song to a close, Jasper looked back at Emilia, and she knew for sure that he was talking about her.

They played the last note, and Emilia immediately stood and navigated her way to the stage. She knew both the bouncers and they guided her up. Jasper was waving at the crowd and heading offstage. She yelled, "Jasper!"

He turned.

For the first time, they looked at each other with a realization of what they shared between them.

They approached each other. "How'd we do?" he asked, speaking loudly as to overcome the crowd.

"It was beautiful. You're beautiful."

"That song was for you if you didn't catch the hint."

"I was hoping so."

That was all the green light he needed, and he went straight for her, kissing her lips in front of this huge crowd of people applauding and yelling for more. He put his hands on her sides and pulled her closer.

They parted lips and met each other's eyes. She felt a sullen feeling come over her, something dark. He saw it in her and said, "What's wrong?"

"I'm broken, Jasper. Why would you want me?"

He firmly grasped her arms above the elbows. "You're not broken. And even if you were broken into a million different pieces, I'd still want you, every little piece. Look at me." She did and he said, "Do you hear me?"

"Yeah." She nodded her head, feeling more free than ever before, free to be herself for once in her life.

He kissed her again, a touch of the lips, an aftershock. He asked, "So what now?"

She took his hands. "You and me, Jasper Simpson. You and me."

"That's exactly what I was thinking."

The house lights came on around them.

52

A MIRACLE AND A GUN

The hospital squeezed Otis in early Monday morning for an MRI. Dr. Jezewski was as anxious as Otis for an explanation. They'd have to wait a couple of days for the results, though, so Otis headed back home where Joan waited for him, a date involving bicycles ahead. Passing Henry's house, he noticed Cody was gone again. Maybe this time that poor dog really had gotten away.

Every time he passed his neighbor's house, Otis revisited Thanksgiving morning and the loss of his wine. The police had nothing. No witnesses, no fingerprints, nothing left behind. All Otis had to go on is what Brooks had said about Henry indicating guilt with his shit-eating grin. That information wasn't going to do a damn thing in a court of law.

What was Otis going to do? Go beat it out of Henry? Unlikely. All he could do was hope that Henry and his wife would leave Red Mountain, because Otis damn well intended to die there. Otis had insurance and would be reimbursed for the lost wine, but it was the vintage that couldn't be replaced. And now that he could smell and taste again—in fact he could taste better than he had in years—he'd tasted what was left of this vintage. Brooks was right: the wines were stunning.

At least I have Joan, he thought. *At least I have her.* That's what mattered most. He climbed out of his truck and headed into the house. The chickens were in their normal spot near the woodpile, nesting in the dirt, bathing in the sun. Hearing a chain dragging along the ground, he turned. There was Cody, the Australian Shepherd, running to him.

"Hey, guy." The dog ran up as Otis knelt to greet him. "You have to run a lot farther than my house to get away from that son of a bitch." He rubbed Cody's ears, and Cody pushed into his hands, loving the attention. He licked Otis's pant leg and barked.

"I wish I knew what you were saying."

The dog barked again.

Otis barked back. The dog loved it and barked again. They traded barks back and forth, and Otis grinned and gave the dog a big hug. "I'd love to keep you. You have to know that."

That's when Henry came stumbling down the gravel drive yelling, "Cody! Cody!"

"Here we go again," Otis said. "You getting me in another fight?"

Cody barked.

Otis stood and squinted his eyes at Henry. It was the first time Otis had seen him in weeks, though Otis had pictured the bastard in his mind, imagining breaking down the man's door. But what good would that do? He'd feel better for a minute, but he'd probably get thrown in jail just like Brooks and Shay, and he'd miss out on precious moments with Joan.

Watching Henry coming up that drive in his overalls, stumbling drunk, fired up Otis's anger.

"I need you to get off my land. We've been through this before."

"I'm just getting my dog," Henry mumbled through the gap in his teeth, clearly a six-pack deep already. His eyes glowed demon red, like there might be more running through his veins than beer.

"Not today, Henry. Not on my property. How about you call him from your place and see if he comes?"

"Funny, old man." He looked at his dog, gritting his decaying teeth. "Cody! Get your ass over here."

"Get the hell off my land! You may have gotten away with dumping my wine out, but today you're not going to be so lucky."

"Cody!"

The dog moved his eyes from one man to the other, torn between listening to his owner and staying with Otis. Otis knelt back down and held Cody's collar. "You stay with me, pal."

"Get your hands off my dog!" Henry hissed.

Otis pointed his finger. "I'll ask you again. Walk your ass back home."

Henry reached under the bib of his overalls and drew a handgun, probably the same one he'd held on Brooks and Shay at Thanksgiving. "Let go of my dog!" he yelled, pointing the gun at Otis's chest.

Otis let go of Cody and instinctively raised his hands in the air. "Now, calm down, Henry."

"Get over here, you dumb-ass dog!"

Cody didn't move.

Otis knelt down again and touched the dog. "You'd better go home. Save this fight for another day."

Cody buried himself in between Otis's legs. Otis looked back up at Henry. "I don't even know why you want the poor dog. He clearly doesn't like you."

Henry steadied his aim. "You step back and get away from my dog."

"What is it I've done to you anyway? You go and empty out my wine, trying to destroy my livelihood. Now, you pull a gun on me. What is it with you?"

"You really don't know, do you?"

"I really don't."

"You people." He shook his head. "You people move onto our land, you wine people. Trying to move us out so you can get rich. I'm not putting up with it."

"We *people* are making you all rich. This land, your land, is worth fifty times what it would be had we not come here."

"I grew up on this land. I raised my boys on this land. You think I want to sell? They'll just keep raising property taxes until I have to.

I'm tired of all these people coming in here and running off my neighbors, planting more and more vines. This land used to be beautiful. Now it's a goddamn nightmare. Soon it'll be fucking Disney World, with hotels and restaurants and golf courses. Soon I won't even be able to piss outside."

"Move a few miles down the road. It looks the same."

"Why don't you people move a few miles down the road? The wine's not going to change."

"That's where you're wrong. There's something about this place, this specific mountain, the wines here, and I'd do anything if I could open your eyes to it." Otis knew he was wasting his words but found himself saying them anyway.

"I'm done talking. Step away from my dog or I'll shoot you dead."

Henry's face was getting redder, almost as red as his eyes. Otis knew it was time to step away. He backed up a few feet. Holding the gun up at Otis, Henry moved toward the dog, reaching down for the collar. Cody snapped at Henry and let out a long growl. Henry pulled back. "What are you doing?"

He reached down again, and Cody chomped down on Henry's hand. Henry jerked back up and ripped his hand out of Cody's mouth, revealing deep punctures and a few heavy drops of blood. Henry cursed and reared back to kick Cody.

Otis moved as quickly as he could to stop him, but Henry kicked Cody full on in the chest with his boot. Cody yelped as he landed several feet away onto his back.

Before Otis could reach them, Henry got his gun up in the air, pointed back at Otis's chest. Otis backed off, throwing his hands in the air. "You can't go kicking that dog on my property."

"No? What are you going to do about it?" Henry was fuming now, his gun hand shaking badly. Otis wondered if he was high on something. Cody got up and moved farther away, casting an eye toward Henry.

Otis shook his head and backed up, knowing there was nothing he could do. He said, "You're a coldhearted bastard."

The door to the house opened, and both men and the dog turned. Joan was standing there.

"Go inside, Joan," Otis said. "I'll be there in a minute."

Joan looked at them, one by one. She smiled at Otis, and it was at that moment he realized the seriousness of the situation.

"Joan, go back inside."

Joan looked over at the neighbor and said, "Henry, please go home."

Henry moved the gun toward Joan and pointed it at her head. He said, "You heard him. Go back inside."

"Put that gun down!" Otis said. Then, much less aggressively, "Please, Henry. Put that gun down. She's my baby."

A shot rang out. Joan fell.

Otis ran as fast as he could toward her, barely hearing Henry in the background, going, "Shit! I didn't mean to pull the trigger. Shit!"

Otis ran up the steps and slid onto the stone porch next to her. She was bleeding from her neck, coughing velvet blood into a gathering puddle. Her eyes were open and blankly looking up.

"Call 911!" Otis yelled. "Call 911!" He realized there was no one else there. He felt the adrenalin kick in and he began to shake, but he had to focus. He ran to his truck, noticing Henry stumbling home. Otis got his phone out of the cup holder and stabbed at the numbers. *711.* No, his fingers were shaking. *834.* No. *912.* He couldn't dial! He put the phone down on the seat and steadied his right hand with his left. He desperately focused and finally stabbed out the correct digits.

He ran back to her. Joan was now breathing in short, sharp gasps. Everything he had was going away; dying. She was dying, leaving the world. *No, no, no, no.*

53

HERE'S MOMMY!

Brooks hadn't gone in to work yet. It was almost eleven on Monday morning. Jake and his brother and his dad had been calling him all day. Noise, noise, noise. Everywhere, noise.

He was sitting on the couch staring at the ceiling, the cable news on in the background blabbing politics. If Abby were on the couch next to him, she'd either be nodding her head or yelling at the TV, depending on the talking head. Brooks didn't know what to do with his life. He'd made the decision about Abby and that felt like the right one, but what about everything else? Most importantly, what was he going to do about work and Red Mountain?

He got up to answer a knock on the door, not bothering to button his shirt. He pulled the door open.

He'd seen her pictures in his dad's wallet, and he'd been amazed by her idle beauty. Not the kind that made Marilyn Monroe famous, but not cute either. Somewhere in between. His mother was beautiful like an eagle flapping her wings up high in the western sky.

Past her beauty, though, beyond what she'd want anyone to see, Brooks saw a sadness in her wildflower-blue eyes. Perhaps Brooks could see the truth of her because they shared the same blood. There was even sadness in the way her white hair fell to her slightly drooping shoulders. The whole world was pulling her down. He saw a rusted red and brown heartbreak pumping through the veins near her cheeks and eyes and through her neck.

What do you say to your mother when you've never met her? They stared at each other, wading through a deep pool of curiosity, taking in the loved one they'd never had.

She finally spoke. "I'm so sorry, Brooks."

It's so easy to be sorry, he thought. All you have to do was to say the words. Anyone can be sorry. He could be sorry. But how do you forgive?

He nodded to her, no words available.

She smiled awkwardly. "Can I come in?"

He moved aside and she eyed her surroundings. "It's beautiful," she said. "And really clean. You are your father's son, aren't you?"

Still, he had nothing to say.

She turned back to him as he stood in the foyer, bouncing his eyes around, grasping for reality. She said, "I guess the ball's in my court, isn't it?" She approached him and whispered, "Say something."

"Mom," he said tentatively, as if trying it on for size.

"Yes, I'm your mom." She looked at him, waiting for him to open up. She took his hand. Her fingers were long and bony, but they were warm, like a mother's should be. "I'm sorry it's taken me this long. I've wanted to meet you since the day Charles found you. But it wasn't that easy. I'm so ashamed. I left you alone. I abandoned you." She looked to be so past the crying that all she had left was the pain.

"You didn't abandon me," Brooks said. "Don't think that." He'd accepted this fact years ago. "You put me up for adoption. It's different. You did what was best for me."

Still holding his hand, she said, "You're right. We did what we thought was best for you. But still. You can't really know."

"That was a long time ago."

"I hurt every day." She brushed the side of his head with her warm hand. "You're okay, aren't you?"

"Sometimes." He wanted to sound stronger but she'd caught him at a bad time.

"Can we sit down?"

"Yeah," he said, leading her to the same couch where he'd been lying.

"Look, I'm not going to pretend to be your mother. Your parent. I don't deserve that. But you need to know that I love you, even after being absent from your life for so long. I always have and always will, even if you tell me to walk out of your life right now."

She sighed. "Charles told me what's going on. With you. With your fiancée. With your work. With your brother. It's all too much. I know. Allow me, my son, to say something. Will you let me do that?"

"Why not?"

"If there's one thing I could have taught you, if there's one thing I could have said to you before we left you, it's this." She sat up some and turned toward him. "The closer you get to people, the harder it is to love them. But you have to love them anyway. You have to work at it. And you can't walk away from them. That's what love is. As these words come out of my mouth, I realize I'm in no place to say them, but I'm saying them anyway."

Noise, noise, noise. It was the same noise coming out of everyone's mouths.

She said, "When your father turned Shay away—when he went to prison—it almost ended us. I felt so much anger toward your father. But it was all miscommunication and sickness and pain. He didn't mean the things he said to your brother. He was hurting inside. His dad—your grandfather—was in and out of prison, and your father struggled with that. He still does."

"Why was my grandfather in prison?"

"Beating your grandmother. Beating Charles. Time and time again. He was a drunk."

"Why didn't they leave him? Why didn't she take Charles and run?"

"That would be the better story, wouldn't it?" Moving on, she said, "Shay didn't mean the things he said either. I had to learn to forgive them both. I was able to do that. I just was never able to forgive myself for letting you go."

"You have to forgive yourself."

"I know." She sat back. "Will you forgive Abby?"

"One day."

"I don't know her. But your father's told me about her. Brooks, she sounds like the kind of woman worth giving a second chance."

His phone rang on the coffee table in front of him, and Otis's name lit up on the display.

"One minute, please," he told her. "I need to answer this."

"Of course."

Otis whispered, "I need you," and that's all it took for Brooks to be running out the door, mumbling to his mother that they'd have to talk later.

54

SOMETIMES SURPRISES

Margot spent the sunny Monday morning with Shay, making plans for the sanctuary. They would build the stable and the coop on the far east side near the water well, and Margot made it clear she wanted housing fit for royalty. Then they'd build a shelter for the tractor and hay farther to the right. Shay said he'd have all the construction done in two months. Right about the same time Épiphanie was set to open. She knew better than to believe timelines, but Ron sure had built back her faith in men.

She meandered back along the dirt road, visiting with several of the hens who were testing her property line. At the inn, she found Ron working on the fountain, his knees on the ground, his right hand holding a screwdriver. Along the pathway to the front door, he'd built a stone wall, and on the wall hung the porcelain fountain. It featured a young girl made of stone with flowers in her hair, standing on her toes, drinking. Well, she was about to be drinking, once Ron got the water started.

"Is it making sense?" she asked.

He turned to her, and as was his custom, removed his wide-brimmed hat. "Yeah, I think I have it. You mind flipping the switch?"

He'd installed the switch on the back side of the fountain. She flipped it and heard the water start to flow.

"Look at that!"

Margot came back around the stone wall and looked at the young girl, who was finally getting her drink of water. "Good job. Thank you."

He stood up and brushed the dirt off his jeans. Dust clouded around his knees before falling to the ground. "Saw Tanner Henderson at Home Depot today."

She hadn't heard that name in a while. She'd even started to forget about her old contractor. "Oh, boy."

"He was in the checkout lane next to me."

"Did you say anything to him?" Margot knew Ron wasn't afraid to speak his mind.

"I saw him pocketing a pack of Juicy Fruit."

"What? Stealing?"

"Yep. He didn't think anyone was watching. I turned to the employee checking me out and told her. She got the manager involved."

"Can you get arrested for stealing chewing gum?"

"Who knows? I didn't bother sticking around. Either way, he won't be welcomed back. Tough to work in construction and be blackballed from Home Depot. Just proves how much of a bonehead he is."

"Maybe he'll learn one day. I really don't wish him ill. I just hope he stops taking advantage of people."

"Yeah. Anyway, he's not worth wasting any more words on today. I have something I'd like to ask you." Ron pinched his mustache and asked, "Could I take you out?"

The question floored her, and she immediately looked down at his left hand. No ring. "Aren't you married?" she asked.

"I haven't been married for a long time."

"But you were wearing a ring."

"My wife died three years ago. I left the ring on. Until last week, when I decided I was ready. I wanted to ask you out."

Margot was confused, but then started thinking, *Oh, my god! He's asking me out. Now calm yourself. Don't throw yourself at him. Act nonchalant.* She nodded her head, when what she really wanted to do was start skipping in circles. She looked at him with Margot 2.0 eyes and said, "I'd like that."

"Great," he said, smiling. "Great."

"Where are we going?" she asked.

"To be honest, I don't know of a place worthy of you around here."

Wow, he knew what to say. "I'm not that picky."

"But I want to make sure it's right. Let me think on it. Are you free tomorrow night?"

"I am."

"Seven o'clock. I'll pick you up."

She said goodbye and strolled back to the house. That's when she got the call from Brooks Baker.

55

THE REAL ME

Emilia left her science class and came around the corner to see Jasper waiting by her locker. He had his earphones in, but when he saw her, he pulled them out.

"Excuse me," he said in his British accent. "I'm darting around looking for my girlfriend. Have you seen her?" He raised his hands and tickled the air with his fingers. "A very nice figure. Stunning lips like budding tulips. Teeth as white as freshly fallen snow. Eyes the color of evergreens."

Using her own British accent, she said, "Was it that cute brunette who just passed by?" Only with Jasper Simpson would she have the guts to try out her awful dialect.

"Could be," he said, staying in character, his accent spot on. "She's a real spitfire. Hard to miss."

Emilia pointed with her thumb over her shoulder. "That had to be her."

"Well, thanks then." Jasper smiled and continued on past another set of lockers. She turned to watch him go and after he'd gone about twenty feet, he turned back. She tilted her head, watching him. He surprised her by waving and dipping around a corner to another hallway. She burst into a laugh that came all the way from her core.

"The nerve," she said to herself, eyeing the corner.

After almost a full minute, he popped his head back around. Not his body, just his head. And he winked. Yes, he knew she'd still be waiting for him.

She shook her finger at him.

Jasper returned and took her hands and kissed her lips like there was no one else in that hallway. That's the way he made her feel. Like there was no one else on earth.

After the next class, she checked her phone. Margot and her mother had both left voice mails. She listened to the first message and started running toward the double doors.

56

A MOUNTAIN OF LOVE

They wandered into Joan's stark white room at Kadlec Hospital.

Otis.

Margot. Jasper.

Jake. Carmen. Emilia. Luca.

Brooks.

It was nine o'clock at night, almost eleven hours after she'd been shot, though Otis felt like it had been days. Unable to think about himself for a moment, he hadn't even gone for a sip of water. A nurse had forced him to drink some coffee and eat a sponge cake.

Her surgeon already operated on Joan twice. It wasn't looking good. He had been very clear about that, saying she may not make it through the night. Otis had been in and out a few times but only now at this moment had the nurse led everyone else in from the waiting room.

Joan was in a coma. Her right clavicle had been shattered, though her spine was intact. She'd lost a tremendous amount of blood. Her brain had suffered from a lack of blood and oxygen, and they couldn't be sure of the damage.

The police had arrested Henry Davidson, and he'd go to jail for a long time. But Otis wasn't spending much time hating the man. He was devoting the majority of his energy to loving Joan.

Her friends circled around her, getting a glimpse of her pale face, all of them for the first time seeing the most alive person they knew running out of time, the constant beep of the heart monitor the only signal of life.

Otis found himself strong and hopeful, though prepared to lose her. Before knowing Joan, he might have been a wreck. But there was a strange sense in the core of him that knew it was going to be okay, even if she breathed her last breath on that bed. He knew she'd be all right. And he had to be strong, because he wasn't the only one losing her. So many people were losing her, not just in that room, but surely countless others out there, ones he'd never met, ones whose lives she'd changed as well.

Even as their healer lay there weak and dying, white and cold, she gave him courage. She was so much more than her flesh. He took her hand and in that very quiet room, he said to the group, "I'm not sure if she can hear us, but I'd like for those who care to, to say something."

"Yes," Margot said. "I'm sure she'd love that."

"Maybe we could all hold hands too," Otis said, reaching out. He took Joan's almost lifeless right hand. On the other side of the bed, Margot closed the circle by taking Joan's other hand. Otis felt a great power in their unity, in that circle.

"I'll go first," Otis said, looking at his lover's face, at the lips he'd kissed, at the lids covering the eyes he'd gazed into so many times. "You gave me a new life. It's as simple as that. I know you'd say that you didn't do anything, that I did it all myself, but really, you're the one who woke me up." He shook his head. "Boy, you're something special. I love you. With all my heart. And I want to marry you and I want to go on this trip with you. Don't make me go at it alone. Not yet. Not when we're just getting started." He smiled. "I want to eat spinach and kale and daffodils with you. I want to go on more crazy dates and do things no one our age would do. I want to see what else you have up your sleeve, Joan Tobey." An overwhelming sadness rose from his heart and pushed out through his red eyes and dry mouth, leaving him breathless. "Come back. You hear me? Come back."

Otis looked back at everyone, the heartbreak palpable.

Margot spoke up. "I'd like to say something." She looked at Joan. "You woke me up too, Joan. You showed me the *Om*, the great *Om*, the reason for being. Oh, God, where would I be without you?" She cackled, nervously. "If these people even knew how bad I was, right? Come back to us, my dear friend. The world needs you. We love you. I love you."

Each of them said their words to Joan, even Luca, who made the room laugh softly. When the laughing wilted back to sadness, Otis said, "We're waiting on you, baby. Come on back." He lost his breath, heaving air, gasping for it, and his eyes watered, and he coughed and cried. He said the only words he had left to say. "We all believe."

Otis shut his eyes and lifted his head to the ceiling, to the moon. Squeezing his friends' hands tighter, unifying their circle, he howled. He howled like he was outside in his vineyard on all fours at midnight, the leader summoning his pack. He howled again and again, calling out to Joan's soaring spirit, asking his mate to come back to him for just a few more minutes, a few more days, a few more years.

Please. One last lap before eternity; one more chance to say goodbye.

Ahhhhhhhh-ooooooooooo!

As the echo of Otis's howl subsided, a surge of energy ran through his hand, and Joan softly squeezed his palm. Otis gasped and looked down. Though her eyes were still closed, he knew she was on her way back to him.

If you enjoyed this story, please take a moment to leave a short review on Amazon.com. It makes a world of difference.

~

For other books in this series, free stories, updates, and my newsletter sign-up, visit boowalker.com.

boowalker

ACKNOWLEDGMENTS

Without my wife, I'd have quit creating art years ago. Thanks, Mikella, my shaman, for believing in me and putting up with me. Please don't tell anyone how much you contributed to this book; they may take my name off the cover. You continually remind me of the great *Om* and the endless depths of life and art and love.

Riggs, you've reminded me of what's important in life. I hope it shows in my writing. What great fun we have ahead of us, my son.

Thank you to my dear family and friends, especially my mother-in-law, Patty, for trudging through the early drafts, offering wonderful criticism, and selflessly promoting my work.

Thank you, Nancy Beaty, for offering your superb editing skills.

Thanks to my west coast family, the Hedges, for taking me in and teaching me everything I know about wine.

Thank you, Leila Meacham, for lighting the fire for this book and encouraging me to push a little harder and dig a little deeper. I'll never forget your generosity, and I promise you I'll pass it forward one day.

And a giant thank you to everyone who reads my books. Art doesn't exist without an audience.

BOOK CLUB GUIDE FOR RED MOUNTAIN

Who is your favorite character? Who is your least favorite character?

Who would you cast as the main characters in the movie of *Red Mountain*?

What were the strongest wants/desires of Otis, Margot, Emilia, and Brooks?

In *Red Mountain*, Boo switches points of view in each chapter? Did you find this device an effective way to tell this story or was it too confusing?

Would you consider Red Mountain to be a character itself?

Do you disagree with Jake taking Carmen back?

How did Aunt Morgan affect Otis?

What was Joan's purpose in the novel?

Talk about the following minor characters: Aunt Morgan, Shay, Abby, Jake, Carmen, Luca, Brooks's parents, Jasper, Mr. Massey. What purpose did they serve?

Did this book change the way you think about wine?

Toward the end, Brooks's mom tells him: "The closer you get to people, the harder it is to love them. But you have to love them anyway. You have to work at it. And you can't walk away from them. That's what love is." How does this message pertain to the entire story?

Knowing the author did not initially intend on writing a sequel, do you think Red Mountain could have been a stand-alone novel? (Boo asks, bracing for criticism.)

What questions were left unanswered?

If you had to make assumptions as to what happened after the end of the novel, what would they be?

Would you consider the power of belief to be a strong element in *Red Mountain*? If so, how would that pertain to this somewhat controversial ending?

Do you find any other books/authors to be similar to Boo and his book?

Have you read any other books by Boo? How is *Red Mountain* different?

Bonus Question:

Did you wonder what Joan was doing at the doctor's office when she ran into Otis?

Notable passages worthy of discussion:

1) Otis crossed his arms and put his head down. "If only all beginnings didn't come with endings."

Morgan touched his arm. "You can't think that way."

"It's all I've ever known. My life is one big black cat crossing in front of me."

2) Growing and making wine was the purest of art forms: to work the land all year—to work with the land all year—to bleed and sweat and toil through the seasons, to bring in the harvest and guide the juice all the way to a bottle, and to share that bottle with the world. To share the fruit of a time and place. To help people smile.

3) It was about committing to a piece of land, to an area; not simply by planting vines, but by building a community, an ecosystem where animals thrive, where healthy children are raised with great ambition; a place that people talk about all over the globe, a place chefs come to open restaurants in hopes of finding that perfect pairing or perhaps connecting with farmers to bring back an old heirloom grain. It was about creating a magical environment so that when people tasted the wines at a later time in another place, they would be transported to Red Mountain and all its greatness.

4) Joan says, "I believe there's no good to be found in reliving memories, especially those times that hurt. And there's certainly no sense in dreading things that might not ever happen."

5) Joan says, "We're going to practice visualization. If you can create something in your mind, you can create it in your physical world as well. I want you to picture yourself on this day a year from now. Picture where you are. Where you want to be. Picture what you're wearing. All the way to your socks and shoes. What are you doing? Who are you with? What do you smell? What do you feel like? Every

detail. That's you. That can be your reality. I practice this every day. I create my own reality. We all do."

*Apropos the above thought, Emilia fears that if she isn't able to picture something, something or someone else will draw her destiny. How do you, the reader, feel about this notion?

ABOUT BOO

Bestselling author Boo Walker initially tapped his creative muse as a songwriter and banjoist in Nashville before working his way west to Washington State, where he bought a gentleman's farm on the Yakima River. It was there amongst the grapevines and wine barrels that he fell in love with telling stories that now resonate with book clubs around the world. Rich with colorful characters and boundless soul, his novels will leave you with an open heart and a lifted spirit.

Always a wanderer, Boo currently lives in Cape Elizabeth, Maine with his wife and son. He also writes thrillers under the pen name Benjamin Blackmore. You can find him at boowalker.com and benjaminblackmore.com.